W9-ARP-766

Praise for *Long, Last, Happy:*

"The biggest literary badass you've never heard of."

—*The Boston Phoenix*

"One of those young writers who is brilliantly drunk with words and could at gunpoint write the life story of a telephone pole."

—Jim Harrison

"One of the most valuable voices of the New South . . . For years, Hannah had been the only writer willing to push the limits of language and narrative in quite the way William Faulkner did: He was willing, that is, to risk being misunderstood, to risk offending, to risk failing; he had the artistic courage to try to do more than he or prose could possibly do."—Noel Polk, *San Francisco Chronicle*

"His stories are like nothing I'd read before or since. . . . They duck like [Muhammad] Ali."

—Askold Melnyczuk

"What's remarkable about these stories is their density, how much they pack into a concise space. . . . Hannah revels in the flexibility the short story offers, the way it can zero in or stretch out wide."

—David L. Ulin, *Los Angeles Times*

"It's a shame that Hannah has so little contemporary competition, because his readers may be out of shape for such richness, such relentless, hell-bent writing."

—Ben Marcus

"The dark maestro of southern lit."

Details

"Barry was, and will always be, essential—as a writer and as a man with an exquisite, deep soul."

—Amy Hempel

"Hannah's lines invigorate and intoxicate. . . . Hannah was a storyteller, an enchanter with a refined eye for the outrageous and an ecstatic worldliness worthy of Rabelais."

—Justin Taylor, *The New York Times Book Review*

"A poetic wail that is both distinctly Southern and all his own ... Hannah will live on because of the dynamic and innovative prose of the fever-dream stories."
— Mike Fischer, *Milwaukee Journal Sentinel*

"No one has ever written, and no one ever will write, like Barry Hannah ... I can't imagine any serious American writer not owning this book, or anyone reading it without a sense of awe."
— Tom Grimes, *The Outlet (Electric Literature Blog)*

"Each of Hannah's stories is ... an extraordinary event of diction and light, music and life. ... His novels and short stories are on par, I believe, with works by Beckett, Hemingway, and Camus, writers he adored, and in Hannah's last work can be found all the startling insights, situations, language, and narrative complexities that our greatest writers are known for."
— John Oliver Hodges, *The Oxford American*

"Shows why Hannah's regarded as one of the best. Hannah's wit is caustic, shot through with social commentary and gleefully interspersed with bursts of slapstick comedy."
— *Publishers Weekly* (starred review)

"'In Mississippi it is difficult to achieve a vista,' wrote the late laureate Hannah of his native state. He was wrong: he provided some of the best vistas in American literature, as this collection of short fiction ably shows."
— *Kirkus Reviews*

"[A] wonderland of stories ... of active, vibrant, nearly throbbing fiction."
— Brad Hooper, *Booklist* (starred review)

"Though working in the Southern Gothic tradition of William Faulkner and Flannery O'Connor, Hannah is, ultimately, unlike either of them, with a wilder, more darkly comic edge, a Southern and an American original."
— Lawrence Rungren, *Library Journal*

★ ★ ★ ★ ★ ★ ★ ★ ★ ★ ★ ★ ★ ★

Long, Last, Happy

★ ★ ★ ★ ★ ★ ★ ★ ★ ★ ★ ★ ★ ★

★ ★

Long, Last, Happy

New and Selected Stories

★ ★

Barry Hannah

Grove Press
New York

Printed in the United States of America
Published simultaneously in Canada

ISBN-13: 978-0-8021-4550-5

Grove Press
an imprint of Grove/Atlantic, Inc.
841 Broadway
New York, NY 10003

Distributed by Publishers Group West

www.groveatlantic.com

11 12 13 14   10 9 8 7 6 5 4 3 2 1

In Memory of Barry and Susan Hannah

I look down at my hand. It's not a gun. It's only a pencil. I am not going anywhere.

—from "Idaho"

Ladies and Gentlemen,
It's all power and light.

—from "Power and Light"

Contents

★ ★ ★ ★ ★ ★ ★ ★ ★ ★ ★ ★ ★ ★ ★ ★ ★

1964–1978
Airships and Before

★ ★ ★ ★ ★ ★ ★ ★ ★ ★ ★ ★ ★ ★ ★ ★

Trek

Our host energetically stamped the brake and whipped our station wagon into a space that seemed to me to have burst out of the metallic desert from nowhere. Although assured by our host that we were indeed lucky, I held doubt as to our advantage. In fact, a single backward glance convinced me that we were no farther than a red light from our host's home. The host never looked back, strangely enough, so convinced was he that we were indeed lucky. We unloaded the asses and Negroes from the back end of our car and managed to get a look at the map and have a cigarette while the Negroes loaded the donkeys' backs. The noise of passing caravans and their personnel almost obliterated our host's admonitive plea, which I thought, from what I could hear between the jacking of the asses and the work songs of the Negroes, was well put and persuaded me, after a perusal of the horizon and the frustrations involved between our intended ascent and its gleam, that we should and would just have to stick together, that is that part of his speech which I was able to hear persuaded me, for the jacking of the asses, the lament of the eunuchs, the cries of the Lost, the general din of the vulgar in their ascent ahead were overpowering.

After a short while of walking, I settled into the comfort that we were in the hands of competence with our host. He indeed was directing our little sortie ably, never once flinching from the cries

3

of desperate souls who burst wide and panic-eyed from the aisles of cars, stumbling along in opposite direction to us, earnestly tilting their compasses to the light, grappling or dragging collapsed or semicollapsed wives and children wailing behind them, nor either from the occasional and increasingly frequenter parties heading back toward us either gasping resolutely or displaying on crudely lettered and upraised billboards: "There is no use" and "Turn back now, Brother." We encountered even several of those pathetic shades of men running bearded and half-naked among the chrome searching for their cars, their families, a hint of the Outer or Inner Passage, or those more pitiable skeletons who had lost all hope, babbling, imploring alms, or deliriously polishing their underwear. These, our host explained, as he beat away one of these very safe refugees from the tail of our caravan (they had been known to pillage supplies or even masquerade as eunuchs in desperate hope of attaching themselves to the successful caravan), were the ones probably befouled by imperfect compasses, lost maps, of cars identical with many others, the Lost. He hastened to add, and I could easily see his point, they were giving the game a bad name.

Meanwhile the Negroes faithfully prodded the asses and hummed pep songs. Three of the poor fellows fainted under their bales, those always seeming especially ponderous to me—until one of the perspiring Negroes explained to me that within the sheaves of burlap and wire was housed our liquor. I fully understood and appreciated then and could not help admiring our host for his elaborate and clever concealment of bliss. Two of the darkies, by the way, gave no indication of ever reviving and so our able host, over the protests of the eunuchs who I understood later were strictly and conscientiously union, recruited two of the Lost, floundering into our route, more than eager to take up the burdens. We proceeded then down and across infinite aisles, up grade, the entire first night of the journey. All the way the surrounding clamor alerted us to the need for sticking together, which was constantly the admonition of our great host. The humble music of the bearers had noticeably changed into a vigorous dialectic chant diatribing the impossible incompetency of the ofay. Deaf to this prejudice, the two Lost, as it were, the laboring minority, and dumb except through energetic eyes, peered passionately toward the horizon and its dull glow, from which sprung our Hope.

Since dawn hid the glow of our destination, we rested then, and fell to singing songs to the glory of our team. The clamor around us, nevertheless, sustained itself in the merchants who dared venture as far back as we were, screaming their offers, which entailed, at what I thought to be highly irregular fees, such entities as the True Maps, relics from the Destination itself, survival pamphlets, Dexedrine and other narcotics stimulating fervor and perseverance, and even such optimistic and far-flung symbols of the Contest itself as partisan flags, medals, and swords.

Night fell finally and we each rushed for our binoculars. Sure enough, in the very far East, lights again charged the air and the resilience of our destination hung even brighter on the horizon. Our host persuaded our caravan into action, enthusing each constituent with optimism and hope. Beside us, the anxious eyes of the two Lost fairly trembled in their sockets. Generally, the great inverse exodus gathered its paraphernalia around us, sending up a terrific din and repleting with victory and other earnest shouts. At this time we encountered a strange party intersecting our particular aisle. They were, doubtless, members of the Filthy Rich, for they snobbed us, high upon the backs of camels. I did think their transport indeed rare and their garb was fine, I'm sure, although of a longer cut than ours, and very elaborate you may be sure, even to the degree that they were thoroughly out of mode.

These fellows looked earnest enough, however, and so I ceased to suspicion their intent. There was not time, actually, for me to make their acquaintance since our relations with them were terminated when a darker member of their trio prodded his camel alongside our train and addressed our host.

"Is this then the light in the East?" he implored, whisking the curtains back from his face, which displayed solemnity and an almost inordinate degree of wiseness. "Is this then the light of the promised?" he again asked. I must admit he was incoherent to me and must have been to our host, for he threatened them against using our aisle and our dexterity of voyage. "Alas, we have come from afar," one of the other two lamented rather anachronistically. And while I sympathized with our host and held faith in his judgment I suspected that we should have been more courteous to this party, for actually, if it must be known what I was thinking, I feared they were UN delegates gone astray, as I have also heard is not inordinate. The fellows, at least, left passively and disappeared over the next promontory shortly, for their camels were swifter than our own caravan. The incident, however, did not cease to impress its moment on my mind for the remainder of the journey; the thought of the Three hunting back and forth between cars, scrounging the aisles unshaved and desperate as members of the Lost disturbed me, for I knew it would not breed any too good international relations to have them doing so.

After perhaps another two hours our host halted the train and had eunuchs lay our gear into a large square pile, perhaps twelve or fifteen feet high, on which he climbed with their help. So enthused was he over something he saw in his large binoculars that he toppled headlong off the platform and twisted his neck. The two of the Lost shivered and vomited with anxiety, poor fellows, and lifted themselves up on tiptoes to glimpse something over the hill. "What?" our entire train asked in unison. "Is it?" "Perhaps?"

Our joyous host leaped from the ground and held up his arms. Silence, except for the enthusiastic, staccato moans of the two Lost, thrilled the train.

"I have seen it," he uttered simply. "The stadium is just over the hill a few miles." With this announcement we shook hands, even congratulated the eunuchs, and for the occasion split one of the bales. Around us, the shouts of similar discoverers thrilled the air, there was much song and dance, with liquor flowing freely. I can say there was only one sad incident that wonderful night. The two Lost, in the head of expectation, completely lost their wits, broke from the train, ignoring the whip of our host, and scampered over the hills like goats. "A common temptation," the host had termed it in his Preparation for the Journey speech, and I was glad I had listened. Scanning the metallic jungle of rooftop aerials and infinite aisles and ways, the host offered a toast. I drank, but probably with less gusto than the rest because I realized we wouldn't, nor anybody except other fans on chance in their journeys, ever see those two of the Lost again.

Water Liars

WHEN I AM RUN DOWN AND FLOCKED AROUND BY THE WORLD, I GO down to Farte Cove off the Yazoo River and take my beer to the end of the pier where the old liars are still snapping and wheezing at one another. The lineup is always different, because they're always dying out or succumbing to constipation, etc., whereupon they go back to the cabins and wait for a good day when they can come out and lic again, leaning on the rail with coats full of bran cookies. The son of the man the cove was named for is often out there. He pronounces his name Far*tay,* with a great French stress on the last syllable. Otherwise you might laugh at his history or ignore it in favor of the name as it's spelled on the sign.

I'm glad it's not my name.

This poor dignified man has had to explain his nobility to the semiliterate of half of America before he could even begin a decent conversation with them. On the other hand, Farte, Jr., is a great liar himself. He tells about seeing ghost people around the lake and tells big loose ones about the size of the fish those ghosts took out of Farte Cove in years past.

Last year I turned thirty-three years old and, raised a Baptist, I had a sense of being Jesus and coming to something decided in my life—because we all know Jesus was crucified at thirty-three. It had all seemed especially important, what you do in this year, and holy with meaning.

On the morning after my birthday party, during which I and my wife almost drowned in vodka cocktails, we both woke up to the making of a truth session about the lovers we'd had before we met each other. I had a mildly exciting and usual history, and she had about the same, which surprised me. For ten years she'd sworn I was the first. I could not believe her history was exactly equal with mine. It hurt me to think that in the era when there were supposed to be virgins she had allowed anyone but *me,* and so on.

I was dazed and exhilarated by this information for several weeks. Finally, it drove me crazy, and I came out to Farte Cove to rest, under the pretense of a fishing week with my chum Wyatt.

I'm still figuring out why I couldn't handle it.

My sense of the past is vivid and slow. I hear every sign and see every shadow. The movement of every limb in every passionate event occupies my mind. I have a prurience on the grand scale. It makes no sense that I should be angry about happenings before she and I ever saw each other. Yet I feel an impotent homicidal urge in the matter of her lovers. She has excused my episodes as the course of things, though she has a vivid memory too. But there is a blurred nostalgia women have that men don't.

You could not believe how handsome and delicate my wife is naked.

I was driven wild by the bodies that had trespassed her twelve and thirteen years ago.

My vacation at Farte Cove wasn't like that easy little bit you get as a rich New Yorker. My finances weren't in great shape; to be true, they were about in ruin, and I left the house knowing my wife would have to answer the phone to hold off, for instance, the phone company itself. Everybody wanted money and I didn't have any.

I was going to take the next week in the house while she went away, watch our three kids and all the rest. When you both teach part-time in the high schools, the income can be slow in summer.

No poor-mouthing here. I don't want anybody's pity. I just want to explain. I've got good hopes of a job over at Alabama next year. Then I'll get myself among higher paid liars, that's all.

Sidney Farte was out there prevaricating away at the end of the pier when Wyatt and I got there Friday evening. The old faces I recognized; a few new harkening idlers I didn't.

"Now, Doctor Mooney, he not only saw the ghost of Lily, he says he had intercourse with her. Said it was involuntary. Before he knew what he was doing, he was on her making cadence and all their clothes blown away off in the trees around the shore. She turned into a wax candle right under him."

"Intercourse," said an old-timer, breathing heavy. He sat up on the rail. It was a word of high danger to his old mind. He said it with a long disgust, glad, I guess, he was not involved.

"MacIntire, a Presbyterian preacher, I seen him come out here with his son-in-law, anchor near the bridge, and pull up fifty or more white perch big as small pumpkins. You know what they was using for bait?"

"What?" asked another geezer.

"*Nuthin.* Caught on the bare hook. It was Gawd made them fish bite," said Sidney Farte, going at it good.

"Naw. There be a season they bite a bare hook. Gawd didn't have to've done that," said another old guy, with a fringe of red hair and a racy Florida shirt.

"Nother night," said Sidney Farte, "I saw the ghost of Yazoo hisself with my pa, who's dead. A Indian king with four deer around him."

The old boys seemed to be used to this one. Nobody said anything. They ignored Sidney.

"Tell you what," said a well-built small old boy. "That was somethin when we come down here and had to chase that whole high school party off the end of this pier, them drunken children. They was smokin dope and two-thirds a them nekid swimmin in the water. Good hunnerd of em. From your so-called *good* high school. What you think's happnin at the bad ones?"

* * *

I dropped my beer and grew suddenly sick. Wyatt asked me what was wrong. I could see my wife in 1960 in the group of high schoolers she must have had. My jealousy went out into the stars of the night above me. I could not bear the roving carelessness of teenagers, their judgeless tangling of wanting and bodies. But I was the worst back then. In the mad days back then, I dragged the panties off girls I hated and talked badly about them once the sun came up.

"Worst time in my life," said a new, younger man, maybe sixty but with the face of a man who had surrendered, "me and Woody was fishing. Had a lantern. It was about eleven. We was catching a few fish but rowed on into that little cove over there near town. We heard all these sounds, like they was ghosts. We was scared. We thought it might be the Yazoo hisself. We known of some fellows the Yazoo had killed to death just from fright. It was over the sounds of what was normal human sighin and amoanin. It was big unhuman sounds. We just stood still in the boat. Ain't nuthin else us to do. For thirty minutes."

"An what was it?" said the old geezer, letting himself off the rail.

"We had a big flashlight. There came up this rustlin in the brush and I beamed it over there. The two of em makin the sounds get up with half they clothes on. It was my own daughter Charlotte and an older guy I didn't even know with a mustache. My *own* daughter, and them sounds over the water scarin us like ghosts."

"My Gawd, that's awful," said the old geezer by the rail. "Is that the truth? I wouldn't've told that. That's terrible."

Sidney Farte was really upset.

"This ain't the place!" he said. "Tell your kind of story somewhere else."

The old man who'd told his story was calm and fixed to his place. He'd told the truth. The crowd on the pier was outraged and discomfited. He wasn't one of them. But he stood his place. He had a distressed pride. You could see he had never recovered from the thing he'd told about.

I told Wyatt to bring the old man back to the cabin. He was out here away from his wife the same as me and Wyatt. Just an older guy with a big hurting bosom. He wore a suit and the only way you'd know he was on vacation was he'd removed his tie. He didn't know where the bait house was. He didn't know what to do on vacation at all. But he got drunk with us and I can tell you he and I went out the next morning with our poles, Wyatt driving the motorboat, fishing for white perch in the cove near the town. And we were kindred.

We were both crucified by the truth.

Love Too Long

MY HEAD'S BURNING OFF AND I GOT A HEART ABOUT TO BUST OUT OF my ribs. All I can do is move from chair to chair with my cigarette. I wear shades. I can't read a magazine. Some days I take my binoculars and look out in the air. They laid me off. I can't find work. My wife's got a job and she takes flying lessons. When she comes over the house in her airplane, I'm afraid she'll screw up and crash.

I got to get back to work and get dulled out again. I got to be a man again. You can't walk around the house drinking coffee and beer all day, thinking about her taking her brassiere off. We been married and divorced twice. Sometimes I wish I had a sport. I bought a croquet set on credit at Penney's. First day I got so tired of it I knocked the balls off in the weeds and they're out there rotting, mildew all over them, I bet, but I don't want to see.

Some afternoons she'll come right over the roof of the house and turn the plane upside down. Or maybe it's her teacher. I don't know how far she's got along. I'm afraid to ask, on the every third night or so she comes in the house. I want to rip her arm off. I want to sleep in her uterus with my foot hanging out. Some nights she lets me lick her ears and knees. I can't talk about it. It's driving me into a sorry person. Maybe Hobe Lewis would let me pump gas and sell bait at his service station. My mind's around to where I'd do nigger work now.

I'd do Jew work, Swiss, Spanish. Anything.

She never took anything. She just left. She can be a lot of things—she got a college degree. She always had her own bank account. She wanted a better house than this house, but she was patient. She'd eat any food with a sweet smile. She moved through the house with a happy pace, like it meant something.

I think women are closer to God than we are. They walk right out there like they know what they're doing. She moved around the house, reading a book. I never saw her sitting down much, unless she's drinking. She can drink you under the table. Then she'll get up on the spot of eight and fix you an omelet with sardines and peppers. She taught me to like this, a little hot ketchup on the edge of the plate.

When she walks through the house, she has a roll from side to side. I've looked at her face too many times when she falls asleep. The omelet tastes like her. I go crazy.

There're things to be done in this world, she said. This love affair went on too long. It's going to make us both worthless, she said. Our love is not such a love as to swell the heart. So she said. She was never unfaithful to me that I know. And if I knew it, I wouldn't care because I know she's sworn to me.

I am her always and she is my always and that's the whole trouble.

For two years I tried to make her pregnant. It didn't work. The doctor said she was too nervous to hold a baby, first time she ever had an examination. She was a nurse at the hospital and brought home all the papers that she forged whenever I needed a report. For example, when I first got on as a fly in elevated construction. A fly can crawl and balance where nobody else can. I was always working at the thing I feared the most. I tell you true. But it was high pay out there at the beam joints. Here's the laugh. I was light and nimble, but the sun always made me sick up there under its nose. I got a permanent suntan. Some people think I'm Arab. I was good.

When I was in the navy, I finished two years at Bakersfield Junior College in California. Which is to say, I can read and feel fine things and count. Those women who cash your check don't cause any distress to me, all their steel, accents and computers. I'll tell you what

I liked that we studied at Bakersfield. It was old James Joyce and his book *The Canterbury Tales*. You wouldn't have thought anybody would write "A fart that well nigh blinded Absalom" in ancient days. All those people hopping and humping at night, framming around, just like last year at Ollie's party that she and I left when they got into threesomes and Polaroids. Because we loved each other too much. She said it was something you'd be sorry about the next morning.

Her name is Jane.

Once I cheated on her. I was drunk in Pittsburgh. They bragged on me for being a fly in the South. This girl and I were left together in a fancy apartment of the Oakland section. The girl did everything. I was homesick during the whole time for Jane. When you get down to it, there isn't much to do. It's just arms and legs. It's not worth a damn.

The first thing Jane did was go out on that houseboat trip with that movie star who was using this town we were in in South Carolina to make his comeback film. I can't tell his name, but he's short and his face is old and piglike now instead of the way it was in the days he was piling up the money. He used to be a star and now he was trying to return as a main partner in a movie about hatred and back-stabbing in Dixie. Everybody on board made crude passes at her. I wasn't invited. She'd been chosen as an extra for the movie. The guy who chose her made animalistic comments to her. This was during our first divorce. She jumped off the boat and swam home. But that's how good-looking she is. There was a cameraman on the houseboat who saw her swimming and filmed her. It was in the movie. I sat there and watched her when they showed it local.

The next thing she did was take up with an architect who had a mustache. He was designing her dream house for free and she was putting money in the bank waiting on it. She claimed he never touched her. He just wore his mustache and a gold medallion around his neck and ate yogurt and drew houses all day. She worked for him as a secretary and landscape consultant. Jane was always good about trees, bushes, flowers and so on. She's led many a Spare That Tree campaign almost on her own. She'll write a letter to the editor in a minute.

Only two buildings I ever worked on pleased her. She said the rest looked like death standing up.

The architect made her wear his ring on her finger. I saw her wearing it on the street in Biloxi, Mississippi, one afternoon, coming out of a store. There she was with a new hairdo and a narrow halter and by God I was glad I saw. I was in a bus on the way to the Palms House hotel we were putting up after the hurricane. I almost puked out my kidneys with the grief.

Maybe I need to go to church, I said to myself. I can't stand this alone. I wished I was Jesus. Somebody who never drank or wanted nooky. Or knew Jane.

She and the architect were having some fancy drinks together at a beach lounge when his ex-wife from New Hampshire showed up naked with a single-shot gun that was used in the Franco-Prussian War—it was a quaint piece hanging on the wall in their house when he was at Dartmouth—and screaming. The whole bar cleared out, including Jane. The ex-wife tried to get the architect with the bayonet. She took off the whole wall mural behind him and he was rolling around under tables. Then she tried to cock the gun. The policeman who'd come in got scared and left. The architect got out and threw himself into the arms of Jane, who was out on the patio thinking she was safe. He wanted to die holding his love. Jane didn't want to die in any fashion. Here comes the nude woman, screaming with the cocked gun.

"Hey, hey," says Jane. "Honey, you don't need a gun. You got a hell of a body. I don't see how Lawrence could've left that."

The woman lowered the gun. She was dripping with sweat and pale as an egg out there in the bright sun over the sea. Her hair was nearabout down to her ass and her face was crazy.

"Look at her, Lawrence," said Jane.

The guy turned around and looked at his ex-wife. He whispered: "She was lovely. But her personality was a disease. She was killing me. It was slow murder."

When I got there, the naked woman was on Lawrence's lap. Jane and a lot of people were standing around looking at them. They'd fallen back in love. Lawrence was sucking her breast. She wasn't a bad-looking sight. The long gun lay off in the sand. No law was needed. I was just humiliated. I tried to get away before Jane saw me, but I'd been drinking and smoking a lot the night before and I gave out this ninety-nine-year-old cough. Everybody on the patio except Lawrence and his woman looked around.

But in Mobile we got it going together again. She taught art in a private school where they admitted high-type Negroes only. And I was a fly on the city's first high-rise parking garage. We had so much money we ate out even for breakfast. She thought she was pregnant for a while and I was happy as hell. I wanted a heavenly blessing—as the pastors say—with Jane. I thought it would form the living chain between us that would never be broken. It would be beyond biology and into magic. But it was only eighteen months in Mobile and we left on a rainy day in the winter without her pregnant. She was just lean and her eyes were brown diamonds like always, and she had begun having headaches.

Let me tell you about Jane drinking punch at one of the parties at the University of Florida where she had a job. Some hippie had put LSD in it and there was nothing but teacher types in the house, leaning around, commenting on the azaleas and the evil of the administration. I never took any punch because I brought my own dynamite in the car. Here I was, complimenting myself on holding my own with these profs. One of the profs looked at Jane in her long gown, not knowing she was with me. He said to another: "She's pleasant to look at, as far as *that* goes." I said to him that I'd heard she was smart too, and had taken the all-Missouri swimming meet when she was just a junior in high school. Another guy spoke up. The LSD had hit. I didn't know.

"I'd like to stick her brain. I'll bet her brain would be better than her crack. I'd like to have her hair falling around my honker. I'd love to pull on those ears with silver loops hanging around, at, on, above—what is it?—*them*."

This guy was the chairman of the whole department.

"If I was an earthquake, I'd take care of her," said a fellow with a goatee and an ivory filter for his cigarette.

"Beauty is fleeting," said his ugly wife. "What stays is your basic endurance of pettiness and ennui. And perhaps, most of all, your ability to hide farts."

"Oh, Sandra!" says her husband. "I thought I'd taught you better. You went to Vassar, you bitch, so you wouldn't say things like that."

"I went to Vassar so I'd meet a dashing man with a fortune and a huge cucumber. Then I came back home, to assholing Florida and you," she said. "Washing socks, underwear, arguing with some idiot at Sears."

I met Jane at the punch bowl. She was socking it down and chatting with the librarian honcho who was her boss. He was a Scotsman with a mountain of book titles for his mind. Jane said he'd never read a book in thirty years, but he knew the hell out of their names. Jane truly liked to talk to fat and old guys best of all. She didn't ever converse much with young men. Her ideal of a conversation was when sex was nowhere near it at all. She hated all her speech with her admirers because every word was shaded with lust implications. One of her strange little dreams was to be sort of a cloud with eyes, ears, mouth. I walked up on them without their seeing and heard her say: "I love you. I'd like to pet you to death." She put her hand on his poochy stomach.

So then I was hitting the librarian in the throat and chest. He was a huge person, looked something like a statue of some notable gentleman in ancient history. I couldn't do anything to bring him down. He took all my blows without batting an eye.

"You great bastard!" I yelled up there. "I believed in You on and off all my life! There better be something up there like Jane or I'll humiliate You! I'll swine myself all over this town. I'll appear in public places and embarrass the shit out of You, screaming that I'm a Christian!"

We divorced the second time right after that.

Now we're in Richmond, Virginia. They laid me off. Inflation or recession or whatever rubbed me out. Oh, it was nobody's fault, says the boss. I got to sell my third car off myself, says he. At my house, we don't eat near the meat we used to, says he.

So I'm in this house with my binoculars, moving from chair to chair with my cigarettes. She flies over my house upside down every afternoon. Is she saying she wants me so much she'd pay for a plane to my yard? Or is she saying: Look at this, I never gave a damn for anything but fun in the air?

Nothing in the world matters but you and your woman. Friendship and politics go to hell. My friend Dan three doors down, who's also unemployed, comes over when he can make the price of a six-pack.

It's not the same.

I'm going to die from love.

★ ★

Testimony of Pilot

★ ★

WHEN I WAS TEN, ELEVEN AND TWELVE, I DID A GOOD BIT OF MY PLAY
in the backyard of a three-story wooden house my father had bought
and rented out, his first venture into real estate. We lived right across
the street from it, but over here was the place to do your real play.
Here there was a harrowed but overgrown garden, a vine-swallowed
fence at the back end, and beyond the fence a cornfield which belonged to someone else. This was not the country. This was the town,
Clinton, Mississippi, between Jackson on the east and Vicksburg on
the west. On this lot stood a few water oaks, a few plum bushes, and
much overgrowth of honeysuckle vine. At the very back end, at the
fence, stood three strong nude chinaberry trees.

In Mississippi it is difficult to achieve a vista. But my friends
and I had one  at the back corner of the garden. We could see
across the cornfield, see the one lone tin-roofed house this side of the
railroad tracks, then on across the tracks many other bleaker houses
with rustier tin roofs, smoke coming out of the chimneys in the late
fall. This was niggertown. We had binoculars and could see the colored children hustling about and perhaps a hopeless sow or two with
her brood enclosed in a tiny boarded-up area. Through the binoculars one afternoon in October we watched some men corner and beat
a large hog on the brain. They used an ax and the thing kept running
around, head leaning toward the ground, for several minutes before

19

it lay down. I thought I saw the men laughing when it finally did. One of them was staggering, plainly drunk to my sight from three hundred yards away. He had the long knife. Because of that scene I considered Negroes savage cowards for a good five more years of my life. Our maid brought some sausage to my mother and when it was put in the pan to fry, I made a point of running out of the house.

I went directly across the street and to the back end of the garden behind the apartment house we owned, without my breakfast. That was Saturday. Eventually, Radcleve saw me. His parents had him mowing the yard that ran alongside my dad's property. He clicked off the power mower and I went over to his fence, which was storm wire. His mother maintained handsome flowery grounds at all costs; she had a leaf-mold bin and St. Augustine grass as solid as a rug.

Radcleve himself was a violent experimental chemist. When Radcleve was eight, he threw a whole package of .22 shells against the sidewalk in front of his house until one of them went off, driving lead fragments into his calf, most of them still deep in there where the surgeons never dared tamper. Radcleve knew about the sulfur, potassium nitrate and charcoal mixture for gunpowder when he was ten. He bought things through the mail when he ran out of ingredients in his chemistry sets. When he was an infant, his father, a quiet man who owned the Chevrolet agency in town, bought an entire bankrupt sporting goods store, and in the middle of their backyard he built a house, plain painted and neat, one room and a heater, where Radcleve's redundant toys forevermore were kept—all the possible toys he would need for boyhood. There were things in there that Radcleve and I were not mature enough for and did not know the real use of. When we were eleven, we uncrated the new Dunlop golf balls and went on up a shelf for the tennis rackets, went out in the middle of his yard, and served new golf ball after new golf ball with blasts of the rackets over into the cornfield, out of sight. When the strings busted we just went in and got another racket. We were absorbed by how a good smack would set the heavy little pills on an endless flight. Then Radcleve's father came down. He simply dismissed me. He took Radcleve into the house and covered his whole body with a belt. But within the week Radcleve had invented the mortar. It was a steel pipe into which a flashlight battery fit perfectly, like a bullet into a muzzle. He had drilled a hole for the fuse of an M-80 firecracker at the base, for the charge. It was a grand cannon, set up on a stack of bricks at the back of my dad's property, which was the free place to play. When it shot, it would back up violently with thick smoke and you could hear the flashlight battery whistling off. So that morning when I ran out of the house protesting the hog sausage, I told Radcleve to bring over the mortar. His ma and dad were in Jackson for the day, and he came right over with the pipe, the batteries and the M-80 explosives. He had two gross of them.

Before, we'd shot off toward the woods to the right of niggertown. I turned the bricks to the left; I made us a very fine cannon carriage pointing toward niggertown. When Radcleve appeared, he had two pairs of binoculars around his neck, one pair a newly plundered German unit as big as a brace of whiskey bottles. I told him I wanted to shoot for that house where we saw them killing the pig. Radcleve loved the idea. We singled out the house with heavy use of the binoculars.

There were children in the yard. Then they all went in. Two men came out of the back door. I thought I recognized the drunkard from the other afternoon. I helped Radcleve fix the direction of the cannon. We estimated the altitude we needed to get down there. Radcleve put the M-80 in the breech with its fuse standing out of the hole. I dropped the flashlight battery in. I lit the fuse. We backed off. The M-80 blasted off deafeningly, smoke rose, but my concentration was on that particular house over there. I brought the binoculars up. We waited six or seven seconds. I heard a great joyful wallop on tin. "We've hit him on the first try, the first try!" I yelled. Radcleve was ecstatic. "Right on his roof!" We bolstered up the brick carriage. Radcleve remembered the correct height of the cannon exactly. So we fixed it, loaded it, lit it and backed off. The battery landed on the roof, blat, again, louder. I looked to see if there wasn't a great dent or hole in the roof. I could not understand why niggers weren't pouring out distraught from that house. We shot the mortar again and again, and always our battery hit the tin roof. Sometimes there was only a dull thud, but other times there was a wild distress of tin. I was still looking through the binoculars, amazed that the niggers wouldn't even come out of their house to see what was hitting their roof. Radcleve was on to it better than me. I looked over at him and he had the huge German binocs much lower than I did. He was looking straight through the cornfield, which was all bare and open, with nothing left but rotten stalks. "What we've been hitting is the roof of that house just this side of the tracks. White people live in there," he said.

I took up my binoculars again. I looked around the yard of that white wooden house on this side of the tracks, almost next to the railroad. When I found the tin roof, I saw four significant dents in it. I saw one of our batteries lying in the middle of a sort of crater. I took the binoculars down into the yard and saw a blonde middle-aged woman looking our way.

"Somebody's coming up toward us. He's from that house and he's got, I think, some sort of fancy gun with him. It might be an automatic weapon."

I ran my binoculars all over the cornfield. Then, in a line with the house, I saw him. He was coming our way but having some trouble with the rows and dead stalks of the cornfield.

"That is just a boy like us. All he's got is a saxophone with him," I told Radcleve. I had recently got in the school band, playing drums, and had seen all the weird horns that made up a band.

I watched this boy with the saxophone through the binoculars until he was ten feet from us. This was Quadberry. His name was Ard, short for Arden. His shoes were foot-square wads of mud from the cornfield. When he saw us across the fence and above him, he stuck out his arm in my direction.

"My dad says stop it!"

"We weren't doing anything," says Radcleve.

"Mother saw the smoke puff up from here. Dad has a hangover."

"A what?"

"It's a headache from indiscretion. You're lucky he does. He's picked up the poker to rap on you, but he can't move farther the way his head is."

"What's your name? You're not in the band," I said, focusing on the saxophone.

"It's Ard Quadberry. Why do you keep looking at me through the binoculars?"

It was because he was odd, with his hair and its white ends, and his Arab nose, and now his name. Add to that the saxophone.

"My dad's a doctor at the college. Mother's a musician. You better quit what you're doing. . . . I was out practicing in the garage. I saw one of those flashlight batteries roll off the roof. Could I see what you shoot 'em with?"

"No," said Radcleve. Then he said: "If you'll play that horn."

Quadberry stood out there ten feet below us in the field, skinny, feet and pants booted with black mud, and at his chest the slung-on, very complex, radiant horn.

Quadberry began sucking and licking the reed. I didn't care much for this act, and there was too much desperate oralness in his face when he began playing. That was why I chose the drums. One had to engage himself like suck's revenge with a horn. But what Quadberry was playing was pleasant and intricate. I was sure it was advanced, and there was no squawking, as from the other eleven-year-olds on sax in the band room. He made the end with a clean upward riff, holding the final note high, pure and unwavering.

"Good!" I called to him.

Quadberry was trying to move out of the sunken row toward us, but his heavy shoes were impeding him.

"Sounded like a duck. Sounded like a girl duck," said Radcleve, who was kneeling down and packing a mudball around one of the M-80s. I saw and I was an accomplice, because I did nothing. Radcleve lit the fuse and heaved the mudball over the fence. An M-80 is a very serious firecracker; it is like the charge they use to shoot up those sprays six hundred feet on July Fourth at country clubs. It went off, this one, even bigger than most M-80s.

When we looked over the fence, we saw Quadberry all muck specks and fragments of stalks. He was covering the mouthpiece of his horn with both hands. Then I saw there was blood pouring out of, it seemed, his right eye. I thought he was bleeding directly out of his eye.

"Quadberry?" I called.

He turned around and never said a word to me until I was eighteen. He walked back holding his eye and staggering through the cornstalks. Radcleve had him in the binoculars. Radcleve was trembling . . . but intrigued.

"His mother just screamed. She's running out in the field to get him."

I thought we'd blinded him, but we hadn't. I thought the Quadberrys would get the police or call my father, but they didn't. The upshot of this is that Quadberry had a permanent white space next to his right eye, a spot that looked like a tiny upset crown.

I went from sixth through half of twelfth grade ignoring him and that wound. I was coming on as a drummer and a lover, but if Quadberry happened to appear within fifty feet of me and my most tender, intimate sweetheart, I would duck out. Quadberry grew up just like the rest of us. His father was still a doctor—professor of history—at the town college; his mother was still blonde, and a musician. She was organist at an Episcopalian church in Jackson, the big capital city ten miles east of us.

As for Radcleve, he still had no ear for music, but he was there, my buddy. He was repentant about Quadberry, although not so much as I. He'd thrown the mud grenade over the fence only to see what would happen. He had not really wanted to maim. Quadberry had played his tune on the sax, Radcleve had played his tune on the mud grenade. It was just a shame they happened to cross talents.

Radcleve went into a long period of nearly nothing after he gave up violent explosives. Then he trained himself to copy the comic strips, *Steve Canyon* to *Major Hoople*, until he became quite a versatile cartoonist with some very provocative new faces and bodies that were gesturing intriguingly. He could never fill in the speech balloons with the smart words they needed. Sometimes he would pencil in "Err" or "What?" in the empty speech places. I saw him a great deal. Radcleve was not spooked by Quadberry. He even once asked Quadberry what his opinion was of his future as a cartoonist. Quadberry told Radcleve that if he took all his cartoons and stuffed himself with them, he would make an interesting dead man. After that, Radcleve was shy of him too.

When I was a senior we had an extraordinary band. Word was we had outplayed all the big AAA division bands last April in the state contest. Then came news that a new blazing saxophone player was coming into the band as first chair. This person had spent summers in Vermont in music camps, and he was coming in with us for the concert season. Our director, a lovable aesthete named Richard Prender, announced to us in a proud silent moment that the boy was joining us tomorrow night. The effect was that everybody should push over a seat or two and make room for this boy and his talent. I was annoyed. Here I'd been with the band and had kept hold of the taste among the whole percussion section. I could play rock and jazz drum and didn't even really need to be here. I could be in Vermont too, give me a piano and a bass. I looked at the kid on first sax, who was going to be supplanted tomorrow. For two years he had thought he was the star, then suddenly enters this boy who's three times better.

The new boy was Quadberry. He came in, but he was meek, and when he tuned up he put his head almost on the floor, bending over trying to be inconspicuous. The girls in the band had wanted him to be handsome, but Quadberry refused and kept himself in such hiding among the sax section that he was neither handsome, ugly, cute or anything. What he was was pretty near invisible, except for the bell of his horn, the all-but-closed eyes, the Arabian nose, the brown hair with its halo of white ends, the desperate oralness, the giant reed punched into his face, and hazy Quadberry, loving the wound in a private dignified ecstasy.

I say dignified because of what came out of the end of his horn. He was more than what Prender had told us he would be. Because of Quadberry, we could take the band arrangement of Ravel's *Boléro* with us to the state contest. Quadberry would do the saxophone solo. He would switch to alto sax, he would do the sly Moorish ride. When he played, I heard the sweetness, I heard the horn which finally brought human *talk* into the realm of music. It could sound like the mutterings of a field nigger, and then it could get up into inhumanly careless beauty, it could get among mutinous helium bursts around Saturn. I already loved *Boléro* for the constant drum part. The percussion was always there, driving along with the subtly increasing triplets, insistent, insistent, at last outraged and trying to steal the whole show from the horns and the others. I knew a large boy with dirty blond hair, name of Wyatt, who played viola in the

Jackson Symphony and sousaphone in our band—one of the rare closet transmutations of my time—who was forever claiming to have discovered the central *Boléro* one Sunday afternoon over FM radio as he had seven distinct sexual moments with a certain B., girl flutist with black bangs and skin like mayonnaise, while the drums of Ravel carried them on and on in a ceremony of Spanish sex. It was agreed by all the canny in the band that *Boléro* was exactly the piece to make the band soar—now especially as we had Quadberry, who made his walk into the piece like an actual lean Spanish bandit. This boy could blow his horn. He was, as I had suspected, a genius. His solo was not quite the same as the New York Phil's saxophonist's, but it was better. It came in and was with us. It entered my spine and, I am sure, went up the skirts of the girls. I had almost deafened myself playing drums in the most famous rock and jazz band in the state, but I could hear the voice that went through and out that horn. It sounded like a very troubled forty-year-old man, a man who had had his brow in his hands a long time.

The next time I saw Quadberry up close, in fact the first time I had seen him up close since we were eleven and he was bleeding in the cornfield, was in late February. I had only three classes this last semester, and went up to the band room often, to loaf and complain and keep up my touch on the drums. Prender let me keep my set in one of the instrument rooms, with a tarpaulin thrown over it, and I would drag it out to the practice room and whale away. Sometimes a group of sophomores would come up and I would make them marvel, whaling away as if not only deaf but blind to them, although I wasn't at all. If I saw a sophomore girl with exceptional bod or face, I would do miracles of technique I never knew were in me. I would amaze myself. I would be threatening Buddy Rich and Joe Morello. But this time when I went into the instrument room, there was Quadberry on one side, and, back in a dark corner, a small ninth-grade euphonium player whose face was all red. The little boy was weeping and grinning at the same time.

"Queerberry," the boy said softly.

Quadberry flew upon him like a demon. He grabbed the boy's collar, slapped his face, and yanked his arm behind him in a merciless wrestler's grip, the one that made them bawl on TV. Then the boy broke it and slugged Quadberry in the lips and ran across to my side of the room. He said "Queerberry" softly again and jumped for the door. Quadberry plunged across the room and tackled him on the threshold. Now that the boy was under him, Quadberry pounded the top of his head with his fist made like a mallet. The boy kept calling him "Queerberry" throughout this. He had not learned his lesson. The boy seemed to be going into concussion, so I stepped over and touched Quadberry, telling him to quit. Quadberry obeyed and stood up off the boy, who crawled on out into the band room. But once more the boy looked back with a bruised grin, saying "Queerberry." Quadberry made a move toward him, but I blocked it.

"Why are you beating up on this little guy?" I said. Quadberry was sweating and his eyes were wild with hate; he was a big fellow now, though lean. He was, at six feet tall, bigger than me.

"He kept calling me Queerberry."

"What do you care?" I asked.

"I care," Quadberry said, and left me standing there.

We were to play at Millsaps College Auditorium for the concert. It was April. We got on the buses, a few took their cars, and were a big tense crowd getting over there. To Jackson was only a twenty-minute trip. The director, Prender, followed the bus in his Volkswagen. There was a thick fog. A flashing ambulance, snaking the lanes, piled into him head on. Prender, who I would imagine was thinking of *Boléro* and hearing the young horn voices in his band—perhaps he was dwelling on Quadberry's spectacular gypsy entrance, or perhaps he was meditating on the percussion section, of which I was the king—passed into the airs of band director heaven. We were told by the student director as we set up on the stage. The student director was a senior from the town college, very much afflicted, almost to the point of drooling, by a love and respect for Dick Prender, and now afflicted by a heartbreaking esteem for his ghost. As were we all.

I loved the tough and tender director awesomely and never knew it until I found myself bawling along with all the rest of the boys of the percussion. I told them to keep setting up, keep tuning, keep screwing the stands together, keep hauling in the kettledrums. To just quit and bawl seemed a betrayal to Prender. I caught some girl clarinetists trying to flee the stage and go have their cry. I told them to get the hell back to their section. They obeyed me. Then I found the student director. I had to have my say.

"Look. I say we just play *Boléro* and junk the rest. That's our horse. We can't play "Brighton Beach" and "Neptune's Daughter." We'll never make it through them. And they're too happy."

"We aren't going to play anything," he said. "Man, to play is filthy. Did you ever hear Prender play piano? Do you know what a cool man he was in all things?"

"We play. He got us ready, and we play."

"Man, you can't play any more than I can direct. You're bawling your face off. Look out there at the rest of them. Man, it's a herd, it's a weeping herd."

"What's wrong? Why aren't you pulling this crowd together?" This was Quadberry, who had come up urgently. "I got those little brats in my section sitting down, but we've got people abandoning the stage, tearful little finks throwing their horns on the floor."

"I'm not directing," said the mustached college man.

"Then get out of here. You're weak, weak!"

"Man, we've got teen-agers in ruin here, we got sorrowville. Nobody can—"

"Go ahead. Do your number. Weak out on us."

"Man, I—"

Quadberry was already up on the podium, shaking his arms.

"We're right here! The band is right here! Tell your friends to get back in their seats. We're doing *Boléro*. Just put *Boléro* up and start tuning. *I'm* directing. I'll be right here in front of you. You look at *me!* Don't you dare quit on Prender. Don't you dare quit on me. You've got to be heard. *I've* got to be heard. Prender wanted me to be heard. I am the star, and I say we sit down and blow."

And so we did. We all tuned and were burning low for the advent into *Boléro,* though we couldn't believe that Quadberry was going to remain with his saxophone strapped to him and conduct us as well as play his solo. The judges, who apparently hadn't heard about Prender's death, walked down to their balcony desks.

One of them called out "Ready" and Quadberry's hand was instantly up in the air, his fingers hard as if around the stem of something like a torch. This was not Prender's way, but it had to do. We went into the number cleanly and Quadberry one-armed it in the conducting. He kept his face, this look of hostility, at the reeds and the trumpets. I was glad he did not look toward me and the percussion boys like that. But he must have known we would be constant and tasteful because I was the king there. As for the others, the soloists especially, he was scaring them into excellence. Prender had never got quite this from them. Boys became men and girls became women as Quadberry directed us through *Boléro*. I even became a bit better of a man myself, though Quadberry did not look my way. When he turned around toward the people in the auditorium to enter on his solo, I knew it was my baby. I and the drums were the metronome. That was no trouble. It was talent to keep the metronome ticking amidst any given chaos of sound.

But this keeps one's mind occupied and I have no idea what Quadberry sounded like on his sax ride. All I know is that he looked grief-stricken and pale, and small. Sweat had popped out on his forehead. He bent over extremely. He was wearing the red brass-button jacket and black pants, black bow tic at the throat, just like the rest of us. In this outfit he bent over his horn almost out of sight. For a moment, before I caught the glint of his horn through the music stands, I thought he had pitched forward off the stage. He went down so far to do his deep oral thing, his conducting arm had disappeared so quickly, I didn't know but what he was having a seizure.

When *Boléro* was over, the audience stood up and made meat out of their hands applauding. The judges themselves applauded. The band stood up, bawling again, for Prender and because we had done so well. The student director rushed out crying to embrace Quadberry, who eluded him with his dipping shoulders. The crowd was still clapping insanely. I wanted to see Quadberry myself. I waded through the red backs, through the bow ties, over the white bucks. Here was the first-chair clarinetist, who had done his bit like an angel; he sat close to the podium and could hear Quadberry.

"Was Quadberry good?" I asked him.

"Are you kidding? These tears in my eyes, they're for how good he was. He was too good. I'll never touch my clarinet again."

The clarinetist slung the pieces of his horn into their case like underwear and a toothbrush.

I found Quadberry fitting the sections of his alto in the velvet holds of his case.

"Hooray," I said. "Hip damn hooray for you."

Arden was smiling too, showing a lot of teeth I had never seen. His smile was sly. He knew he had pulled off a monster unlikelihood.

"Hip hip hooray for me," he said. "Look at her. I had the bell of the horn almost smack in her face."

There was a woman of about thirty sitting in the front row of the auditorium. She wore a sundress with a drastic cleavage up front; looked like something that hung around New Orleans and kneaded your heart to death with her feet. She was still mesmerized by Quadberry. She bore on him with a stare and there was moisture in her cleavage.

"You played well."

"Well? Play well? Yes."

He was trying not to look at her directly. Look at *me*, I beckoned to her with full face: I was the *drums*. She arose and left.

"I was walking downhill in a valley, is all I was doing," said Quadberry. "Another man, a wizard, was playing my horn." He locked his sax case. "I feel nasty for not being able to cry like the rest of them. Look at them. Look at them crying."

True, the children of the band were still weeping, standing around the stage. Several moms and dads had come up among them, and they were misty-eyed too. The mixture of grief and superb music had been unbearable

A girl in tears appeared next to Quadberry. She was a majorette in football season and played third-chair sax during the concert season. Not even her violent sorrow could take the beauty out of the face of this girl. I had watched her for a number of years—her alertness to her own beauty, the pride of her legs in the majorette outfit—and had taken out her younger sister, a second-rate version of her and a wayward overcompensating nymphomaniac whom several of us made a hobby out of pitying. Well, here was Lilian herself crying in Quadberry's face. She told him that she'd run off the stage when she heard about Prender, dropped her horn and everything, and had thrown herself into a tavern across the street and drunk two beers quickly for some kind of relief. But she had come back through the front doors of the auditorium and sat down, dizzy with beer, and seen Quadberry, the miraculous way he had gone on with *Boléro*. And now she was eaten up by feelings of guilt, weakness, cowardice.

"We didn't miss you," said Quadberry.

"Please forgive me. Tell me to do something to make up for it."

"Don't breathe my way, then. You've got beer all over your breath."

"I want to talk to you."

"Take my horn case and go out, get in my car, and wait for me. It's the ugly Plymouth in front of the school bus."

"I know," she said.

Lilian Field, this lovely teary thing, with the rather pious grace of her carriage, with the voice full of imminent swoon, picked up Quadberry's horn case and her own and walked off the stage.

I told the percussion boys to wrap up the packing. Into my suitcase I put my own gear and also managed to steal drum keys, two pairs of brushes, a twenty-inch Turkish cymbal, a Gretsch snare drum that I desired for my collection, a wood block, kettledrum mallets, a tuning harp and a score sheet of *Boléro* full of marginal notes I'd written down straight from the mouth of Dick Prender, thinking I might want to look at the score sheet sometime in the future when I was having a fit of nostalgia such as I am having right now as I write this. I had never done any serious stealing before, and I was stealing for my art. Prender was dead, the band had done its last thing of the year, I was a senior. Things were finished at the high school. I was just looting a sinking ship. I could hardly lift the suitcase. As I was pushing it across the stage, Quadberry was there again.

"You can ride back with me if you want to."

"But you've got Lilian."

"Please ride back with me . . . us. Please."

"Why?"

"To help me get rid of her. Her breath is full of beer. My father always had that breath. Every time he was friendly, he had that breath. And she looks a great deal like my mother." We were interrupted by the Tupelo band director. He put his baton against Quadberry's arm.

"You were big with *Boléro,* son, but that doesn't mean you own the stage."

Quadberry caught the end of the suitcase and helped me with it out to the steps behind the auditorium. The buses were gone. There sat his ugly ocher Plymouth; it was a failed, gay, experimental shade from the Chrysler people. Lilian was sitting in the front seat wearing her shirt and bow tie, her coat off.

"Are you going to ride back with me?" Quadberry said to me.

"I think I would spoil something. You never saw her when she was a majorette. She's not stupid, either. She likes to show off a little, but she's not stupid. She's in the History Club."

"My father has a doctorate in history. She smells of beer."

I said, "She drank two cans of beer when she heard about Prender."

"There are a lot of other things to do when you hear about death. What I did, for example. She ran away. She fell to pieces."

"She's waiting for us," I said.

"One damned thing I am never going to do is drink."

"I've never seen your mother up close, but Lilian doesn't look like your mother. She doesn't look like anybody's mother."

I rode with them silently to Clinton. Lilian made no bones about being disappointed I was in the car, though she said nothing. I knew it would be like this and I hated it. Other girls in town would not be so unhappy that I was in the car with them. I looked for flaws in Lilian's face and neck and hair, but there weren't any. Couldn't there be a mole, an enlarged pore, too much gum on a tooth, a single awkward hair around the ear? No. Memory, the whole lying opera of it, is killing me now. Lilian was faultless beauty, even sweating, even and especially in the white man's shirt and the bow tie clamping together her collar, when one knew her uncomfortable bosoms, her poor nipples. . . .

"Don't take me back to the band room. Turn off here and let me off at my house," I said to Quadberry. He didn't turn off.

"Don't tell Arden what to do. He can do what he wants to," said Lilian, ignoring me and speaking to me at the same time. I couldn't bear her hatred. I asked Quadberry to please just stop the car and let me out here, wherever he was: this front yard of the mobile home would do. I was so earnest that he stopped the car. He handed back the keys and I dragged my suitcase out of the trunk, then flung the keys back at him and kicked the car to get it going again.

My band came together in the summer. We were the Bop Fiends . . . that was our name. Two of them were from Ole Miss, our bass player was from Memphis State, but when we got together this time, I didn't call the tenor sax, who went to Mississippi Southern, because Quadberry wanted to play with us. During the school year the college boys and I fell into minor groups to pick up twenty dollars on a weekend, playing dances for the Moose Lodge, medical-student fraternities in Jackson, teenage recreation centers in Greenwood, and such as that. But come summer we were the Bop Fiends again, and the price for us went up to $1,200 a gig. Where they wanted the best rock and bop and they had some bread, we were called. The summer after I was a senior, we played in Alabama, Louisiana and Arkansas. Our fame was getting out there on the interstate route.

This was the summer that I made myself deaf.

Years ago Prender had invited down an old friend from a high school in Michigan. He asked me over to meet the friend, who had been a drummer with Stan Kenton at one time and was now a band director just like Prender. This fellow was almost totally deaf and he warned me very sincerely about deafing myself. He said there would come a point when you had to lean over and concentrate all your hearing on what the band was doing and that was the time to quit for a while, because if you didn't you would be irrevocably deaf like him in a month or two. I listened to him but could not take him seriously. Here was an oldich man who had his problems. My ears had ages of hearing left. Not so. I played the drums so loud the summer after I graduated from high school that I made myself, eventually, stone deaf.

We were at, say, the National Guard Armory in Lake Village, Arkansas, Quadberry out in front of us on the stage they'd built. Down on the floor were hundreds of sweaty teenagers. Four girls in sundresses, showing what they could, were leaning on the stage with broad ignorant lust on their minds. I'd play so loud for one particular chick, I'd get absolutely out of control. The guitar boys would have to turn the volume up full blast to compensate. Thus I went deaf. Anyhow, the dramatic idea was to release Quadberry on a very soft sweet ballad right in the middle of a long ear-piercing run of rock-and-roll tunes. I'd get out the brushes and we would astonish the crowd with our tenderness. By August, I was so deaf I had to watch Quadberry's fingers changing notes on the saxophone, had to use my eyes to keep time. The other members of the Bop Fiends told me I was hitting out of time. I pretended I was trying to do experimental things with rhythm when the truth was I simply could no longer hear. I was no longer a tasteful drummer, either. I had become deaf through lack of taste.

Which was—taste—exactly the quality that made Quadberry wicked on the saxophone. During the howling, during the churning, Quadberry had taste. The noise did not affect his personality; he was solid as a brick. He could blend. Oh, he could hoot through his horn when the right time came, but he could do supporting roles for an hour. Then, when we brought him out front for his solo on something like "Take Five," he would play with such light blissful technique that he even eclipsed Paul Desmond. The girls around the stage did not cause him to enter into excessive loudness or vibrato.

Quadberry had his own girlfriend now, Lilian back at Clinton, who put all the sundressed things around the stage in the shade. In my mind I had congratulated him for getting up next to this beauty, but in June and July, when I was still hearing things a little, he never said a word about her. It was one night in August, when I could hear nothing and was driving him to his house, that he asked me to turn on the inside light and spoke in a retarded deliberate way. He knew I was deaf and counted on my being able to read lips.

"Don't . . . make . . . fun . . . of her . . . or me. . . . We . . . think . . . she . . . is . . . in trouble."

I wagged my head. Never would I make fun of him or her. She detested me because I had taken out her helpless little sister for a few weeks, but I would never think there was anything funny about Lilian, for all her haughtiness. I only thought of this event as monumentally curious.

"No one except you knows," he said.

"Why did you tell me?"

"Because I'm going away and you have to take care of her. I wouldn't trust her with anybody but you."

"She hates the sight of my face. Where are you going?"

"Annapolis."

"You aren't going to any damned Annapolis."

"That was the only school that wanted me."

"You're going to play your saxophone on a boat?"

"I don't know what I'm going to do."

"How . . . how can you just leave her?"

"She wants me to. She's very excited about me at Annapolis. William [this is my name], there is no girl I could imagine who has more inner sweetness than Lilian."

I entered the town college, as did Lilian. She was in the same chemistry class I was. But she was rows away. It was difficult to learn anything, being deaf. The professor wasn't a pantomimer—but finally he went to the blackboard with the formulas and the algebra of problems, to my happiness. I hung in and made a B. At the end of the semester I was swaggering around the grade sheet he'd posted. I happened to see Lilian's grade. She'd only made a C. Beautiful Lilian got only a C while I, with my handicap, had made a B.

It had been a very difficult chemistry class. I had watched Lilian's stomach the whole way through. It was not growing. I wanted to see her look like a watermelon, make herself an amazing mother shape.

When I made the B and Lilian made the C, I got up my courage and finally went by to see her. She answered the door. Her parents weren't home. I'd never wanted this office of watching over her as Quadberry wanted me to, and this is what I told her. She asked me into the house. The rooms smelled of nail polish and pipe smoke. I was hoping her little sister wasn't in the house, and my wish came true. We were alone.

"You can quit watching over me."

"Are you pregnant?"

"No." Then she started crying. "I wanted to be. But I'm not."

"What do you hear from Quadberry?"

She said something, but she had her back to me. She looked to me for an answer, but I had nothing to say. I knew she'd said something, but I hadn't heard it.

"He doesn't play the saxophone anymore," she said.

This made me angry.

"Why not?"

"Too much math and science and navigation. He wants to fly. That's what his dream is now. He wants to get into an F-something jet."

I asked her to say this over and she did. Lilian really was full of inner sweetness, as Quadberry had said. She understood that I was deaf. Perhaps Quadberry had told her.

The rest of the time in her house I simply witnessed her beauty and her mouth moving.

I went through college. To me it is interesting that I kept a B average and did it all deaf, though I know this isn't interesting to people who aren't deaf. I loved music, and never heard it. I loved poetry, and never heard a word that came out of the mouths of the visiting poets who read at the campus. I loved my mother and dad, but never heard a sound they made. One Christmas Eve, Radcleve was back from Ole Miss and threw an M-80 out in the street for old times' sake. I saw it explode, but there was only a pressure in my ears. I was at parties when lusts were raging and I went home with two girls (I am medium handsome) who lived in apartments of the old two-story 1920 vintage, and I took my shirt off and made love to them. But I have no real idea what their reaction was. They were stunned and all smiles when I got up, but I have no idea whether I gave them the last pleasure or not. I hope I did. I've always been partial to women and have always wanted to see them satisfied till their eyes popped out.

Through Lilian I got the word that Quadberry was out of Annapolis and now flying jets off the *Bonhomme Richard,* an aircraft carrier headed for Vietnam. He telegrammed her that he would set down at the Jackson airport at ten o'clock one night. So Lilian and I were out there waiting. It was a familiar place to her. She was a stewardess and her loops were mainly in the South. She wore a beige raincoat, had red sandals on her feet; I was in a black turtleneck and corduroy jacket, feeling significant, so significant I could barely stand it. I'd already made myself the lead writer at Gordon-Marx Advertising in Jackson. I hadn't seen Lilian in a year. Her eyes were strained, no longer the bright blue things they were when she was a pious beauty. We drank coffee together. I loved her. As far as I knew, she'd been faithful to Quadberry.

He came down in an F-something Navy jet right on the dot of ten. She ran out on the airport pavement to meet him. I saw her crawl up the ladder. Quadberry never got out of the plane. I could see him in his blue helmet. Lilian backed down the ladder. Then Quadberry had the cockpit cover him again. He turned the plane around so its flaming red end was at us. He took it down the runway. We saw him leap out into the night at the middle of the runway going west, toward San Diego and the *Bonhomme Richard*. Lilian was crying.

"What did he say?" I asked.

"He said, 'I am a dragon. America the beautiful, like you will never know.' He wanted to give you a message. He was glad you were here."

"What was the message?"

"The same thing. 'I am a dragon. America the beautiful, like you will never know.'"

"Did he say anything else?"

"Not a thing."

"Did he express any love toward you?"

"He wasn't Ard. He was somebody with a sneer in a helmet."

"He's going to war, Lilian."

"I asked him to kiss me and he told me to get off the plane, he was firing up and it was dangerous."

"Arden is going to war. He's just on his way to Vietnam and he wanted us to know that. It wasn't just him he wanted us to see. It was him in the jet he wanted us to see. He *is* that black jet. You can't kiss an airplane."

"And what are we supposed to do?" cried sweet Lilian.

"We've just got to hang around. He didn't have to lift off and disappear straight up like that. That was to tell us how he isn't with us anymore."

Lilian asked me what she was supposed to do now. I told her she was supposed to come with me to my apartment in the old 1920 Clinton place where I was. I was supposed to take care of her. Quadberry had said so. His six-year-old directive was still working.

She slept on the fold-out bed of the sofa for a while. This was the only bed in my place. I stood in the dark in the kitchen and drank a quarter bottle of gin on ice. I would not turn on the light and spoil her sleep. The prospect of Lilian asleep in my apartment made me feel like a chaplain on a visit to the Holy Land; I stood there getting drunk, biting my tongue when dreams of lust burst on me. That black jet Quadberry wanted us to see him in, its flaming rear end, his blasting straight up into the night at mid-runway—what precisely was he wanting to say in this stunt? Was he saying remember him forever or forget him forever? But I had my own life and was neither going to mother-hen it over his memory nor his old sweetheart. What did he mean, *America the beautiful, like you will never know?* I, William Howly, knew a goddamn good bit about America the beautiful, even as a deaf man. Being deaf had brought me up closer to people. There were only about five I knew, but I knew their mouth movements, the perspiration under their noses, their tongues moving over the crowns of their teeth, their fingers on their lips. Quadberry, I said, you don't have to get up next to the stars in your black jet to see America the beautiful.

I was deciding to lie down on the kitchen floor and sleep the night, when Lilian turned on the light and appeared in her panties and bra. Her body was perfect except for a tiny bit of fat on her upper thighs. She'd sunbathed herself so her limbs were brown, and her stomach, and the instinct was to rip off the white underwear and lick, suck, say something terrific into the flesh that you discovered.

She was moving her mouth.

"Say it again slowly."

"I'm lonely. When he took off in his jet, I think it meant he wasn't ever going to see me again. I think it meant he was laughing at both of us. He's an astronaut and he spits on us."

"You want me on the bed with you?" I asked.

"I know you're an intellectual. We could keep on the lights so you'd know what I said."

"You want to say things? This isn't going to be just sex?"

"It could never be just sex."

"I agree. Go to sleep. Let me make up my mind whether to come in there. Turn out the lights."

Again the dark, and I thought I would cheat not only Quadberry but the entire Quadberry family if I did what was natural.

I fell asleep.

Quadberry escorted B-52s on bombing missions into North Vietnam. He was catapulted off the *Bonhomme Richard* in his suit at 100 degrees temperature, often at night, and put the F-8 on all it could get—the tiny cockpit, the immense long two-million-dollar fuselage, wings, tail and jet engine, Quadberry, the genius master of his dragon, going up to twenty thousand feet to be cool. He'd meet with the big B-52 turtle of the air and get in a position, his cockpit glowing with green and orange lights, and turn on his transistor radio. There was only one really good band, never mind the old American rock-and-roll from Cambodia, and that was Red Chinese opera. Quadberry loved it. He loved the nasal horde in the finale, when the peasants won over the old fat dilettante mayor. Then he'd turn the jet around when he saw the squatty abrupt little fires way down there after the B-52s had dropped their diet. It was a seven-hour trip. Sometimes he slept, but his body knew when to wake up. Another thirty minutes and there was his ship waiting for him out in the waves.

All his trips weren't this easy. He'd have to blast out in daytime and get with the B-52s, and a SAM missile would come up among them. Two of his mates were taken down by these missiles. But Quadberry, as on saxophone, had endless learned technique. He'd put his jet perpendicular in the air and make the SAMs look silly. He even shot down two of them. Then, one day in daylight, a MiG came floating up level with him and his squadron. Quadberry couldn't believe it. Others in the squadron were shy, but Quadberry knew where and how the MiG could shoot. He flew below the cannons and then came in behind it. He knew the MiG wanted one of the B-52s and not mainly him. The MiG was so concentrated on the fat B-52 that he forgot about Quadberry. It was really an amateur suicide pilot in the MiG. Quadberry got on top of him and let down a missile, rising out of the way of it. The missile blew off the tail of the MiG. But then Quadberry wanted to see if the man got safely out of the cockpit. He thought it would be pleasant if the fellow got out with his parachute working. Then Quadberry saw that the fellow wanted to collide his wreckage with the B-52, so Quadberry turned himself over and cannoned, evaporated the pilot and cockpit. It was the first man he'd killed.

The next trip out, Quadberry was hit by a ground missile. But his jet kept flying. He flew it a hundred miles and got to the sea. There was the *Bonhomme Richard,* so he ejected. His back was snapped but, by God, he landed right on the deck. His mates caught him in their arms and cut the parachute off him. His back hurt for weeks, but he was all right. He rested and recuperated in Hawaii for a month.

Then he went off the front of the ship. Just like that, his F-6 plopped in the ocean and sank like a rock. Quadberry saw the ship go over him. He knew he shouldn't eject just yet. If he ejected now he'd knock his head on the bottom and get chewed up in the motor blades. So Quadberry waited. His plane was sinking in the green and he could see the hull of the aircraft carrier getting smaller, but he had oxygen through his mask and it didn't seem that urgent a decision. Just let the big ship get over. Down what later proved to be sixty feet, he pushed the ejection button. It fired him away, bless it, and he woke up ten feet under the surface swimming against an almost overwhelming body of underwater parachute. But two of his mates were in a helicopter, one of them on the ladder to lift him out.

Now Quadberry's back was really hurt. He was out of this war and all wars for good.

Lilian, the stewardess, was killed in a crash. Her jet exploded with a hijacker's bomb, an inept bomb which wasn't supposed to go off, fifteen miles out of Havana; the poor pilot, the poor passengers, the poor stewardesses were all splattered like flesh sparklers over the water just out of Cuba. A fisherman found one seat of the airplane. Castro expressed regrets.

Quadberry came back to Clinton two weeks after Lilian and the others bound for Tampa were dead. He hadn't heard about her. So I told him Lilian was dead when I met him at the airport. Quadberry was thin and rather meek in his civvies—a gray suit and an out-of-style tie. The white ends of his hair were not there—the halo had disappeared—because his hair was cut short. The Arab nose seemed a pitiable defect in an ash-whiskered face that was beyond anemic now. He looked shorter, stooped. The truth was he was sick, his back was killing him. His breath was heavy-laden with airplane martinis and in his limp right hand he held a wet cigar. I told him about Lilian. He mumbled something sideways that I could not possibly make out.

"You've got to speak right at me, remember? Remember me, Quadberry?"

"Mom and Dad of course aren't here."

"No. Why aren't they?"

"He wrote me a letter after we bombed Hué. Said he hadn't sent me to Annapolis to bomb the architecture of Hué. He had been there once and had some important experience—French-kissed the queen of Hué or the like. Anyway, he said I'd have to do a hell of a lot of repentance for that. But he and Mom are separate people. Why isn't *she* here?"

"I don't know!"

"I'm not asking you the question. The question is to God."

He shook his head. Then he sat down on the floor of the terminal. People had to walk around. I asked him to get up.

"No. How is old Clinton?"

"Horrible. Aluminum subdivisions, cigar boxes with four thin columns in front, thick as a hive. We got a turquoise water tank; got a shopping center, a monster Jitney Jungle, fifth-rate teenyboppers covering the place like ants." Why was I being so frank just now, as Quadberry sat on the floor downcast, drooped over like a long weak candle? "It's not our town anymore, Ard. It's going to hurt to drive back into it. Hurts me every day. Please get up."

"And Lilian's not even over there now."

"No. She's a cloud over the Gulf of Mexico. You flew out of Pensacola once. You know what beauty those pink and blue clouds are. That's how I think of her."

"Was there a funeral?"

"Oh, yes. Her Methodist preacher and a big crowd over at Wright Ferguson funeral home. Your mother and father were there. Your father shouldn't have come. He could barely walk. Please get up."

"Why? What am I going to do, where am I going?"

"You've got your saxophone."

"Was there a coffin? Did you all go by and see the pink or blue cloud in it?" He was sneering now as he had done when he was eleven and fourteen and seventeen.

"Yes, they had a very ornate coffin."

"Lilian was the Unknown Stewardess. I'm not getting up."

"I said you still have your saxophone."

"No, I don't. I tried to play it on the ship after the last time I hurt my back. No go. I can't bend my neck or spine to play it. The pain kills me."

"Well, *don't* get up, then. Why am I asking you to get up? I'm just a deaf drummer, too vain to buy a hearing aid. Can't stand to write the ad copy I do. Wasn't I a good drummer?"

"Superb."

"But we can't be in this condition forever. The police are going to come and make you get up if we do it much longer."

The police didn't come. It was Quadberry's mother who came. She looked me in the face and grabbed my shoulders before she saw Ard on the floor. When she saw him she yanked him off the floor, hugging him passionately. She was shaking with sobs. Quadberry was gathered to her as if he were a rope she was trying to wrap around herself. Her mouth was all over him. Quadberry's mother was a good-looking woman of fifty. I simply held her purse. He cried out that his back was hurting. At last she let him go.

"So now we walk," I said.

"Dad's in the car trying to quit crying," said his mother.

"This is nice," Quadberry said. "I thought everything and everybody was dead around here." He put his arms around his mother. "Let's all go off and kill some time together." His mother's hair was on his lips. "You?" he asked me.

"Murder the devil out of it," I said.

I pretended to follow their car back to their house in Clinton. But when we were going through Jackson, I took the North 55 exit and disappeared from them, exhibiting a great amount of taste, I thought. I would get in their way in this reunion. I had an unimprovable apartment on Old Canton Road in a huge plaster house, Spanish style, with a terrace and ferns and yucca plants, and a green door where I went in. When I woke up I didn't have to make my coffee or fry my egg. The girl who slept in my bed did that. She was Lilian's little sister, Esther Field. Esther was pretty in a minor way and I was proud how I had tamed her to clean and cook around the place. The Field family would appreciate how I lived with her. I showed her the broom and the skillet, and she loved them. She also learned to speak very slowly when she had to say something.

Esther answered the phone when Quadberry called me seven months later. She gave me his message. He wanted to know my opinion on a decision he had to make. There was this Dr. Gordon, a surgeon at Emory Hospital in Atlanta, who said he could cure Quadberry's back problem. Quadberry's back was killing him. He was in torture even holding up the phone to say this. The surgeon said there was a seventy-five/twenty-five chance. Seventy-five that it would be successful, twenty-five that it would be fatal. Esther waited for my opinion. I told her to tell Quadberry to go over to Emory. He'd got through with luck in Vietnam, and now he should ride it out in this petty back operation.

Esther delivered the message and hung up.

"He said the surgeon's just his age; he's some genius from Johns Hopkins Hospital. He said this Gordon guy has published a lot of articles on spinal operations," said Esther.

"Fine and good. All is happy. Come to bed."

I felt her mouth and her voice on my ears, but I could hear only a sort of loud pulse from the girl. All I could do was move toward moisture and nipples and hair.

Quadberry lost his gamble at Emory Hospital in Atlanta. The brilliant surgeon his age lost him. Quadberry died. He died with his Arabian nose up in the air.

That is why I told this story and will never tell another.

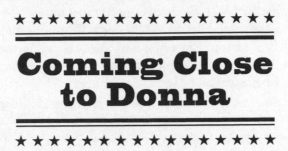

Coming Close to Donna

★ ★ ★ ★ ★ ★ ★ ★ ★ ★ ★ ★ ★ ★ ★ ★

FISTFIGHT ON THE OLD CEMETERY. BOTH OF THEM WANT DONNA, square off, and Donna and I watch from the Lincoln convertible.

I'm neutral. I wear sharp clothes and everybody thinks I'm a fag, though it's not true. The truth is, I'm not all that crazy about Donna, that's all, and I tend to be sissy of voice. Never had a chance otherwise—raised by a dreadfully vocal old aunt after my parents were killed by vicious homosexuals in Panama City. Further, I am fat. I've got fat ankles going into my suede boots.

I ask her, "Say, what you think about that, Donna? Are you going to be whoever wins's girlfriend?"

"Why not? They're both cute," she says.

Her big lips are moist. She starts taking her sweater off. When it comes off, I see she's got great humpers in her bra. There's a nice brown valley of hair between them.

"I can't lose," she says.

Then she takes off her shoes and her skirt. There is extra hair on her thighs near her pantie rim. Out in the cemetery, the guys are knocking the spunk out of each other's cheeks. Bare, Donna's feet are red and not handsome around the toes. She has some serious bunions from her weird shoes, even at eighteen.

44

My age is twenty. I tried to go to college but couldn't sit in the seats long enough to learn anything. Plus, I hated English composition, where you had to correct your phrases. They cast me out like so much wastepaper. The junior college system in California is tough. So I just went back home. I like to wear smart clothes and walk up and down Sunset Strip. That will show them.

By now, Donna is naked. The boys, Hank and Ken, are still battering each other out in the cemetery. I look away from the brutal fight and from Donna's nakedness. If I were a father, I couldn't conceive of this from my daughter.

"Warm me up, Vince. Do me. Or are you really a fag like they say?"

"Not that much," I say.

I lost my virginity. It was like swimming in a warm, oily room—rather pleasant—but I couldn't finish. I thought about the creases in my outfit.

"Come in me, you fag," says she. "Don't hurt my feelings. I want a fag to come in me."

"Oh, you pornographic witch, I can't," says I.

She stands up, nude as an oyster. We look over at the fight in the cemetery. When she had clothes on, she wasn't much to look at. But naked, she is a vision. She has an urgent body that makes you forget the crooked nose. Her hair is dyed pink, but her organ hair isn't.

We watch Hank and Ken slugging each other. They are her age and both of them are on the swimming team.

Something is wrong. They are too serious. They keep pounding each other in the face past what a human could take.

Donna falls on her knees in the green tufted grass.

She faints. Her body is the color of an egg. She fainted supine, titties and hair upward.

The boys are hitting to kill. They are not fooling around. I go ahead in my smart bell-bottom cuffed trousers. By the time I reach them, they are both on the ground. Their scalps are cold.

They are both dead.

"This is awful. They're *dead*," I tell Donna, whose eyes are closed.

"What?" says she.

"They killed each other," says I.

"Touch me," she says. "Make me know I'm here."

I thrust my hand to her organ.

"What do we do?" says I.

She goes to the two bodies, and is absorbed in a tender unnatural act over the blue jeans of Hank and Ken. In former days, these boys had sung a pretty fine duet in their rock band.

"I can't make anybody come! I'm no good!" she says.

"Don't be silly," I say. "They're dead. Let's get out of here."

"I can't just get out of here! They were my sweethearts!" she screams. "Do me right now, Vince! It's the only thing that makes sense."

Well, I flung in and tried.

A half year later, I saw her in Hooper's, the pizza parlor. I asked her how it was going. She was gone on heroin. The drug had made her prettier for a while. Her eyes were wise and wide, all black, but she knew nothing except desperation.

"Vince," she said, "if you'd come lay your joint in me, I wouldn't be lost anymore. You're the only one of the old crowd. Screw me and I could get back to my old neighborhood."

I took her into my overcoat, and when I joined her in the street in back of a huge garbage can, she kept asking: "Tell me where it is, the cemetery!"

At the moment, I was high on cocaine from a rich woman's party.

But I drove her—that is, took a taxi—to the cemetery where her lovers were dead. She knelt at the stones for a while. Then I noted she was stripping off. Pretty soon she was naked again.

"Climb me, mount me, fight for me, fuck me!" she screamed.

I picked up a neighboring tombstone with a great effort. It was an old thing, perhaps going back to the nineteenth century. I crushed her head with it. Then I fled right out of there.

Some of us are made to live for a long time. Others for a short time. Donna wanted what she wanted.

I gave it to her.

Dragged Fighting from His Tomb

IT WAS A ROUT.

We hit them, but they were ready this time.

His great idea was to erupt in the middle of the loungers. Stuart was a profound laugher. His banjo-nigger was with him almost all the time, a man who could make a ballad instantly after an ambush. We had very funny songs about the wide-eyed loungers and pickets, the people of negligent spine leisuring around the depots and warehouses, straightening their cuffs and holding their guns as if they were fishing poles. Jeb loved to break out of cover in the clearing in front of these guards. He offered them first shot if they were ready, but they never were. It was us and the dirty gray, sabers out, and a bunch of fleeing boys in blue.

Except the last time, at Two Roads Junction in Pennsylvania.

These boys had repeaters and they were waiting for us. Maybe they had better scouts than the others. We'd surprised a couple of their pickets and shot them down. But I suppose there were others who got back. This was my fault. My talent was supposed to be circling behind the pickets and slaying every one of them. So I blame myself for the rout, though there are always uncertainties in an ambush. This time it was us that were routed.

We rode in. They were ready with the repeating rifles, and we were blown apart. I myself took a bullet through the throat. It didn't take me off my mount, but I rode about a hundred yards out under a big shade tree and readied myself to die. I offered my prayers.

"Christ, I am dead. Comfort me in the valley of the shadow. Take me through it with honor. Don't let me make the banshee noises I've heard so many times in the field. You and I know I am worth more than that."

I heard the repeating rifles behind me and the shrieks, but my head was a calm green church. I was prepared to accept the big shadow. But I didn't seem to be dying. I felt my neck. I thrust my forefinger in the hole. It was to the right of my windpipe and there was blood on the rear of my neck. The thing had passed clean through the muscle of my right neck. In truth, it didn't even hurt.

I had been thinking: Death does not especially hurt. Then I was merely asleep on the neck of my horse, a red-haired genius for me and a steady one. I'd named him Mount Auburn. We took him from a big farm outside Gettysburg. He wanted me as I wanted him. He was mine. He was the Confederacy.

As I slept on him, he was curious but stable as a rock. The great beast felt my need to lie against his neck and suffered me. He lay the neck out there for my comfort and stood his front heels.

A very old cavalryman in blue woke me up. He was touching me with a flagstaff. He didn't even have a weapon out.

"Eh, boy, you're a pretty dead one, ain't you? Got your hoss's head all bloody. Did you think Jeb was gonna surprise us forever?"

We were alone.

He was amazed when I stood up in the saddle. I could see beyond him through the hanging limbs. A few men in blue were picking things up. It was very quiet. Without a thought, I already had my pistol on his thin chest. I could not see him for a moment for the snout of my pistol.

He went to quivering, of course, the old fool. I saw he had a bardlike face.

What I began was half sport and half earnest.

"Say wise things to me or die, patriot," I said.

"But but but but but but," he said.

"Shhh!" I said. "Let nobody else hear. Only me. Tell the most exquisite truths you know."

He paled and squirmed.

"What's wrong?" I asked.

A stream of water came out the cuff of his pants.

I don't laugh. I've seen pretty much all of it. Nothing a body does disgusts me. After you've seen them burst in the field in two days of sun, you are not surprised by much that the mortal torso can do.

"I've soiled myself, you gray motherfucker," said the old guy.

"Get on with it. No profanity necessary," I said.

"I believe in Jehovah, the Lord; in Jesus Christ, his son; and in the Holy Ghost. I believe in the Trinity of God's bride, the church. To be honest. To be square with your neighbor. To be American and free," he said.

"I asked for the truths, not beliefs," I said.

"But I don't understand what you mean," said the shivering home guard. "Give me an example."

"You're thrice as old as I. You should give *me* the examples. For instance: Where is the angry machine of all of us? Why is God such a blurred magician? Why are you begging for your life if you believe those things? Prove to me that you're better than the rabbits we ate last night."

"I'm better because I know I'm better," he said.

I said, "I've read Darwin and floundered in him. You give me aid, old man. Find your way out of this forest. Earn your life back for your trouble."

"Don't shoot me. They'll hear the shot down there and come blow you over. All the boys got Winchester repeaters," he said.

By this time he'd dropped the regiment flag into a steaming pile of turd from his horse. I noticed that his mount was scared too. The layman does not know how the currents of the rider affect that dumb beast he bestrides. *I've seen a thoroughbred horse refuse to move at all under a man well known as an idiot with a plume. It happened in the early days in the streets of Richmond with Wailing Ott, a colonel too quick if I've ever seen one. His horse just wouldn't move when Ott's boys paraded out to Manassas. He screamed and there were guffaws. He even cut the beast with his saber. The horse sat right down on the ground like a deaf beggar of a darky. Later, in fact during the battle of Manassas, Colonel Ott, loaded with pistols, sabers and even a Prussian dagger, used a rotten outhouse and fell through the aperture (or split it by his outlandish weight in iron) and drowned head down in night soil. I saw his horse roaming. It took to me. I loved it and its name (I christened it afresh) was Black Answer, because a mare had just died under me and here this other beast ran into my arms. It ran for me. I had to rein Black Answer to keep him behind General Stuart himself. (Though Jeb was just another colonel then.) I am saying that a good animal knows his man. I was riding Black Answer on a bluff over the York when a puff went out of a little boat we were harassing with Pelham's cannon from the shore. I said to Black Answer, "Look at McClellan's little sailors playing war down there, boy." The horse gave a sporty little snort in appreciation. He knew what I was saying.*

It wasn't a full fifteen minutes before a cannonball took him right out from under me. I was standing on the ground and really not even stunned, my boots solid in the dust. But over to my right Black Answer was rolling up in the vines, broken in two. That moment is what raised my anger about the war. I recalled it as I held the pistol on the old makeshift soldier. I pulled back the hammer. I recalled the eyes of the horse were still bright when I went to comfort it. I picked up the great head of Black Answer and it came away from the body very easily. What a deliberate and pure expression Black Answer retained, even in death.

What a bog and labyrinth the human essence is, in comparison. We are all overbrained and overemotioned. No wonder my professor at the University of Virginia pointed out to us the horses of that great fantast Jonathan Swift and his Gulliver book. Compared with horses, we are all a dizzy and smelly farce. An old man cannot tell you the truth. An old man, even inspired by death, simply foams and is addled like a crab.

"Tell me," I said, "do you hate me because I hold niggers in bondage? Because I do not hold niggers in bondage. I can't afford it. You know what I'm fighting for? I asked you a question."

"What're you fighting for?"

"For the North to keep off."

"But you're here in Pennsylvania, boy. You attacked *us*. This time we were ready. I'm sorry it made you mad. I'm grievous sorry about your neck, son."

"You never told me any truths. Not one. Look at that head. Look at all those gray hairs spilling out of your cap. Say something wise. I'm about to kill you," I said.

"I have daughters and sons who look up to me," he said.

"Say I am one of your sons. Why do I look up to you?" I said.

"Because I've tried to know the world and have tried to pass it on to the others." He jumped off the horse right into the droppings. He looked as if he were venturing to run. "We're not simple animals. There's a god in every one of us, if we find him," he said.

"Don't try to run. I'd kill you before I even thought," I said. His horse ran away. It didn't like him.

On the ground, below my big horse Mount Auburn, the old man was a little earthling in an overbig uniform. He kept chattering.

"I want a single important truth from you," I said.

"My mouth can't do it," he said. "But there's something here!" He struck his chest at the heart place. Then he started running back to the depot, slapping hanging limbs out of his way. I turned Mount Auburn and rode after. We hit the clearing and Mount Auburn was in an easy prance. The old man was about ten yards ahead, too breathless to warn the troops.

In an idle way I watched their progress too. Captain Swain had been killed during our ambush. I saw the blue boys had put his body up on a pole with a rope around his neck, a target in dirty gray. His body was turning around as they tried out the repeaters on him. But ahead of me the old man bounced like a snow-tail in front of Mount Auburn. We were in a harrowed field. The next time I looked up, a stand of repeaters was under my left hand three strides ahead. I was into their camp. Mount Auburn stopped for me as I picked up a handful of the rifles by the muzzles.

The old man finally let out something.

"It's a secesh!" he shouted.

Only a couple looked back. I noticed a crock of whiskey on a stool where the brave ones were reloading to shoot at Captain Swain again. I jumped off Mount Auburn and went in the back door of the staff house. I kicked the old man through the half-open door and pulled Mount Auburn into the room with me, got his big sweaty withers inside. When I looked around I saw their captain standing up and trying to get out his horse pistol. He was about my age, maybe twenty-five, and he had spectacles. My piece was already cocked and I shot him square in the chest. He backed up and died in another little off-room behind his desk. A woman ran out of the room. She threw open the front door and bullets smacked into the space all around her. She shut the door. A couple of bullets broke wood.

"Lay down," I said.

She had a little derringer double-shot pistol hanging in her hand. The old man was lying flat on the floor behind the desk with me.

The woman was a painted type, lips like blood. "Get down," I told her. She was ugly, just lips, tan hair, and a huge bottom under a petticoat. I wondered what she was going to try with the little pistol. She lay down flat on the floor. I asked her to throw me the pistol. She wouldn't. Then she wormed it across to us behind the big desk. She looked me over, her face grimy from the floor. She had no underwear and her petticoat was hiked up around her middle. The old man and I were looking at her organ.

"Wha? War again?" she said. "I thought we already won."

The woman and the old man laid themselves out like a carpet. I knew the blue boys thought they had me down and were about ready to come in. I was in that position at Chancellorsville. There should be about six fools, I thought. I made it to the open window. Then I moved into the window. With the repeater, I killed four, and the other two limped off. Some histrionic plumehead was raising his saber up and down on the top of a pyramid of cross ties. I shot him just for fun. Then I brought up another repeater and sprayed the yard.

This brought on a silence. Nothing was moving. Nobody was shooting. I knew what they were about to do. I had five minutes to live, until they brought the cannon up. It would be a canister or the straight big ball. Then the firing started again. The bullets were nicking the wall in back of me. I saw Mount Auburn behind the desk. He was just standing there, my friend, my legs. Christ, how could I have forgotten him? "Roll down, Auburn!" I shouted. He lay down quick. He lay down behind the thick oak desk alongside the slut and the old man.

Then what do you think? With nothing to do but have patience until they got the cannon up, somebody's hero came in the back door with a flambeau and a pistol, his eyes closed, shooting everywhere. Mount Auburn whinnied. The moron had shot Auburn. This man I overmurdered. I hit him four times in the face, and his torch flew out the back door with one of the bullets.

I was looking at the hole in Auburn when the roof of the house disappeared. It was a canister blast. The sound was deafening. Auburn was hurting but he was keeping it in. His breaths were deeper, the huge bold eyes waiting on me. I had done a lead-out once before on a corporal who was shot in the buttocks. He screamed the whole time, but he lives now, with a trifling scar on his arse, now the war is over. You put your stiletto very hard to one side of the hole until you feel metal—the bullet—and then you twist. The bullet comes out of the hole by this coiling motion and may even jump up in your hand.

So it was with the lead in Auburn's flank. It hopped right out. The thing to do then is get a sanitary piece of paper and stuff it into the wound. I took a leaf from the middle of the pile of stationery on the captain's table, spun it, and rammed it down.

Auburn never made a complaint. It was I who was mad. I mean, angry beyond myself.

When I went out the front door with the two repeaters, firing and levering, through a dream of revenge—fire from my right hand and fire from my left—the cannoneers did not expect it. I knocked down five of them. Then I knelt and started shooting to kill. I let the maimed go by. But I saw the little team of blue screeching and trying to shoot me, and I killed four of them. Then they all ran off.

There was nothing to shoot at.

I turned around and walked back toward the shack I'd been in. The roof was blown off. The roof was in the backyard lying on the toilet. A Yank with a broken leg had squirmed out from under it.

"Don't kill me," he said.

"Lay still and leave me alone," I said. "I won't kill you."

Mount Auburn had got out of the house and was standing with no expression in the bare dirt. I saw the paper sticking out of his wound. He made an alarmed sound. I turned. The Yank with a broken leg had found that slut's double-barreled derringer. I suppose she threw it up in the air about the time the roof was blown over.

He shot at me with both barrels. One shot hit my boot and the other hit me right in the chin, but did nothing. It had been misloaded or maybe it wasn't ever a good pistol to begin with. The bullet hit me and just fell off.

"Leave me alone," I said. "Come here, Auburn," I called to the big horse. "Hurt him."

I went back in the house while Mount Auburn ran back and forth over the Yank. I cast aside some of the rafters and paper in search of the old man and the slut. They were unscathed. They were under the big desk in a carnal act. I was out of ammunition or I would have slaughtered them too. I went out to the yard and called Mount Auburn off the Yank, who was hollering and running on one leg.

By the time the old man and the slut got through, I had reloaded. They came out the back slot that used to be the door.

"Tell me something. Tell me something wise!" I screamed.

He was a much braver man than I'd seen when I'd seen him in the shade of the tree.

"Tell me *something*. Tell me *something wise!*" I screamed.

"There is no wisdom, Johnny Reb," the old man said. "There's only tomorrow if you're lucky. Don't kill us. Let us have tomorrow."

I spared them. They wandered out through the corpses into the plowed rows. I couldn't see them very far because of the dirty moon. I was petting Mount Auburn when Jeb and fifteen others of the cavalry rode up. Jeb has the great beard to hide his weak chin and his basic ugliness. He's shy. I'm standing here and we've got this whole depot to plunder and burn. So he starts being chums with me. Damned if I don't think he was jealous.

"You stayed and won it, Howard, all on your own?" he says.

"Yes, sir. I did."

"There's lots of dead Christians on the ground," he said. "You've got blood all over your shirt. You're a stout fellow, aren't you?"

"You remember what you said to me when you came back and I was holding Black Answer's head in my hands when he'd been shot out from under me?"

"I recall the time but not what I said," said Jeb Stuart.

"You said, 'Use your weeping on people, not on animals,'" I said.

"I think I'd hold by that," said Stuart.

"You shit! What are we doing killing people in Pennsylvania?" I screamed.

"Showing them that we can, Captain Howard!"

They arrested me and I was taken back (by the nightways) to a detention room in North Carolina. But that was easy to break out of.

I rode my horse, another steed that knew me, named Vermont Nose.

I made it across the Mason-Dixon.

Then I went down with Grant when he had them at Cold Harbor and in the Wilderness. My uniform was blue.

I did not care if it was violet.

I knew how Stuart moved. We were equal Virginia boys. All I needed was twenty cavalry.

I saw him on the road, still dashing around and stroking his beard.

"Stuarrrrrrrrt!" I yelled.

He trotted over on his big gray horse.

"Don't I know this voice?" he said.

"It's Howard," I said.

"But I sent you away. What uniform are you wearing?"

"Of your enemy," I said.

They had furnished me with a shotgun. But I preferred the old Colt. I shot him right in the brow, so that not another thought would pass about me or about himself or about the South, before death. I knew I was killing a man with wife and children.

I never looked at what the body did on its big horse.

Then Booth shot Lincoln, issuing in the graft of the Grant administration.

• • •

I am dying from emphysema in a Miami hotel, from a twenty-five-year routine of cigars and whiskey. I can't raise my arm without gasping.

I know I am not going to make it through 1901. I am the old guy in a blue uniform. I want a woman to lie down for me. I am still functional. I believe we must eradicate all the old soldiers and all their assemblies. My lusts surpass my frame. I don't dare show my pale ribs on the beach. I hire a woman who breast-feeds me and lets me moil over her body. I've got twenty thousand left in the till from the Feds.

The only friends of the human sort I have are the ghosts that I killed. They speak when I am really drunk.

"Welcome," they say. Then I enter a large gray hall, and Stuart comes up.

"Awwww!" he groans. "Treason."

"That's right," I say.

In 1900 they had a convention of Confederate veterans at the hotel, this lonely tall thing on the barbarous waves. I was well into my third stewed mango, wearing my grays merely to be decorous. I heard a group of old coots of about my age hissing at a nearby table. It became clear that I was the object of distaste.

I stood up.

"What is it?" I asked them.

I was answered by a bearded high-mannered coot struck half dead by Parkinson's disease. He was nodding like a reed in wind. He rose in his colonel's cape. Beside him his cane clattered to the floor.

"I say I saw you in the road, dog. I'm a Virginian, and I saw it by these good eyes. You killed Jeb Stuart. *You!* Your presence is a mockery to us of the Old Cause."

"Leave me alone, you old toy," I said.

I raised my freckled fists. His companions brought him down.

When the convention left, I dressed in my grays again and walked to the beach. Presently Charlie came out of the little corral over the dune, walking Mount Auburn's grandchild. If President Grant lied to me, I don't want to know. I have proof positive that it came from a Pennsylvania farm in the region where we foraged and ambushed.

It was an exquisitely shouldered red horse, the good look in its eye.

Charlie let me have the rein and I led the animal down to the hard sand next to the water. It took me some time to mount. My overcoat fell over his withers.

"You need any help, Captain Howard?" Charlie asked.

"I don't need a goddamned thing except privacy," I said.

There was nothing on the beach, only the waves, the hard sand, and the spray. The beauty I sat on ran to the verge of his heart-burst. I had never given the horse a name. I suppose I was waiting for him to say what he wanted, to talk.

But Christ is his name, this muscle and heart striding under me.

★ ★

Midnight and I'm Not Famous Yet

★ ★

I WAS WALKING AROUND GON ONE NIGHT, AND THIS C-MAN—I SAW HIM open the window, and there was a girl in back of him, so I thought it was all right—peeled down on me and shot the back heel off my boot. Nearest I came to getting mailed home when I was there. A jeep came by almost instantly with a thirty cal mounted, couple of allies in it. I pointed over to the window. They shot out about a box and a half on the apartment, just about burned out the dark slot up there. As if the dude was hanging around digging the weather after he shot at me. There were shrieks in the night, etc. But then a man opened the bottom door and started running in the street. This ARVN fellow knocked the shit out of his buddy's head turning the gun to zap the running man. Then I saw something as the dude hit a light: he was fat. I never saw a fat Cong. So I screamed out in Vietnamese. He didn't shoot. I took out my machine pistol and ran after the man, who was up the street by now, and I was hobbling without a heel on my left boot.

Some kind of warm nerve sparklers were getting all over me. I believe in magic, because, million-to-one odds, it was Ike "Tubby" Wooten, from Redwood, a town just north of Vicksburg. He was leaning on a rail, couldn't run anymore. He was wearing the uniform of our army with a patch on it I didn't even know what was. Old Tubby would remember me. I was the joker at our school. I once pissed in a Dixie cup and eased three drops of it on the library radiator. But Tubby was so serious, reading some photo magazine. He peeped up and saw me do it, then looked down quickly. When the smell came over the place, he asked me, Why? What do you want? What profit is there in that? I guess I just giggled. Sometimes around midnight I'd wake up and think of his questions, and it disturbed me that there was no answer. I giggled my whole youth away. Then I joined the army. So I thought it was fitting I'd play a Nelda on him now. A Nelda was invented by a corporal when they massacred a patrol up north on a mountain and he was the only one left. The NVA ran all around him and he had this empty rifle hanging on him. They spared him.

"I'm a virgin! Spare me!"

"You, holding the gun? Did you say you were a virgin?" said poor Tubby, trying to get air.

"I am a virgin," I said, which was true, but hoping to get a laugh, anyway.

"And a Southern virgin. A captain. Please to God, don't shoot me," that fat boy said. "I was cheating on my wife for the first time. The penalty shouldn't be death."

"Why'd you run from the house, Tubby?"

"You know me." Up the street they had searchlights moved up all over the apartment house. They shot about fifty rounds into the house. They were shooting tracers now. It must've lit up my face; then a spotlight went by us.

"Bobby Smith," said Tubby. "My God, I thought you were God."

"I'm not. But it seems holy. Here we are looking at each other."

"Aw, Bobby, they were three beautiful girls. I'd never have done the thing with one, but there were *three*." He was a man with a small pretty face laid around by three layers of jowl and chin. "I heard the machine gun and the guilt struck me. I had to get out. So I just ran."

"Why're you in Nam, anyway?"

"I joined. I wasn't getting anything done but being in love with my wife. That wasn't doing America any good."

"What's that patch on you?"

"Photography." He lifted his hands to hold an imaginary camera. "I'm with the Big Red. I've done a few things out of helicopters."

"You want to see a ground unit? With me. Or does Big Red own you?"

"I have no idea. There hasn't been much to shoot. Some smoking villages. A fire in a bamboo forest. I'd like to see a face."

"You got any pictures of Vicksburg?"

"Oh, well, a few I brought over."

The next day I found out he was doing idlework and Big Red didn't care where he was, so I got him over in my unit. I worried about his weight, etc., and the fact he might be killed. But the boys liked a movie-cameraist being along and I wanted to see the pictures from Vicksburg. It was nice to have Tubby alongside. He was hometown, such as he was. Before we flew out north, he showed me what he had. There was a fine touch in his pictures. There was a cute little Negro on roller skates, and an old woman on a porch, a little boy sleeping in a speedboat with the river in the background. Then there was a blurred picture of his wife naked, just moving through the kitchen, nothing sexy. The last picture was the best. It was John Whitelaw about to crack a golf ball. Tubby had taken it at Augusta, at the Masters. I used to live about five houses away from the Whitelaws. John had his mouth open and his arms, the forearm muscles, were bulked up plain as wires.

John was ten years older than me, but I knew about him. John Whitelaw was our only celebrity since the Civil War. In the picture he wore spectacles. It struck me as something deep, brave, mighty and, well, modern; he had to have the eyeglasses on him to see the mighty thing he was about to do. Maybe I sympathized too much, since I have to wear glasses too, but I thought this picture was worthy of a statue. Tubby had taken it in a striking gray-and-white grain. John seemed to be hitting under a heroic deficiency. You could see the sweat droplets on his neck. His eyes were in an agony. But the thing that got me was that John Whitelaw *cared* so much about what he was doing. It made me love America to know he was in it, and I hadn't loved anything for nigh three years then. Tubby was talking about all this "our country" eagle and stars mooky and had seen all the war movies coming over on the boat. I never saw a higher case of fresh and crazy in my life.

But the picture of John at Augusta, it moved me. It was a man at work and play at the same time, doing his damnedest. And Whitelaw was a beautiful man. They pass that term "beautiful" around like pennies nowadays, but I saw him in the flesh once. It was fall in Baton Rouge, around the campus of LSU. He was getting out of a car with a gypsyish girl on his hand. I was ten, I guess, and he was twenty. We were down for a ball game, Mississippi vs. Louisiana, a classic that makes you goo-goo eyed when you're a full-grown man if your heart's in Dixie, etc. At ten, it's Ozville. So in the middle of it, this feeling, I saw Whitelaw and his woman. My dad stopped the car.

"Wasn't that Johnny Whitelaw?" he asked my grandfather.

"You mean that little peacock who left football for golf? He ought to be quarterbacking Ole Miss right now. It wouldn't be no contest," said my grandfather.

I got my whole idea of what a woman should look like that day . . . and what a man should be. The way John Whitelaw looked, it sort of rebuked yourself ever hoping to call yourself a man. The girl he was with woke up my clammy little dreams about, not even sex, but the perfect thing—it was something like her. As for Whitelaw, his face was curled around by that wild hair the color of beer; his chest was deep, just about to bust out of that collar and bow tie.

"That girl he had, she had a drink in her hand. You could hardly see her for her hair," said my grandfather.

"Johnny gni him vomething Cajun," said my father.

Then my grandfather turned around, looking at me like I was a crab who could say a couple of words. "You look like your mother, but you got gray eyes. What's wrong? You have to take a leak?"

Nothing was wrong with me. I'd just seen John Whitelaw and his girl, that was all.

Tubby had jumped a half-dozen times at Fort Bragg, but he had that heavy box harnessed on him now and I knew he was going down fast and better know how to hit. I explained to him. I went off the plane four behind him, cupping a joint. I didn't want Tubby seeing me smoking grass, but it's just about the only way to get down. If the Cong saw the plane, you'd fall into a barbecue. They've killed a whole unit before, using shotguns and flame bullets, just like your ducks floating in. You hear a lot of noise going in with a whole unit in the air like this. We start shooting about a hundred feet from ground. If you ever hear one bullet pass you, you get sick thinking there might be a lot of them. All you can do is point your gun down and shoot it all out. You can't reload. You never hit anything. There's a sharpshooter, McIntire, who killed a C shooting from his chute, but that's unlikely. They've got you like a gallery of rabbits if they're down there.

I saw Tubby sinking fast over the wrong part of the field. I had two chutes out, so I cut one off and dropped over toward him, pulling on the left lines so hard I almost didn't have a chute at all for a while. I got level with him and he looked over, pointing down. He was doing his arm up and down. Could have been farmers or just curious rubbernecks down in the field, but there were about ten of them grouped up together, holding things. They weren't shooting, though. I was carrying an experimental gun, me and about ten of my boys. It was a big, light thing; really, it was just a launcher. There were five shells in it, bigger than shotgun shells. If you shot one of them, it was supposed to explode on impact and burn out everything in a twenty-five-yard radius. It was a mean little mother of phosphorus, is what it was. I saw the boys shooting them down into the other side of the field. This stuff would take down a whole tree and you'd chute into a quiet smoking bare area.

I don't know. I don't like a group waiting on me when I jump out of a plane. I almost zapped them, but they weren't throwing anything up. Me and Tubby hit the ground about the same time. They were farmers. I talked to them. They said there were three Cong with them until we were about a hundred feet over. The Cong knew we had the phosphorus shotgun and showed ass, loping out to the woods fifty yards to the north when me and Tubby were coming in.

Tubby took some film of the farmers. All of them had thin chin beards and soft hands because their wives did most of the work. They essentially just lay around and were hung with philosophy, and actually were pretty happy. Nothing had happened around here till we jumped in. These were fresh people. I told them to get everybody out of the huts because we were going to have a thing in the field. It was a crisis point. A huge army of NVA was coming down and they just couldn't avoid us if they wanted to have any run of the valley five miles south. We were there to harass the front point of the army, whatever it was like.

"We're here to check their advance," Tubby told the farmers.

Then we all collected in the woods, five hundred and fifty souls, scared out of mind. What we had going was we knew the NVA general bringing them down was not too bright. He went to the Sorbonne and we had this report from his professor: "Li Dap speaks French very well and had studied Napoleon before he got to me. He knows Robert Lee and the strategy of Jeb Stuart, whose daring circles around an immense army captured his mind. Li Dap wants to be Jeb Stuart. I cannot imagine him in command of more than five hundred troops."

And what we knew stood up. Li Dap had tried to circle left with twenty thousand and got the hell kicked out of him by idle navy guns sitting outside Gon. He just wasn't very bright. He had half his army climbing around these bluffs, no artillery or air force with them, and it was New Year's Eve for our side.

"So we're here just to kill the edge of their army?" said Tubby.

"That's what I'm here for, why I'm elected. We kill more C's than anybody else in the Army."

"But what if they take a big run at you, all of them?" said Tubby.

"There'll be lots of cooking."

We went out in the edge of the woods and I glassed the field. It was almost night. I saw two tanks come out of the other side and our pickets running back. Pock, pock, pock from the tanks. Then you saw this white glare on one tank where somebody on our team had laid on with one of the phosphorus shotguns. It got white and throbbing, like a little star, and the gun wilted off of it. The other tank ran off a gully into a hell of a cow pond. You wouldn't have known it was that deep. It went underwater over the gun, and they let off the cannon when they went under, raising the water in a spray. It was the silliest looking thing. Some of them got out and a sergeant yelled for me to come up. It was about a quarter mile out there. Tubby got his camera, and we went out with about fifteen troops.

At the edge of the pond, looking into flashlights, two tank-men sat, one tiny, the other about my size. They were wet, and the big guy was mad. Lot of the troops were chortling, etc. It was awfully damned funny, if you didn't happen to be one of the C-men in the tank.

"Of all the fuck ups. This is truly saddening." The big guy was saying something like that. I took a flashlight and looked him over. Then I didn't believe it. I told Tubby to get a shot of the big cursing one. Then they brought them on back. I told the boys to tie up the big one and carry him in.

I sat on the ground, talking to Tubby.

"It's so quiet. You'd think they'd be shelling us," he said.

"We're spread out too good. They don't have much ammo now. They really galloped down here. That's the way Li Dap does it. Their side's got big trouble now. And, Tubby, me and you are famous."

"Me, what?"

"You took his picture. You can get some more, more arty angles on him tomorrow."

"Him?"

"It's Li Dap himself. He was in the tank in the pond."

"No. Their general?"

"You want me to go prove it?"

We walked over. They had him tied around a tree. His hands were above his head and he was sitting down. I smelled some hash in the air. The guy who was blowing it was a boy from Detroit I really liked, and I hated to come down on him, but I really beat him up. He never got a lick in. I kicked his rump when he was crawling away and some friends picked him up. You can't have lighting up that shit at night on the ground. Li Dap was watching the fight, still cursing.

"Asshole of the mountains." He was saying something like that. "Fortune's ninny."

"Hi, General. My French isn't too good. You speak English. Honor us."

He wouldn't say anything.

"You have a lot of courage, running out front with the tanks."
There were some snickers in the bush, but I cut them out quick. We
had a real romantic here and I didn't want him laughed at. He wasn't
hearing much, though. About that time two of their rockets flashed
into the woods. They went off in the treetops and scattered.

"It was worthy of Patton," I said. "You had some bad luck.
But we're glad you made it alive."

"Kiss my ass."

"You want your hands free? Oliver, get his ropes off the tree."
The guy I beat up cut him off the tree.

"You scared us very deeply. How many tanks do you have
over there?"

"Nonsense," he said.

"What do you have except for a few rockets?"

"I had no credence in the phosphorus gun."

"Your men saw us use them when we landed."

"I had no credence."

"So you just came out to see."

"I say to them never to fear the machine when the cause is
just. To throw oneself past the technology tricks of the monsters and
into his soft soul."

"And there you will win, huh?"

"Of course. It is our country." He smiled at me. "It's relative
to your war in the nineteenth century. The South had slavery. The
North must purge it so that it is a healthy region of our country."

"You were out in the tank as an example to your men?"

"Yes!"

All this he needed was a plumed hat.

"Sleep well," I said, and told Oliver to get him a blanket and
feed him, and feed the tiny gunner with him.

When we got back to my dump, I walked away for a while, not wanting to talk with Tubby. I started crying. It started with these hard sobs
coming up like rocks in my throat. I started looking out at forever,
across the field. They shot up three more rockets from the woods
below the hill. I waited for the things to land on us. They fell on the

tops of trees, nothing near me, but there was some howling off to the right. Somebody had got some shrapnel.

I'd killed so many gooks. I'd killed them with machine guns, mortars, howitzers, knives, wire, me and my boys. My boys loved me. They were lying all around me, laying this great cloud of trust on me. The picture of John Whitelaw about to hit that ball at Augusta was jammed in my head. There was such care in his eyes, and it was only a golf ball, a goddamned piece of nothing. But it was wonderful and peaceful. Nobody was being killed. Whitelaw had the right. He had the beloved American right to the pursuit of happiness. The tears were out of my jaws then. Here we shot each other up. All we had going was the pursuit of horror. It seemed to me my life had gone straight from teenage giggling to horror. I had never had time to be but two things, a giggler and a killer.

Christ, I was crying for myself. I had nothing for the other side, understand that. North Vietnam was a land full of lousy little Commie robots, as far as I knew. A place of the worst propaganda and hypocrisy. You should have read some of their agitprop around Gon, talking about freedom and throwing off the yoke, etc. The gooks went for Communism because they were so ignorant and had nothing to lose. The South Vietnamese, too. I couldn't believe we had them as allies. They were such a pretty and uniformly indecent people. I once saw a little taxi boy, a kid is all, walk into a medevac with one arm and a hand blown off by a mine he'd picked up. These housewives were walking behind him in the street, right in the middle of Gon. Know what they were doing? They were laughing. They thought it was the most hysterical misadventure they'd ever seen. These people were on our side. These were our friends and lovers. That happened early when I got there. I was a virgin when I got to Nam and stayed a virgin, through a horde of B-girls, the most base and luscious-lipped hustlers. Because I did not want to mingle with this race.

In an ARVN hospital tent you see the hurt officers lined up in front of a private who's holding in his guts with his hands. They'll treat the officer with a bad pimple before they treat the dying private. We're supposed to be shaking hands with these people. Why can't we be fighting for some place like England? When you train yourself to blow gooks away, like I did, something happens, some kind of popping returning dream of murder-with-a-smile.

I needed away. I was sick. In another three months I'd be zapping orphanages.

"Bobby, are you all right?" said Tubby, waddling out to the tree I was hanging on.

"I shouldn't ever've seen that picture of John Whitelaw. I shouldn't've."

"Do you really think we'll be famous?" Tubby got an enchanted look on him, sort of a dumb angel look in that small pretty face amid the fat rolls. It was about midnight. There was a fine Southern moon lighting up the field. You could see every piece of straw out there. Tubby, by my ass, had the high daze on him. He'd stepped out here in the boonies and put down his foot in Ozville.

"This'll get me major, anyhow. Sure. Fame. Both of us," I said.

Tubby said: "I tried to get nice touches in with the light coming over his face. These pictures could turn out awfully interesting. I was thinking about the cover of *Time* or *Newsweek*."

"It'll change your whole life, Tubby," I said.

Tubby was just about to die for love of fate. He was shivering.

I started enjoying the field again. This time the straws were waving. It was covered with rushing little triangles, these sort of toiling dots. Our side opened up. All the boys came up to join within a minute and it was a sheet of lightning rolling back and forth along the outside of the woods. I could see it all while I was walking back to the radio. I mean humping low. Tubby must've been walking straight up. He took something big right in the square of his back. It rolled him up twenty feet in front of me. He was dead and smoking when I made it to him.

"C'mon, I've got to get the pictures," he said.

I think he was already dead.

I got my phosphorus shotgun. Couldn't think of anything but the radio and getting it over how we were being hit, so we could get dragons—helicopters with fifty cals—in quick. The dragons are nice. They've got searchlights, and you put two of them over a field like we were looking at, they'd clean it out in half an hour. So I made it to the radio and the boys had already called the dragons in, everything was fine. Only we had to hold them for an hour and a half until the dragons got there. I humped up front. Every now and then you'd see somebody use one of the experimental guns. The bad thing was that it lit up the gunner too much at night, too much shine out of the muzzle. I took note of that to tell them when we got back. But the gun really smacked the gook assault. It was good for about seventy-five yards and hit with a huge circle burn about the way they said it would. The gooks' first force was knocked off. You could see men who were still burning running back through the straw, hear them screaming.

I don't remember too well. I was just loitering near the radio, a few fires out in the field, everything mainly quiet. Copters on the way. I decided to go take a look at Li Dap. I thought it was our boys around him, though I didn't know why. They were wearing green and standing up plain as day. There was Oliver, smoking a joint. His rifle was on the ground. The NVA were all around him and he hadn't even noticed. There were so many of them—twenty or so—they were clanking rifles against each other. One of them was going up behind Oliver with a bayonet, just about on him. If I'd had a carbine like usual, I could've taken the bayoneteer off and at least five of the others. Oliver and Li Dap might've ducked and survived.

But I couldn't pick and choose. I hardly even thought. The barrel of the shotgun was up and I pulled on the trigger, aiming at the bayoneteer.

I burned them all up.

Nobody even made a squeak.

There was a flare and they were gone.

Some of my boys rushed over with guns. All they were good for was stomping out the little fires on the edges.

When we got back, I handed over Tubby's pictures. The old man was beside himself over my killing a general, a captured general. He couldn't understand what kind of laxity I'd allowed to let twenty gooks come up on us like that. They thought I might have a court-martial, and I was under arrest for a week. The story got out to UPI and they were saying things like "atrocity," with my name spelled all over the column.

But it was dropped and I was pulled out and went home a lieutenant.

That's all right. I've got four hundred and two boys out there—the ones that got back—who love me and know the truth, who love me *because* they know the truth.

It's Tubby's lost fame I dream about.

The army confiscated the roll and all his pictures. I wrote the Pentagon a letter asking for a print and waited two years here in Vicksburg without even a statement they received the note. I see his wife, who's remarried and is fat herself now, at the discount drugstore every now and then. She has the look of a kind of hopeless cheer. I got a print from the Pentagon when the war was over and it didn't matter. Li Dap looked wonderful—strained, abused and wild, his hair flying over his eyes while he's making a statement full of conviction.

It made me start thinking of faces again.

Since I've been home I've crawled in bed with almost anything that would have me. I've slept with high school teachers, Negroes and, the other night, my own aunt. It made her smile. All those years of keeping her body in trim came to something, the big naughty surprise that the other women look for in religion, God showing up and killing their neighbors, sparing them. But she knows a lot about things and I think I'll be in love with her.

We were at the John Whitelaw vs. Whitney Maxwell play off together. It was a piece of wonder. I felt thankful to the wind or God or whoever brought that fine contest near enough by. When they hit the ball, the sound traveled like a rifle snap out over the bluffs. When it was impossible to hit the ball, that is exactly when they hit it.

My aunt grabbed hold of my fingers when the tension was almost up to a roar. The last two holes. Ah, John lost. I looked over the despondency of the home crowd.

Fools! Fools! I thought. Love it! Love the loss as well as the gain. Go home and dig it. Nobody was killed. We saw victory and defeat, and they were both wonderful.

★ ★

Knowing He Was Not My Kind Yet I Followed

★ ★

IT MAKES ME SICK WHEN WE KILL THEM OR RIDE HORSES OVER THEM. My gun is blazing just like the rest of them, but I hate it.

One day I rode up on a fellow in blue and we were both out of ammunition. He was trying to draw his saber and I was so outraged I slapped him right off his horse. The horseman behind me cheered. He said I'd broken the man's neck. I was horrified. Oh, life, life—you kill what you love. I have seen such handsome faces with their mouths open, their necks open to the Pennsylvania sun. I love stealing for forage and food, but I hate this murdering business that goes along with it.

Some nights I amble in near the fire to take a cup with the boys, but they chase me away. I don't scold, but in my mind there are the words: All right, have your way in this twinkling mortal world.

Our Jeb Stuart is never tired. You could wake him with a message any time of night and he's awake on the instant. He's such a bull. They called him "Beauty" at West Point. We're fighting and killing all his old classmates and even his father-in-law, General Philip St. George

Cooke. Jeb wrote about this man once when he failed to join the Confederacy: "He will regret it but once, and that will be continuously."

Gee, he can use the word, Jeb can. I was with him through the ostrich feathers in his hat and the early harassments, when we had nothing but shotguns and pretty horses. He was always a fool at running around his enemy. I was with him when we rode down a lane around a confused Yank picket, risking the Miniés. But he's a good family man too, they say.

I was with him when he first went around McClellan and scouted Porter's wing. That's when I fell in love with burning and looting. We threw ourselves on railroad cars and wagons, we collected carbines, uniforms and cow steaks that we roasted on sticks over the embers of the rails. Jeb passed right by when I was chewing my beef and dipping water out of the great tank. He had his banjo man and his dancing nigger with him. Jeb has terrific body odor along with his mud-spattered boots, but it rather draws than repels, like the musk of a woman.

When we were celebrating in Richmond, even I was escorted by a woman out into the shadows and this is why I say this. She surrendered to me, her hoop skirt was around her eyebrows, her white nakedness lying under me if I wanted it, and I suppose I did, because I went laboring at her, head full of smoke and unreason. I left her with her dress over her face like a tent and have no clear notion of what her face was like, though my acquaintance Ruppert Longstreet told me in daylight she was a troll.

That was when young Pelham set fire to the Yank boat in the James with his one Napoleon cannon. We whipped a warship from the shore. Pelham was a genius about artillery. I loved that too.

It's killing close up that bothers me. Once a blue-suited man on the ground was holding his hands out after his horse fell over. This was at Manassas. He seemed to be unclear about whether this was an actual event; he seemed to be asking for directions back to his place in a stunned friendly way. My horse, Pardon Me, was rearing way high and I couldn't put the muzzle of my shotgun at him. Then Jeb rode in, plumes shivering. He slashed the man deep in the shoulder with his saber. The man knelt down, closing his eyes as if to pray. Jeb rode next to me. What a body odor he had. On his horse, he said:

"Finish that poor Christian off, soldier."

My horse settled down and I blew the man over. Pardon Me reared at the shot and tore away in his own race down a vacant meadow—fortunate for me, since I never had to look at the carnage but only thought of holding on.

After McClellan placed himself back on the York, we slipped through Maryland and here we are in Pennsylvania. We go spying and cavorting and looting. I'm wearing out. Pardon Me, I think, feels the lunacy even in this smooth countryside. We're too far from home. We are not defending our beloved Dixie anymore. We're just bandits and maniacal. The gleam in the men's eyes tells this. Everyone is getting crazier on the craziness of being simply too far from home for decent return. It is like Ruth in the alien corn, or a troop of men given wings over the terrain they cherished and taken by the wind to trees they do not know.

Jeb leads us. Some days he has the sneer of Satan himself.

Nothing but bad news comes up from home, when it comes.

Lee is valiant but always too few.

All the great bullies I used to see out front are dead or wounded past use.

The truth is, not a one of us except Jeb Stuart believes in anything any longer. The man himself the exception. There is nobody who does not believe in Jeb Stuart. Oh, the zany purposeful eyes, the haggard gleam, the feet of his lean horse high in the air, his rotting flannel shirt under the old soiled grays, and his heroic body odor! He makes one want to be a Christian. I wish I could be one. I'm afraid the only things I count on are chance and safety.

The other night I got my nerve up and asked for him in his tent. When I went in, he had his head on the field desk, dead asleep. The quill was still in his hand. I took up the letter. It was to his wife, Flora. A daguerreotype of her lay next to the paper. It was still wet from Jeb's tears. At the beginning of the letter there was small talk about finding her the black silk she'd always wanted near Gettysburg. Then it continued: "After the shameful defeat at Gettysburg," etc.

I was shocked. I always thought we won at Gettysburg. All the fellows I knew thought we had won. Further, he said:

"The only thing that keeps me going on my mission is the sacred inalienable right of the Confederacy to be the Confederacy, Christ Our Lord, and the memory of your hot hairy jumping nexus when I return."

I placed the letter back on the table. This motion woke him.

I was incredulous that he knew my first name. He looked as if he had not slept a second.

The stories were true.

"Corporal Deed Ainsworth," he said.

"Sorry to wake you, General."

"Your grievance?" he said.

"No one is my friend," I mumbled.

"Because the Creator made you strange, my man. I never met a chap more loyal in the saddle than you. God made us different and we should love His differences as well as His likenesses."

"I'd like to kiss you, General," I said.

"Oh, no. He made me abhor that. Take to your good sleep, my man. We surprise the railroad tomorrow."

"Our raids still entertain you?" I asked.

"Not so much. But I believe our course has been written. We'll kill ten and lose two. Our old Bobbie Lee will smile when we send the nigger back to him with the message. I'll do hell for Lee's smile."

The nigger came in the tent about then. He was highfalutin, never hardly glanced at me. They had a magnificent bay waiting for the letters. Two soldiers came in and took an armload of missives from General Stuart's trunk, pressing them into the saddlebags. The nigger, in civilian clothes, finally looked at me.

"Who dis?" he said.

"Corporal Deed Ainsworth; shake hands," said General Stuart.

I have a glass shop in Biloxi. I never shook hands with any nigger. Yet the moment constrained me to. He was Jeb's best minstrel. He played the guitar better than anything one might want to hear, and the banjo. His voice singing "All Hail the Power" was the only feeling I ever had to fall on my knees and pray. But now he was going back down South as a rider with the messages.

"Ain't shaking hands with no nancy," said the nigger. "They say he lay down with a Choctaw chief in Mississip, say he lick a heathen all over his feathers."

"You're getting opinions for a nigger, George," said Jeb, standing. "I don't believe Our Lord has room for another nigger's thoughts. You are tiring God when you use your mouth, George."

"Yessuh," said George.

"Do you want to apologize to Corporal Ainsworth?"

"I real sorry. I don't know what I say," the nigger said to me. "General Jeb taught me how to talk and sometimes I justs go on talking to try it out."

"Ah, my brother George," Jeb suddenly erupted.

He rushed to the nigger and threw his arms around him. His eyes were full of tears. He embraced the black man in the manner of my dreams of how he might embrace me.

"My chap, my chum. Don't get yourself killed," said Jeb to George. "Try to look ignorant when you get near the road pickets, same as when I found you and saved you from drink."

"I loves you too, General Jeb. I ain't touched nothing since you saved me. Promise. I gon look ignorant like you say, tills I get to Richmond. Then I might have me a beer."

"Even Christ wouldn't deny you that. Ah, my George, there's a heaven where we'll all prosper together. Even this sissy, Corporal Ainsworth."

They both looked at me benevolently. I felt below the nigger.

George got on the horse and took off South.

At five the next morning we came out of a stand of birches and all of us flew high over the railroad, shooting down the men. I had two stolen repeaters on my hip in the middle of the rout and let myself off Pardon Me. A poor torn Yank, driven out of the attack, with no arm but a kitchen fork, straggled up to me. We'd burned and killed almost everything else.

Stuart rode by me screaming in his rich bass to mount. The blue cavalry was coming across the fire toward us. The wounded man was stabbing me in the chest with his fork. Jeb took his saber out in the old grand style to cleave the man from me. I drew the pistol on my right hip and put it almost against Jeb's nose when he leaned to me.

"You kill him, I kill you, General," I said.

There was no time for a puzzled look, but he boomed out: "Are you happy, Corporal Ainsworth? Are you satisfied, my good man Deed?"

I nodded.

"Go with your nature and remember our Savior!" he shouted, last in the retreat.

I have seen it many times, but there is no glory like Jeb Stuart putting spurs in his sorrel and escaping the Minié balls.

They captured me and sent me to Albany prison, where I write this.

I am well fed and wretched.

A gleeful little floorwipe came in the other day to say they'd killed Jeb in Virginia. I don't think there's much reservoir of self left to me now.

This earth will never see his kind again.

Behold the Husband in His Perfect Agony

IN THE ALLEYS THERE WERE SIGHS AND DERISIONS AND THE SLIDE OF dice in the brick dust. His vision was impaired. One of his eyes had been destroyed in the field near Atlanta as he stood there with his binoculars.

Now he was in Richmond.

His remaining eye saw clearly but itched him incessantly, and his head turned, in necessity, this way and that. A clod of dirt struck him, thrown by scrambling children in the mouth of the alley he had just passed. False Corn turned around.

He thanked God it wasn't a bullet.

In the next street there was a group of shoulders in butternut and gray jabbering about the Richmond defenses. He strolled in and listened. A lieutenant in his cups told False Corn what he wanted to hear. He took a cup of acorn coffee from a vendor.

A lovely woman hurried into a house, clicking her heels as she took the steps. He thought of his wife and infant son. They lived in a house in Baltimore. His wife was lively and charming. His son was half Indian, because he, False Corn, was an Indian himself, of the old Huron tribe, though he looked mostly Caucasian.

Now he wore a maroon overcoat that hit him at midknee. In his right pocket were the notes that would have got him killed if discovered by the law or the soldiers.

He turned and went uptown, climbing the hill from the railroad.

False Corn's contact was a Negro who pretended, days, to be mad on the streets. At nights he poisoned the bourbon in the remaining officers' saloons, where colonels and majors drank from the few remaining barrels. Then he loped into a spastic dance—the black forgettable fool—while home-front leaders gasped and collapsed. Apparently the Negro never slept, unless sleep came to him in the day and was overlooked as a phase of his lunacy by passersby, who would rather not have looked at all.

Isaacs False Corn, the Indian, the spy, saw Edison, the Negro, the contact, on the column of an inn. His coat was made of stitched newspapers. Near his bare feet, two dogs failed earnestly at mating. Pigeons snatched at the pieces of things in the rushing gutter. The rains had been hard.

False Corn leaned on the column. He lifted from his pocket, from amongst the notes, a half-smoked and frayed cheroot. He began chewing on the butt. He did not care for a match at this time. His cheroot was a small joy, cool and tasteless.

"Can you read?" False Corn asked Edison.

"Naw," said Edison.

"Can you remember?"

"Not too good, Captain."

"I'm going to have to give you the notes, then. Goddamn it."

"I can run fast. I can hide. I can get through."

"Why didn't you run out of Virginia a long time ago?"

"I seen I could do more good at home."

"I want you to stop using the arsenic. That's unmanly and entirely heinous. That's not what we want at all."

"I thought what you did in war was kill, Captain."

"Not during a man's pleasure. These crimes will land you in a place beyond hell."

"Where's that? Ain't I already been there?"

"The disapproval of President Lincoln. He freed you. Quit acting like an Italian."

"I do anything for Abe," Edison said.

"All you have to do is filter the lines. I mean, get through."

"That ain't no trouble. I been getting through long time. Get through to who?"

"General Phil Sheridan, or Custer. Here's the news: *Jeb Stuart is dead.* If you can't remember anything else, just tell them Stuart is dead. In the grave. Finished. Can you remember?"

"Who Jeb Stuart be?" asked Edison, who slobbered, pretending or real.

"Their best horse general. If you never get the notes to them, just remember: Stuart is dead."

False Corn stared into the purpled white eyes of Edison. One of the dogs, ashamed, licked Edison's toes. It began raining feebly. False Corn removed his overcoat.

"All my notes are in the right pocket. Can you remember the thing I told you, even if you lose the notes?"

"Stuart is dead. He down," said Edison.

Passersby thought it an act of charity. False Corn placed the coat on Edison's shoulders. What an incident of noblesse oblige, they thought. These hard times and look at this.

False Corn shivered as the mist came in under the gables. He chewed the cigar. Edison rushed away from him up the street, scattering the dogs and pigeons. Do get there, fool, the Indian thought.

False Corn's shirt was light yellow and soiled at the cuffs. On his wrist he wore a light sterling bracelet. It was his wife's and it brought her close to him when he shook it on his arm and felt its tender weight. He plunged into the sweet gloom of his absence from her, and her knees appeared to his mind as precious, his palms on them.

In the front room of the hotel a number of soldiers were sitting on the floor, saying nothing. Some of them were cracking pecans and eating them quickly. There was no heat in the building, but it was warmer and out of the mist.

His eye itched. He asked where there might be water. A corporal pointed. He found a bucket in the kitchen. The water was sour.

When he finished the cup, he found a man standing on his blind side. The man held a folded paper in his game hand. His other arm was missing. The brim of his hat was drawn down.

"Mister False Corn?" the man said.

He shouldn't have known the name. No one else in Richmond was supposed to know his true name. False Corn was swept by a chill. He wished for his pistol, but it was in the chest in his garret, back in the boardinghouse. He took the note.

It read: "Not only is Gen. Stuart dead. The nigger is dead too." It was in a feminine script and it was signed "Mrs. O'Neal."

When he looked up, the one-armed man was gone. False Corn pondered whether to leave the kitchen. Since there was nothing else to do, he did. Nobody was looking at him as he made his way out of the lobby. He had determined on the idea of a woman between two mean male faces, the trio advancing before he opened the door.

But he was on the street now.

Nothing is happening to me, he thought. There's no shot, no harsh shout.

It will be in my room, decided False Corn, opening the door of the garret. Yes, there. There it sits. Where's the woman?

A bearded man was sitting on the narrow bed, holding a stiff brown hat between his legs. False Corn's pistol was lying on the blanket beside the man's thigh. The man was thin. His clothes were sizes large on him. But his voice was soft and mellow, reminiscent.

"Shut the door. I've known you since Baltimore, my friend."

"Who are you?" False Corn said.

"An observer. Mrs. O'Neal. Your career is over."

This *voice*, thought False Corn. He stood carefully, a weary statue with severely combed black hair to his nape, center-parted. This man is little, he thought. I can murder him with my hands if he drops his guard, thought False Corn.

"You have a funny name, a big pistol, and you've been quite a spy. We know all the women you've been with."

"Then you know nothing. I've been with no women."

"Why not? A man gets lonely."

"I've been more hungry than lustful in these parts. I have a wife, a child."

I can kill him if he gets too easy, thought False Corn.

"I think I'll end you with your own pistol. Close your eyes and dream, Isaacs. I'll finish it off for you."

"All right," False Corn said. "The rain has made me sleepy. Allow me to get my robe."

He picked his robe off the hook without being shot. The robe was rotten at the elbows and smelled of wet dog. But it was familiar to him.

"What a wretched robe," said the man in that reminiscent voice.

False Corn took a match off his dresser. Isn't this just to light my cigar? There was a flat piece of dynamite in the collar of the robe. He bent to the side, cupping his hands, and lit the fuse. The fuse was only an inch long. He removed the robe.

"You've caught your shoulder on fire, you pig," cried the man. But it wasn't a man's voice now.

False Corn threw the robe toward the voice and fell to the door. No shot rang out. He fumbled at the latch. He saw the robe covering the man's face. The man was tearing the robe away. His beard dropped, burning, to the floor. False Corn shut the door and lay on the planks of the upper hallway.

There was a shudder and an utterance of rolling light that half split the door. False Corn's face was pierced by splinters. His good eye hardly worked for the blood rushing out of his eyebrow.

The thing was still alive. It was staggering in the doorway. Its limbs were naked and blackened. Its breasts were scorched black. It was a woman, hair burned away. False Corn kicked the thing in the thigh. It collapsed, face to the floor.

It was Tess, his wife. She looked at him, her mouth and eyes alive.

"I was your wife, Isaacs, but I was Southern," she said.

By that time a crowd of the sorrowful and the inept had gathered.

Mother Rooney Unscrolls the Hurt

MOTHER ROONEY OF TITPEA STREET, THAT LITTLE FIFTY YARDS OF dead-end crimped macadam east off North State, crept home from the Jitney Jungle in the falling afternoon of October 1965. She had on her high-laced leather sneakers and her dress of blue teacup roses; she had a brooch the size of an Easter egg pinned on at her booby crease; she clutched a wrapped-up lemon fish filet, fresh from Biloxi, under her armpit.

Mother Rooney had been served at the Jitney by Mimsie Grogan, an ancient girl who had converted back in the thirties to Baptist. Mimsie would hiss at her about this silly disgusting ritual of Fridays as she wrapped the fish. Mother Rooney was Catholic. She was old, she had been being Mother Rooney so long. In the little first-story bathroom of her great weird house no spray she bought could defeat the odor of reptile corpses stewed in mud. Her boarder boys, all gone now for a month, would sometimes come in late and use her bathroom to vomit in, not being able to climb the stairs and use their own. And sometimes they were not able to use even hers well. There would be whiskey and beer gravy waiting for her on the linoleum. Just unspeakable. Yet the natural smell of her toilet would be overcoming the other vileness, she could not deny it. A couple of the young men smarties would openly confess, in the way of complaining about the unbearably reeking conditions among which they were forced to puke last night, that they were the ones. One of them even arranged his own horrid bountiful vomit into a face with a smile, such as a child might draw, and *this* she had to confront one morning at six o'clock as she came to the chilly tiles to relieve herself. Nobody confessed to that. But she caught on when she heard all the giggling up in the wings, at this hour in the morning. She wasn't deaf, and she wasn't so slow. The boys were sick and tired of her flushing the toilet and waking them all up every morning. Her toilet sounded like a volcano. Yes, Mr. Monroe had voiced that complaint before. He said it sounded as if this old house's back was breaking at last, it couldn't stand the tilt anymore. It woke them all up, it made them all goggle-eyed, everybody stayed stiff for two hours in their beds. Nobody wanted to be the one to make the move that finally broke it in two and sent them all collapsing down the hill into the Mississippi State Fairgrounds. What a way to wake up, Mr. Monroe complained. The situation here is uninhabitable. I don't know a man upstairs who isn't planning to move out of here as soon as he sees an equal rent in the paper.

She promptly brought down the rent to fifteen a month, and the boys all showed up downstairs Saturday night to celebrate, spilling wine and whiskey, which were illegal in this state, everywhere, and grabbing her ruggedly around her weary little rib cage and huffing smoke and rotten berries into her face, calling her the perfect landlady; but profanity began to be used in the dining room, and she was eager to remind them that hard liquor such as three or four of them were drinking was against the law in the state of Mississippi. The party got quiet. They all took their hands off her. They left like mice, not a backward look. She was so sorry to have ruined this party. It was too loud, it was drunken, but one thing had been agreeable to her. Their hugging on her had been good. The hugging. So many big boys had put their arms around her ribs and had not hurt her. She didn't feel a thing there, nary a lingering of pain, but a warm circle of her body Mother Rooney rubbed against. Oh oh, it was like old flannel cloth that had fingers. Give me that, honeys, she thought. Keep me. Watch me. Watch me, witness me make my old way till one day I've got my eyes closed and you'll . . . I'll keep you here at twenty-five cents a month, but you'll have to discover me dead, feel me with those large hands, you will circle me, wrap me, you boys made of flannel cloth. Some mornings Mother Rooney would pretend and lie toes-up in her bed past six-thirty, having to tee-tee agonizingly, but not going to the toilet and flushing it on time, and getting all she could out of her own old flannel gown. By seven the pain in her bladder would take her almost to true death.

Mother Rooney of Titpea Street came on.

Her boys had all left her now. Like mice. Not a whisper since. Some of them had said they'd write her every day. But not a line. Not a hint even as to whose facilities they were throwing up in nowadays. Her boys were lost in unknown low-rent holes of Jackson, the big midstate town of Mississippi. They had broken up their tribe. They . . .

She was deafened by thought; she'd kept it inside so long, there was a rumble. First thing she knew, she was at the doorknob leaning too hard; she broke the glass doorknob and the door gave. Still, she was a deaf-mute. If sound would come back to her, she could maybe hold on with her sneakers at the top of the hall. That retrograde dance at the top of her perilously drooping lobby, it couldn't come. She saw ahead of her the boards that were smooth as glass; she saw the slick boards beckoning her like a well down past the gloom of the stairs. The fish bundle jumped out of her arms and broke out of its paper and lit on the boards, scooting downward like a pound of grease. No sound would come to her. She flopped in her skirts; her face turned around for a second. She got a look at the wasted orange trees and a look at the sky. It was so chilly and smoky, but quiet. Then her sound came back to her. She was falling.

She put her arms out for flight. She kept her knees together. She knew she was gone. She knew she would snap. She forecast for herself a lonely lingering coughing up of spinal fluid—she could hear all her sounds now—when *fock,* landing on the fish binding, she hit facedown on the boards as if entering water in a shallow dive.

The back of the house was black, such a black of hell's own pit. Something was trying to stop her from going down there. Her breasts burned. The brooch had caught the wood and stopped her.

How wonderful of the brooch to act like a brake, Mother Rooney thought. She had slid only to the edge of the stairwell.

She might have butted through the kitchen door, clear out the back of the house and down the kudzu hill, where there was death by snakes at most, terror by entwinement and suffocation at least.

The house stood, slanting backward but not seriously dismantled yet, over a kudzu-covered cliff that dwindled into red clods upon the grounds of the Mississippi State Fair and Livestock Exhibition. Mother Rooney lived in only the bottom story of the brown middle box between two three-story tubular wings with yellow shingles. The brown box was frosted gingerbread-style in white wooden agates and scrolls, and had a sharp roof to it. In the yellow towers, upstairs, was nobody. She had her stove, pot, couch, bed and dining room, where the boarders ate.

But they were gone.

Her husband Hoover was dead since 1947.

Meager breezes of human odor fell and rose on the stairs.

Once last week she took herself up the stairs of the left wing and opened a room and buried her face in a curtain saturated still with cigarette smoke. She got *in* the curtain. This time she did not weep. She just held on, getting what she could.

Her rugs moved backward against the baseboards. You dropped a ball of yarn and it took off downhill; you spilled some tea and it streaked away from the dining room, over the threshold hump, and vaporized in the kitchen. The boards were really slick. But she would not nail things down or put gripper mats around everywhere. She wouldn't surrender. The only concession she made to the house was the acceptance of the sneakers from Harry Monroe, the medical student, who told her they were strictly the newest development from the university, already tested and broken in for her. What they were, were wrestling shoes Monroe and his partner, Bobby Dove Fleece, had stolen off a dead woman in the emergency room, a lady wrestler who had been killed down at City Auditorium. Mother Rooney could make it, with these sneakers, even though her feet didn't breathe well in them.

She lay hurt more than she then knew beside the stairs, and felt only as usual, surrounded by the towering vacant wings of her house.

Now this horror that she had not personally cultivated at all, this queer renewal of sights and sounds in the air—ghosts—was with her.

Mr. Silas was whispering to her in the dining room. "You are living in the cocked twat of the house. This house has its legs in the air. Not only is it ugly, it's an outrage, Mother. It's a woman's thing cocked beggingly between big old thighs. My shocked friends ask why I live here. I answer that it's what I can afford. I was homeless driving my motorbike and saw the 'Rooms' sign. I chose at night. All I wanted was a pillow. Once on the porch, I fell in."

"She snatched our money and gave us lard to eat," said Bobby Dove Fleece.

This young man thought he was a genius. All of them were naughty, her boys.

The house tilted all of six inches. A black gap of air stood between the bottom of the porch and the top of the ferny foundation. A sweet waft of ruining potatoes hung in the gap. Hoover had buried the pile for winter-keeping in 1945. Was he ruining so sweetly in his grave? Mother Rooney wondered. Or did his soul lie like a dead putrescent snake in the plumbing under her commode? as she often thought.

But Jerry Silas, leaping from his motorcycle toward the cocked porch, smelled *sperm*, blowing him over from under the house: haphazard nature had approximated the smell with a rotting compost of yams.

Nature will always scandalize, Silas had told her. And since he was bare chested, as usual in the house, Mr. Silas had flexed all his upper body, a girl-murdering suavity in his eyes, and made the muscles of his chest, stomach and arms stand out most vulgarly in front of her.

Oh, Mother Rooney wished Mr. Silas and all the young men back now, filling the wings and the upstairs with cigar and cigarette smoke, music, whoops, nonsense, coming down and arranging themselves noisily around her table to eat what they called her Texas pie—because it was so ugly, they said. And she, scooping out the brown stringy beef and dumplings and setting it on their plates with insulted vigor, *flak*! Oh, they kept her at the edge of weeping or of praying; she was hurt in her cook's heart.

Some juice spattered on Mr. Delph, the young pharmacist, and he announced, wiping it away: "Fellows, Mother Rooney is not being a Christian again."

They made her uncertain of even her best dishes, her squash casserole, her oyster patties. When they first had begun this business, she lingered in the kitchen while tears ran off her cheeks into her milky desserts.

But for them just to be here she wished, calling her anything they wanted to. Let them mimic Father Putee behind his back as he advises my poor carnal body, the two of us seated on the couch in the dining room.

Mother Rooney regained the picture of that rascal Mr. Worley, the student at Millsaps College. He was loitering up the stairway listening to Father Putee, and she saw him, dressed only in underwear for her benefit. When Father Putee would finish a sentence, Mr. Worley would snap the waist of his underwear and look upward to heaven. Finally, Father Putee, an old person himself, heard the underwear snap, and turned. But by then Worley was gone, and Harry Monroe was in his place, sitting fully dressed, waving his hand. "Hi, padre. I'm just chaperoning you two."

Let them, let them, she wished.

Let them take me to another movie at the Royal Theater, telling me it is an epic of the Catholic faith, and then we sit down and see all of that Bulgarian woman in her nightgown prissing about until that sordid beast eats her neck, the moon in the window. Let them ride me by St. Thomas's Church, as Mr. Worley says in the backseat to Mr. Hammack, the young man who tunes organs, and asking it again to Mr. Delph: "Don't you hate a fish-eater? Hammack, Delph, don't you?" They go on and on, pretending to be rural hard-shells, then stop the car under the shadowy cross in the street. "Let's kill a fish-eater." They ask me to find them one, describing how they will torture one like they did in the Middle Ages, only nastier, and especially an old woman fish-eater. Maybe let her live for a few weeks until she has to beat on the door with her own leg bone to be heard from the street.

Then let them all come down to the table in their underwear, all except Mr. Monroe, who is in on the joke so far as to have his shirt off. I'm in the kitchen and see Mr. Silas stand up and say this: "Predinner game tonight! Here it is! If any old, creeping, venereal-ized, moss-covered turtle of a Catholic scab-eating bimbo discarded from Pope Gregory's lap and rejected by the leprous wino in back of the Twentieth Century Pool Hall comes in here serving up any scum-sucking plate of oysters of a fish-eating Friday night, we all pull off our jockey shorts and wave them over our heads, okay?" "Yahhhhh!" the rest of them agree, and I peep around and see Mr. Silas putting the written-up piece of paper in his elastic underwear. I wait, wait, not sure of anything except I am getting the treatment from them for asking each one if he was a Catholic by any chance when they first boarded with me. Then: "But where *is* our sweet Mother Rooney?" I hear Mr. Silas chiming, lilting. "With her charming glad old heart, the beam in her eye of a reconciled old age? Her mushrooms and asparagus, blessed by the Lord? Her twinkling calluses, proud to tote the ponderous barge of householdery? Benedictions and proverbs during the neat repast, and an Irish air or two over the piano after-wards, to bed at nine?" says Harry Monroe. "To flush at six," says Bobby Dove Fleece.

I sneak in, for I did want music in the house, and had bought the secondhand piano for the corner over there. I know well that Mr. Hammack can play. I did hope in my heart that someone could play and young men would sing around it. At least they are not doing what Mr. Silas threatened they would. And I ask, "Are you really going to sing some Irish songs afterwards?"—passing the fried oys-ters. Blind drooping of the eyes as if they'd never seen me before. Mr. Silas, who works at Wright's Music Store and is a college graduate, asks, "Do the Irish have a music, Harry?" Mr. Monroe took a lot of courses in music at his college. "They have a uniform national fart," Mr. Monroe replies.

I'm already crying, steaming red in the face over the hot oys-ters. I don't care about Irish; I'm not Irish, for mercy's sake, nor originally Roman Catholic. I just wanted music, any kind of music. I just wanted music, and I tell them that.

"Sorry," Mr. Monroe ventures to say. And they all eat quickly in silence, running back to the wings and upstairs without a word. Next day they all come back from work and school and don't give me a word. Only Mr. Monroe comes down at evening to eat some soup left from lunch.

But then, of course, the call from the police the next night, saying they know, they have been following the crude public display of nudity I allow in my boardinghouse, and that there have been complaints about vulgarism. Then I know it must be Mr. Silas, whose light is on. I see as I put down the phone and look up at the left wing. Just to check, just to be sure, still scared from perhaps hanging up on the real police, I walk up there, though it takes a lot of breath.

But knocking, there is no answer, and I open the door and right in the way is Mr. Silas naked, stiff and surprised, but he seems to be proud at the same time. But how did he do it?

I ease the door to. There's only one phone in the house, mine. Mr. Silas cries out vulgarly behind the door; he's lifting his weights, his barbells—and what sounds, what agony or pleasure of his body.

Yes, let my boys come back to me with all that. Even Harriman Monroe, who drove them all from the house, who told my boys to leave. Let slim Harry, who turned just a wee bit prig on us all, come back. Dear heart, though, he was hurt by the loss of a musical career. And Bobby Fleece mentioned to me privately that Harry Monroe was not making it as a medical student, either. Harry does not take care of his health in the meantime. He breaks out with red spots on the face. I tried to feed him, diet him on good vegetables at night. I asked him what he ate in the day, and he answered me. Women, he said. Whereas Mr. Silas used to sneak down to eat everything I have left. It was a secret between us, how much Mr. Silas ate. It went to six pounds a day.

The brooch was standing up like the handle of a dagger. It had unclasped. It had not behaved. The pin of it was sunk three inches in her bosom. Where it went into her was purple and mouth-looking. An unlucky bargain—the biggest bauble ever offered on the counters of the Emporium, uptown. It had been designed for a crazy czarina who could yank it off her chest and fend back lechers in the alley.

Mother Rooney surged up on her haunch bones. She worked her lips together to make them twinkle with spittle. She shucked off her ugly shoes by rubbing each ankle against the other, folded in her legs under the moon in blue roses of her hip, pushed herself against the stairwell. In general, she arranged the corpse so that upon discovery it would not look dry, so that it would not look murdered or surprised in ugliness.

At least, she thought, no bag of fluid inside her has ruptured. No unspeakable emission like that. She wondered about the brooch. Do you pull it out? The body would be prettier without it. But her boys had made her conscious of her body. She was a sack whose seams were breaking, full of organs, of bitter and sour fermenting fluids. Her body threatened to break forth into public every second.

Concerning the brooch, she feared blood, a hissing of air, perhaps a rowdy blood bubble so big it would lift her out of the hall, through the doorway, into the street.

Oh, such alarm, such wild notoriety!

Oh, Mother Rooney hurt like a soldier.

She remembered from the movies at the Royal: Don't talk. Each word a drop of blood into the lungs. And what about thinking? Mother Rooney had always conceived of mental activity as a whirlpool of ideas spinning one's core. Wouldn't that action send bloodfalls to her lungs and elsewhere? She imagined her body filling up with blood because she was really thinking.

The deep itch of the pin came now.

She saw the pin running, shish-kebabing, through her heart, lungs, spleen, pancreas, liver, esophagus, thorax, crop, gizzard, gullet —remembering all that apparatus, wet, hot and furcated, she had pulled out of chickens in the 1930s. Then she thought of the breast, drumstick, pulley bone, and oh!—that hurt thinking that, because the pulley bone snapped and often punched into the hand.

So thinking it could be either way—a lung wound or shish kebab—she guessed she had better stop this whirlpool mental activity, for safety. It could be that shish kebab wasn't definitely fatal because, once the pin was pulled out, all the organs might flap back to their places and heal. But she dreaded feeling them do this inside her, and so she left the pin alone.

It came to her then that she might make her brain like a scroll, and that by just the tiniest bit of mental activity she might pull it down in tiny snatches at a time and dwell on the inch that was offered by the smallest little tug of the will, like the scrolled maps in schoolrooms. Perhaps she could survive then, tensing her body in a petite, just a petty, hope.

First was Hoover, the son of a sewage-parts dealer who fled Ireland in 1915; Roman Catholic Hoover Rooney, bewildered by snot and asthma. Then there was Hoover Second, his working son in overalls. Wasn't there something holy about the unsanitariness of their brick and board cottage on Road of Remembrance Street? How the yard grass was shaggy, and the old creamed tea from breakfast time was found in chipped cups with five or six cigarettes floating on top like bleached creatures from a cow pond's bottom; their black Ford with plumbing manuals in the backseat which smelled like a gymnasium with a melting-butter smell over that. Sometimes Hoover stopped at stop signs—I remember once in front of the King Edward Hotel—and a wine bottle rolled under my bare foot. I was tired, and when Hoover drove up to the lumberyard where I was a secretary, I would hop in and pull my shoes and stockings right off. Then one day Hoover grabbed my foot, and holding it in his lap, he took what he told me was his dead mama's ring and put it on my little toe and said, "Baaaa!" I told him it degraded her memory. And he eased my foot out of his lap, started the car, and I had to hold my foot in the air to keep the ring from falling on the dirty floorboard, because Hoover grabbed my body and held me really hurtfully, so I couldn't get my hands free. How he laughed, making his face orange. With those desperado sideburns and slit eyes, he looked like something from Halloween. He had a hot metal body odor that came up close to the degree of unpleasantness. He smeared my mouth with his hairy lips and chin. I felt like I was eating down steel filings, and forgot I was thirty and he just a boy of early twenties. I laughed.

For being Annie Broome of Brandon, Mississippi, supposed to be at my Aunt Lily's promptly after work every day to eat our supper together, supposed to attend Wednesday night church with her this evening. I saw my daddy drilling Hoover with a glare like at a snake doctor or a vegetarian. But I never told Mother or Daddy much at all, just sent them one of Hoover's postcards with an airplane picture of the shores of Ireland on it, and told them I'd been converted and that Hoover was the one. Then, back in the car with Hoover, I quiver in that red moan against his marvelous hard tongue.

Plus all the other strange hours I felt like the robber queen. I called in sick to the lumberyard. Hoover picked me up at eight. He and his papa didn't start off the day till ten.

She lay cold in the hall of the old house. She waved her ring finger at the whirlpool. Stop. Blood, she thought, fell out of her mind into her lungs. If she could just shape her mind with a timid effort requiring no breath, she could beckon the scroll, easing it down in millimeters. Flies had found her. She fought them, thinking.

That malt cereal that the old man ate every morning, it got on his cuffs and his newspapers from Dublin, and he wore his napkin like a bib, tucked under his neck, which glucked with the tea and cereal. His yellow cheeks and red beard, they should've sent him home to shave at one o'clock, but he was not American yet; more like a Mongolian with his thin eye slits; then his brogue so thick you imagined he carried heavy cereal always in his throat, had to choke back a slug of it to talk. He did not care and tinkled loudly with the door of the bathroom open while he talked to Hoover and me about religions, the mediocre number of them. It shocked him. There were only a hundred-odd Catholics in all Jackson then, 1916. Hoover courted me on the settee. I waited for the old man to flush, but he never did. I thought about that yellow water still lying there and saw green Ireland floating in it. The hairy lawn of the house, and Hoover's body odor, and the whole milky stink of the house, they cut on me very sharp. And Hoover's breath was of some iron pipeline.

I was happy, sucked right into the church, because I got its feeling. In St. Thomas's it was clean, dark, cooling and beautiful, with wood rafters of cedar, gloomy green pictures of Jesus, St. Thomas and the Jordan River in glass. Also, it was tiny and humiliating. It was a thrill to cover your head with a scarf because you were such a low unclean sex, going back to Eve, I guess, making man slaver in lust for you and not be the steward he was meant to be. You were so deadly, you might loop in the poor man kneeling next to you with your hair. I saw Hoover bending on the velvet rail. I felt peculiarly trickful, that this foreign cluck would moo and prance for a look at my garters, that his slick hair would dry and stand up in heat for me. In St. Thomas's I was thrown on that heap of navels, hair and rouge that makes the flesh-pile Woman, which even the monks have to trudge through waist-deep, I thought, before they finally ascend to sacredness. God told me this, and I blushed, knowing my power.

So I thought, that day when Hoover and I sat on his couch at one o'clock, thirty years old and smoking my first cigarette and drinking *tea,* that when he began playing sneaky-devious at my parts, with a whipped look on his face, this wasn't Catholic or Irish from what I knew of them, and that it was more Mississippi Methodist in Brandon, Mississippi, with the retreat at Lake Pelahatchie and Grady Rankin working at me with his pitiful finger, and I told Hoover my opinion, leaving out Grady and so on. We both jumped through our eyes at each other then. We were soggy and rumpled as when you are led to things, and I let him, I did, let him do the full act, hurting on his bed beyond what God allows a woman to hurt. God pinched off all but a thimble-worth of pleasure in that act for me. I mean, as long as I had Hoover my husband. But I let out oaths of pleasure and Hoover in that silly position . . . sometimes I take my mind up to the moon and see Hoover in that position, moving, with nothing under him. I laugh. The hunching doodlebug, ha ha ha! I was in this filthy house doing this, with an Irish Catholic. He said America was an experiment. He said I was safe in the oldest religion of historical mankind. On his bed I believed him: my hurt and fear turned to comfort.

Oh, but Papa Rooney wasn't proud of his boy for getting his wings on me. The old man was really there at the door watching us. He'd become more an American. He'd come in to shave, and was here on us viewing Hoover in that silly position and me too. He called me names I'll never forgive, and Hoover too. He cried, and threw cups on the floor, and lay down on the couch, talking about what he'd seen and on and on. I was numb awhile, but then I started moving, low-pedaling around the house, while Hoover sat on the bed looking at his bare feet. I found the broom and swept up the teacups and then swept the rug right beside Papa Rooney, put all the dirty lost glassware in the sink, filled it with hot water. I mopped the tiles in the kitchen and flew into the bathroom at the bowl and sink. I scraped them all with only a towel and water, then found the soap and started using that everywhere. I went back in the halls, I fingered the dust out of the space heater. I found a bowl of cereal under the bed with socks and collars lying in it. I made the old man's room spanking clean. I made a pile for his stained underwear in the back closet. Then it was four o'clock in the afternoon. I sat down by Papa Rooney, who was still on the couch. He looked tearfully at me. "Annie, my boibee!" he said, and smothered me into his arms, asking forgiveness for what he had said. We went and sat by Hoover, while the old fellow told us about our marriage. I was scared. There seemed no other way, with Papa Rooney and his arms over our shoulders.

Except for Papa Rooney watching us all the way up the aisle, I doubt we would've married; we did. Through the ceremony we were both scared of—with Father Remus talking words of comfort over our heads to Mother and Daddy, who hung back and were shocked—we tied the knot.

Mother Rooney's head stood wide open in the twirl of remembrance. Blood, eye juice and brain fluid roared down to her lungs, she thought. Too hard, too hard, her thoughts. There were noises in the house as the wind blew on the windows, which were loose in their putty. The hallway was dark. It was her box. No light now; her coffin space.

Mother Rooney shrieked, "Be loud on the organ! Pull my old corpse by a team of dogs with a rope to my toe down Capitol Street, and let Governor White peep out of his mansion and tell them to drag that old sourpuss Annie to the Pearl River Swamp. Oh, be heavy on the organ!" She shocked herself, and she remembered that Papa Rooney had died insane too, thinking that Jackson was Dublin.

The hell with the scroll! "Everything!" she howled.

The old man went crazy in a geographic way at the last, at St. Dominic's Hospital. He shouted out the names of Dublin and Chicago and Jackson streets as if he was recalling one town he knew well. He injured his son Hoover, behaving this way. Hoover became lost; he saw the blind eyes of his daddy and heard the names of the streets. His daddy didn't know where they were. But Annie also recalled the sane old fellow at his last, how he'd fallen in love with her; loved her cleanliness and order; loved America, because he was getting rich easily and enlarged the sewage-parts house so that now Hoover was a plumbing contractor too. Papa Rooney told her he was in love with peace and money and her—Annie.

Annie made Hoover build her a house, a house that would really be a place, so Hoover would know where he was. He seemed to, when the house was up. There was actually no reason for Hoover to go insane, because, unlike his father, he loved the aspects of his job. He loved clear water running through a clot-free pipe. He loved the wonder of nastiness rinsed and heaved forever out of sight; he loved the dribbling water replacing it in the bowl, loved the fact that water ran hot and cold; he loved thermostats. He adored digging down to a pipe, breaking it and dragging the mineral crud and roots from it, and watching the water flush through, spangling. He got high and witty watching that one day at twilight, and the slogan came to him, like a smash to Hoover's mind: "The Plumber's Friend." That was how he advertised his firm in the *Clarion Ledger* for twenty years.

Hoover went jumping hard and erect to the gingerbread house with yellow towers, driving home with his first ad in his pocket. On Titpea, he saw the house lit up in all quarters; knew his gentle Annie waited in one room. He knew he must have the wings full of baby sons, soon. Annie opened the door for him. He took her body. He was almost gagged by the odor of flowers and her supper of spaghetti, which was very new then, but he blasted her; bucked her upstairs, and perished hunching her to the point he didn't know when his orgasm was, but kept on hunching in a trance. He knew she was frail as a peaflower. He liked to snap her and squeeze her.

Oh! Certainly, how much, how so, so much Hoover wanted to be both a plumber's friend and a father, every evening. And Hoover Second came, finally, hurting more than any of those books told, because those books were written by men in some far-off tower, and they couldn't know. The intern leaned on her stomach. Great Lord! The nuns held her. They giggled. "He's looking for another baby, dear."

There could be no doubt that Hoover was. Again and again, and something was wrong. Not just that Mother Rooney couldn't have any more babies, as she couldn't, but Hoover's desire to be both a plumber's friend and a father was destroying her. The dearie loved plumbing, but he got to see less of it every year. The company was big and he had to employ many men in the expansion. He could do nothing but sit at his desk and inventory and buy and sell, in his business suit, and he didn't have the old man's love for pure money. How many times, she asked, how many times did I see him leaning over the toilet bowl smiling at the water? How many times did he deliberately break some rod or other in the tanks at home, or rip something out that wasn't brand new, so he could drive down to the place in the night for a part? How many times did he look at me as if I was brand new too, and had worked once, then fagged off?

Bless his heart, he had to remember the night of what we both thought was Hoover Second's right vigorous making, the night he came home with his first ad in his pocket. Oh, I knew in my heart without doubt that was when, because the pains of the entrance and the exit almost matched up. Pity his name, poor Hoover had to remember that he had had a little dirt from the pipeline on his breeches that night, and that he stunk some from heaving away and watching the men work. Lovely, wronged, one-son Hoover Rooney, heaving away and mating me, he had smeared my legs with mending compound off his ankles. Charming Hoover, who began showing up late in twilight absolutely negrified with pitch spots and sweat beads and his business suit done in forever with gunk. I knew what the dear was doing, that he was leaving the office at noon to parade out on one of his jobs among his plumbers, who probably didn't want him out there. He peered into the deepest and filthiest work going, careful to lift a pipe for some Negro, stumble against the roofing tar, for luck and because he desired so to be a plumber's friend. He came in manly and proud of his day's work's grime, looking like he wanted to break my back. Through the years he tried different combinations of filth and ruined bundles of suits, for luck, but he had no more with me. I had shoved out the boy that I had, for mercy's sake, and I tried to tell him so with my hurting eyes. It would not take—get in that silly position till Christ came!

Then Hoover went insane, yes, long before Hoover Second was killed and the house began tilting. In the middle thirties, when he was losing money every day, he almost gave me up and turned on the house. He sat on the dainty loveseat in the lobby when he came in, and soiled that, then lay back in the studio upstairs on my Persian divan with cornets and red iris on it, rolling the suet off his breeches until the pretty pattern was blurred; slept silently away in both wings with his rusty cheeks hard on the linen, for I could see the half a face Hoover left behind in the mornings, the big fans of palm grease where his hands had known my guest towels, and the wallpaper of clover flowers, but especially on my lovely fat pillows, everywhere. Oh, Hoover, you were late for supper *again,* hung down so heavy with dirt. You were private and sulky and unhungry. You were so ugly and angry when I opened one of the doors on you, as if you'd been found out in your love's rendezvous. Pretty soon you had the house back like the cottage on Road of Remembrance, where you could've grown agricultural products on the floor.

You had a place again, dearest, and I had none, but only Hoover Second that you almost forgot, wanting Third through Four Thousandth. I loved, loved. What could I do, though? Little Hoover. I see him most of all for his feet and little toes, hot and dimpling from the bath water, and his steamy curling hair, his tiny wet marks on my rug. It was always him just coming from the water that I . . . like a fish you pull up, wondering what? And there the marvelous slippery rascal is, breathing something else than you breathe. Christ, the horror as he grew up and I saw he did, he did breathe something else. Oh, in the earlier days when Big Hoover attacked me in gangs, every one of them more mindless and slaughtering, hurting, ahhhhh; when he draped on me afterward, nicking his dirty fingernails together, and he was heavy as the island of Ireland and had just tried to mash the whole country into me, and he would smoke then, roughhousing his cigarettes and letting them fall in pieces all over the bed. Well, I see too Hoover Second nestling by me after his bath, and think that my little baby, who didn't even know he had his man's business between his legs, was left to me when I was almost too tired to look at him and love. But I did, and I cupped his infant's peabud in my hand and held the softest most harmless unhurting thing in the world, and fell asleep in beauty.

I watched it stalk and grow too, and shiver—that funny time when he was open and proud with it and had just found it out. We called it Billy. Nuzzling against my side, he would want to know which neighbors had Billy. He asked if the air, clowns, toy soldiers and Cream of Wheat had Billy. I told him no, and we divided the world like that, with Billy and no Billy. He would kid me then, and ask about rocks, mud, the Jitney Jungle, underwear, as he hiccupped with the jollies. I guess he was telling his first racy jokes.

Sure enough, the days came so very soon when he hid his boyhood sprout from me, and it brought on a sweet pinch in my heart to see him finger away and snap up his pants with a rude look when I burst in on him unawares in the bathroom. There were two hurting worlds for me to endure. Big Hoover, coming at me with his never-faulty club with the head of an apple as he stands red and greasy as an Indian of naked insanity; his world, so slow and grinding. Little Hoover, slipping away just out of hand-reach in all the rooms of my big house, so I seem to see only his heels in the cruel scuffed leather of his shoes. And he was gone, a teenager and suspicious.

I was snagged, and only my unwanted hands to look at.

Came that afternoon quiet as a bird's breath when the world itself blew up, and all through the house there lay newspapers with inch-high letters on them about the war. Hoover dropped them on the floors and they filled up our Plymouth, so you made a dusty crackling sound climbing in upon the seats. We drove to St. Joseph's School. There he stood under that oak near the storm fence and the basketball court, in a ring of friends, talking quietly. All of Jackson was so quiet and breezeless. We couldn't hear the boys, but I know it was about the military situation. You thought they should be in the classrooms, that they were hatching something illegal and were hoodlums. Hoover Second was tall and not so pretty now, and in his large wool pants he looked skinny and just a little stupid. He noticed us; his eyes were black and hard. He felt called on to spit, and he did. He waved to his friends. Then, now, he was up in the left wing packing, and didn't want me near him, I knew, because the war idea made him even more a man. Oh, I thought he was through, though, and I was innocent and walked up to kiss him, crying already, and hung on his small bones for half a minute because I knew I had it coming to me.

It was mine too, that three-second vision of Hoover Second partially blind without his steel glasses and naked on his feet, when

I bumped the door to his room open. He held his underwear in one hand and his other hand rested in the groove below the belly where it joins to the legs; he was pink from his bath. And yes, he was tenderly awful with his coiling wet hair, his dim eyes that felt toward me at the door. Who are you, Mother? he seemed to say. He stepped quickly into his underwear and abided my weeping weight, rushing upon him. "What is it?" he says. I wanted to say, "This is it: that you, something like you, should have been the one, that I was made for somebody like you; that what I see of your muscles and hair and your crumpled stalk tells me somebody like you would have been kind and right, that I'm crying now for how safe the world is with your skinny tenderness in it, how delicate its girls must be to deserve you, how lucky they'll be, how Europe seems like a rough metal planet to eat you on its cold soil or in its foggy air. Please, please, don't you meet any of Hoover's nieces in Ireland, who would eat you just as quick as the Nazis, and you watch out for, you step around Ireland and Irish like the plague. Oh, Hoover, baby, you hide in the tiny dark unfindable corners and ditches and clouds and cupboards of Europe, and do come back to your mama and she will find you a girl."

I do not believe all the terror Hoover Second was supposed to be in his airplane, because I know he couldn't see to do it; that he unloaded a record amount of bombs on German cities and set them afire; that he flew unofficial missions to "grind them to powder." He was so happy in the photograph with his crew. I believe that he was shot at unmercifully, and that he came back a hero with his legs full of brutal powdered lead, dug up in Europe's cold earth. Big Hoover told me once, trying to twist the knife over my not being pregnant— we were out of church and behind Mrs. Pitcaithly with her brood of boys and saw them wait in the cold weather for a taxi—"A mother is the sum of her children." Very cute and salty, Hoover, but you will wish to explain to me how this charming saying applies to me all the way through. You tell me Hoover Second has gone off as a soldier, and I would say, all right, that's me, I would've gone off too. Then you tell me Hoover Second was a war hero, risking himself, going beyond orders in an airplane called the Ugly Fierce Sparrow, to put the bombs in Hitler's lap, and I say again, all right, this might be an undiscovered hero fool part of his mama. But tell me, Hoover, if you were pushing on, what part of me was it that came back to Jackson wounded but out of the crisis, and tinkered together a wreck the Civil Air Patrol gave him for twenty dollars, that Piper thing which pooted and fluttered over Jackson and swooped over the towers of this very house, then proceeded to drop here and there—on the grounds of the capitol building, on the governor's mansion, on St. Thomas's, on Millsaps' campus, on Main Street Jackson, on the football game in Clinton—white unspooling rolls of toilet paper that he had stolen out of the basement of St. Joseph's High School; and enjoyed the scandal and the protest that the *Clarion* wrote up about it, until they found out who it was: a *veteran* with a rich sense of humor! Then the schoolchildren ran out on the playgrounds at lunch period, hoping hoping hoping that he would drop a roll of rump-wiperage down their throats; and the whole town, running out to caress the paper, to find the real spool dropped from Jackson's man of the air. What part of me ran to the airport every morning, couldn't even finish his cup of coffee, like he was still on some schedule? What act have I done at my wildest is there that would remind you of Hoover Second's crash and irresponsible burn on the tennis courts of Mississippi College, when there were miles of flat unpopulated fields all over the county for him to choose from? Find me somewhere in the sum of the parts of that burned airplane, dearest, and think again on that charming saying "the sum of her children." The little coeds, with their rackets, were telling the police how Hoover Second had come down on them repeatedly, how they had to scamper, and the preacher students were still pronouncing on the wreck when we arrived, two hours later. I sat down on the courts and I was never in a more foreign land than on the scorched tennis courts at the scene.

We die, Mother Rooney thought. Even me, in this cold hall, by accident. But God—Goddamn it, yes! for you, Hoover, to hike off with a broken heart and die of self-inflicted plumber's pneumonia when the house did tilt, it seems, a week after Hoover Second's crash. But I know it wasn't. I got three more mooning years from you, who never looked at the boy in his life except as the first number of numbers that didn't come. For you to die, Goddamn it, for *you* to be the one, with everybody saying: "Sure. Completely understandable. He's borne that grief." All your dirt started piling up in the back of the house, didn't it? Your heart was broken, it had been stretched so much when the men with the jacks couldn't do anything about the tilt. Godarooney, Goddamn. Thanks for not omitting to fill the bathroom with colorful phlegm when you went. Thank God we didn't live on together and dredge up memories of false romance from our past. Don't think, dear, that I missed those scrubby melancholy kisses of old age.

Mother Rooney had never taken even an aspirin, and now she was harsh and proud.

She heard Harry Monroe's English Ford outside, with its drizzling ruptured halt at the curb. It was a ghost again, she thought. But she thought of how Harry Monroe had cured her of being afraid every October when the fair came and when she thought she heard something down the hill in back calling her—Mother! Mother! Mother! Harry took her out in the backyard and proved to her that what she was hearing was the men getting the cattle out of the trucks, and when they didn't move right, the men would lay on with sticks and shout, "Motherfucker!"

"It's just the Four-H boys saying *motherfucker*," Harry explained. Mr. Harry Monroe thought he was being such a clever learned adviser to her. But from Bobby Dove Fleece she knew Mr. Harriman Monroe wasn't making it as a medical student.

Harry Monroe was really there in the doorway.

He called, "Mother Rooney?" He wore his sophomore lab coat as a cape on his shoulders; he had a fat little book in one hand and a bottle of wine in the other. He was handsome in an old public way. His face was not smooth. He had wanted to play the horn more than know all he was forced to know at the med center of Ole Miss.

He found her. He saw Mother Rooney regarding him. He hit the light switch, and he saw her cartoon yellow hair in its old bun, her bunions shining through her stockings, and the white, blue-rosed dress.

Mother Rooney crooned, "I'm gone, Harriman. You pull off your clothes and let me get a look at you, baby. You were the one, but you always just hurt me. I deserve this. Don't you be shy. I walked in on Jerry Silas completely naked one night. He was so muscular. He was a wonder. I have seen young men. You aren't the first. Don't you be ashamed, Mister Monroe."

Harry Monroe said, "I know you saw Silas. He's on the porch. I'm going to take his ass tonight. Don't you lose control now."

"You ran my boys away. You ruined this house."

Mother Looney, he thought. He shut the door and locked it to keep Silas and the other fellow out. "I'm the only one that did care a little," he said to her. He knelt by her and saw the brooch buried in her and the blood dripping down the old ravine of her breasts. He didn't want her to see him blanch. He thought she was in shock. "I brought you this bottle of wine. I saw Silas at the Dutch Bar and we thought we'd surprise you tonight. You must take up drinking." He peered at the wound some more. "I brought this book, the *Merck Manual*. You can read in it and tell your own disease by the symptoms. You can advise the doctors."

Aw hell, Monroe thought. The bottle of wine was a third drunk, and the *Merck Manual* was an old one he'd got out of the pharmacology trash basket.

"You were always ugly to me. Is Jerry Silas out there? I want to see him. I have a crush on him," she said.

She's with it. She's not in shock, Monroe thought.

"I'm not going to let them in," he said.

Two men were outside the door, falling on the porch and yelling to him.

"You don't like Silas, Mother. We all knew he was . . . he lifted weights. Didn't just lift them. The weights possessed him. He sent off for special underwear and for red oil to rub on his body. He bought a camera that he could activate from across the room while he lay on his bed, flexing. He'll kill himself when his stomach muscles start sagging."

Oh, but they didn't sag, Mother Rooney thought, when I walked in on him and he was naked and stiff, but twinkling in his eyes so joyously that it was clear he couldn't hurt a woman in all his health, either. He would have been tender, friendly, out-of-doors with you. Oh, he maketh me to lie down in green pastures, but where was he and where was his pasture? And, yes, he restoreth my soul, but all I got was used up. And, yes, his rod and staff, they comfort me—and they would have, but where was he, and where was the comfort I was entitled to? My cup runneth over with hurt-juice.

"Mr. Silas wanted me to be thirty again," Mother Rooney said.

Monroe leaned on the stairwell with his head in his hands. He yelled out to the porch for them to shut up. He opened the *Merck Manual* and began turning pages.

"You cannot like him. You cannot like any of us. We were the ugliest people as a group. Didn't you see how marked out for losing we all were? Hammack, Worley, Delph. I sometimes wondered how all we shits got ganged up in this—this beautiful house. But especially you can't like Silas. Silas breathes out a smell of broiler shanties and rotten pine, and he is always sweating. He's lost his job at the music store, but he flourishes on, trying in different ways to prove that he is not from Fig Newton, Mississippi, that a certain type of mass-produceable chicken wasn't named after his father."

"You are very sharp toward others," Mother Rooney said.

"Oh, I know, me," Harry Monroe said. "A man who was so bad in music he was booted out of the Jackson symphony, and now almost failing med school."

"But you keep on being so cruel to me. You won't open the door and let me see those boys. There are *two* boys out there, aren't there?"

"One of them isn't a boy," Monroe said.

It was strange to him to hear the two on the porch, still savagely drunk, and to realize that he himself, who had put down more than any of them, was now sober as Mother Rooney was.

He said, "The fellow with Silas is seventy years old. He was at the Dutch Bar and we thought we'd bring him over as a—a gift, a present to you. The old guy is ready to be your companion from now on out; he already has a crush on you, Mother. Listen!"

She had begun to rise, hissing at him.

"I know it's horrible now. But I and Silas wanted to make amends to you, really. We are so sorry for what happened in this house. You know, it started with the little joking insults, and then it grew to where hurting you was a cult. You really occupied us. Especially those of us who were taking a lot of bad traffic in the shit of the outer world and were originally endowed with a great amount of rottenness in our personal selves. The next thing would've been murdering you. I always felt the police were ready to break in any minute."

"You prissy little scholar. I could've taken it," Mother Rooney said. "You don't know the hurt that's come to me. It tells me I'm alive, hurting."

Monroe looked at her forlornly. "Do you think you can take that pin wound in your chest now?"

"I don't know." Mother Rooney sank, remembering the pin. What to do? Monroe wondered. He drew away into the dining room and sat on the couch. "Puncture" was all he remembered. He was very busy with the *Merck,* after making the phone call. She heard the pages ruffling and Harry mumbling.

". . . do not bleed freely and the point of entry seals quickly, making the depths of the wound ideal for the propagation of infective agents. Tract should be laid open and excised and *débridement* carried out in the manner described under Contaminated Incised Wounds."

Mother Rooney also heard a loud mauling at the door.

Silas and the old guy were making a ram attack on it. Monroe yelled unspeakably filthy words at them. His pages were still rippling. Then he threw the book out through the front bay window and there was a horrendous collapsing of glass. Then the ambulances came squalling up Titpea. By mistake, two of them came to the same house. Monroe ran on. There were steps and voices and the red lights outside.

Mother Rooney bellowed, "Is it the police, Harriman? I always thought they'd come in and stop Hoover's cruelty to me. I thought they should have been at the tennis courts at Hoover Second's crash, declaring it illegal and unfair, and restoring him to me. But they never came. They're worthless. Tell them that if they try to get in the door."

Harry Monroe studied the standing brooch on her chest. Do you pull it out? And because the brooch looked silly sticking in the old lady, he walked to her quickly and snapped it out, then flung it down the hall at the back of the house.

He unlocked the door, and there was big Mr. Silas, asking, "What is occurring? I've got the lover here." The old man was riding piggyback on Silas's huge shoulders; he had combed his white hair back with his own drunkardly, lonely spit, using his fingers, and he was scared to death. The two men waddled in, looking at Mother Rooney.

Monroe ran at Silas and slugged him in the eyes and Silas abandoned the old guy and fell into the dining room upon Monroe. A brawl could be heard by Mother Rooney. The table went over. Silas was reaching for Monroe, who kicked away and whimpered, and that was what the brawl amounted to.

The old boy lay dazed in the lobby, fallen where he was shucked off Silas. He had landed hard and didn't move. Then his body, with its ruined hairdo, started sliding on the slick boards, face up, down toward Mother Rooney. He moved on down and she saw he was really a red old drunk.

The first ambulance crew thought he was the one and rolled him out expertly. The second crew noticed the woman bleeding. But she was standing now, and went out to the ambulance walking. One of the ambulance men had to go in and break off Silas from Monroe, and now Monroe was another case, and Mother Rooney sat beside him and petted him, all the way to the hospital.

★★★★★★★★★★★★★★★★★★

1979–1985
Captain
Maximus

★★★★★★★★★★★★★★★★★★

Getting Ready

He was forty-eight, a fisherman, and he had never caught a significant fish. He had spent a fortune, enough for two men and wives, and he had been everywhere after the big one, the lunker, the fish bigger than he was. His name was Roger Laird, better off than his brother, who went by the nickname "Poot."

Everywhere. Acapulco, Australia, Hawaii, the Keys. Others caught them yesterday and the weather was bad today and they were out of the right bait. Besides, the captain was sick and the first mate was some little jerk in a Def Leppard T-shirt who pulled in the big grouper that Roger hung because Roger was almost pulled overboard. Then the first mate brought some filets packed in ice to Roger's motel door. The mate Roger was ill with sunburn and still seasick.

Roger had been paying money all day for everything and so when he went to bed, ill, he inserted a quarter for the Magic Fingers.

Something went wrong.

The bed tossed around worse than the boat in four feet of waves.

There was vomit all over the room and when Roger woke up, hearing the knock on the door, he opened the ice chest and looked at the big grouper filets and before he could do anything about it, he threw up on the fish, too, reeling blindly and full of bile back to the bed, which was still on, bucking. His wife was still asleep—but when

107

she heard the new retching sounds from Roger, him trying to lie down, she thought something amorous was up and would have gone for him except for the filthy smell he had.

She crawled away.

Mrs. Reba Laird was a fine woman from Georgia, with her body in trim. She had looked up the origin of the Laird name. In Scots, it means landholder. She knew there was an aristocratic past to her husband, for she herself had found out that her side of the family were thieves and murderers brought over by Oglethorpe to populate and suffer from the jungles of Georgia. She thought Roger was a wonderful lover when he wasn't fishing.

Roger eschewed freshwater fishing in Louisiana, where the Lairds lived now, except for the giant catfish in a river near the Texas border. He got a stout pole, a big hook, and let it down weighted with ocean lead and a large wounded shad. He had read all the fishing tips in *Field & Stream* and he knew those giants were down there because there were other men fishing right where he was with stiff rods and wounded live shad.

The man to Roger's right hooked into one and it was a tussle, tangling all the lines out—so Roger felt the mother down there, all right.

When they got the fish out, by running a jeep in and hooking the line to the bumper, it was the weight of ninety pounds.

The jeep backed over Roger's brand-new fishing rod and snapped it into two pieces and ground his fishing reel into the deep muck. Roger saw the fish and watched them wrench it up, hanging from the back bar of the jeep. He was amazed and excited—but the fish was not his. Still, he photographed it with his Polaroid. But when Roger added up the day, it had cost him close to three hundred dollars for a Polaroid picture.

The thing about it was that Roger was not dumb. He was handsome, slender, gray at the temples, with his forehair receding to reveal an intelligent cranium, nicely shaped like that of a tanned, professional fisherman.

Roger watched the Southern TV shows about fishing— Bill Dance, others—and he had read the old Jason Lucas books, wherein Lucas claims he can catch fish under any conditions, even chopping holes in the ice in Wisconsin at a chill degree of minus fifty and taking his limit in walleye and muskie. Also, Roger had read Izaak Walton, but he had no use for England and all that olden shit.

It was a big saltwater one he wanted, around the Gulf of Mexico where he lived. On the flats near Islamorado, Roger had hung a big bonefish. However, he was alone and it dragged the skiff into some branches where there were several heavy cottonmouth moccasins.

He reached for the pistol in his kit. One of the snakes, with its mouth open, had fallen in the boat. Roger shot the stern floor out of the boat. As the boat sank, all his expensive gear in it, Roger Laird kept going down, reloading, firing at the trees, and when he went underwater he thought he saw the big bonefish under the water, which was later, as he recalled, a Florida gar. He could see underwater and could hold his breath underwater and was, withal, in good shape. But the .25 automatic shot underwater rather startled the ears, and the bullet went out in slow motion like a lead pellet thrown left-handed by a sissy. So Roger waded out of the water, still firing a few rounds to keep Nature away from him. Then got his wind back and dove in to recover his radio.

The Coast Guard came and got him.

Roger's father, Bill Laird, was a tender traveler of eighty years in his new Olds 98. Old Mr. Laird found remarkable animals all over the land. Behind a service station in Bastrop, Louisiana, he saw a dog playing with a robin. The two of them were friends, canine and bird. They had been friends a long time. Grievously, one day the dog became too rough and killed the bird. The men at the service station were sort of in mourning. They stared at the nacreous eyes of the bird on the counter. The dog was under the counter, looking up sorrowfully at the corpse.

Nothing of this should have occurred.

Roger thought of his father, who had always loved animal life and was quite a scholar on the habits of anything on land that roved on four legs.

Well, where was Roger now?

Roger was at Mexico Beach, thirty miles south of Panama City. He was out of money and had brought only a Zebco 33 with a stiff fiberglass rod. He had no money for bait, and he was just helping pay for some of the groceries for George and Anna Lois and their son and daughter-in-law, who had a baby. The house was old and wooden, with a screen porch running around two sides; a splendid beach house owned by Slade West, a veteran of Normandy, who had once kept a pet lion there. The lion started chasing cars when the Florida boom hit, and he had to give it to a zoo.

At the moment, Roger was alone in the house. He was looking out over the ocean at some crows. The crows hung around, although it was not their place. They fetched and quacked in the air and were rolled by sea breezes off the mark.

Somebody's dog from down the way came in and rolled privately in the sea oats. What a lark, all to himself, he was having! Feet in the air and twisting his back in the sand and the roots! But the heavy dangerous trucks going by were just feet from the dog. The dog was playing it very close.

Yesterday, Roger had caught a crab on his line that reminded him of himself. The crab was aging well and, dumb as hell, was holding on till the very, very last, where Roger might drag him in out of the water if he wanted him. The crab was in the surf, clamped on the shrimp and hook, trying to prove something. While the crab was looking at Roger and deciding on the moment, the dog dashed into the water and tore the crab to pieces with its jaws.

Roger had never seen anything like this. Not only was Roger stunned, he had now caught a dog! So he ran down the beach lickety-split with a loose line—so the hook wouldn't hurt the dog's lips. Roger offered abject apologies, pulling the last ten from his wallet to pay the vet bill.

Next door to the house where Roger was staying was an ugly little brick house fenced in as if somebody would want to take something from it. The owner and occupant was a Mr. Mintner, possibly a vampire. Roger had never seen Mr. Mintner come out into the sun and all the plant signs around the house were dead and dry. Parked outside was a Harley-Davidson golf cart, and at 11 p.m. three nights ago Roger had seen Mr. Mintner crank up the golf cart and come back from the Minute Market with several bloody-looking steaks and beef bouillon cubes and some radishes. Roger saw all this in the dim outside light of Mr. Mintner's. He saw Mr. Mintner in a black golf outfit and black boots, and his arms were pale almost to luminescence. There was a story that his heart had been broken by a woman years ago and that he had never recovered.

Roger had a fascinated aversion to this Mintner and believed that he should be hauled away and made to eat with accountants.

Roger, with no financial resources at the time, cleaned up the house and read some of the *National Geographic* and *Discover* magazines around the place. He had brought along his fisherman's log, in which there was not one entry, only some notes on the last pages where it said NOTES.

He looked out at the green softly rolling ocean again. There were a lot of things out there in "the big pond," as *McClane's New Standard Fishing Encyclopedia* called the Gulf. There were things like marlin and sailfish and cobia(ling) and bluefish. As for the little ocean catfish, Roger had caught his weight twenty times over of them.

They were trash and insignificant.

Today George and his son Steve were out casting in the surf and catching some small whiting. Roger waded into the water, feeling the warm wash over his sneakers, and then stood straddle legged, arms behind his back, rather like a taller Napoleon surveying an opposing infantry horde from an unexpected country of idiots.

Two-thirds of the world was water, wasn't it?

There were king mackerel out there, too, and big snapper. But Roger had no funds to hire a boat, and all his wonderful gear was back in Louisiana in his garage, every line coiled perfectly, every hook on every lure honed to surgical sharpness, every reel oiled and soundless. As for what Roger had here at Mexico Beach, it was the cheap Zebco with a light-medium–weight rod, the whole thing coming out of a plastic package from T.G.&Y. at a price of twenty-four dollars—such a rig as you would buy a nephew on his eleventh birthday.

Roger's friend George Epworth was having a good time with his son Steve. They were up to their hips in water, casting away with shrimp on the hook. They caught a ground mullet, which Roger inspected. This kind of mullet is not the leaping vegetarian that is caught with a net only. Roger looked on with pursed lips. Then there were some croakers, who gave them a little tussle. It was fine kid sport, with the surf breaking right around the armpits of the fellows. Steve's wife, Becky, had made a tent over their baby, and Anna Lois, newly a grandmother, was watching the baby and reading from one of Slade West's encyclopedias of sea life. George was a biochemist back at Millsaps College in Jackson. Anna Lois worked for the state crime lab, and their ocean time was precious. They liked *everything* out here and knew a good bit about sea chemistry. Roger envied them somewhat. But he had only a fever for the big one, the one to write home about, the one to stuff, varnish, and mount, whereas none of these fish were approaching a pound, though they were beautiful.

Roger was wondering what in the deuce was so *wrong* with him and his luck now.

Not just the fish.

Not just the fact that his Reba had gone a bit nuts when menopause came on her.

Not just the fact that she bought a new dress *every* day, and from high-priced boutiques, and that she stayed in the bathroom for an hour, making up—but that she emerged in earrings and hose and high heels only to sit on the couch and stare at the wall across from her. Not at a mirror, not at a picture, not at the television, not smoking anymore, not drinking, not reading—which she had loved— just sitting there with a little grieving smile on her face. She wasn't grouchy. She just sat, staring with the startling big gray eyes that had charmed Roger to raving for her back in college days. They'd just had their twenty-fifth anniversary, Roger and Reba.

Further, his luck with money recently. Why, he'd had near a hundred-fifty thousand in the bank, and they were thinking about living on interest for the first time ever when *bang,* the offshore-drilling speculation in which they had the stock exploded and the money was gone.

It made Roger so tired he had not the energy to track down the reasons.

As for Nature, Roger was tiring, too. He had a weary alliance with Nature—the roses, the wisteria, and the cardinals and the ori-oles and the raccoons round the deck on the rear of his dutch-roofed little castle. But he was not charmed much now when he went out there and looked.

Were his senses shutting down? He who had never had to use even reading glasses and about whom everyone said he looked a decade younger than he was? At least?

Roger Laird was about to turn and go back to his room, shut the curtains, write in his fishing log *something* that might give him an idea as to what was wrong with him, when something happened out beyond the breakers.

He saw it roll, and he saw a fin of some kind stand up.

Then it rolled again!

A rising shower of small fish leapt up and the gulls hurried over, seconded by the crows, quacking but not knowing how to work the sea as the gulls did.

The big fin came up again!

Roger's eyes narrowed and the point of his vision met on the swirl of water as if on the wrong end of a pair of Zeisses. Given the swirl, the fish was seven to nine feet long at the smallest.

Roger looked slyly around to see if any of his friends, the Epworths, had noticed it. But they were otherwise occupied and had not.

Roger looked again, bending as if to find a nice conch shell like a lady tourist, and the thing rolled again!

The birds were snapping the moiling little minnows, the crows missing and having to move out heavy on the flap because of their sogged feathers.

Then there was no activity.

Roger walked back with the Epworths, helping to carry the Lui ki l uf finh they intended to roast over charcoal for lunch. The baby was put to bed. Steve and his wife lay on the divan walching thu uuuµ opera *General Hospital*. The local weather and fishing report came on. The man with big spectacles said the weather was fine but the fishing was no good, apologizing to the world for the ocean this week.

After they had eaten the smoked fish and salad and the oysters Rockefeller, everybody was sleepy except Roger—who pretended sleepiness and went to his room. It was a half hour he waited there, studying the Zebco outfit in the corner. Then you could hear nothing in the house, and he, despite himself, began making phony snoring noises.

Barefooted, he scooted to the kitchen and found the plastic bowl of bait shrimp. He eased the door to, not even the sound of a vacuum sucking on rubber. Then he put on his sneakers and, holding the Zebco unit, he slipped out into the driveway.

Roger was about halfway down the drive, aiming straight for the sea, when a loud voice from the little ugly redbrick house horrified him.

"*You!*"

It was Mr. Mintner, shouting from his window.

The pale man was holding the windowsill, speaking with his nose practically against the screen.

"Getting any?" shouted Mintner.

There was a horrifying derisive laugh, like rolling tin, and then the window came down with a smash, Mintner receding into the dark of the room. It was two in the afternoon and the house was totally unlit.

Roger was not certain that there had been a man at all. Perhaps it was just a voice giving body to something waxen and then vanishing.

He had never been a coward. But he was unsettled when he reached the sea. He had some trouble tying on the hook. It was not even a sea hook. It was a thin golden bass hook that came with the Zebco kit. He put the bell weight on and looked out, yearning at the blue-gray hole where the creature had shown.

There was not a bird in sight. There was no whirl and leaping of minnows. The water was as dead as a pond some bovine might be drinking from.

Roger stayed near the water—waiting, getting ready.

Then he cast—a nice long cast—easy with this much lead on the line, and the rig plumped down within a square yard of where he'd seen the fish.

He tightened the line and waited.

There was a tug but small and he knew it was a crab. He jerked the line back, cursing, and reeled in. The shrimp was gone. He looked in the plastic bowl and got the biggest shrimp there, peeled it, and ran it onto the hook, so that his bait looked like a succulent question mark almost to the geometry.

This time he threw long but badly, way over to one side.

It didn't matter.

He knew it didn't matter. He was just hoping that that crab-eating dog wouldn't show up, and he hadn't even tightened his line when it hit.

It was big and it was on.

He could not budge it, and he knew he'd snap the line if he tried.

He forgot how the drag worked. He forgot everything. Everything went into a hot rapid glared picture, and he was yanked into the sea, past his knees, up to his waist, then floundering, swimming, struggling up.

Then he began running knee-deep and following the fish.

Jesus—oh, thank you, please, please, yes—holy Christ, it was coming toward him now! He reeled in rapidly. He had gone yards and yards down the beach.

It came on in. He could pull it in. It was coming. It was bending the rod double. But it was coming. He had it. Just not be dumb and lose it.

It surfaced. A sand shark. About four feet long and fifteen pounds. But Roger had never seen anything so lovely and satisfying. He grabbed the line and hauled it toward him, and there it was, white bellied and gray topped, and now he had it on the sand and it was *his*, looking like a smiling tender rocket from the deep, a fish so young, so handsome, so perfect for its business, and so unlucky.

By this time a crowd had gathered, and Roger was on his knees in the sand, sweating profusely and with his chest full of such good air it was like a gas of silver in him.

The crowd began saying things.

"I'll kill him with this flounder gig! Everybody stand back!" said one of the young men.

"Ooo! Ugg!" said a young somebody else.

George Epworth was on the beach by then.

"That was something. I watched you through the binoculars. That was something." George Epworth knelt and watched the shark heaving away.

"Would you unhook him for me?" Roger Laird asked.

George Epworth reached down, cut the line, and pulled the hook out backward through the shank, leaving only a tiny hole.

A man who had been cutting up drift logs for a fire said, "I'll do the honors. They're good to eat, you know."

The man was raising his axe and waiting for Roger to move away.

"Not mine, you don't!" Roger screamed, and then he picked up the shark by the tail and threw it way out in the water. It turned over on its back and washed in as if dying for a few minutes, whereupon it flipped over and eased into the deep green.

When Roger Laird got back to Louisiana, he did not know what kind of story to tell. He only knew that his lungs were full of the exquisite silvery gas.

Reba Laird became better. They were bankrupt, had to sell the little castle with the dutch roof. She couldn't buy any more dresses or jewelry. But she smiled at Roger Laird. No more staring at the wall.

He sold all his fishing gear at a terrible loss, and they moved to Dallas, address unknown.

Then Roger Laird made an old-fashioned two-by-four pair of stilts eight-feet high. It made him stand about twelve feet in the air. He would mount the stilts and walk into the big lake around which the rich people lived. The sailing boats would come around near him, big opulent three-riggers sleeping two families belowdecks, and Roger Laird would yell:

"Fuck you! Fuck you!"

Even Greenland

I WAS SITTING RADAR. ACTUALLY DOING NOTHING.

We had been up to seventy-five thousand to give the afternoon some jazz. I guess we were still in Mexico, coming into Miramar eventually in the F-14. It doesn't much matter after you've seen the curvature of the earth. For a while, nothing much matters at all. We'd had three sunsets already. I guess it's what you'd call really living the day.

But then,

"John," said I, "this plane's on fire."

"I know it," he said.

John was sort of short and angry about it.

"You thought of last-minute things any?" said I.

"Yeah. I ran out of a couple of things already. But they were cold, like. They didn't catch the moment. Bad writing," said John.

"You had the advantage. You've been knowing," said I.

"Yeah. I was going to get a leap on you. I was going to smoke you. Everything you said, it wasn't going to be good enough. I was going to have a great one, and everything you said, it wasn't going to be good enough," said he.

"But it's not like that," said I. "Is it?"

He said, "Nah. I got nothing, really."

★　★　★

117

The wings were turning red. I guess you'd call it red. It was a shade against dark blue that was mystical flamingo, very spaceylike, like living blood. Was the plane bleeding?

"You have a good time in Peru?" said I.

"Not really," said John. "I got something to tell you. I haven't had a 'good time' in a long time. There's something between me and a good time since, I don't know, since I was twenty-eight or like that. I've seen a lot, but you know I haven't quite *seen* it. Like somebody's seen it already. It wasn't fresh. There were eyes that had used it up some."

"Even high in Mérida?" said I.

"Even," said John.

"Even Tibet, where you met your wife. By accident a beautiful American girl way up there?" said I.

"Even," said John.

"Even Greenland?" said I.

John said, "Yes. Even Greenland. It's fresh, but it's not fresh. There are footsteps in the snow."

"Maybe," said I, "you think about in Mississippi when it snows, when you're a kid. And you're the first up and there's been nobody in the snow, no footsteps."

"Shut up," said John.

"Look, are we getting into a fight here at the moment of death? We going to mix it up with the plane on fire?"

"Shut up! Shut up!" said John. Yelled John.

"What's wrong?" said I.

He wouldn't say anything. He wouldn't budge at the controls. We might burn but we were going to hold level. We weren't seeking the earth at all.

"What is it, John?" said I.

John said, "You son of a bitch, that was *mine*—that snow in Mississippi. Now it's all shot to shit."

The paper from his notepad was flying all over the cockpit, and I could see his hand flapping up and down with the pencil in it, angry.

"It was mine, *mine*, you rotten cocksucker! You see what I mean?"

The little pages hung up on the top, and you could see the big moon just past them.

"Eject! Save your ass!" said John.

But I said, "What about you, John?"

John said, "I'm staying. Just let me have *that* one, will you?"

"But you can't," said I.

But he did.

Celeste and I visit the burn on the blond sand under one of those black romantic worthless mountains five miles or so out from Miramar base.

I am a lieutenant commander in the reserve now. But to be frank, it shakes me a bit even to run a Skyhawk up to Malibu and back.

Celeste and I squat in the sand and say nothing as we look at the burn. They got all the metal away.

I don't know what Celeste is saying or thinking, I am so absorbed myself and paralyzed.

I know I am looking at John's damned triumph.

Ride, Fly, Penetrate, Loiter

My name is Ned Maximus, but they call me Maximum Ned.

Three years ago, when I was a drunk, a hitchhiker stabbed me in the eye with my own filet knife. I wear a patch on the right one now. It was a fake Indian named Billy Seven Fingers. He was having the shakes, and I was trying to get him to the bootleggers off the reservation in Neshoba County, Mississippi. He was white as me—whiter, really, because I have some Spanish.

He asked me for another cigarette, and I said no, that's too many, and besides you're a fake—you might be gouging the Feds with thirty-second-part maximum Indian blood, but you don't fool me.

I had only got to the *maximum* part when he was on my face with the fish knife out of the pocket of the MG Midget.

There were three of us. Billy Seven Fingers was sitting on the lap of his enormous sick real Indian friend. They had been drinking Dr. Tichenors Antiseptic in Philadelphia, and I picked them up sick at five in the morning, working on my Johnnie Walker Black.

The big Indian made the car seem like a toy. Then we got out in the pines, and the last thing of any note I saw with my right eye was a Dalmatian dog run out near the road, and this was wonderful in rural Mississippi—practically a miracle—it was truth and beauty like John Keats has in that poem. And I wanted a dog to redeem my life, as drunks and terrible women do.

But they wouldn't help me chase it. They were too sick.

So I went on, pretty dreadfully let down. It was the best thing offering lately.

I was among dwarves over in Alabama at the school, where almost everybody dies early. There is a poison in Tuscaloosa that draws souls toward the low middle. Hardly anybody has honest work. Queers full of backbiting and rumors set the tone. Nobody has ever missed a meal. Everybody has about exactly enough courage to jaywalk or cheat a wife or a friend with a quote from Nietzsche on his lips.

Thus it seemed when I was a drunk, raving with bad attitudes. I drank and smiled and tried to love, wanting some hero for a buddy: somebody who would attack the heart of the night with me. I had worn out all the parlor charity of my wife. She was doing the standard frigid lockout at home, enjoying my trouble and her cold rectitude. The drunkard lifts sobriety into a great public virtue in the smug and snakelike heart. It may be his major service. Thus it seemed when I was a drunk, raving with bad attitudes.

So there I was, on my knees in the pebble dust on the shoulder of the road, trying to get the pistol out of the trunk of my car.

An eye is a beautiful thing! I shouted.

An eye is a beautiful thing!

I was howling and stumbling.

You frauding ugly shit! I howled.

But they were out of the convertible and away. My fingers were full of blood, but it didn't hurt that much. When I finally found the gun, I fired it everywhere and went out with a white heat of loud horror.

I remember wanting a drink terribly in the emergency room. I had the shakes. And then I was in another room and didn't. My veins were warm with dope, the bandage on. But another thing— there was my own personal natural dope running in me. My head was very high and warm. I was exhilarated, in fact. I saw with penetrating clarity with my lone left eye.

It has been so ever since. Except the dead one has come alive and I can see the heart of the night with it. It throws a grim net sometimes, but I am lifted up.

Nowadays this is how it goes with me: ride, fly, penetrate, loiter.

I left Tuscaloosa—the hell with Tuscaloosa—on a Triumph motorcycle black and chrome. My hair was long, leather on my loins, bandanna of the forehead in place, standard dope-drifter gear, except for the bow and arrows strapped on the sissy bar.

No guns.

Guns are for cowards.

But the man who comes near my good eye will walk away a spewing porcupine.

The women of this town could beg and beg, but I would never make whoopee with any of them again.

Thus it seemed when I was a drunk.

I was thirty-eight and somewhat Spanish. I could make a stand in this chicken house no longer.

Now I talk white, Negro, some Elizabethan, some Apache. My dark eye pierces and writhes and brings up odd talk in me sometimes. Under the patch, it burns deep for language. I will write sometimes and my bones hurt. I believe heavily in destiny at such moments.

I went in a bar in Dallas before the great ride over the desert that I intended. I had not drunk for a week. I took some water and collected the past. I thought of my books, my children, and the fact that almost everybody sells used cars or dies early. I used to get so angry about this issue that I would drag policemen out of their cars. I fired an arrow through the window of my last wife's, hurting nothing but the cozy locked glass and disturbing the sleep of grown children.

It was then I took the leap into the wasteland, happy as Brer Rabbit in the briars. That long long, bloated epicene tract "The Waste Land" by Eliot—the slideshow of some snug librarian on the rag—was nothing, unworthy, in the notes that every sissy throws away. I would not talk to students about it. You throw it down like a pickled egg with nine Buds and move on to giving it to the preacher's wife on a hill while she spits on a photograph of her husband.

I began on the Buds, but I thought I was doing better. The standard shrill hag at the end of the bar had asked me why I did not have a ring in my ear, and I said nothing at all. Hey, pirate! she was shrieking when I left, ready to fire out of Dallas. But I went back toward Louisiana, my home state, Dallas had sickened me so much.

Dallas, city of the fur helicopters. Dallas—computers, plastics, urban cowboys with schemes and wolf shooting in their hearts. The standard artist for Dallas should be Mickey Gilley, a studied fraud who might well be singing deeply about ripped fiberglass. His cousin is Jerry Lee Lewis, still very much from Louisiana. The Deep South might be wretched, but it can howl.

I went back to the little town in the pines near Alexandria where I grew up. I didn't even visit my father, just sat on my motorcycle and stared at the little yellow store. At that time I had still not forgiven him for converting to Baptist after Mother's death.

I had no real home at all then, and I looked in the dust at my boots, and I considered the beauty of my black and chrome Triumph 650 Twin, '73 model, straight pipes to horrify old hearts, electricity by Lucas. I stepped over to the porch, unsteady, to get more beer, and there she was with her white luggage, Celeste, the one who would be a movie star, a staggering screen vision that every sighted male who saw the cinema would wet the sheets for.

I walked by her, and she looked away, because I guess I looked pretty rough. I went on in the store—and now I can tell you, this is what I saw when my dead eye went wild. I have never been the same since.

The day is so still, it is almost an object. The rain will not come. The clouds are white, burned high away.

On the porch of the yellow store, in her fresh stockings despite the heat, her toes eloquent in the white straps of her shoes, the elegant young lady waits. The men, two of them, look out to her occasionally. In the store, near a large reservoir, hang hooks, line, Cheetos, prophylactics, cream nougats. The roof of the store is tin.

Around the woman the men, three decades older, see hot love and believe they can hear it speak from her ankles.

They cannot talk. Their tongues are thick. Flies mount their shoulders and cheeks, but they don't go near her, her bare shoulders wonderful above her sundress. She wears earrings, ivory dangles, and when she moves, looking up the road, they swing and kiss her shoulders almost, and the heat ripples about but it does not seem to touch her, and she is not of this place, and there is no earthly reason.

The men in the store are stunned. They have forgotten how to move, what to say. Her beauty. The two white leather suitcases on either side of her.

"My wife is a withered rag," one man suddenly blurts to the other.

"Life here is a belligerent sow, not a prayer," responds the other.

The woman has not heard all they say to each other. But she's heard enough. She knows a high point is near, a declaration.

"This store fills me with dread. I have bleeding needs," says the owner.

"I suck a dry dug daily," says the other. "There's grease from nothing, just torpor, in my fingernails."

"My God, for relief from this old charade, my mercantilia!"

"There is a bad God," groans the other, pounding a rail. "The story is riddled with holes."

The woman hears a clatter around the counter. One of the men, the owner, is moving. He reaches for a can of snuff. The other casts himself against a bare spar in the wall. The owner is weeping outright.

He spits into the snuff in his hands. He thrusts his hands into his trousers, plunging his palms to his groin. The other man has found a length of leather and thrashes the wall, raking his free hand over a steel brush. He snaps the brush to his forehead. He spouts choked groans, gasping sorrows. The two of them upset goods, shatter the peace of the aisles. The man with the leather removes his shoes. He removes a shovel from its holder, punches it at his feet, howls and reattacks his feet angrily, crying for his mute heels.

"My children are low-hearted fascists! Their eyebrows meet! The oldest boy's in San Diego, but he's a pig! We're naught but dying animals. Eve and then Jesus and us, clerks!"

The owner jams his teeth together, and they crack. He pushes his tongue out, evicting a rude air sound. The other knocks over a barrel of staves.

"Lost! Oh, lost!" the owner spouts. "The redundant dusty clock of my tenure here!"

"Ah, heart pie!" moans the other.

The woman casts a glance back.

A dog has been aroused and creeps out from its bin below the counter. The owner slays the dog with repeated blows of the shovel, lifting fur into the air in great gouts.

She, Celeste, looks cautiously ahead. The road is still empty.

The owner has found some steep plastic sandals and is wearing them—jerking, breaking wind, and opening old sores. He stomps at imagined miniature men on the floor. The sound—the snorts, cries, rebuffs, indignant grunts—is unsettling.

The woman has a quality about her. That and the heat.

I have been sober ever since.

I have just told a lie.

At forty, I am at a certain peace. I have plenty of money and the love of a beautiful red-haired girl from Colorado. What's more, the closeness with my children has come back to a heavenly beauty, each child a hero better than yours.

You may see me with the eye patch, though, in almost any city of the South, the Far West, or the Northwest. I am on the black and chrome Triumph, riding right into your face.

Fans

WRIGHT'S FATHER, A SPORTSWRITER AND A HACK AND A SHILL FOR THE university team, was sitting next to Milton, who was actually blind but nevertheless a rabid fan, and Loomis Orange, the dwarf who was one of the team's managers. The bar was out of their brand of beer, and they were a little drunk, though they had come to that hard place together where there seemed nothing, absolutely nothing to say.

The waitress was young. Normally, they would have commented on her and gone on to pursue the topic of women, the perils of booze, or the like. But not now. Of course it was the morning of the big game in Oxford, Mississippi.

Someone opened the door of the bar, and you could see the bright wonderful football morning pouring in with the green trees, the Greek-front buildings, and the yelling frat boys. Wright's father and Loomis Orange looked up and saw the morning. Loomis Orange smiled, as did Milton, hearing the shouts of the college men. The father did not smile. His son had come in the door, swaying and rolling, with one hand to his chest and his walking stick in the other.

Wright's father turned to Loomis and said, "Loomis, you are an ugly distorted little toad."

Loomis dropped his glass of beer.

"*What?*" the dwarf said.

"I said that you are ugly," Wright said.

"How could you have said that?" Milton broke in.

Wright's father said, "Aw, shut up, Milton. You're just as ugly as he is."

"What've I ever did to you?" cried Milton.

Wright's father said, "Leave me alone! I'm a writer."

"You ain't any kind of writer. You an alcoholic. And your wife is ugly. She's so skinny she almost ain't even there!" shouted the dwarf.

People in the bar—seven or eight—looked over as the three men spread, preparing to fight. Wright hesitated at a far table, not comprehending.

His father was standing up.

"Don't, don't, don't," Wright said. He swayed over toward their table, hitting the floor with his stick, moving tables aside.

The waitress shouted over, "I'm calling the cops!"

Wright pleaded with her: "Don't, don't, don't!"

"Now, please, sit down everybody!" somebody said.

They sat down. Wright's father looked with hatred at Loomis. Milton was trembling. Wright made his way slowly over to them. The small bar crowd settled back to their drinks and conversation on the weather, the game, traffic, etc. Many of the people talked about J. Edward Toole, whom all of them called simply Jet. The name went with him. He was in the Ole Miss defensive secondary, a handsome figure who was everywhere on the field, the star of the team.

Wright found a seat at the table. He could half see and he looked calmly at all of them. His voice was extremely soft, almost ladylike, very Southern. Wright was born-again, just like Jet, who led the team in prayer before every game.

"Let's talk about Jet. I know him well," Wright began.

His father shifted, embarrassed. "We know that, Son."

"I grew up with that boy," he went on.

"Wright, we know . . ."

"We shared the normal boyhood things together. We were little strangers on this earth together. We gamboled in the young pastures. We took our first forbidden pleasures together"—he winked—"our first cigarette, our first beer." Wright paused, shyly. "I shared my poetry with him."

"God," said Wright's father.

"We met when he and the other boys chased me down the beach with air rifles, shooting me repeatedly on my bare back, legs, and ears until they had run me to earth. He was always large and swift. He used to pinch me in the hall and pull out my T-shirt so that it looked as if I had breasts. He used to flatulate at his desk and point at me. In point of the fair sex, there was always a gag from this merry lad. He took my poems and revised them into pornographic verse, complete with sketches, mind you, and sent them to my sweetheart—"

"Son," pleaded Wright's father.

"Oh, I even tried the field with him myself, though thin of leg. He was a champion already, only a sophomore at Bay High. I will say that he, ha ha, taught me very well how to fumble on return of punts and kickoffs. For such was I used—as swift fodder for the others."

Loomis and Milton were entranced. Wright's father was breathing very heavy and looking at the floor.

"*Wright.*" This time he was almost demanding.

"Those smashes of his! I certainly, ha ha, coughed up the ball and often limped into the showers. One afternoon while no one was looking, he clipped me from behind, right on the concrete floor."

Wright was smiling meekly as his voice trailed off. And when he went on, it was quieter but very even.

"We won all the games. I say we, though I stood on the sidelines or played in the band—French horn. I remember his beautiful mother watching from the stands, but what I mainly remember was Jet, with all his tackles and interceptions. He was All-State his junior year, then went on to duplicate that his senior, ultimately receiving, as you know, a full scholarship to the university here, where fate—or most likely God—brought my family and me to this fair city, my father finding employment and I a convenient although irregular education."

Wright's father's hands were over his face.

"It's back to the night of our senior graduation from Bay High, that night you are familiar with—"

"Yes, Goddamn it, we are familiar!" said his father.

"Wait. I want to hear the story again," said Loomis Orange.

"Yeah. Again," said Milton.

"That night, knowing I had my new Vespa motor scooter as a present from my father and mother, Jet and some of the boys waited at the end of the drive out from the auditorium. Still wearing my robe, my mortarboard under my arm, I cranked up that lovely red Vespa for all it could rip. I was in a hurry to change and join Jet and the others out at the lake party. They were in the bushes on either side of the road with a rope lying hidden between them. Well, they 'clotheslined' me. The rest is history."

"Yes, Son! We *know* about that and your condition, bless your heart. Let's—"

Wright's father rose as if to go.

"Then . . ."

"*Then?*" said Loomis. He put his short arms on the table. He wore a bulky child's-size Izod shirt.

"*Then? Then?*" said the father. He sat back down.

"The best, I suppose, in a way, ha ha. At the end of the summer, when I was out of the hospital and all was said and done, Jet and I made a private trip to the Biloxi Yacht Club. We were interested in a boat. Or rather, as I usually did, I followed his interests. It was late in the afternoon and there had been a bumper crop of shrimp— so many they were falling off the boat. The sharks had followed the boats in and they'd called off swimming.

"A man on the dock was balling up hamburger meat full of razor blades, in chunks about the size of horse apples, and throwing them in the water. The water would churn and a fan of blood would rush out of the shark's head. This brought the others to it. The water was white and thrashing. Heads and half bodies floated up and snapped back down. Then the alligator gars got into it and it was bleeding paradise. That was Jet's phrase. Oh, he could do the smart phrase now and then, using a British term or some such.

"It was *bleeding paradise*, he said. After he finished saying this over and over again, he asked me what I thought. Thought about *what?* I said. And Jet got very sad and looked out over the water at the red sun. Then he pushed me in."

"He pushed you *in?* In the *water?*" said Milton, who was the only one at the table who could respond in words.

"Yes," said Wright. There was a bit of hurt in his eyes, but they retained an even, soft gleam. "But there is the further beautiful thing."

"He pushed you in the water, Son?"

"Yes. But last year I saw him on campus. I knew that he'd been born-again and I wanted to congratulate him. You know what he said to me as he rubbed that big Sugar Bowl ring on those great sun-browned fingers of his? He put his arm on my shoulder and said to me, 'Wright, I'm sorry.'"

There was business to do, the game to see, or feel, so the four of them slowly left the bar, tapping, wobbling, huffing, and met Wright's mother on the corner, then went up to the stadium to wait for Jet to kill them.

★ ★

1986–1993
Bats Out of Hell

★ ★

High·Water Railers

THE PIER SHOOK UNDER HIS FEET, WRAPPED IN SOCKS AND SANDALS. He wore huge gabardine shorts and was blue-white in the legs. Yeah, our time's about over, and I was counting the things I hadn't done last night, things I regretted, sins of omission; omitted to *sin*, I mean, ha! He was going on. Lewis, ninety-one, had watched some four-foot square of water for three years. He was still intrigued by what the lake gave up. Storms had been rough through the late winter and spring. This was an oxbow lake. The flooding from the great continental river washed splendid oddities into the channel, some of them carnivorous, some of them simply bottom suckers of astounding girth, armored with scales of copper. Lewis shook with both palsy and wonder when fish this rare were dragged up or just spotted rolling.

His fine sea-size rig was cast out with a six-inch red and white bobber; two fathoms under was a hooked shrimp from a frozen bag he'd brought down. Lewis had a theory that with hurricanes—they'd had two just lately a hundred-fifty miles south—sea life pushed up into the high reaches of the river, then flooded even into this lake and Farte Cove. He considered himself an ichthyologist of minor parts and kept a notebook with responses to fish life in it. There were no entries or dates when he did not catch or witness interesting water life. Like a great many days in a man's life, those days he'd just as soon did not occur at all. He wanted a lot of the exotic and a minimum of the ordinary.

Lewis turned and was deeply unimpressed by old Ulrich staggering onto the pier. This man featured himself a scientist or at least an aerocrat, though Lewis thought him a fraud afloat on a sea of wide misunderstanding. Ulrich was in the process of "studying" blue herons, loons and accipiters in flight and for some nagging reason was interested in the precise *weight* of everybody he met. He thought it happily significant that the old had lighter, hollower, more aerodynamic bones, such as birds had. Having been witness to the first German jet aircraft in the war, a specter he had never recovered from, he "drew on" this reflection time and again, apropos of almost zero, thought Lewis. Unfortunately, he had also been blown a goodly distance by Hurricane Camille in 1969. Ulrich was old *then*, but claimed also to be wiser in special "hurricane minutes" and inflicted this credential here and there, at any time, during his seminar at the end of the pier. There was no gainsaying the man with his "brief flight" and "hurricane minutes." The body was preparing the elderly for the "flight of the soul," said Ulrich. Why, he expected to weigh about thirty-five pounds when he died, just a bit of mortal coil dragged away protesting like a hare under an eagle.

Another annoyance to Lewis—who actually loved Ulrich; almost all the old loved each other at the end of the pier—was that Ulrich, eighty-nine, showed no signs of bad health even though he lit up one Kent after another. This, Ulrich attributed—wouldn't it be—to a "scientific diet" such as that literally eaten by birds. The diet of birds was indicated come the senior years. A final annoyance was that Ulrich cherished the word *acquit,* as in "let me acquit myself" or "he acquitted himself well." Though Lewis ignored this as often as possible, he wondered why Ulrich should think a person was perpetually on trial when he opened his mouth, especially given the blather that flew out Ulrich's own. Ulrich, too, was interested in piscatorial life, though fish were "base and heavy," mere "forage in the pastures of the deep." Ignore, look away, pleaded Lewis to himself.

Many eutrophic lakes, their food chains unbalanced by man or nature, simply died. But this old oxbow had come back in the nineties. Bass, sunfish, perch, bluegill, gar, buffalo, carp, and now small alligators popped the surface. Big shad fled and recovered in shoals. Rare wading birds attended the shores and shallows. Hunted duck and geese veterans rested and paddled with only the great moccasins and turtles to fear. The water was a late-spring black, with sloughs going to tannin. Three unrecovered human bodies were somewhere out there, victims of March lightning. In a bad storm, the huge lake could imitate an inland sea, all three-foot whitecaps and evil sail-wrappers. It would also flood quickly and drive mink and nutria to the back roads, where one could make ladies' coats from the roadkill.

Next, Sidney Farte, of the old cove family who owned the boat and bait house, came out, barely, humbled by shingles and roaring ulcers, giving a sniff of propriety to the pier, which he did not own but had watched for fifty-seven years through the replacement and repiling in the seventies. The man who'd had the benches and the rail fixed for the elderly was a kind man—Wooten—now dead and discussed only by that one inexorable trait of his, his kindness in little things and big. Nobody knew what experience had produced this saint, and his perfection attracted none of them, so terrible would be the strain, especially considering the fact that Wooten had not been stupid, not at all. Some said that he had been president of a small Baptist college, but for some reason nobody had ever directly put the question to him. There was a holy air about the man, no denying, that brooked none of your ordinary street questioning. Wooten never quoted anybody or any source. He spoke only for himself, and not very often. Such a man—well, even if something enormous and ugly had happened in his past, it would seem rude to know it. Wooten was a tiny man, maybe five-four, with snow-white hair that turned boyishly fore and aft in the wind. He stepped very softly. Next you knew, he was beside you, looking at what you were looking at in respectful quiet.

Ulrich had said that the lake was now Wooten's college, but Wooten himself would never have expressed anything as pompous as that.

"The water looks so fresh and deep this morning!" Wooten would say, a curious sweet medicinal smell reaching you on his breath.

Sidney Farte did not care for his virtue, was made sullen by it, but did not dare attack "Cardinal Wooten" (as he called him under his breath) around the others. He was glad when the fellow passed on. Now Sidney could get back to the regular profanity of his observations. Sidney was having a bad time in his old age, but he rather adored his bad time. Also afflicted with serious deafness, he did not enjoy the reprieve from noise as other old people did, but hurled this way and that, certain that whispered conspiracies and revenges were afoot. The soreness in his chest predicted the weather, which Sidney inevitably pronounced rotten: tornadoes, more flooding and thunder, every kind of spiteful weather. A sunny day filled him with mild horror and suspicion. Sidney had endured lately a sorry, sorry thing, and all of them knew it. A male grandchild of his had won a scholarship to a mighty eastern university, Yale, and was the object of a four-year gloat by Sidney, who had no college. The young man upon graduation had come over to visit his grandfather for a week, at the end of which he pronounced Sidney "a poisonous, evil old man who ought to be ashamed of yourself." This statement simply whacked Sidney flat to the ground. He was still trying to recover and was much more silent than in previous springs. Ulrich and Lewis both worried about him, used to his profanity as a sort of walking milieu against which they fished and breathed.

The other oldster of the core on the rail was late. This was Peter Wren, brother of the colonel who made Wake Island gallant against the Japanese and a chronic prevaricator whose lies were so gaudy and wrapped around they might have been a medieval tapestry of what almost or never happened. He had of course suborned the history of his brother and his constant perjuries held a real fear of the truth, lest the whole tissue of lies crumble when it came forward. It was getting where it seemed dangerous to risk even a simple declarative sentence about the weather or time of day, and Pete Wren was likely to misstate even that. "It's really wanting to rain, you know. Must be near noon"—when the sky was full blue and the time was about ten, latest. People took him to be majorly misinformed, but it was not that: he lived in fear of rupture from the tangled web. So finally he came out with his expensive ultralight rig and crickets. Wren was a partisan of the bluegill, for which—it was heard—he held the state record, but he'd casually eaten the fish without registering it. He was breeding a special kind of mutant cricket in his wire keep that would take the record fish again. There were enormous bluegills in the lake, in fact, and even a liar could catch them. Wren had taken home a pound-and-a-quarter one late one evening, but he claimed it had interbred with a German trout and had disqualified itself.

"Morning, gents," said Wren to the three at the rail. They waited for his maiden lie of the day. Something impossible about his sleep, perhaps.

"A car hit him and that queer just flew away," he said.

"Say it again?" asked Lewis.

"Oh, I rented a video of *Last Exit to Brooklyn* last night. A queer ran out in the road, a car hit him, and that queer just flew straight up in the air away."

"Could I see that?" asked Ulrich, intensely concerned with the flight of human beings.

"I might have lost the tape."

"Already lost it, Wren?"

"It could be in there among my volumes of Shakespeare. I've got all ninety-five of his stories and plays. Given to me by my grandson, who just adores me."

Though he meant nothing by it, Sidney Farte was insulted, recalling the anathema of his own grandson last spring. This began his day vilely, even lower.

"You diarrhea-mouth cocksucker," he said.

"Here now, so early," objected Lewis. A ninety-one-year-old man didn't want to hear such filth announcing the day. That was the sort of thing they did in that vicious far-north horror, New York City. The saintly Wooten had established a certain spirit on the pier that was not recanted at his death. Sidney heard nothing beyond a direct blast in the ear, which Wren was determined to give him. He actually began feeling better now, recovering his purchase on the island of unconscious profanity that was his.

"Puts me in mind of Icarus," said Ulrich.

"Like everything," said Sidney. "Shit, I knew a rat once could fly. Throw that sumbitch cheese in the air. Shit in the air too."

"You look thin today, Sidney. What's your weight?" asked Ulrich, lighting another Kent.

He jumped into something running parallel in his brain: "Thing to do is wait out the pain. Most times it'll pass of itself. Modern man has not let the body heal itself. The downfall was aspirin."

"What in hell are you talking about?"

"Rock and roll kills a lot of men early. We know for a fact that the presence of rock and roll electrons in the air causes plane crashes. Some of that hip-hop stuff will take the wing right off your jumbo jet. Even makes cancer, too. They're looking into it."

"These people you say 'looking into' shit. Count 'em, it just about leaves only us on the pier that ain't doing a survey."

"It's the age of high-priced nosiness all right," said Lewis, whose bobber was going under as if a sucking thing were on. He let out an audible breath in sympathy. "Something's on my shrimp, gentlemen."

"I want to see this sea creature," said Peter Wren, throat red with prevarication.

The huge bobber submerged and disappeared in the black-ish green, down to legend they hoped, and the men hovered together into one set of eyes three hundred and twenty-three years old. The bobber came back up again, but Lewis raised the line and the shrimp was gone. Wren began rigging for bluegill, excited.

"A turtle or a gator'd bite shrimp," said Sidney.

"I suspect sturgeon," said Lewis. "They can breathe both salt and fresh. And they migrate long distances."

"Your human being is made like the shark. If he quits moving and doing, he perishes," said Ulrich.

"Now *shark*. I'll eat any shark you catch raw," said Wren. Though a liar, Wren was a man of some sartorial taste. He suddenly observed Ulrich with a jump. Ulrich wore a brown Eisenhower jacket over blue-striped polyester bell-bottom pants—something truly ghastly from the seventies, such as on a boulevarding pimp. Through a flashback of several connected untruths, Wren was visited by a haze of nausea, for everything wicked had happened to him in the seventies. He had lost his wife, his business; thieves had stolen his collection of guns. Music was provided by those skinny, filthy Lazaruses, the Rolling Stones. Carter had given away everything to the blacks and hippies; brought blue jeans to the White House. Every adult became a laughingstock and fool. Old Ulrich here was dressing right into the part. How Wren despised him now for his encyclopedic near-information. The world was in such a sorry state, it made a man lie sometimes to be sane. He tossed his line out grimly. Ulrich had ruined the fishing.

The lake, just alive, now seemed bright warm and dead, just a stretch of empty liquid at midmorning. A bad quality of light had suddenly come over. All of them felt it, like that mean gloom one feels after a pointless argument with one's wife. Nobody spoke for thirty minutes, hearing the call of an unnamed flat accidie.

At last Lewis, back to his daybreaking thought about what he regretted having never done, his sin of omission, spoke. He asked the others what bothered them in this area. Lunchtime loomed— pleasant ritual of the hungry sun. More and more they talked about food, except for Sidney Farte, often too sick to eat.

"I guess what I missed most was having a significant pet," said Lewis. "I was always talked out of them. Would be nice to have an old dog hearkening toward the end with me."

"I guess I missed the Big Money," said Ulrich. "That could have been sweet. Imagine the studies one could pursue. Perfecting one-man propulsion. I could have been the Howard Hughes of individual flight."

"I wish I'd had a heart," blurted Sidney Farte. "I didn't even cry at my wife's funeral. Knew I should, but I just couldn't. My children looked long and expectant at me. Hell, I was like that as a little boy. Look on the worst things without a blink, eyes so dry they hurt. Something left out of me at birth. Begun lying 'cause there wasn't nothing in true life that moved me."

The confession was so astounding to the rest, who had known Farte for a decade and a half, that reply was occluded. His health must be sincerely bad. They all felt a surrender. Now noon, it became darkly clouded; something dangerous and honest seemed to be in the air. Peter Wren had a fish on, but was just ignoring it, reckoning on Sidney Farte. But it was Wren's turn.

"That I could have sex with a child," he said.

"My ugly God," said Lewis.

"I mean a youngish girl, say fourteen. That she would adore me. I would be everything to her."

Was he now adjusting himself to a public? they wondered. Or was he inwardly a vile old criminal, collecting photographs and near to wearing a garter belt? Fourteen was suddenly too legitimate, hardly a story at all. In their youth, fourteen was open season. There were many mothers at age fifteen, already going to fat. Four memories raked through the deep ashes of their desire.

"Shit, I *had* that," said Sidney.

"Was she tight? Did she cavort for you?" asked Wren.

"Yes and yes. Couldn't get enough. I tell you—"

"Shhh!" said Lewis.

Behind them, someone had lightly shaken the pier. In her tennis shoes, she had crept up unheard. The small vibration of the boards was all the warning Lewis had of her. She was right behind Sidney, attentive. It was Melanie, Wooten's widow, the only woman ever to insist on coming among the men at the end of the pier. Farte despised having her near. The others could not quite decide. Something was always suspended when she came around. A sort of startled gentility set in, unbearable to Farte, like sudden envelopment by a church.

"We were talking horses, Mrs. Wooten," said Lewis.

She'd brought them a snack of homemade sugar cookies. You could smell vanilla on her. She was an industrious person who had begun blowing glass animals after the death of her husband. That she came out there was somewhat aggressive, they felt, and she had begun talking a lot more since Wooten passed, finding a hobby and her tongue at about the same time.

"No, you weren't talking horses. Don't mind me, don't you dare. I like man talk."

"Cloudy noon," Ulrich offered.

"Aren't you going to pull your fish in?" the old lady asked Wren.

When he got the fish reeled in, they saw it was a Gaspergou, a frog-eyed crossbreed of bass and bream nobody had seen in ages. Everybody but the sulking Farte was fascinated.

"That's your unlikely combination, a mutant, absolutely," said Ulrich, "the predator and the predatee, crossbred. The eater and the eaten." As Wren unhooked it and laid it out on the planks,

Ulrich continued, in an excess of philosophy: "An anomaly of the food chain, hardly ever witnessed. We've got the aquatic equivalent of a fox and a chicken here, on your food chain. Reminds you of man himself. All our funereal devices are a denial of the food chain—our coffins, our pyres, our mausoleums, our pyramids. Pitifully declaring ourselves exempt from the food chain. Our arrogance. But we aren't, we're right in it. Nits, mites and worms will have us. Never you doubt it."

They munched the sugar cookies and Ulrich was confident he had produced a deep silence with his gravity.

"I'm not that innocent, lads," said Melanie Wooten. "*I've* cavorted. I was a looker, my skin they said seemed not to have any pores at all. Wootie was lucky. The man stayed grateful, all his life."

"Is that what made him so kind?" asked Lewis.

He acknowledged, looking at her firmly for the first time, that she was no liar. Her skin was still fine for a woman in her seventies. There was a blonde glow to her. Her lips were full and bowed—quite beautiful, like a lady in films. The way she broke into life here toward the end he found admirable too. Many women of his generation remained huddled mice. You could not even imagine them straight in their coffins.

"I hope so," said Melanie. "His gratitude. Without, I hope, sounding proud."

"Not at all," said Lewis. "Gratitude is what marks the higher being, doesn't it?"

"But the thing came over him toward the end, which I've never much discussed. It came on just like diabetes. My love had nothing to do with it. In his seventies he turned gay. Isn't that something? All those male students—he had a different infatuation every week. Poor Wootie. They fired him from the college. He couldn't control himself."

"*What?*" asked Sidney Farte, rather meanly. She knew the problem.

"He turned homosexual. *Homosexual,*" she emphasized, as if in a lecture to a pupil.

"Is it true?" asked Lewis.

They were not looking anywhere in particular, the others, when they noticed Lewis was weeping. He shook a little, and his long white face was drawn up in hurt.

"What is it?" Ulrich and Wren begged. "What's wrong?"

"I want a *dog*. I want a *dog*. I get so lonely, nothing anybody can do about it," Lewis cried out like a child.

"Well now, a dog can be *had*. Let's be about getting you a dog," said Ulrich.

"Certainly," Melanie said, taking Lewis's hand. "Did I upset you?"

"Just a dog," Lewis sniffled.

"By all that pukes, get the man a dog," said Sidney.

"That's a dream you hardly have to defer," said Wren. "*That* can be most painlessly had."

They went back up the pier together, Melanie indicating the way to her station wagon. All in, they set out over to Vicksburg to find Lewis a dog.

★ ★

Two Things, Dimly, Were Going at Each Other

★ ★

THE OLD MAN OFF FORTY YEARS OF MORPHINE WAS FASCINATED BY guns. He was also a foe of dogs everywhere. They were too servile, too slavering, too helplessly pack-bent when not treacherous. The cat was the thing. Coots cut at the evening with his cane and wanted to "see a death" in the big city. He had been crazy for death these many years, writing about it and studying it in thick manuscripts. Many, hordes, died in his fictions. He dressed in a suit, often a three-piece, and looked to be a serious banker, with a Windsor knot in his tie. The scratch of the lower Midwest was in his voice. He was looking for a billiards parlor in Manhattan. In these blocks he had heard one rumored.

He knew of an afflicted man playing billiards—Latouche, ninety, a barely retired surgeon. The grofft was getting him. It was a rare Central American disease, making one hunt like a dog, bark and whine, the face becoming wolfish. The old man, Coots, despised the even older Latouche. There was just something, something— what?—about the man, perhaps his comfort, an obtuseness. And, sealing it, he owned a proud Hungarian sheepdog. The thing had gruesomely licked Coots at an underground firing range where he and Latouche shot their exotic weapons. It was their only similarity, this love of handguns. The old men would ardently blast away for hours, exchanging Italian, German, South African and Chinese pieces, barrels all heated up so that they would have made a pop of steam if tossed in water. Hunting and ordering correct calibers was a main part of their lives. Latouche was more the weapons technician, while Coots revered the history of each piece, or even more precisely, what kind of hole in what men in what time, entrance and exit; what probable suffering.

In Mexico once when he was young, Coots had shot his wife "inadvertently when the black thing was on me" as they were sporting around with the idea of William Tell, a glass on her head. Coots was drunk, but he insisted on "the black thing." He believed in spells and even more in guns as he got old. He believed he could think spells on enemies and bring hideous luck to them, or so he wrote in his chilly fictions, where homicide and orgasm were inevitably concurrent and hundreds died in rages of lust and murder; a holocaust of young men perishing was always at least in the background, like wallpaper in a shrine. It was an ancient and beloved tyranny of the cosmos in which desirable bodies were given up religiously.

Coots, queer not gay, was an old-timer who hated "fairies" almost as much as women, or so he wrote. "Queens" were anathema, down there with the dreaded "cunts." His manly Midwestern prose would scratch out at them. Physically he was a coward, and as he aged in the big city, his paranoia had a field day and became quite adorable to Coots cultists, who were always at him for interviews. His prose was no hoax. He wrote beautifully, especially when he was telling a straight clean story—something "linear." But too much of this thirties stuff annoyed him and he was apt to launch off into his "genius"—spiteful incoherence, cut-up blather, free-floating time pirates corn-holing each other, etc. He was, though, dead accurate about the century often in this "shotgunning"—it seemed to thousands anyway—as only, perhaps, an old shy queer full of hate can be.

Coots had murdered nobody else (his wife's accident had cost him a few days in a Mexican jail), but he was proud of the three dogs he had shot in a great city park one twilight, two German shepherds and a Rottweiler, just last year. Their hides were on the wall of the composing room in his "bunker," a windowless warehouse apartment tremendously padlocked in a cheap nasty section of town. Coots had claimed an attack, and the young amanuensis with him (they were not lovers) did not deny it. There had been high adventure in secreting the gun, getting the animals back to the apartment in three separate taxis, and arranging for their skinning with a jubilant cultist now ten years on methedrine. The legend got out to everybody with whom the cultist had a beer, hundreds. Alcoholism was necessary to balance his speed habit, but nothing balanced his tongue. The story had all three animals, escaped from a wealthy high-altitude widow hag on Riverside Drive, tearing unprovoked at Coots's legs, with the amanuensis sprawled in terror, and Coots fast-drawing a .44 from his Abercrombie & Fitch raincoat. Coots, swarmed by his interviewers and even by *Time,* demurred, but there were the three hides on the wall, head shots, no hole in the pelt. Of peculiar literary satisfaction was the fact that the methedrined skinner died a week later, as if taken off by a curse from the shy hermitic Coots.

Coots was now thinking he had successfully hexed Latouche, a man who at eighty-nine had never had a day of bad health, and now the grofft on him, horrible and unlucky. Latouche was of an almost alarming breed. He seemed never to have made a mistake. Neither with his surgery (famous), his wives (he had outlived two fine women devotedly in love with him), his clothes, his money, his charities (quiet and enormous), or his prosperous handsome doctor sons. At billiards he was a wizard and put away other wizards one fourth his age, some of them precocious millionaires of his pat tern. The great violent, greedy and rude city had not put one line of worry on his face. He had been a gallant chief of surgery in World War II, at forty-one, with Patton's racing Third Army, but could have been queer Hitler's Aryan model. Even in his forties he seemed to be the one for whom Grable showed her amazing legs; he could have been her kiddish admirer and our hope for Over There, Lucky Strike thrust into sidelips with the dash of veteranship forced on him. Latouche could have ridden on sheer image, but insisted instead on Johns Hopkins, Harvard, and the Sorbonne, to emerge a surgeon, powerful before age thirty: athlete (impossible endurance, perfect fingers), intellectual (four ontological approaches named for him), and doting lover, amazingly of his beautiful wives alone. Also he had written about guns, and could outshoot Coots, who was almost twenty years younger.

After retirement, Latouche became a student of man, fresh as a ten-year-old. It was the one thing he'd neglected, mankind. He was making fast time, of course, as usual. His Hungarian sheepdog, his curly pal, was allowed everywhere, even restaurants. Latouche was that kind of darling. Folks loved to have him around and hear his voice, kind and modest, and he could have lived free on what people bought for and gave him. He lived in an apartment on Wall Street very near the waterfront, where men loaded and unloaded international goods. Because he was such a distinguished widower, emblem of a nobler time, the owners of the building allowed him to stay on the top floor in a building where everything else was business. With more dedication than others with telescopes, he began watching the men on the docks, studying the poor, the bitter, the disheveled, the union apes, some with bursting muscles, some gone all punk and crooked with labor. He might have seen Coots down there, with his young amanuensis dickering for morphine, heroin, hashish, opium, or just espresso, Player's cigarettes, and Stolichnaya, with a man of trade. Dr. Latouche knew nothing much of drugs. He had never done much biochemistry. Fifty years ago he had quit cigarettes. His three cold martinis every evening, no matter where he was, were the only rise he required. He had been close to being an addict of surgery but why not? He did not like drugs, even when he prescribed them in small amounts. Dr. Latouche had never even had a real headache. In his medicine cabinet were Epsom salts, Pepto-Bismol, iodine, and, for visitors, aspirin.

Coots might have looked back up at Latouche's apartment window, maybe swallowing a Bucet with a fresh cup of espresso if nothing better was to be had. He, just lately, knew where Latouche lived. He was very much on his case, narrowing. Latouche might have mistaken the gaunt, tall Coots in his suit for an owner, a big legitimate importer. Outside his addiction, morphine now beaten, Coots insisted on having his things in order. The shooting of his wife had finally convinced him deeply against sloppiness. The worst of it was the mess. He led a tidy, controlled life. He despised what controlled him. His books railed against control, didn't they, despite the obliquity? Conspiracies of control were the target for his massed attacks, using stacked cords of bodies out front, behind, flanking. Up at seven for his stomach exercises; fruit, espresso, and pumpernickel toast; cold shower, then hot briefly, beating last night's cigarette residue from his lungs like Tarzan with a habit; speed-reading the London and New York *Times*es, especially for dire foreign and space alien occurrences, then more deliciously the personals; next perhaps a novel urged on him by some hopeful who'd pierced through his secretary, a matter of fifteen minutes (Coots had speed-read by sixth grade in St. Louis without realizing it was unnatural). His mind brilliantly plundered the book, storing entire sentences, shucking the rest like a piece of green corn, only a few nuggets in there. Coots cared very little for creative writing other than his own, and was blithely unconscious of any real American literary scene—a part of his charm to his adorers. He would write very slowly and often beautifully, clearheaded, trusting only hashish or a minor barbiturate, with his mild Benson & Hedges cigarettes. At times he would quit one or the other to exercise his control. Coots had lost a rough twenty years stoned, in Tangiers, New Orleans, New York and Mexico, filthy on a mattress, and he wanted to make them count.

Some had called him a genius since the fifties. Now he was a man of adequate means and invited everywhere for very little reason except the sight of him, alive and gray and imperturbable, a miracle of crotchety survival, beyond space and time. By late afternoon, through with his "studies"—diseases, drugs, hieroglyphics (he had no facility with languages and was deaf to music)—he'd be tired, and walk off the funk in the company of his secretary on interesting streets, wanting to "see a death" near him. His cane, really a sheath for a long stiletto, tapped along merrily. New York was getting too expensive, but he had always loved the hate and Byzantine corruption not only as metaphor but directly inhaling them so as to store them as power. He had been among natives and occult literatures and believed in magic as flatly as in chemistry. He had experienced rare days when he could do no wrong. He would sail an envelope, eyes blind, and it would smack right into the wastebasket. He would drop his razor and the thing would tumble perfectly to his toe, clipping a nail that needed it. On his tape recorder certain meaningful phrases would rise in volume for no technical reason, and they would be important to his life and work. He could fast for a week and be stronger. On the streets he was almost sure that if the enemy were persuasive enough, he could cause "a death" and pass by as an innocent bystander. The evidence of this had come clear years ago when an absurdly rude landlady had looked at him and fallen dead right on the stair landing outside his door, the hexed "gash." At night, eating with friends and admirers, some of them world-famous actors and musicians, he was polite and attentive. He would not lie, and he refused to be cajoled into being "strange" by some fresh fool who had misunderstood him entirely. Most of the world was perfectly obvious to him. He would not romanticize the "alien." In his own case, he'd never romanticized being a junkie. Contemporaries in drug and drink had dropped around him like flies—into morgue or loony bin—but a certain dim ingeniousness and regularity had dragged him through, so that his gray eminence punched out like a face on Mount Rushmore. For several thousands worldwide, Coots was one of the true fathers of the century. And greatly tested by calamity. His wife, then their son shooting up like Pop (amphetamines), but lasting only till thirty, liver all gone. Coots was not stone. He fell in love with forlorn helplessness, even now, and would cry like a woman when penetrated by some dreams. Dr. Latouche was in his dreams—not love, not envy, but what? Coots was driven, as not in decades.

When he found the billiards club, an establishment for the Arrived, he snorted. The Britishness. These atavistic beasts he'd had fun with in his violent satires, but even those books were old. He reckoned he looked MP enough to get in and was very pleased when the deskman, young, collegiate, recognized him and waved to the back rooms where all the fun was, offering him the place. It was dark green and woody, pungent with hearthsmoke, with jolly music from somewhere like England happening. Low voices drifted from separate parlors. Coots had no opinion of billiards at all, but the place made him a little homesick for St. Louis in the thirties: innocent American pool tables, the first taste of tobacco, the swoon. He was a boy then, just graduated from the neighborhood pond, with sunbrowned cheeks, a string of bullheads, and a cane pole with black cotton line. Learning to be idle and mock, forever. The heft of the cue stick always made it seem like a good thing to knock with. Even Harvard never dragged that feeling from him. The pool hall had a real wood fire you could spit in and watch.

The first players to his right were neither one Latouche. Coots could tell by their faces that they were dumbed by privilege and bucks, and he hissed straight at them, feeling the hidden stiletto in his cane. How a sweep of it across the throat would tumble them, gasping *Why? Why?* Queer angels would then move down on them with a coup de grace of quick sodomy. Coots's grandfather was a rich inventor and Coots had never been without a constant monthly sum, but the frigid regard of certain wealthy raised a fire from balls to crown in him. And where was Latouche? In another parlor, vainly ignoring active grofft by placing himself in public at billiards. Coots had only, with delight, *heard* of grofft in his Central American travels, where he'd made himself fit enough to penetrate the wilds in search of a storied hallucinogen. The drug was a retching bust, but the grofft tales were very interesting. Latouche must have *been* there to contract grofft. Coots had never heard of a white man with it.

A man near ninety could not have pushed into the deeps down there. Coots remembered the horrible misunderstandings with natives, the dangerous approach through a white-water creek, the malarial bottoms, where mosquitoes *were* the air. He had written solemnly about his explorations, but in the back of his mind he'd since wondered if he was thoroughly had by the tribesmen. Some foliage had moved, a barking human face emerged briefly, and the thing had run off lowly like a pointer, having smelled or seen that Coots was not the right thing. *Grofft!* shouted the natives, turninud. He didn't understand what was going on, but he was alarmed too, near killed by a fer-de-lance before he snapped out of it. In the University of Mexico medical library he had looked up the pathology. But the entry on grofft read as if it didn't belong, as if it had been written in dread by a haunted mystic of the seventeenth century. The cause: probably the bite of a grofftite—the breath or saliva. Etiology? Symptoms: lupine facial features and doglike barking and whining; quadruped posture; hebephrenia; extremely nervous devotion to a search, general agitation, constant disappointment; lethargy, then renewal. Treatment:

Nobody of any medical skill had ever run down a grofftite. History: The skeletons of grofftites had been seen (and avoided) in places near and far from settlements; no uniformity in demise except bones of the fingers, forehead, and sometimes neck were often (twelve cases reported) fractured, the teeth broken; head in three cases planted to jaw depth in dirt, as if thrown violently from a high elevation. And *this*: Grofftites have lived up to fifty years after being stricken. It was claimed infants were taken off by grofftites but these might be mere Indian tales or manipulative responses to the urban interlocutors. *N.B.*: Indians have demanded money to imitate a grofftite.

Coots, peering hard at old Latouche in the last parlor now, suspected it might be a powerful drug that induced grofftism. He was in the country of powerful brews, and he could not shake the idea that it was a vaguely religious, maybe even saintly condition, drunk deliberately down by the devout, enough *d*'s to go direct to disease, the divine. The sight of noble old Latouche, cuing the ball and doing something smooth with it, was making Coots silly.

Thinking back through the years, he had known very, very few people of pure virtue, if that was Latouche's case. In his suit Coots felt rude and small. Latouche—another endearing trait—wore wonderful clothes, but he was a bit sloppy and misfit in them. They loved his rumpled way, his scuffed shoes, the speck of sauce on his tie. What an agreeable granddad of a guy.

The doctor was playing a young man with a built-up physique. The young man wore a blazer. Ribbed socks—Coots noticed—with spangling black loafers. He acted familiar with old Latouche. Coots wondered if Latouche was the ward of this muscular stooge.

"Good evening, our genius," said Latouche, surprised. "You're a billiards man too?"

"Hardly. Just a watcher. Lifelong."

"Order you a drink?"

"Too early. Perhaps a tonic with lime."

"We're just talking about the rumors that God is a woman. What do the literary people say about that?"

"When wasn't it? It's a neurotic hag demanding worship while it lays a pox down. An obtuse monster, a self-worshiping fiend. I know gods, Doctor."

"Should have guessed you'd have an opinion. This is Riley Barnes, Coots. Barnes, the author. Barnes knows your work. I've been reading you. Some difficulty, I confess, for an old sawbones. I liked the surgeon using the plumber's friend in a heart operation. I'd suppose you've known some awfully bad doctors. So have I, but—"

"You have literary interest?" Coots asked Barnes. "I've seen you before, haven't I?"

"Yes sir," said Barnes, knowing Coots too. "I'm a stevedore. The docks."

"You know, I'd spotted Riley. Somehow I thought I must meet him. So I did. Very fortuitous circumstance. I watched him through a telescope. How could I have guessed he was a literary man and wild for billiards? The city always surprises you," explained Latouche.

Coots had written about men like Barnes, one of his physical type of boy. He had them falling through space, ejecting incandescent sperm while being hanged by the neck . . . Old duffer consuls would gobble it up. Sacrifice of the young to evil, entrenched needs. The way the world worked.

"You and your friend bought . . . commodities down there. I was in different clothes," said Barnes. "Didn't think you'd recognize me, sir. Anyway, it's an honor. I know people who'd pay to be here."

"Go on with your game, please," said Coots to the young man. Was he in his late twenties? Coots wondered. Straight. Off a mural of American Labor in an old union hall, dusty hoarse Commies around being ass-fucked by shark-skinned fat union bosses with stogies. Brando, *On the Waterfront*. What we pansies would have given to jump *his* bones. Stop. Latouche is the mission. The doctor did boom a little depressed, anxious, behind the jolly front. In the old days I'd have shucked him for drugs. Exactly the kind of croaker we'd set up till thoroughly burned down. Some of them were so stupidly moral they believed they were helping my endless kidney stones. Could be literary because I was so good at those riffs. Multiple personalities I developed. Then no personality at all when sick—protoplasm, whimpering, completely dishonored. Working the subways for drunks, at my best. New York, New York! Never again, knock on wood. Paper cup of coffee dissolving at the edge with spit. Ketchup on crackers, free at the Automat, for weeks. Harvard education. Unfit to attack Hitler or Tōjō, thank God.

"How's your dog, Doctor? It isn't here?"

"No." Latouche looked guilty, furtive. "Had to bury her. She got something, poor girl. They didn't know what."

Coots came alive, took a seat in a padded drugstore chair copied from the thirties.

"Was a Hungarian breed, something, wasn't it?"

"I wouldn't talk about the dog, Mr. Coots," interjected Barnes. Latouche *was* his charge, then.

"It's fine, Riley. Really." Latouche grasped the billiard table, his fingers going white over the felt edge.

"I'm a cat man, myself," said Coots. Could he now detect Latouche trembling, his eyes rolling back into his head? Delicious, better than his first horror movies with Lon and Bela in St. Louis.

"Can't stand them!" yelled Latouche. He shot back—reloaded, rather, thought Coots. "Sneaky, conniving! . . . the *odor* of cat piss! Doesn't that tell you something?" Agitated, pushing the insane, this beat the medical libraries cold. ("A death"?) But I don't have the full persuasion for a spell, really, Coots decided. What do I hate about the man? My own grandfather? Grand patricide? Biting the hand that.

"I'll have to ask you, Mr. Coots." Barnes again. My word, so rapidly the nurse, all the jargon.

"No. I want this resolved and confessed!" shouted Latouche. "Secrets are killing me!"

The cue stick, released, fell over, *plump*, on the rug. Both his hands were on the table now.

"I buried Nana, I had Nana buried with my wives, between them, in Forest Hills cemetery! Riley did it for me!"

"That isn't so bad, Latouche. Isn't there a law, though? The Indians, you know . . . the Egyptians . . ."

"We didn't ask. I did it at night," said Riley Barnes.

"He's got grofft, doesn't he?"

"How'd you know?" Barnes bolstered Latouche. "Oh yes. Your travels. Would you know how it's treated? Dr. Latouche, bless him, believes he can just ignore it away."

Latouche was slavering and attempting to drop to the floor, while Barnes was resisting, gently, though all his big muscles were needed. The doctor certainly had his right man. Barnes seemed to care deeply for him. Coots smiled less than he wanted to, hands crossed on his stiletto cane in front, the boulevardier.

"I don't think this is a mind-over-matter case, Barnes"— Latouche actually whimpered like a dog now—"though by what I've observed, the doctor has *civilized* the disease. Perhaps strength of character. Or just being un-Indian, highly Western. I recall the small-pox didn't kill that many of us, but wiped out whole tribes of the Sioux. We've antibodies, but—"

Barnes sadly let the doctor go and raced to the door, pulling it to and locking. The doctor went around the table on all fours, sniffing and pointing, heedless of them. Why was this, Coots asked himself, so charming to him?

Why did Latouche pique such high disgust? Was he an old lifetime closet fairy and Coots knew it? Many great professionals were, no great mystery. Then was it the hypocrisy Coots loathed? The laurels and friendships gained by an, at least, eighty-year false front? But he did not really think Latouche was gay. Some deeply sick, hidden gays were fascinated by weapons, especially on the right wing, the loud NRA and all that, but not Latouche, who loved the technology more than the blast. Latouche acquainted himself with past heroes in dangerous times, as did Coots, who owned in his locker one of Billy the Kid's purported old irons. But Latouche liked to balance the loads, better.

Latouche was all around the room now, scraping at the door and whimpering urgently. Something was out there he had to hunt. Coots thought of a feverish liver-spotted thing whirling in its cage, wanting the quail fields. He had witnessed that once in Texas when he was a failed marijuana farmer. The face of the doctor was working classically, too. His cheeks closed forward, lupine, more than could be done by a well man. Then came the barks and worried low growls, the mutter of need, almost ecstatic.

"How did he get into the Honduran wilds?" asked Coots.

"He didn't. I went for him. The Indians were known for pro-digious strength. Please don't let on, Mr. Coots. You're a man of the world, the cosmos. It shouldn't shock you. I'd found a healthy young Indian, I thought. He'd had a fatal accident. I took his blood and brought it back chilled. We transfused Dr. Latouche."

"Extraordinary. Why?"

"It had worked for one of his old colleagues. The man's ninety-five now, in glowing health. Down there, the laws . . . deep back in there, there *are* no laws. You can *buy* somebody. Never mind, I had the boat connections and the way, so I did it for him. There aren't many Latouches in the world. Like there aren't many of you. He'd been low, depressed, feeble, didn't believe in drugs. This is corny, but he's the grandfather I never had, and the father who left me. I didn't want to lose him right after I'd found him."

"Commendable. So this is the 'secret'?"

"Yes."

"But, my God, boy, he's a horror. How can you have him out here in public playing at billiards?"

"He goes a long time without spells. He's set off by mental . . . imagery, I think. Especially dogs. Or their enemies. Cats, awful. And sometimes blacks, unfortunately, although Dr. Latouche doesn't have a racist bone in his body."

"He's going to quit this after a while, then?"

"If things go right. But the spells are getting longer. We've got to keep him locked in here. I'm sorry."

"Not at all. I've no other business. So he gave you money, he paid you . . ."

"Mr. Coots, you'd imagine, but Dr. Latouche doesn't even have that much money. He's given it all away. He should have a better apartment, servants, but he's got none of it. Thousands are *alive* because of Dr. Latouche."

"And he looks a young seventy."

"Doesn't he? I think it's all love and happy work, Mr. Coots."

"*William*. You think so? And nobody knows any more than I do about the disease?"

"Looked everywhere. Only one doc in New York had ever *heard* of it. It's never been treated in South America. We can only be grateful his is milder, so far. If you believe this, Dr. Latouche wants to begin a fund to go in and cure those few pitiful Indians. Not for himself, not in his lifetime."

"Yet an Indian . . . died. For him."

"That's the worst way to put it. And it was my choice."

Coots lit a Player's. He needed a strong hit. Fifty years of cigarettes now, with no drastic trouble. He was enjoying the smoke no less than the first good inhale in St. Louis. In that pool hall, he remembered now, a strange old man from nowhere had put his hand on his shoulder and said to him, "My lad, you will write masterpieces." One of those magic episodes that had punctuated his life. Now Latouche was grievously scuttling and digging at the floor with his long elegant surgeon's fingers.

"I don't know why you're here, sir. But you are the thing, I hope. Obviously you know medicine and magic. I've read all your books. What can we do?"

"The Indians did nothing. I believe they revered and, I know, feared the grofftites."

"Your guess would be better than any doctor's, I'd bet."

"I could try something." Coots was into the grim clinical zone he often elected for himself. It was obvious he could have been a fine MD, given any ambition to heal. The other, too. He grabbed at the pertinent file in his head. The delight of the fit was wearing out. He had lost his spite somewhere.

"You might try slapping him a hard one. Be a bigger dog. Canines respond to bald aggression. They're pack animals."

"I doubt I could—"

"Do it. Don't hold back. Otherwise, you could drench yourself with bitch urine. But he might just hump you and bite your back."

Barnes did reach down, turning the doctor's cheeks up, and slap him powerfully, then shut his eyes in pity.

It worked.

Soon enough, Latouche was biped, straightening his tweedy suit back to its original loose rumple, pulling down his vest and replacing his watch chain across the front in the old style. His medical fraternity pin hung there, a small vanity. He was national president in the fifties, the decade of Coots's first grand fame and obscenity trial.

The French, who like their authors sick, fell on his book in droves. Coots stayed shyly and happily away, grogged in morpheus. It had taken him years and the help of friends, but the thing was out and he was going to make some money. Manslaughterer, junkie, thief, queer, layabout—the outer and under had won through. He was regent guru of the beatniks, like it or not.

"Little phase there. I seem to have left you. My cheek smarts. Did I fall?" Latouche wanted to know.

"A little," said Riley Barnes quickly.

"Old men get tired. Don't they, Coots? Are you sometimes just *tired?*"

"Yes indeed."

"I think it's martini time. Can almost taste it already, terribly cold, with big white onions. Would you, Riley? What's your pleasure, Coots?"

"The same. Sounds perfect."

"All right, then. Don't want to try the stick?"

"No. Let's sit in the booth and talk, guns maybe. Hard decisions about the forty-four/forty-five."

Coots noticed Latouche did not have that detestable turkeyness under the throat that the old often do. Even in his thinness Coots had one gaining on him. A thing that the aging imp Capote attempted to cure by fellatio, he'd heard. They sat.

"Good. I have one. An eighteenth-century heavy handgun. Short piece, cap and ball, of course. Never shot."

"Bring it on down to the range next Tuesday. We'll rig it."

The martinis came, with Barnes, who had a light beer, imported. A health man. How long was his dick? The drinks were sublime, just the ticket. Coots opened up even more. He was narrowing on the question of his own spite.

"I have the Billy the Kid gun," he said.

"You don't. There is no Billy the Kid gun."

"But there is. I'll show it to you. You must come down to my fort. Say Tuesday instead of the range."

Barnes spoke up, delighted. "He's known for not inviting many, Dr. Latouche. You should feel honored. This could be a legendary evening for us."

Coots looked at the boy, who had become too chummy.

"How about just an old-timers' chat, the two of us?" said Coots. "This is no rebuke, Barnes."

"Sorry. Not at all. I go to the gym, anyway, when he goes shooting. I could be nearby, however."

"Then it's fixed. I'm feeling better all the time," said Latouche. "Let me ask you something. Why did Billy the Kid kill so many?"

"¿Quien es?" chuckled Coots. These were the Kid's last words before being gunned down by Pat Garrett. "I'm not sure. It was a sort of war, the Lincoln County thing. It wasn't twenty-one, not nearly that. But I'd imagine it got in his blood, very early, when he was attacked by a bully with a knife. Rather like a drug addiction. I've studied killers. Now let me ask you: When you shoot, who are you shooting, mentally? What kind of enemies does a man like you have?"

The old doctor was surprised. "Well . . . quite zero. It's *all* mental, a sport."

"Come now. You're too good at it. Some emotion belongs, surely."

"I've no enemies I know of."

"Life has treated you nicely. No malpractice suit, say, totally unjust. The lawyers. You've known *women*. Some yapping gash that bilked you. Tell me too, that somewhere in the world of money there wasn't . . . And you were in the war, no?"

Coots hardly ever beseeched this much. Even when directly interviewed, for money, he'd not shown this zeal.

"Downrange there you must see some Nazi, some Commie, hippie, queer, black mugger, proponent of socialized medicine, or, really, man a—" Coots almost said Jew, as a joke. He looked at Riley Barnes, intense and worshipful, vastly enjoying, and lucky. "Mengele, a Stalin, a Klansman."

"Not at all. I'm afraid you're making me sound like a man of no passion. What do *you* shoot, Coots?"

"Everything. Old age."

This created high giggles in the other two. Poor men, was he that interesting to them? A scholar, a dreamer, and rather a drudge is what Coots thought he was. He yearned for the character of William Bonney.

"I suppose people who don't hate don't write," said the doctor. "With surgery, I was rarely conscious of a person. Another thing entirely. Never have I felt the necessity, either, to interpret the universe. It was mainly just one piece of work, then another."

"Then who would you rather have been, Latouche? Please think."

"Umm. Well, actually . . . Methuselah. I'm not ready to go. I've known hardly a day I've not truly enjoyed. Even the war, I was always up bright and early. Even, do not mistake me, the morning of my wives' funerals. You've made me honest. Is that your function?"

"But, my man, you have . . ." Coots reflected and checked on Riley Barnes, who was writing something down on a billfold tablet. "You have *grofft*. The only man in North America."

Barnes flashed up, eyes sorrowful. He might want to strike Coots. When he masturbated, looking in the mirror, did he insert his finger in his anus to intensify it? Could he entice women into rim jobs? Many muscle men—*vide* your obsessive weightlifters in the big house—were "anally retentive," thanks, Sigmund. And sex was a way of keeping, owning lovers, having them to play with in the bank vault later. As opposed to the looser lostness of the mere pussy, which invited death and servility. Barnes's big stevedore's hand was on Latouche's wrist.

"Yes, I have it. But luckily, it seems, just a mild touch. I've not been on all fours yet. No barking. Riley watches me honestly."

As with a thirty-year quart-a-day man he'd once met at the Maple Leaf Bar in New Orleans: "I have no drinking problem, Coots." Skin flaking off from the burst veiny patches of his face, yellow as a crayon, and his tongue black.

"Then Tuesday night at seven, Latouche."

"Delighted. I'll have Riley bring me around in my vintage Hudson. Now there's an item you might like. Spotless. Forest green. Purrs like a"—Barnes harder on his wrist—"sewing machine."

"The Hudson and Billy the Kid's gun," said Barnes in wonder. "A great American evening."

A couple days later Coots flew to Kansas with his amanuensis, Horton. They planned to live there soon, and had already bought a small clapboard house with a picket fence and a porch in the university town. Coots hoped he might teach a class there, though there was some lack of enthusiasm from the older faculty, to whom he was a profane dope fiend and pederast who wrote gibberish. His secretary friend was attempting to broker him into a place. Coots could use the money. It was a sorry scandal that they would exclude him. In several apparent ways he was a conservative. He loved the plains of the Midwest and was fascinated by the Old West and its worthy guns. He knew Native American culture (Custer's stuffed horse, Comanche, was in the university museum); had the notes for two large books wherein he would explore the West in space-time narratives and by way of his "cut-up" method—not montage, he insisted, but more: common threads of magic in random clippings from various sources, sometimes announced into his tape recorder and retranscribed. He'd not yet got all from cannabis that he intended, either. Coots was a hard worker, putting to shame the energies of the senior faculty, with their emeritus rose beds and sailing vacations.

It was hard for Horton not to get angry about the matter, though Coots accepted the landscape and *l'état* gladly as they were away from wearying, impolite and expensive New York. The main point was he was old, damn it, and had been everywhere. He'd never had a thing against roots and a calm place, there was no crime in that. And there would be wide and free places to shoot. He could have a cat or two, his favorite creatures. He was so much like them it was nearly like having children. "The furred serpent," Egyptians called them.

He did not tell Horton about Latouche.

Lawrence, Kansas, occupied them. Coots breathed in his "square" neighborhood: perfect, superb. The air might give him a few more years, a few more books. The scratchy, potent West. The "Johnsons"—trustworthy, minding their own business, nonjudgmental, quick to ally with a fellow in trouble, salt of the earth, loving of land, their house was yours, etc.—Coots had the forgotten shock of being waved at by citizens who didn't know him from Adam. Howdy. Partners in the given day. Suitably, it came a "gusher" while they were there. The rain smelled sweet, rich. Thinking of the golden wheat lapping it up, breadbasket of the world, amber fields of, sun-browned boy with a string of bullheads, home-dried cut cane pole with black cotton line, drilled piece of corncob for a bobber, Prince Albert tin with nightcrawlers in wet leaves for bait.

Horton liked seeing the old fellow this happy.

They were out in Latouche-land too. Latouche was originally from Ellsworth.

It was the land of generals—Eisenhower, Bradley. And Frank James rode through Lawrence itself with the guerrilla slaughterers and Quantrill. Then Coots and T. S. Eliot over in St. Louis, not far from Twain. Ah, dreamed Coots on his porch, his thin hair blowing, to have fucked Huck when the country was young, about to strangle itself in the Big One, sun-swollen teenage corpses in the cornfield. Sherman sodomizes the South. John Brown began here first, Kansas, bloody Kansas, my Kansas. What did Latouche think of it? Had Latouche ever thought much at all?

The doctor was at his door and they walked out to see the Hudson purring at the curb. Barnes, in gym suit, was at the wheel saluting him. The Hudson was a gem all right. A space fiction of 1950, drop-shaped, chubby, svelte too. Barnes yelled something about being careful, he'd see Latouche at midnight. Coots noticed his massive legs. That boy could really hurt you if he wanted. Without him, the car gone, Latouche seemed smaller, with snowier hair, cautious and unbalanced. Coots helped him down the stairs to "the bunker," leaning on the sharp door—like a vault door. Coots gasped, weak himself. Safe inside, Latouche took the sofa and looked about, out of his overcoat. They were alone. Horton was away for the night.

"I've brought this mini–tape recorder, if you don't mind. It's for Riley's sake," said Latouche.

Coots minded. His words were worth a great deal lately. The BBC thing, and NPR. He was to play a junkie priest in a movie soon too. Might as well ham it up toward the end.

Something had clicked one strange tired morning a month ago—he'd been very, very tired, from no direct cause. Coots was going to die soon, the fatigue told him quietly. Some ancient soft voice like that of the unknown man in the pool hall, but this was not an "episode." This was the dead and dry tone of the inevitable. He didn't know when he'd die, but something announced the beginning of the last lap. The public flies were on him, even worse.

"I thought you'd bring your forty-four/forty-five," he said coolly. Coots could wither, with his scratchy voice and small eyes.

"But I did, in the other pocket." Latouche drew the handsome brute out, size of a good man's organ, laying it on the coffee table next to the minirecorder, a Toshiba. He punched it on. Coots's anger left when he spied the weapon. Lovely little highwayman's surprise, lovely.

"I've loaded the thing. Can't quite figure why," said Latouche.

"The mean streets. It's a bad area."

"No." Latouche stared at Coots as if lost. He seemed really to have no idea why the thing was loaded. Septagonal barrel?

"Barnes knows you have a loaded gun?"

"No. He's a deep pacifist, for gun control. New York law, of course."

"I think he killed an Indian for you." Coots smiled at the little reels turning inside the machine.

"He told you?"

"I gather things. Pretty nasty, and unethical, medically speaking, you know."

"Oh, I do. It's all a bad mysterious thing. And my fault. I found out that Riley has a dangerous loyalty to me. Almost an innocence. If only I could take it back. I'm very shallow with people, I'm afraid."

"But I suppose you've been paid back. The blood of a very wrong Indian. Hmm?"

"Yes. And that wasn't my first transfusion. I've had two others —one for each of my marriages—each done legally. Good Swiss blood, very."

"What do you mean, *for?*"

"For Maggie and Verna both. I was slowing down and I did it for us. To keep up, to prance, to dance. They were both a good deal younger and I couldn't give them an old coot dead on his lounge chair at the end of the day."

"And they worked?"

"My word, yes! You couldn't keep me down. It was amazing, scary, truly. I romanced them, read in erotic books" (Latouche blushed), "rowed down the river with them in the bow. I pleased them constantly, not just with flowers and gifts. In fact—"

"Just a second. I'll have the martinis out. Save this."

Coots prepared the martinis with more care than usual, dropping in Latouche's big white onions, specially bought that afternoon. He waited longer, too, to diffuse the agitation the nonagenarian had got himself into. Coots—Saul on the road to Tarsus—suddenly had an overwhelming light on him; nothing like this had happened to him before. He *liked* Latouche, thoroughly. True friendship was attacking him. He was very afraid the fellow would get too wound up and stumble into the names, the "imagery," and say *cat* or *dog—wolf? snake? Negro? quail?* He was close to saying everything, and in danger. He waited almost impolitely long. When he went out with the tray he stared at the gun. Let's get that thing away, Coots decided. Which is what he did, turning it in his other hand admiringly, his martini hand freezing.

"Fine heft. A real buried treasure. The recoil must be a consideration. Jim 'Awkins and Long John Silver, eh?"

"What?"

"*Treasure Island.* Stevenson. What did you *do* as a boy in Kansas?"

"Oh, sure now. Even I read that one once, I think."

"I dreamed of almost nothing but pirates, myself."

"I dreamed of, can you believe it, Kansas itself. Simply repictured what was around me. The wheatfields, the blizzards, the combines, the awful summer sun. For dreams in my sleep, I never had any. I never dream."

"You've got to be kidding. A man would die, flat out."

"But it's true. Freud would've had no use for me."

"Well, surgery did. But what a fact."

"The transfusions, though—" began Latouche.

"My friend, this is startling too. Yours worked. Mine didn't. I tried to kick morphine with one. No go."

Latouche couldn't know that he had Coots entirely. Coots had a young healthy crush on him, wanting nothing.

"I'm very sorry." Latouche drank deep. Coots was saddened by the unusual sloppiness, gin down the doctor's chin, untended. "But my transfusions, let me tell you, I think, I know—poor Maggie, poor Verna—I was *too* much. How they loved me! What a heavenly benefit, their love. I could not leave them alone, Coots. Finally, I— now I say, the bed, the bed, the bed, the bed. The dances, the bicycling, the jogging, the too long mountain hikes in rain—they loved it for *me*. Then always the bed, the couch, the shower, even the garage, every which way, all hours! Then I'd be up with their breakfast, waking them. I'd have written up an oncological technique while they slept! Too much, too much! They died."

"What?"

Latouche's pathetic unlined face was sopped with gin, dropping down like a beard of tears and slobber.

Coots dragged his handkerchief out and kneeled to attend Latouche, dabbing away, kinder than a nurse.

"My friend, my friend," he sympathized in his great scratch, softened.

"It's true. I killed them. They were just worn out, is all. Still lovely, both, still should have been in the fine bloom of a woman's middle age, that arousing . . ."

"But one would suppose that one often destroys the loved one. *I* have destroyed. Have been destroyed," Coots said, trying to aid.

"I don't mean your . . . fictions, your creative writing! I mean *destroyed!*"

"Yes, but guilt, must . . ."

"I don't know what brought me to shout it out. I don't know why that pistol is loaded. Something made . . . *You*. It's you, Coots. You demand terrible buried things, somehow. Calamities. Isn't that it?"

"That's not a condition of our friendship.

Latouche calmed down and smiled. "We *are* friends, aren't we? All our strangenesses and our differences. We are, yes?"

"Doubtless, friends. And for that I'll get a fresh one for you. Take it easy. All is locked, here in the bunker."

Latouche saw the big secured door and nodded, instantly more solid himself.

This drink Coots did thoroughly, a spring in his step, close again to that sun-browned boy with his string of bullheads, his Prince Albert tin filled with nightcrawlers.

When he came out, Latouche was gone and the door was thrown open. There had been a noise in his writing room, and now only Latouche's things were left, his tape recorder, gun, and overcoat across the arm of the sofa. The front door was unlocked; it must have been thrown open very rapidly, speed quieting the noise.

Coots shut his eyes and knew. He'd forgotten, forgotten, forgotten, entirely the dog hides on the wall of his writing room: the Rottweiler's black one, and the German shepherds' speckled gray. Latouche must have stepped inside, looked, then fled, feeling hunted himself. On the spoor.

Horton's Honda Express, the little city motorbike, was next to the front entranceway, helmet on the seat. Coots knew he should take this. He'd handled it perfectly many times. It would be required, he was positive.

He labored with the big two-by-twelve board on the stairs that served Horton as a ramp. His own long smart overcoat on, helmeted—Horton's humor insisted on a dove aviary painted all over the helmet—and buckled in, he cranked the scooter and rushed precariously upward through exhaust clouds to the sidewalk, then out bumping off the curb, an old man from hell. Wouldn't you know, his pesty neighbor, the junkie dentist Newcomb, antithesis of Latouche, hooked possibly on everything and ever determined to visit, was right in his way, and was knocked down by Coots and the whirling machine. Coots cursed with his last cigarette breath, despising this low absurdity. He thought he saw Latouche three blocks up as the street was otherwise empty. Something was scrambling ahead on all fours, head down, trailed by its suspenders, white shirttails out.

It was Latouche. Coots ran over his jacket in the street. Then there was a boot, an old Wellington boot, straight up, abandoned. Poor man! Coots could hardly breathe—the pity, the terror, the love, and the effort with that board. His adrenaline, if it was there, was wondering where to go. He could hardly get air down. Latouche was faster, or through asthmatic illusion Coots thought he was, and he turned back the accelerator all the way. The doctor was running up into the middle of the city. Soon he'd be lost in neon and street strollers, sloths, pimps, bus-stop criminals, sluts. Coots could see citizens spotting the sidewalks, increasingly, a quarter mile up.

At last his respiration and vision were easier. How fast could a dog run? He looked at the speedometer: thirty mph, and he still wasn't gaining on him. What kind of dog was Latouche? Something Central American and predacious. Please not a greyhound, pushing forty! The motorbike could hit that speed too, but barely. How, then, could he catch Latouche?

He didn't know it but he passed Riley Barnes, early out of the gym, coming toward him in the Hudson. Barnes flinched and soon U-turned. Coots's frail head in the bird helmet was unmistakable. By the time he came even, Coots was narrowing his eyes, an elderly cavalry scout in spectacles. Latouche had run into the crowd. He was gone. There was only reckoning with his speed now and trying to stay up even. If Latouche took a turn, it was hopeless. The motorbike wobbled into higher speed, but the traffic would have him soon. Coots felt pure hate for humankind, especially New Yorkers, too cowardly to stay in their rooms; they must be out with their autos, part of the clot, rubbernecking at each other—like dogs. Dogs! Packs of them sniffing, licking balls, consorting in dumb zeal, not a clue, not an inward reflection. The mayor and the police should be shot, for not shooting them. And then this streetlight. He was in a paroxysm of fury.

"Where in the hell are you going, Mr. Coots?" Riley Barnes was next to him at the junction, yelling to him from the high car. "Stop, please."

Coots did.

"He went into the grofft. I swear, Barnes, a horrible inadvertency at my place. He saw some 'imagery' on my wall in another room. He's up there, blocks, incredibly fast."

"Get in the car, quick. He can't be out here!" Barnes was in tears already.

"The car's no good. If he turns, you've no chance. This Honda's the thing. Let me go."

"I'm going too. He's mine."

"Fool. Then get on the back if you can."

"You can handle this?" Great poundage in the rear with Barnes. They sank down.

"I can handle it. Shut up and look."

They were off, riding as if on a wire, given Barnes's body. Every yard was risky and grim. The motorbike wanted to waddle off into the gutter or straight out into the oncoming lanes. Coots's arms were noodles from the effort.

"Don't move! Just look, damn you!" His voice whipped back around the helmeted cheeks.

He looked too, tried to. Hunter of the hunter, pointer of the pointer. It had been ages since he'd labored physically at anything, but Nature had not slighted him in adrenaline. He was handling the cargo nicely after another half mile. But Nature—in Latouche's case, God?—had not slighted the doctor either. Age ninety, ninety! His fitness was uncanny. Coots thought he saw a clot of citizens part, shouting, at something on the ground another three blocks up. Maybe they were gaining a little. Latouche could not be given much more by his heart and lungs. His bootless feet must be awful by now. If only some decent man would just stop him. But where was a decent citizen of New York to be found? It would take a tourist, some Johnson from Kansas.

"Help! Help him!" shouted Barnes, sensing the same.

All Latouche did was gather disgusted glares from both sidewalks.

The thing they feared worst occurred. Plainly, just two blocks up now, a corner crowd parted, faces snapped down, then to the left, some of them pointing down a side street. Latouche had turned. If he began weaving the streets, he was doomed unless he fainted. Coots's grand new friend would be snatched from him by the most horrible chance and he would be forever had by another "black thing" as vile as his wife's death. This plague of one, this Kansan prince of North America, was nearing his end and Coots did not even feel potent enough to be his nurse.

Latouche may have been the only man of pure virtue Coots had ever known. You could not really fornicate somebody to death. That was all just Latouche's elevated code, wasn't it? An anachronism. Guilty for his own vigor, guilty for his own superb gifts. Could be slight atherosclerosis closing on the old gent, who'd buried awesomely too many contemporaries. Left lonely in his luck.

He must have turned yet again. These streets were near empty, and they saw nothing. It would be merely a matter, Coots feared, of patrolling for his corpse, if they were even that fortunate. They'd have to go to the police and do the official. In the precincts they might know Latouche and get on it with more effort.

The motorbike putted—bleakly—as Coots halted it. The weight of Barnes, at rest, nearly threw them over into the road. But he stood them up with his mighty legs spread. He had not expected to stop.

"Go on! Go on!" cried Barnes in a futile voice as Coots removed the helmet. His hair stood out in wisps. The city had never seemed so unnecessary and odious to him. You could forget there was an old-time Greenwich Village, once worth inhabiting, breathing. And a zoo, the museums, Columbia, the fruitful subway where he'd rolled drunks for dope money. You could "raincoat" a stiff, tying the thing over his head with the sleeves, and have the money without violence; it was quite safe, even for the skinny Coots.

He must meditate the point here, a new one. Where did grofftites want to go? Where would they rest? Where *was* the quarry? There had to be something, he figured. While Barnes was calling the police, Coots tried to voodoo it out, but there was no file in his head about this he could turn to. Bad luck. "Spot of bother"—a refrain of the nasty British colonial—rang silly back and forth in his mind. He had no further sources. Barnes was probably worthless, in his grandsonly adoration. Knock down the maze, what could be the rat's desire? Somebody should have injected rats with grofft gland, offered a number of rat gratifications at the end.

The two of them, Coots and the almost whimpering Barnes—as if taking on symptoms in sympathy—stood foolishly beside the Honda peeping around, statues of the bereaved. Coots had had it with impotence, too old and losing too much by it in the past.

"He was talking about his wives, how he'd murdered them, worn them out with love. He sounded hyper, self-flagellating, caused by a quick suck of gin, maybe."

Barnes stood taller and clamped on Coots's wrist, too hard. You fucking monster. Then Barnes kneeled in street clothes with white bucks on his feet, drew a pen from his coat, and began drawing some route on his right shoe.

"What are you doing?"

"He's talked about his wives before. He could barely stand going to the cemetery with flowers for them. And their birthdays ruined him for days. He was chin-up, but I could tell."

"What cemetery?"

"Forest Hills, and the dog is there too. I know how to get in at night."

"That's ages from here. He couldn't make it."

"He could try. It's all we have. I've got a crow's flight route here on my shoe. We've got to go. Look along the way for him."

Damn the horror between here and there, thought Coots. It's the only mission.

The men wobbled along for a while seeing nothing, then hit an expressway where motorbikes were disallowed and Coots put the engine up red-line, clawing for near forty-five, deathly slow against the eighteen-wheelers. They looked along the highway for the doctor's flattened corpse. He could bake flat like a dog before New York got irritated by the smell. Thank the stars, they were soon off it, buffeted by winds of every rolling thing back there.

The landscape became tree-lined, with residential hedges on both sides where dogs could conceivably sleep in the street for a while, as in Kansas. Coots thought of every possible hazard to Latouche on a run even near here. They were too monstrous to confront. He aimed the scooter numbly, dread age tuckering him again in this long helpless mourning. He wondered if Barnes could feel the cap and ball .44/.45 in his overcoat pocket. He'd forgotten it himself and could not recall why he'd pocketed it. Then it came to him—it was exactly the caliber he'd used to nail the dogs, the favored size of the Old West and until lately the modern army. So what? Except that plugging the dogs was the last large physical thing he had done.

There was a narrow screened gate in a northern wall before a gravel path. Barnes simply destroyed the gate before moving instantly a long ways ahead. Happy to be off the Honda, Coots crept like a rag on wasp's legs. It would be best to let Barnes see that there was nothing at the graves, then return to him. On the other hand, deeper into the burial grounds—vast—he noticed cross paths and cul-de-sacs. He might get lost out here, celebrating this fool's errand by his own tragedy. This place at night was a sullen metropolis, its high monuments like a blind skyscape. The roll of it had its own charm, but not now.

He called ahead to Barnes. There was no answer. Coots was at the bottom of a very dark, long hill. He should stop, but he couldn't.

"Not yet, friends. Three or four more books I've got in me, I think," he announced to the brothering tombstones around him. No limit to the elevated vanity of some of them. Who the hell did they think they were, these fat-cat dead? No doubt with hordes of progeny scumming the Northeast. Old tennisers and polo players who should have died at birth, but giving the granite finger to the lowly and the modest who neighbored them. No worse fate than to fall and just be *discovered* out here.

Something let go a howl, canine and terrifying. It was too high for Barnes or Latouche. Too beyond, too nauseating. He stumbled down the hill toward it, however, loving the pistol when he felt it again. Ghoul, I am ready. Eat me, try. Then he heard what was plainly Barnes, near a big tree by the moon, weeping. Oh no. Oh what.

Apparently Barnes had done the howling. He sat at a plot of three stones.

Latouche had got deeply into one of the graves. His head was in it and both arms. He lay there—bloody, barefoot and dead. The name on the stone of the scratched grave was VERNA LOUISE LATOUCHE.

Coots kneeled, arm on the shoulder of the muddy Barnes, who was beating the ground with his hands, sobbing. He turned his face, changed into one hole of grief.

"Imposs—he was already coldish," said Riley Barnes.

"I think, lad, you'll find he's broken his fingers and his jaws. Poor Latouche."

"He was the finest man I've ever known."

"What was his given name?"

"Harold. Harry. I'm just a termite." Barnes was able to quit weeping, slowly. "What are you doing with that gun?"

"I . . . suppose I was going to try and woo him out of it with a piece of familiarity. It's his. He was an uncommon pistoleer."

"That was nice, Coots."

Barnes stood, filthy at the knees and palms. Then he kneeled again and pulled Latouche out of the hole; he was at the depth you'd see when an infantryman was caught out by bombs. Coots looked up at the rushing beardy clouds. He preferred not to see Latouche's face. That would be profane. Barnes, brushing the dirt from the doctor's face, seemed to agree. He would not look at him full-on. They also agreed that officials should be told—the ambulance, hurling lights, Coots could already imagine. This was enough.

There was, of course, the unspoken idea between them that Latouche should not be found like this. The gossip, the ugliness, the possibility of blemish on his life. Neither said anything for a good while until Coots, finally, spoke up.

"Really it's a better death than most. He didn't have to wait for it. More valiant, don't you think? We've got one problem. They won't believe it."

"It doesn't matter. All of him was unbelievable, when you study it."

"You go call. Can you do the Honda?"

"No problem."

"I'd like to stay and watch. A few more minutes with him."

"You're a good man, Mr. Coots. I really never knew that, by your stuff."

"I have my vagrant loyalties."

As he waited, seating himself finally in an ecstasy of relief—so tired, so worse than weary, his right hand in an agony from twisting on the motorbike—he found a Player's cigarette in his coat and lit it. Nature did nothing more, but the city became louder. Horns, screeches, a ball game, airplanes—it was all obscene.

"Oh yes I saw 'a death,' Harry. So Harry—" He stopped.

Coots's eyes became misted and blind. This was all right, this was fitting.

"But what a gap, Harry. What an awful gap you leave. And I only a watcher."

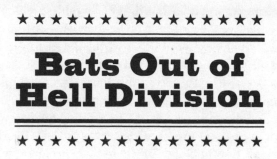

Bats Out of
Hell Division

W<small>E</small>, <small>IN A RAGGED BOLD LINE ACROSS THEIR EYES</small>, <small>COME ON</small>. S<small>HREDS</small> of the flag leap back from the pole held by Billy, then Ira. We, you'd suspect, my posteritites, are not getting on too well. They have shot hell out of us. More properly we are merely the Bats by now. Our cause is leaking, the fragments of it left around those great burned holes, as if their general put his cigar into the document a few times. Thank you mercilessly, Great Perfecter. But we're still out there. We gain by inches, then lose by yards. But back by inches over the night, huff, flap, narg. I am on a first-name basis with five who have had their very trigger fingers blown away—*c'est rien*, mere *bagatelle*. They mutter, these Cajuns. Something about us their cannon doesn't like, to put it mildly. By now you must know that half our guns are no good, either.

Estes—as I spy around—gets on without buttocks, just hewn off one sorry cowardly night. Morton lacks hair, too close to the cannon before he decided on retreat. I have become the scribe—not voluntarily, but because all limbs are gone except my writing arm. Benedict, Ruth and the Captain say I am not unsightly, in my tent with the one armhole out of it, not counting the one for my head. I'm a draped man of some charm, says our benign crone of a nurse,

171

Emmaline. Nobody comes forward to our rear like loyal Emmaline, the only woman to see this much this close. She comes up to the foul hospital, carrying a depth of pity. How, we wonder, does she carry on? "I've seen everything, boys! These milky old eyes have seen it all!" The only real atheist around, she carries love and helplessness forward in a bucket in either hand. We wonder, surely, whether this is the last woman we'll ever see. Maybe they use her to make us fight for home, but which way would that work? Better to think she's part of no plan at all. The best things in life, or whatever you call *this*, happen like that, even I in my old youth have learned. This marks the very thing, most momentous, I am writing about. It's over for me but I can't leave. No. I'd rather just stick here at my niggled work, undismayed by an occasional overshot bomb. I just lean over, disgusted, and think there's not much left of me to hit. Shrapnel blows through my tent-dress every now and then.

The best thing is that on retreat our boys run the rats and shocked wrens and baby rabbits back to me. Out of my tent shoots my arm. Yummy. The creatures had figured me for a goner. The smoke from the enemy's prime ribs, T-bones and basted turkeys floats over here at night sometimes, cruelly, damn the wind. In my long glass I can hardly find a human figure over there among the thick and bristling cannon, and when I do find a face, the smirk on it is killing. That is enough. I whisk back to the rear, wheel rapidly under my dress. Wind blows my tent up and I must resemble some fop's umbrella, rolling in the wheelbarrow. Some of us in that last long entrenchment, I noted, are so narrow against the wind they suffer the advantage of disappearing as targets. One man cuts and eats his own bunions. Corporal Nigg was still in his place, frozen upright, long dead but continuing as the sentry. Who can fire him? Who has time for clerical work? Nigg is present, accounted for, damn you, a soldier's soldier. So Private Ruth brings my journey in the wheelbarrow to its conclusion back at the tent, puffing. Calamity has provided me with perquisites. Some resent me, as they go off to lose an eye or ear and return to chat, lucky this time.

The charge, our old bread and butter, has withered into the final horror of the field, democracy. It is a good thing we are still grassroot-mean, or there would be no impetus left. Referendums for and against the next charge take a long time, collecting ballots down the line, out in the swamp. Every sniper has an opinion, every mule-lackey, every musician. The vote is always in favor, for we are the Bats Out of Hell Division, even if we are down to less than regiment size. These boys can still stir you. When I know something big's afoot, I shriek for Ruth, who rolls me up to jump-off with the shock troops. Nobody is disheartened by my appearance. There are men far, far worse off than I, men unblessed with the ability to write and read; men whose salivation has been taken from them by breathing in one ball of fire too many. Oh Jesus, I'd go rolling out there with them if I could. It's Ruth that holds me back. Otherwise I'd be in the fore, quill high, greeting their cannon—hub to hub they are—a row almost endless of snobs' nostrils, soon to come alive with smoke and flame: grape, canister, ball, bomb, balls and chain. They greet us even with flying glass. I'll never forget the lovely day they took nearly my all. In a way I want to revisit it; a sentimental journey, however, this war has no time for. Ruth won't budge. He has his orders. I, the scribe, have become as important as our general, who is, of no debate, criminally insane just like the rest of them.

Shot to pieces in that rehearsal excursion down to Mexico, the man was buried, but returned out of the very earth once he heard another cracking good one was on. At last, at last! The World War of his dreams. "Thought I'd never live to see it! There *is* a God, and God is *love!*" I have license to exaggerate, as I have just done, but many would be horrified to know how little. He is said to have commented on hearing the first news, "Brother against brother! In my lifetime! Can Providence be truly this good?"

He is dead set on having these battles writ down permanently in ink and will most certainly push me on afterward, whatever befalls, into working up his own biography. There is about enough left of him to drape a horse. Once he's tied on, his voice never stops, and you can hear the wind whistling through him even in the rare interludes of quiet when he has simply blasted away his throat organs. Up and down the line, his raw nagging moans away, overcoming shot and shell; a song eternal, this bawling, in the ears of the ruined but driven. The two colonels and four captains flap around in imitation, one stout captain with a shepherd's crook in hand. He is likely to pull a malingerer out of the trench by the neck with it, and has often pulled up the dead and scolded them and their families. *Audace, avanti, allons mes frères!* Captain Haught is from everywhere. He is the one who told me our colors were inspired by the Russians in Crimea and that there is no more suave concord or color pleasing to our Lord than gray trimmed in yellow. No coward or lay-back, he walks straight up at the front of his unit into the very jaws of their hydra and returns at leisure, starched, unspotted, perfectly whole, armed only with the shepherd's staff. His only flaw is his appetite. It is rumored he has stolen biscuits from corpses right in the middle of an enfilade, and can't be hurried.

There is a man, way forward, who claims to have been shot through the very heart. He has found a hidden place out there, however, some hole in the field, so that he never retreats full and properly, but stops to burrow in like something feral. His boasts are relayed to us in the rear. Soldiers have seen him during battle and do report there is a great dark stain on the left chest of his tunic. Then they see him in the next assault *in media res*. This is what he has said to them: he doesn't want to miss a minute of it because there will never ever be anything like it again. It will set the tone for a century and will be in all the books. Great-grandchildren will still be shaking their heads, overpowered. There *can* never be any repeat of this thing. He saw the first long shadows of it at the one around that church in southern Tennessee and he has been in three worse since. So. They imagine he lives on roots and their liquid in whatever small cellar he has found or dug. Already he is practicing his posture around a stove fueled only by corncobs in an impoverished, riven home. He speaks his tales to gathered neighbors, family and children. They say he has a mirror down there, long as a tailor's, at which he practices. But he can hear our general bawling and their hub-to-hub cannon, and is never tardy for the charge. He is always already into it when his fellow soldiers catch up with him. His name is Beverly Crouch. Crouch has the distinction—whether he's truly been shot through the heart or not—of having been a *white* slave back home, right alongside the Africans with hoe and sack sometimes, but bonding out for other jobs too, wherever the weather and agriculture were better.

Our pathetic cannoneers, the remains of a proud battery of near-geniuses who could shoot the head off a chicken at a mile, speak with great accuracy still but no force, so little shot and shell are left, the main charge yet to come. The conservation they endure in the very heat of battle is almost hysterical. The salvo, that precious Italian concept, seems like some remote advantage in a historical tome. They can hope only to demoralize the other side a little, with an occasional round hitting one of their colonels amid-shoulders. I was never impressed that much by an officer's head blown off beside me, but the general declares this is a huge mournful event "over there," where they are different. The artillerymen are aided in their precision by our forward observer Jones Pierce-Hatton, who has never dressed in anything but civilian clothes, in the beau monde way—gray suit with wide Panama, and binoculars of the Swiss avant-garde. There is a lone enormous tree on a little hump of hill, into the top boughs of which he has fastened a crow's nest. Here is where he looks and rains fire on the enemy. It must be rather godly up there, calling the wrath and precision down on individuals of the indigo persuasion. They really hate him over there. His ladder's been all shot away for a long time. They brought out a line of sharpshooters forward from the ramparts; all of them blazed away upward at him. Now here was a salvo, remarkable, before they were convinced to retire by our own Kentucky experts. Some of these men were hardly anything but eyes, shoulders and trigger fingers. They slipped back gaunt and wispy into their nooks and bowers. The entire top of the tree and especially his crow's nest, all was shredded, much bark and lumber falling down. Somebody yelled up to him, seeing his wide hat come up out of the nest again, asking whether he was hit. There was a long pause.

"Why shit yes! What would you imagine!" But he did not come down and through the days, nobody asked any more questions. Spots of blood, dried, lay around the roots of the trunk where they rigged his food and coffee basket. All he insists on is the coffee, the only real stuff left anywhere over here. He has the canteen that would have gone to the general. Mr. Jones Pierce-Hatton seeks no other reward.

Our only triumph was knocking down their one competing balloon, an airship with basket for the observer underneath, and for this we can thank Granny Nature. The same ill wind that brought us those belly-churning odors of roasting prime meat increased and blew the thing off its anchor, so it wobbled over here right up alongside Jones Pierce-Hatton in his nest. You could hear the cries of dismay from the disheartened passenger as he came alongside the lone enormous tree at bright high noon. Pierce-Hatton shot into the thing with his French double quailing piece, and such a blast of burning air covered the top of this single stick of the forest we reckoned on a momentary view of hell itself (and saw, truly, it was barely a degree worse than what we had).

Somebody called up to Pierce-Hatton to ask whether he was injured. A head wearing nothing but the scorched crown of a hat arose from the hutch.

"Why shit yes! Haven't you got eyes, man?" came the reply.

Something big is afoot. The cannoneers are bringing up the last of the magazine and stacking it. We haven't seen this in weeks, seems years. The thing, our last, comes on at dawn tomorrow. New flags, last in supply, are unrolled. The band has swelled. The deserters, not that many, have returned, but most are in the band. We've never had this enormous a musical outfit before, nor so well instrumented. Fifes, drums long and short, snares, French horns, an Ophicleide, banjos with new woodchuck skin, trumpets and cornets, trombone, four marching violins, and a brand-new man with huge cymbals. They rehearse very softly, but I am told it's a thing from Tchaikovsky they have in mind, a military arrangement of the Concerto for Violin in D, Opus 35. The lines are shaken out, just two fifty-yard-long vanguards. Even three of the camp dogs are with them. We have no rear. The band is right behind them. When I know thoroughly what is up, I double my shrieking at Ruth. We are going, definitely. You bastard, you think I would miss this? I know you've been having it easy. I remind him profanely of his family and tell him I will search them out and write about them badly. So, by God, we are in there too, just ahead of the band. I put my quill away and exchange it for an assault saber. They are lying about everywhere and easy to find.

Is there a better music than the eruption of a true salvo from our beleaguered cannoneers, hub to hub, those ten of them, at the first sparks of dawn in the gray mist? You die for this music. But it lasted only thirty minutes and then we move off in our ghostly ranks, Ruth cursing and whining as he lifts the barrow behind me. Their cannons have not opened yet. They are waiting, waiting, perhaps till the last cynical second, every drop of blood squeezed from their dramatic absence, wrecking us in the mind—they hope. But there is no hesitation and when you see the pitted and shell-raked field, the last quarter mile, suddenly the band up and high in the best enthusiasm, tearing and swelling the heart, we know we have seen heaven. Then their cannon erases their fortifications in serial billows, and the rare banshee music of passing shot that few are privileged to hear seems so thick we have another firmament to breathe, an ozone of the delirious. I am so happy, so happy!

Hardly anybody falls. I tell you we are gaunt! We are almost not there, and we are starting that dear, deep-down precious trot toward them. Their musketry is popping and pecking. Their men are so thick on the line the flame is solid, and it is all we see out of the cannon smoke. Now at last we run; run dear boys, run! I had a chance to look about and the flags, my godly stars and bars, my regimental white cross on blue field, were clustered, gathered to the center. Oh boys, boys! I am shrieking. Up, get it up, my brothers! To them, into them! The general ahead, squalling atop his beast, rides straight into the furnace and our lines go in, and I go in. What a *hell* of a band we've got just behind. You can tell they are committed. They are going ahead too! Oh, happy bayonets high, oh happy, happy, happy! Then we are running in sudden silence. There is mystery and miracle left in this hard century! They are not firing anymore. We are running through stone silence, the grand old yell in our throats, our gray and butternut and naked corpses hurling forward, barely finding their rail fence, their earthen works, their growling ramparts. Bayonets down! Earn heaven, lads! Murder!

But the smoke has cleared off their line and we run up to stare at silent men with their guns down. Somewhere just behind them *their* general is bawling, even over the volume of ours.

There is great confusion, but I am glad I was near the center where General Kosciusky, a Polish-Russian, was screaming at the men in blue.

"Stop it! Stop it! I can't take it anymore. The lost cause! Look at you! My holy God, gray brothers, behold yourself! Cease fire! Cease it all!"

So, you see, we were just staring at their deep and thick line, every soldier in a new blue boat, their general screaming behind them.

"By God, we surrender!" he shouted. "This can't go on. The music. The Tchaikovsky! You wretched specters coming on! It's too much. Too much."

Our general, stunned, went over to take his sword. We, all energy gone in the last run, sagged about. Nothing in history led us to believe we had not simply crossed over to paradise itself and were dead just minutes ago.

In their tent there was a conference. Then their men began stacking arms and bringing forward food to us. You wouldn't believe the victuals. I gorged on honey and oysters fresh from the shell. You could hear a long constant moan of gnawing men as we sat around with plates on our laps, sucking in venison, turkey, porterhouses, piles of fat white beans.

When their general, a splendid tall man, the very replica of the bearded Greek commander, returned to the line and chanced to look down at me in my barrow, he began weeping again, and I am sorry I had nothing but a greasy face and the eyes of a dog to greet him.

Such arms, cannon, even repeating rifles; such almost infinite caissons, so many thrilling flags and handsome plump mules; and thousands of cutlasses and musical instruments—these were all ours. We, the few of the two lines and the band, could not encircle them. We did not know how to guard this host, and just gave up and fell back on more food, whiskey and coffee.

I was, as the scribe, invited into the last conference on dispensation. Our general, held by two orderlies like a towel between them, was still too stunned to gloat. His impossible silence spoke the whole moment. But we must argue a bit on the matter of a name for this battle. There were no landmarks or creeks or churches about; only a family of Germans named Hastenburg who had lived in a house northwest of the field, long obliterated, suggested any proper noun.

It was decided then that this was the Battle of Hastenburg.

★ ★

Evening of the Yarp: A Report by Roonswent Dover

★ ★

DARN IT WERE BORING, WISHT I WERE A HAWK OR CRAB. WHEN I SEEN him first I leapt out of my face for glad cause nothing moving lately but only rabbit nibble and run headfirst into the bottom of the purple cane. Deacon Charles at the VT school say go a head and write like this dont change. He wants to see it quick cause I seen the Yarp. Or somebody like him. Xcuse me please for not correct but I am hard attempting to spell at least sweller it being so important. Of a mountain man/boy nineteen first that day at two-forty-one o'clock afternoon on the watch I found at the road going up to Millsun Okain's house,

The sin of the old people I wondert what it was cause I dint feel it. The evil things of Roonswent Dover which is me werent felt by me like the others cause I had no feltedness of their kind of sin. I found out the Yarp did too.

He was a man hitchhiking where dont nobody come, ever, up a red ditch juncted to a road so dirty and spit out red on the paving. He was a true-looking lean man near hungery looking in a high collar white city shirt but no necktie up on it. I passed him then slapped my thigh, why not, I'm so miserable bored. Maybe this man knewn

179

something markable or a good thing to seek, him wanting a ride up
that ditch where nobody but old woman Skatt lives. Rained down to
gullies, that road, but we figure she be hungery, she walk out of there,
down the mountain with her crooked feet, buffalo toenails and ruint
smell. I backed up and he looked in the window. I say can't you see
no truck nor even tractor could get up that gullied red road? He said
he would go on with me and rest and see Missus Skatt later. He sat
down, no suitcase, bag, nor cane nor hat, just coming out of winter
and going to near freeze this night. Thanks for the lift. You know
where you are? I asked him. Yes I been here plenty time and I know
your Missus Skatt very very well. It doesn't matter much when I get
there sooner or later but I will go with you to the store.

I asted him how he knewn I was going to the store (and I was).
He said life is simple around here and I had the look of a store visit
on me. Nobody much confused him and now he was hungery, feeling
low and getting chill. He gave me a cigar for my trouble and said it
was the kind governors and dictators smoked from Latin America. We
lit up and I was feeling chumly. He asted me would there be music at
the store. This struck me goofy, of course there were a radio at ever
store and a televisioner too. And would there be food? I turned over
to him saying what else would there be in a store to be a store at all,
certain it has food, gas, oil, shells, bait, sardines, herrings, rat cheese,
and two old geezer at a wood stove playing Risk, and Macky Vellens.
He said what, I repeated, he pronounced it better, MacKeyavellea
of course, the writer of the *Prince* they used as a handbook to Risk,
taking on personalities, book falling depart apieces through the gen-
erations. Mr Simpson and Gene James owned it with theyr smart pet
goat that makes change I swear not, only the truth alone.

Then that man, the Yarp, he said shut up. Riding aside me
afortunate my charity, he said Shut Up ragely. It were glum, I werent
happy, but couldnt get mad cause he seem a danger now. I dont want
to hear none of your tales, boy, he kept on it, too many tales come
out of these mountains and everwhere. There shouldnt be any tales.

I said well you can see the goat with his front foot, but he
hissed or spat so I look out the window away from him, stopt talk.

In your mind you thinking you paying for the gas and tires
hauling me. And it was true, what he said.

We had eleven mile to go and it was crooked high down to low then high again, not even a dead dog nor cat nor chicken keep you company under the overhangs of them sweaty rocks. I aint nere liked them and now, getting on dark, the mountains I feel they live and sqeeze in on you to a narrow lane when nobody's around. I nere give up that feeling sinct I was a kid. It aint Arkansas or no real place. Now come sleet specking my poor dusty glass all acracked, which, I didn't like the sun running down either.

We'll have a nice snow tonight, the Yarp adventured. The quiet I was keeping didnt make no call to break it so I remaint quiet. Nineteen or not I was frighted. But if the quiet woulder asked me I woulder said You fool, it's on too late to snow, that sleet is just a peck from some froze cloud way up there. Its April, you fool.

Yes it'll catch Missus Skatt just unfreezing from the winter. She won't have enough wood. I'm sure glad I'm going with you to the warm store, Roonswent Dover.

Yes he called my name. There aint no way of knowing my name and be a stranger cause I go by Bill Dover to everbodys knowlege. I aint got even no license plate on this truck. You can see ten mile clear out here, cant be no stranger as ever came near your house nor your daddy or mommer that you dont know about. Our part of the county can't have no stranger moren ten minutes. So it were cold quiet now, believe it, no heater in my truck only a lantern in case of a mountain accident, lucky if theyr matches in that glove apartment. I couldnt get no speed outer her neither and we aint got to the real high passes yet. We was in a holler and then a vale, pinking out to the sides. There was some sun, a bit, so sudden I got brave.

But you shunt know my name.

He nored me.

You know too many legends, boy. Everbody does. You got to lie to stay halfway interested in yourself, dont you? The imagination is what ruins it. They shouldn't never imagined heaven nor hell. They shoulder taken their years, thats all. You already know the more you think of something aforehand it isn't anything like that at all. They'll be legending though, they'll be doing wrong and doing nothing, bargaining with heaven or hell. They shoulder just taken their years and practiced being dumb, over and over. Already that school is confusing you and hurting your mind, Roonswent Dover, son of Grady and Miriam.

I just fix small engines, I aventured.

You lie!

That last shout was good for another two mile of silents.

It snows here when there aint no snows anywhere else near. We must be higher, higher than all Arkansas and Missouri. In our county the Indian were never pushed out and we has whole fullblood Indians, but they are innocent. All the killing and stealing on tourists or policemen or sometimes a local for peculiar reasons is done not by them. Some said it were womens, womens and girls. A Indian told me that when I was seventeen. Now our Indians are Nini Indians. They fought on the Souths side and had slaves where nare white man here fought for either side, most for not knowing there were a war on and the rest, said my Uncle Rell, because they were drunk or idiots. A Ozark army might have swayed the war, says Rell. Our family wernt interbred but some Ozarkens, come to church and school too, theyr daughters get pregnant by them or theyr sons. So the Indians were defeated, and without slaves they moved up here from like Paragould near the river and sorrowed-out and become puny. Anybody can whip an Indian a head taller than him, a girl could do it. It is still a agony how many years? a thousand years after the War Between the States now the Indian is in deep sorrow even to plant a bean or tote water or feed his dog. They groan out loud all the time, feeble and they hate it, cursing Robert E. Lee who promised them slaves all the future. So theyr homes is tragic, likely to be a stricken old bus or a natural cave or sometimes what I saw, they tooken to living secret under a white man's house that they dug a hole under it. And they are in ever abandoned shack or outhouse, they are in so fast, they might be puny but they are quick, whole families can get on a squat quicker than deer fleas. (The old shacks and cabins here and there was left over from the diamond rush when my pa was a boy.) Reason Im explaining the Indians is they had legends more than us. Theyr chief drives a schoolbus to the VT school and will lie like a mockingbird back and forth to it. The bus dont allow nare radio so that Indian Don Suchi Nini sings to us these stories and believes he is the one who will change them back to real. They still want slaves and Don Nini says the whites better remain strong or, clunk, they be Indian slaves come nigh. When I was littler he had me making my grades and I went to the VT so I wouldnt be no slave. So we know what theyr thinking, and theyr everwhere, slunking round and creeping lenthwise in some Ozark ledge or listening from some nookery, and you cant do nothing about it. Xcept sometimes a girl will kill one, and they are set back in theyr revolution for a few week. I never treated nare Indian bad and most here dont. They might be puny but they scare me, the men dont care whether they got on a dress or overalls, and they will melt right in front of you into a line of trees. So, three mile up from the store on that last bad mountain, this Indian goes across my lights, which, wouldn't you know, is full of snow, active snow, and he was old and naked except for rubber wading boots. It just made me shake. I never seen nare like it, cracking my teeth that way. Then there were a little mountain girl coming after him with a fork hoe, what a dreadsome ancient sneer on her face. They come off the side of the mountain across the road and maintained on down the mountain where nothing but no goat should get a perch, on down to awful black night rock near the pitch of a well.

Oh! I said out. You see that? Hands bout to tear off the steering wheel.

I didnt see anything at all, lad, said him.

Everthing since he got in that truck was mocking me, minding back. Xcept maybe that speech on legends, hell and heaven.

The snow was churning and up in the road, some storm blowing down about three mile high, seemed right from the North Pole, only in our county. But it was, I knewn he was the Yarp in a way already, I bet. He was lost over there in the dark seat and maybe he didnt see that old Indian and girl. Wouldnt you know the engine quit and overheat and I had to coast down, Ive did it before, all the way to the store. Xcept the unsound got to me, in the curves and sliding on them circular threads that does as tires. The quiet was outside and inside and my poor lights was flickering. I knewn Id have already been down twict and back if the Yarp wadn't with me.

You hear about murdering thieving females in these parts, said the Yarp.

I werent going to adventure, Nat Hidey, no I werent. Was peering in the snow which, it was heavier than normal snow and it was gray not good white. A Yarp's eyes of course is suppose to be hot yellow and his skin disappeared from his throat so you can see its tongue long in it and tonsils and open voice box, it makes you sick. I werent going to look over there at all. I werent getting it yet but the Yarps smell of course would be a combination of bull spunk and road kill. Your Yarp suppose to have tiny long bird legs and big long feet too. I was on my way to the store, nailed in my windshield. A Yarp doesnt have to be none of that unless the time come on him. A Yarp has passed for a preacher, you know that. He dont know any breed and he can be an Indian or Kentuckian or live far off in a hospital. But he denominates in black garments, sudden he will lift his coat and you can see all his digestion, everthing he's eaten all chewed and gravyed-up in them tubes and holds and glands, and it makes you sicker. Thered be a baby's foot or one woman saw his stomach and there were a human brain. You can picture me as a hard looker through that windshield.

A Yarp is weak and quick like Indians in the legs, thin, but in the upper body powerful, so this thing throw through the woods and running water and pea gravel top-weighted. It can reach up with its arms and yank you down, but it aint hardly nothing underneath but coot legs and wading feet. My grandpa knewn a family of Yarps, peaceable, but nere eye has set on a whole family sinct his time which was eighty year ago when the Ozarks was founded. A Yarp really belong in Europe or Asia is what my grandpa say, he dont like it here in Arkansas, but some fell off accidental in the boats going out and there we are, they come a Yarping with Vikes and Pilgrims, they dont know no breed. Like the Indian they would be not so scarey if they *was* strong and upright. They is twict the fear to me weak and slimy, hanging down toward the ground like a slug snail, presiding on you specially when they are in groups nearby you, glooming at you, wanting something you cant give but they have to stay after it. That feebletude and they putting hands on you, that belongs more in your nightmares than a strong evil man, it gets your back clammier, your head colder, your heart miserabler.

I coasted on down not talking at all like Im talking now, lights flickering at the snow that were like gray scales, I finally got it, like fish scales, aflapping on the glass. I wouldnt look but he started shaking with cold I guess, commenced knocking on the tin floorboard of my Ford, gruesomish. There hadnt been lights left or right the whole trip, nare cabin nor goodly shack even if there were a light to commit, you hadnt sawn it.

Hurry, lad, the store, said him. I was cold to bones too. When what you know, the engine caught on for maybe cooling down gainst the snow. This thing get a hundred mile on a gallon of water when its good. Will there be music, he asted again. Saying from my choked throat was grievous.

Even if the radio broke they have a televisioner that pull in a music channel all snowy. Out here for the mountains we cant barely get waves, but there is people moving, dancing in the speckled screen we dont know the source, but there be a tiny music at it. The people is sad-looking themselves back and fro specially when the music goes out entire, you just having loud snow and forms pitching and pulling at each other. But I didnt say this to the man I knewn certain were a Yarp, chatting and shifting with cold. I wont it were light enough to see his feet and legs so thin out the right side low of my eyeball.

If there isnt music, lad, we must ride on.

Oh no we dont said I to me.

He knewn already that at the VT school we gathered with Deacon Charles, some nine of us young hillbillies at the head of the willow creek back of the parked schoolbus, the Indian chief Don Nini with us too listening and saying and ahearkening at lunch, seemed it was wouldnt you know subject of females and some studying the old stories and some about the at large way of the world. Some of them had Satan with a fiddle, why Im assaying off again here, the music. He was known to come to a dance out of nowhere and negotiate his fiddle to warp womens and girls. But Deacon who is reasonable in the head and forty-five and run the small engine course said that was made up by jealous male hillbillies whose wives and sweethearts was taken off by a musical stranger. Any slicker could do her, even out of a flat Arkansas town. You might as well say that Satan had a good car or money, which would work better. Deacon knewn the flat delta as well as us in the hills and of course was in the arm service when we was fighting I believe India. He said there werent even half the real tales never that they claim, like youd think a standard Ozark person was going round hardly nothing but a blabbering tale, tales piling up in ever holler and cove. No, and a lots were did pure for government men and university people who wouldnt leave them alone and specially during the Deep Ression. In the Deep Ression times folks often told a tale get the government interested in you as interesting, as workable or feedable or sometimes even free money which they awarded you for not coming off the mountain and mixing in nare cities, which already had too many folks. Some had went to California and messed it up terrible. The governor of California had began a new state and he didnt want nare hillbillies on it. In California they have science that grow eggs on a tree, and them hillbillies so sloppy and shuffling, they dont know how to harvest them down and walk cracking them with their stupid Arkansas feet. Deacon Charles would hold up his banana at lunch and say Whats this? A banana. Well, more than that, friends, youre looking at California, where I shipped out to the East. You say I went west to get East, how? Well, friends, there is a line in the ocean all stormy where everything gets backwards, that's how. They worship whats little, like a stick. Back to the tales, he said when you then dropped the ones said by parents to scare theyr young into formity, you hadnt hardly no real tales left. No, your witches and your haints, there wasn't many of them and the tales told about them got them wrong, my hillbilly geese, all gaggle and tongue. Your active supernaturals aint ever going to get that *apparent,* for one thing. He live on the rim of things and dont want to be discovered. I seen exactly one Yarp and I been searching all my life.

Finally the store, but it looked dim in that rain of snow, just a quarter the light that usually come out of there from Mr Simpson and old Gene James, tall and gray-bald with a bowtie like some girl stood him up sixty years ago. The thing, the Yarp, hopped out and went on in while I gassed up and watered the truck. Ice and snow was already thick and made my truck ghosted. Oh it were freezing and I trembled scared both, not wanting in the store but too cold not to.

The Yarp was over next to the wood stove where they was sitting just staring at the Risk board, no pieces on it. Something was wrong and I were glad theyr was somebody else to share the Yarp with, even nineteen like I am.

He had said something made them stop and frown, Mr Simpson out of a old blanket over him and the smart goat next to the leg of the Yarp. That goat *could* make change for a dollar, signalled with his right foot.

Theyr not believing I am Missus Skatts man, Roonswent, said the Yarp.

Mr Simpson had a face long like a mule's, with magnifying glasses he wore making his eyes huge and swimming at you. He said, That old woman crooked and near eighty and dyes her hair red? She on them inclines like a crab been skint. Aint no young man like you be courting her. Why youd be too young for her *son*.

Before this night is over I will be with her. I have seen her many many times. I have been with her many many times.

Gene James spoke, God made the vaginer of even a plain woman so sweet that even after knucular war and it was the only thing left, the race would be continued. But she cross the line.

How could you get up there? said Mr Simpson.

You cant hardly get up there on a hard summer day, said Gene James. Hed of been the right age if nare man would court her, which, it made you sick to think about. Its froze in on top of being naught but gullies, said James, like that was the law, that was it.

Why I'll walk right up there from here, said the Yarp.

Some dimwits was released on the county about when I was ten from a bus wreck down a iced incline, them that wasnt killed outright. They come from the hatch in Little Rock to spy the Ozarks. Folks liked some of them and took them in and some of them bred, we all knewn. Gene James looked at him and then me like he might be one, this Yarp, just now showing up from torment. You couldn't tell them from normal. But I was busy looking at that mans legs and feets. The feets were long and wide all right, in Ill be hung, dirty white or gray scuffed brogans like an normous baby shoe. You never seen that brand nigh nowhere round here. I liked being clost to my home, three mile on.

Mr Simpson he would wear a gown or womens pedal-pushers, and highheel canvas sandals with bush socks, anything, so he wasnt one to pass judgment, but I was flickering with my eyes at old James wanting him to see the infant boots. Before he could two Ninis came in stomping snow off. They had on blankets and towels and you couldnt tell man or woman or two of the same. Mr Simpson spoke some Nini because he traded with them. One had on a beanie thing on its head with a rubber band under its chin, and it said something so Mr Simpson pointed and the two went back and sat on the one piano bench and the one in the beanie commenct playing the piano, Indian or bad, which was good for seventy-one out of eighty-eight keys. They took up some time from the Yarp question. You thought about the only one ever truly play that thing was away high and rich maybe on Mars by now, Len Simpson. The Yarp was closing his eyes like sweet music was alooning. I was trying to whisper *Yarp* to old James before that thing raised up his coat and made the geezer vomit and die. Gene James was a stubborn born liar, but I was the first to see the Yarp. Now someways out of my fear with four other rightly human persons, I thought I had evened with Deacon Charles. I had a true tale and would be the center of the lunch talkings for a long time. Gene James was only fifth or eighth on what he'd seen true, at eighty or more. The Yarp spoken again.

I've a great hard long love for Missus Skatt. Shes not always what she looks to you, a goat or crab scuttling down that hill of false diamonds from her house. That is a good house, built better than most in the county. And I don't look like this all the time either. Her children is what I love, the young ones. She cooks a sumptuous venison and hare, and has a wheat patch, crushes her own meal herself for larripan bread. We have roasting ears and sweet potatoes right out of the wood ash. Im going to feed myself here.

Before no man could commence his tongue he had come back with a bottle of herrings and sour cream which he put upon a saltine and sucked in, not a crumb left on his palm.

Missus Skatt can lasso a deer. But its her children most I love.

She never had no children. Married but barren or maybe too foul to touch, said Mr Simpson.

She lasso them hares too, ho? said Gene James.

She stares them till theyr hearts break, said the Yarp. That fine house was built by her husband Andrew and shortly he fell dead.

We know all that, the two geezer spoken together.

But you know only a mite. I'm going to tell you of her children and her charming history which will explain why you are sitting here poor, ignorant and stupid with bad backs. For Missus Skatt she runs a sort of charm school you would call it in a town. Unknown to you she has raised every woman in this county. And before her another woman kin to her. While the Indians play that music that I love they cant understand me and even when they stop theyll just look at a mouth moving.

That one without a hat understands American, said Mr Simpson, eyes swole in the magnifying glasses.

But that Indian wont hear a thing. This isnt Indian business.

Then he told a long weirded thing such as I cant hope to repeat only relying on my memory with my simular attempt.

He says all the girl children is drawn to Missus Skatt and sneaks over to her they cant help it, when theyr ten or like that. This was even before the founding of the Ozarks with another woman. Why even right then a girl was hauling wood to her cause she knewn it was cold and she was near out of fuel. All around the girls and the womens learnt at her knee these things: how to pleasure a man so good hed cry for it, how to coy on him, how to get inside him like a mindful tapeworm, because she anointed them with special powerful sexual parts and strong soft arms and eary soothing voices. She coached them when to begin apleading for all they want within the county because they could never go outside the county ever and their men couldnt neither. And how to nag and harangue and beat down and whup their men not raising a little finger, and how to make him worm small and stuck to his spot. You take mind, the Yarp said, that this county aint forever had nothing but tired sorry men droven down like a stake to their patches. They never went off to fight a war even when the whole world needed them to fight evil. Nor none of them was athletes nor only feckless at lumbering or even executing in a automobile. And none ventured out or away and couldnt hardly catch a fish on a spring day with trouts leaping on the bank. Nor with cow nor horse nor goat (the Yarp kicked the goat and Mr Simpson and Gene James seen them whitish baby shoes of a sudden) any count. That they died not only before theyr womens but passed over like sissies mewling and pouting ten years afore they ever hit dirt. You notice how they are coming down level and under the Indians. The Yarp pointed over at the back of that Indian who was playing and sudden he began playing something ghostly like what were wrote by a man with a long beard in a Asian castle and sung by his beautiful daughter.

You notice too the crimes of murder and theft in the nights, all them I tell you now by her womens and girls. Not found by sheriffs nor nobody because the innocence is what she drilled in to them. Right now she is teaching that little wood-hauling girl how to be innocent and quick and steal, you bet. Its a thieves university, the womens, yes your wives too and your children-seeming girls has done it with bloody hand and prestidigitation of the fingers, theyr off with stolen goods, what theyr men dont get them. And sometimes they drop things like the watch Roonswent Dover found. He turned around and his eyes was yellow on me. I couldn't look and down at his knees I see them thin chickeny legs cutting out under his black pants. I just gulped and he was around, said Now this! and he pushed himself right up to Gene James, pulled his coat out.

Old man James took a gander and begun vomiting and then he fell off his chair dead with a whitened head. I was holding my hand over my eyes and didnt know what he was after for a long second. Mr Simpson hed seen but he survived and got up and yelled to them Indians for help but they never even turnt around.

Yes her time has come. Its over for her now. One last night of pleasure and it will be done. This Im getting xactly I think.

You wont tell none of it Simpson because theyll think youve passed to senile and take away your store.

He turned to me. I was ten feet off. The pet goat was nuzzling my legs for comfort and baaing.

And if you tell anybody this you will die, Roonswent. You are going to know whats wrong around here but you cant do nothing about it and that is your eternal curse, which is like that of many a man. But I wont have to worry. Youre of the age where a woman has already touched you and touched you deeply. You think you are being so kind to your mommer taking her a fixed sewing machine but when she takes it you look deep like you've never looked, youll see what is there.

So Im up the hills and mounts, so give me this.

He took a fold-in plastic fishing pole off the wall. It made a stout cane. He went toward the door, red spots on the floor off his infant shoes.

Theyll be out tonight, but just your littler girls. Even I have to swat them off. Youd think not, but I tell you, even Ive been womaned. I aint half the Yarp (he said it!) I used to be.

Therell be a time when the Indians will get the courage too gainst us old white bones. The Yarp went out in the cold snow and turned toward the mountains wed left. But he didnt take all his smell.

Mr Simpson looked horrible miserable.

What did he show you? I asked him.

Miz Skatt's head in his belly, cooking and hollering.

Later in the week me and two, Deacon Quarles and Chief Nini, clambered up the hill and went in the house. There was just, you couldn't believe it, piles of jewelry, watches, radios, knives and ribbons, deputies badges and wigs. Missus Skatt were in her bedroom with a old head and a young body, all laid out nude and peaceful.

So I havent said it, Ive written it and I hope this might make a difference. But I think it wont, not at all. Im got, Im doomed.

But its done for Deacon Charles and he says he will send it on to the governor. That makes me even or better than Deacon Charles, remember.

Mother Mouth

TODAY, VERNON, I NOTICED ELVIS WAS GETTING HAIRY. FINDING THAT, my tongue got hot all the way down to my heart to which it was attached. There was no keeping off the temperature or the *rump rump* noise of my want in my person. We don't go to church hardly anymore except to learn good English. Their music ain't ourn. Ourselves, we suck the air out the radio when it plays the Memphis beam with Negroes, shouts, moans and *rumps* in it. Between ourselves we conceive a sound like a worried panther having lots of mama and baby words. It can't be in a church. We take the airwaves out of our little Philco and spit them back with the mama panther in them. The Philco is all we could afford after you wrote the extra zero on that check and left us for three years in jail.

From now on you are such a disgrace, you understand, that you have absolutely no sway in anything and will only hang in the back or at the rear side to us in disrespect. I, with my dark inset eyes, him and his rustling eyes, we have made a vow, Elvis and I: that we will remain slim and elegant and catlike in our movements until the day he has captured his child bride, who will dye her hair jet black like mine. Then I, then he, will get fat together in blurring of each other toward the end, and we have impacted ourselves so. We like pills when we can get them but our beauty we know can't never last, that's a part of the glory. We can't *be* forty years old. Romance don't really allow forty years of life to what we are. Oh, we might go on as *something*, some shape or mass, but we're not even there anymore, it's burnt up, panther and all.

He will sing about the Teddy Bear, how he wants to be it, and millions of little ears will hear something like never they heard before, down to their feet, and wealth untold will unfold. Every song will be about me, it won't be no real girl, and that is what they will hear and gasp upon and find so magic all to their toes. In pictures you will see him with women, all kinds of gorgeous girls and cute like what ignored him when he was poor and baby-pretty, but you will never ever see love in Elvis's eye for any of them, because it will only be me, and our music together. He'll be looking away like into a mirror all his life but it's me he's looking at. You won't be able to imagine Elvis *ever* looking directly at anybody, it will *always* be off to the side at guess who, the mirror maybe? but more me.

Then I will die and the source will dry up for him. The famous will visit him at some mansion right on Memphis's Main Street, and he will tell these people, in maybe English, "Mama ain't out there no more feeding them chickens in the back." The tears and the crack in his voice will always be there from then on, Vernon—jail trash, you'll be back venaling around like a rodent with an evangelist hairdo, but the money will be *bad*, Vernon, always bad, like that extra zero you wrote on that check—and my boy will get coiled and wrapped and weird inside and out, leaping in flight wild with Tupelo space clothes on him, doing movements that are trying to climb the ladder to heaven where his mama is, and the music gift will still be there, only there ain't nothing worthy to sing no more, and he is making those thrown-out grabbing postures and sweating like with my fluid all over him, becoming a mass, just a groping mass, on the rope—up, up, me waiting for him.

Because there ain't anything like Mama Nooky. Ask all them soldiers that lay dying on the fields of that great war you weren't in.

Rat·Faced Auntie

EDGAR PLAYED THE TROMBONE AND FOR EIGHT YEARS HE WAS A MOST requested boy. Based in Chicago, he did a lot of studio work and homed in the fine, lusty Peets Lambert band. He could step into a serious club and be hailed and dragged onstage by any good band. Even back when, in Georgia at age seventeen, he was more than accomplished on both slide and valve. He favored the copper and silver Bachs. He'd come out of Athens roaring, skipping his high school senior year because he was such a prodigy. Edgar had then got the ear of a jazz fanatic on the university faculty who contracted for his audition in Nashville with Peets Lambert's old big band. It was turning electric and throwing out, ruthlessly, the old players. Lambert had a new sound—jazz/swing, jazz/reggae, jazz/classic, jazz/blues, jazz/country, even. This was simply desperation to survive. The band had not recorded in seven years. Now even the manager was only twenty.

Lambert, a disguised sixty-six, had not made enough to be comfortable from constant tours. He was wearing down, had emphysema, and it was hoped the new Lambert Big Thunder Hounds would get hip and record again. Edgar was approved immediately. He found himself in Chicago with two suitcases, two horns, and ten thousand dollars from Lambert. The band members came from everywhere and almost all were near-adolescent. Edgar loved them. He'd been on the horn so thoroughly since age ten that he'd never been to a scout or church camp or had even played in a high school band, having bypassed them for the Atlanta Symphony at age fourteen. So this was a grand society for him. He loved it, lived it, inhaled it. Immediately he began cigarettes—what the heck?—and staying out late with the guys: hipsters from Los Angeles, nerds from Juilliard, a gal bassist from Jackson, Mississippi—his crush—who hardly spoke except relentlessly and in exquisite taste with her Ampeg fretless. Edgar was in love from their first meeting. He too was shy and awkward, except on his horn, and it took him a year to ask her out, though he watched her religiously during his breaks—how she stood, short and blonde, but somehow with long, heartbreaking legs in black hose as she called on her strings to provide the hard bottom gut of the band. When they *did* record, *did* make money, back down in Muscle Shoals, Alabama, he listened and was caused to tremble by the wanton bass authority that poured from the modest, yes, woman. "All woman," he repeated to himself.

Lambert threatened to throw them out if they took drugs or even drank much. The parents at home loved that about Lambert. He'd returned in fame from a beloved, almost persecuted era in music, and seemed a practical saint to them, a saint of cool when he appeared on television in a turtleneck with his still thick salt-and-pepper hair, beret, and those long genius piano fingers, announcing against drugs nationally. He was one of the first celebrities to do it in the seventies. A victim of cigarettes, he gently pled for the young to avoid his error, though everybody noticed the good man lighting one up in the wings or bathroom every now and then. He looked guilty, though, and nobody said a word. Edgar, with no prior use or education in drugs at all, learned something alarming: Parton Peavey, the black boy on guitar, came into the band daily on heroin and never stopped in the years that Edgar knew him. (He was a fabulous crowd-pleaser in a herd of twenty-six crowd-pleasers—flat-out celestial on an old Fender clawed to pieces, maybe dug out of a burned-down nightclub in the Mississippi Delta, the great bad taste of the fifties left in its remaining blue—Parton Peavey was a star and everybody knew it.) Parton was from east Texas, like the Winters, Stevie Ray and, later, Robert Cray. He would vacation in Beaumont once a month and return with a literal bag of heroin (China White in a one-pound burlap sugar bag). Edgar, drop-jawed, saw him fix himself in a Milwaukee hotel room, calm as putting on a Band-Aid. Didn't he know Lambert would can him instantly? The band was heaven come real to Edgar and he couldn't understand why Parton would do this. But Parton didn't care, it seemed. He played brilliantly, though, and gigged out far more than any of them. The truth was that he was close on being a celebrity at his rail-thin age of twenty-one.

He was so good, or so wanted (guitars owned the world), the suspicion was Peets Lambert couldn't get rid of him, even if he did know. When he let out, peerless amid the stage-packed Big Thunder Hounds, it was a sound such as not heard *any*where. Maybe he was addicted to that, too. Come another year he could fire *Lambert* and buy the band himself. He already had four records. Really, after three years and all that money, it was a miracle he remained with the band at all. He was an imitation of nobody, seemed unconscious of anybody before him, and had his own cult. All this with heroin. Edgar constantly expected him to fall over or go raving, taken off by ambulances and the police, but Parton didn't.

Parton was docile, not sullen or conceited, uneasy with women, and in ways more boyish than Edgar. He was not stupid, but he didn't know one state capital, and when they were headed to a city, he'd only ask, "Up North? Down South?" He seemed barely to have known an ocean, though Beaumont was on the Gulf of Mexico itself. The Pacific off Los Angeles–Venice rather frightened him. He believed, Edgar figured, that the United States didn't end, ever. There was a lot in the world most of them didn't know, some of them near-infantile despite their prodigy, but Peavey took the ticket. Even during his molelike existence in Athens, Edgar had never approached this insulation, practicing upward of twelve hours a day. The thing was, this made Parton Peavey likable, in a strangely hip way, and he began a fad of willful ignorance in the band. People would claim they knew nothing, had never heard of spearmint gum or a pocket calculator. He and Peavey became good friends. Everybody wanted to be close to him. There was a good, young quiet warmth about him, an endless politeness, too. And he was shot full of the world's worst bad, all the time.

The band rose. Edgar had two cars—a Volvo coupe in Chicago and an old vintage Caddy convertible back home in Athens where he got the GED one idle summer at his parents' insistence. He was a minor star down there. Nobody cared much for the trombone, but they respected him as an eccentric phenomenon, and the local paper kept up with him. He affected, newly, an old Harley-Davidson motorcycle and a pet weasel that clung to his neck when he dashed around Chicago and Athens. Edgar had a plain, narrow, long-nosed face. He let his hair grow down to midback, sometimes braiding it twice. He had the necessary headband—chartreuse—and he had a tattoo of an upside-down American flag right at the bottom of his throat where a tie-knot would have been. (His parents gasped when they saw it and he did, too, thirteen years later.) Edgar had always felt behind on his personality. It was near the end of the Vietnam War, so he had to get in fast on his outrage, and a bit louder. He'd gotten tattooed, sober, by the best in a New Orleans parlor, although the old mulatto was an ex-marine and hated the job—"Strictly for money, boy, you got the American right, you got the American right. Play your horn and sport while they dies for you." Somebody gave Edgar books by Kerouac, Bukowski, Brautigan, Hemingway and Burroughs; also the poetry of Anne Sexton, which he liked especially and reread. He was coming on strongly to the bass-playing woman, Snooky, and barely knew that he was capturing her with his new vocabulary stolen from Ms. Sexton. With her and the others his library stopped. He could not conceive needing anything else, ever.

Edgar could afford to get a sitter for his apartment in Chicago, a jazz-smitten female student at the University of Chicago who was just a friend. She took care of his weasel, his Harley and Volvo, his books, his stereo equipment, and his collection of trombone recordings, which dated from the twenties on. Living the trombone had paid off in spades. He could buy and sell most college graduates his age. He had the leisure—holy smoke, he was *playing* all the time already—to take Caribbean vacations, playing trombone with West Indian steel bands (what a sound!) and drummers in Rio (salsa, salsa). The girl, from Louisiana, would boil crawfish for him on his return. He pretended to like them, but it was really Parton they delighted, by the potful, his chin shining with juice. What wonderful friends Edgar had then! Paradise, and Snooky slowly falling in love with him. She had a wild side, of course, especially liking midnight and later on the Harley, whipping around Lake Michigan on the back, hands under his armpits, in a dress with a bare twat underneath, her legs spread, the wind slipping around her joyful "womanity," she said, confessing shyly to him after several rides. That, and the fact she was quietly but increasingly jealous of his house sitter, sitting closer to him and nailing down his thigh with her little hand, were the signals she was going for him in a long way, Edgar thought.

The band went by chartered plane. Snooky was flirted with by everybody, even Parton, but inevitably she'd sit by Edgar, trembling, and he would nurse her fear of flying. Her outfits became sexier and more garish as she was brought out front more and more to riot the house. It was a beloved thing to him that she remained shy and girlish as she aged. They were growing up together, a very privileged American jazz adolescence. In a way, though, to the crowd, Peets Lambert was her pimp. He went *wow* and stroked his chin at the piano when she came out nearly nude in her brief gaudy dress and stiletto heels, hamming with the happy lech smashed by her naughty rig, avuncular (old Peets had seen the wimmens in his time!). The public loved it, the Hollywood Bowl howled. Could it get any better? They did nine encores one night. Edgar played so well some nights that he knew he'd lucked into another whole planet of jazz, just a few of the greats nodding wisely around him. Somebody told Edgar that jazz was the only original American art form. He felt safe in history then.

Most of these nights he was secretly drunk. Edgar, still abhorring Parton's habit, was becoming alcoholic, having never touched drink before age twenty-four. There was no great reason for it. The band was chaster and soberer by a long shot than any of their contemporaries. Some of them, get this, *Rolling Stone* noted, played dominoes and Scrabble at the hotels, enormous bars flowing around them, themselves oblivious, like a bunch of Mormons in the lobby.

Only Edgar and another man, a middle-aged survivor from the last band, a relative of Lambert, hid out in a dark rear booth, drinking, playing nothing but boozy arias back and forth, in prep for the gig. The older man was a veteran. Only vodka would do, maybe a dex on a tired trip, then Listerine and a quick Visine to the eyes before stage time. (Lambert *would* throw you out.) Woodrow, the saxman, assured him that liquor, when controlled, was a friend of music. It was no mystery then that Edgar was playing better. Woodrow argued that he should know, he himself wasn't worth shit, never had been, and had plenty of time to listen, since Lambert rarely used him unless in a loud ensemble. But he knew music and Edgar, you cooking infant, you are away, man. You make other grown trombonists cry. Edgar rejected Woodrow's claim: you're the wise one, the dad, he said. You're the tradition, the years, the true center. Holy smoke, man, you're *football*, or a *church*.

Rolling Stone, concentrating on Parton, Snooky, the maniacal drummer Smith, Edgar and Lambert, had them in a big article called "Revenge of Big Jazz." *Life* did about the same in huge pictures. Parton Peavey had never heard of either magazine. What a gas. He led both features, quoted in his wonderful innocence, drug-thin and solemn in nothing but boxer shorts backstage with a bottle of Geritol in his hand. The following spring their new record, *Quiet Pages from Little Lives*—the loudest thing they'd ever done—went gold. What jazz had done *that* lately?

Edgar let out an unusual, drunken obscenity of approval as they looked at the articles. Snooky was shocked. She accused the house sitter of pushing drinks on Edgar and maybe the black cigarillos, too, cutting into his breath, his life, and so on. The house sitter began crying. Though Edgar denied it, the upshot was that Snooky told the girl to leave. Nasty, but *her* man. This was the final signal. They soon married in her city, Jackson, with Parton and Lambert in attendance. Afterward, Edgar and Snooky began to make love clumsily. They had a long honeymoon in the apartment with only the heavenly gigs to interrupt it. Edgar would look up at the cold black Chicago sky and say, "Thank you." Snooky loved this. She did not notice his drinking. He was such a perfect, gentle, vigorous husband. Nothing could be wrong. On the plane they were treated like two people "going steady" on a high school bus trip. He could swallow nearly a half pint of vodka at once in the jet's restroom.

Lambert got cancer, but he could live with it. For a while the band's celebrity increased because this fact was known. He never missed a show, even during chemotherapy. His piano playing became quieter, more wistful, more classical, his contemporaries noticed, adoring him further, if that were possible.

Then, pop, America forgot them almost wholesale, down to bargain basement at the stores. The band held a two-year discussion about this fact, but nobody could find a reason. Did *Life* kill people? They hated, in all their musicianship, and with saintly Lambert's genius, to have been some vagrant novelty. The jet trips stopped instantly and the hotel rooms were poorer. They ganged up in rooms to make the budget. They traveled in a bus. None of them except Woodrow had saved much. Their foot had been in the door, they were about to step in as permanent guests, then . . . But they had youth and were extremely loyal to each other and to the music. Edgar, who could barely read music, if truth be known, began trying to write for the band with a computer, but he wasn't any good.

Two more records, then studio time became too expensive to make them—that kind of sales. So it was all over America, slowly and much more than anybody wanted. Lambert would fly ahead. Sick and more irritable lately, he'd greet them cheerfully, but his heart was down. All the kids were down. The halls became very thin, half deserted, echoing. Cocaine, more cigarettes, even cough syrup for its codeine became usual. Edgar stayed with the vodka. He'd tried Parton's heroin once, over his protests, but it made him very sick. Snooky and most of them still took nothing.

One night out of Oklahoma City, Edgar had a sort of fit, insanely unlike him. He shouted another withering obscenity, grabbed the steering wheel away from the driver, and raced them off from the rest stop, screaming "I'll take us somewhere! I'll take us somewhere!" He turned the bus over on a curve, laying it down very fast in a long ditch. Everybody was shaken badly. Some had cracked ribs and terrible bruises. But there were no serious injuries except to Parton Peavey. His left hand would never be the same even after three surgeries. Also, something was wrong with the bus insurance—not a dime, and they didn't have enough to get the bus fixed. The band canceled and laid up a month, leaking money.

The third week Lambert called for a band meeting in his small hot room in the motel. He began calmly. Then he insisted Edgar come up front. The general feeling was that Lambert would forgive him. Lambert was that kind of man. But then he saw Edgar was drunk. Edgar and the band had never heard that kind of profanity and hollering from him. Lambert kicked Edgar out and screamed at those, like Smith and Parton, who stood up for him. It was a bitterly sad thing. The worst, thought Edgar. But he was wrong.

Snooky left him. The pets, who'd been disturbed by his behavior, went with her—weasel Ralph and dachshund Funderbird. The house sitter came back. Edgar slept with her mournfully.

Parton, who'd left the band—several others had too—and gone on to solo celebrity (loved by the knowing for his crippled left hand; he was a real vet at twenty-nine now, a dues payer) came by for a last visit. He didn't blame Edgar at all. Further, he was tearful about Edgar's breakup with Snooky, who remained with the little-attended Big Thunder Hounds. He had no solutions, no black Beaumont wisdom, except, "Up to now, Edguh, we been lucky. Don't rush it."

Edgar looked at him through fuzz: a child. He felt much older than Parton. He didn't think he could live at peace like that. He was often breathless and felt dirty around the neck, sweaty, where his tattoo was. An old Dylan thing chased around in his head: "boiled seaweed and a dirty hot dog." Most of the time, he could not even eat *that* down, but it was what he deserved.

He'd made a lot of friends, however, gigging around Chicago, and for a long time he was known as a classy drinking man, an aristocrat of the 'bone, my man. Then he became a student at Northwestern where they had a fine-music program and worshiped pros. He'd heard Snooky was there, studying double bass, but he saw her only twice. Edgar was an uncommon freshman. He'd thought college was the thing to keep him straight, but it wasn't. He felt elderly in the classroom, the reverse of his band experience. He did not know what the rest of them did. Against the odds, he played the clubs till five in the morning, around Rush and out in the burbs where jazz was a discreet rage with the young rich. His appearance in class—blasted, orange, looking thirty—was a miracle. But he pushed on through classes where he was not valued, making poor grades, keeping his mouth shut, and memorizing desperately. He fell down more than once, smashing his head on a desk. A mere pint a day was a masterpiece when he wanted the bar. The house sitter left. There went any order at home. He developed separate dumps of classwork. His refrigerator became green inside with uneaten food as the money got low. By the time he graduated at twenty-seven, thin and trembling, with a sociology major, he was a bum. He had no more time to fool around.

He crashed his old Harley into a pier post after a graduation party he gave himself and the fellow bums on the South Side, where he now lived with his few remaining possessions, a small dusty transistor radio and shower shoes. A lot of his clothes he simply lost. He was thinking an old thought about Snooky when he hit the post, his motorcycle flying out into the water of Lake Michigan. The yachtsmen were highly irritated. When the ambulance came, he still knew nothing. But he remembered what one paramedic said when they were lifting him in, looking at his tattoo: "Look at this piece of shit's throat. Drive slow. He comes out of the booze, he'll scream when to hurry."

His sternum was cracked. For a month afterward he did not drink. The Dilaudid was pretty good, though. When they wouldn't give him any more he had three especially lonely, agonized days. He wrote—why not?—an old aunt who was rich, and lied to her that he was in graduate school and poor. From La Grange came a note and money almost by return mail. What a mystic boon. He drank a great deal on it.

He would retell the story of how he'd had all the clubs going for a while with his "new" sound, but he was a sick drunk by then, the spitty and flat noise duplicating him. Even the avant-garde had found out he was merely drunk, and given him the door. But now his chest hurt too much to play. Plus, both instruments needed fixing.

He liked to travel light anyway, he told the fellows on the corner. Those cases were *heavy,* guys. One of them took him at his word and stole both horns. He knew who'd done it, but he was in such a world now that he just stared with his mouth open at the man and asked him, please, for a slug of port. The man refused. Edgar, forgetting the trombones, said he'd remember this. He wrote his aunt about his graduate studies and here came another money order from La Grange. Guilty, he began making notes on the bums. He used the back of his classwork pages. Some of the bums were long and vibrant narrators. Two of them spoke to Edgar in Russian. He kept scrawling on the page. As payment for their stories he would buy them drinks (sometimes the fellows cleaned up enough to get in a bar, hair combed in a bathroom). They thought he was very classy. The trombone stealer died. One of the narrators kindly took him to the pawnshop and he got his horns back.

He was thirty-four when he finally got treatment and afterwards, why not, he headed back down to Georgia on an Amtrak which went through Jackson, where he looked stupidly around for any sign of Snooky. He kept clothes and toiletries in his horn cases. He wanted, he thought, never to play the horns again. He could smell alcohol in them and they made him sick. But he wanted them near to remember.

Edgar's sobriety did curious things to him. For one thing, he had not realized he was tall. His posture was still poor, though, having been curved over in search of the pavement all those years. He had blood and air in him again, and was still a bit high on withdrawal. His face was plumper, unblotched, his hearing and eyesight better. However, he had the impression he looked suddenly older, thrown forward into his forties at thirty-four. He had intimations that he would die soon, and must hurry. He also felt exceedingly and cheerfully dumb, as a saint or child might feel. He greatly enjoyed not knowing vast lots of things. He could remember nothing from his college "education." Going back to school now under the patronage of his aunt (under the lie that Chicago, foul and windy, made his studies there impossible), he found he could barely write, and did it with his tongue out, counting the letters and misspelling like a fresh rube trying to explain Mars to somebody back home. Women, though his desire was wild from lack, frightened him. He withdrew from music. It hurt him even in restaurants. He discovered himself asleep, eyes wide open, for long periods of time. He guessed he'd nightmared himself haggard with liquor and his body was still catching up, sly fox. He became agoraphobic and would often walk straight out of a room with more than three people in it. Attending class was hard. Then there was one last thing: he was certain that he would do something large, significant and permanent. Yet his imagination was gone, and he supposed it would be a deeply ordinary thing he'd do, after all.

At the little college in La Grange where he pursued his master's degree, depression hit him and he could barely stutter his name. One day he stopped in the hallway of his department in flowing traffic and for several minutes had no real idea where he was. The voices and moving legs around him were suddenly the most poisonous nonsense, but there was nowhere else to go. He was older than everybody again. Later he remembered that with seventeen years in Georgia and seventeen in Chicago he was torn between languages, even whole modes. He hadn't heard Southern spoken by a large group in ages, and it sounded dead wrong, just as the crepe myrtle and warm sun seemed dead wrong. Somebody passed with a Walkman on. He awoke, sickened by the tiny overflow from the earphones. A winsome girl was shaking him by the arm. They were classmates. She, astoundingly, seemed concerned, though she made him afraid.

Next was the matter of his aunt, whose patronage he had never quite understood. He was into her for many thousands already and did not dare count it up until he was a well man. Neither could he face his parents, who had lost him during the years he was a bum. Athens was not far, but it was a century away. They were old people now. The sight of him might kill them.

Long, long ago, his father, who rarely drank, had got loaded on beer to level with the famous hipster his son had become. Edgar was touched. His father, who wrote innocuous historical features for the local paper, seemed bound to drill at the truth about his wealthy older sister, Hadley.

Hadley was rat-faced. She resembled other animals, too, depending on her anger. It was a shame she was so homely and bellicose. A low, crook-backed and turtled thing, her typical expression was the scowl, her typical comment, derision. She scratched the air with snorts and protests. Edgar got it after he'd moved in: "You keep your room like a doghouse!" Edgar thinking it near clinical in classified piles. Nobody could remember her being pleasant to anybody for very long. When she was young she had considerable breasts. Two husbands comforted themselves briefly with them. The husbands may have become husbands mainly for such comfort. But the harshness of her face reasserted itself and the mean gruesomeness of her voice knocked out, in a few months, her breastly charms, and the long rut of acrimony got its habit, driving the last husband pure deaf and happy of it. The old lady had retired from formal religion long ago, blaming the perfume and powder of her contemporaries, widows like her, who gave her "a snarling snootful." Now she listened to the pastor on the radio, but only to keep up a mutter of assault against him. He was too meek and liberal for her. Hadley was a loner first, but not finally. Curiously, she'd had three handsome daughters. She wanted an ear, she demanded an audience, but something that nodded and remained fairly mute. She had worn out her daughters years ago. Her iron-jawed homeliness depressed them. They avoided her except at Christmas and Mother's Day, which she always ruined. They wondered why there was such a long mystery of dispute with her as she was wealthy, safe, air-conditioned, pampered by a forgiving black maid, and hardly threatened by the music, newspapers, widespread fools and widow-harmers she so reviled. Paying for anything especially disgusted her and there was always a furor about some bill. The habits, hairdos, and clothing of her daughters' husbands moved her tongue to little acidic lashes, as if they weren't there, only their shells. The old woman, though, was smart and not just an ignorant blowhard. It seemed she had educated herself to the point of contempt for close to everything; further knowledge was frivolous. She dusted it off with a snarl.

Edgar numbed himself early on. His own rages and countermeasures had cost him soul and ground in the past. He was still a wreck easing himself slowly back into the waters of hope, and with caution he might repair some of the mournful holes. He was dutifully nibbling away in sociology in exchange for his roof, the use of her car, even money for postage. Edgar, on the advice of his counselor, was writing letters of amends to Snooky, Parton, Lambert—still alive!—and delaying the long one to his parents. The old woman knew he'd been a drunk. Said she could smell it in his letters. Hadley relished it, she had him. Edgar would rally up a blank nod and she could scratch away at will. He hid his smoking from her. The day she smelled smoke in her Chrysler would be a loud, nasty one, he reckoned. His elegant garret in the Tudor mansion hid cartons of Larks and ephedrine bottles. The horn cases, necessary, made him sad.

Auntie Hadley had no bad habits. Her enormous love for chocolate was controlled. The single Manhattan she poured herself at six-thirty, correctly just preceding dinner, was all she ever had. He wondered why she bothered. He could have had twelve to establish his thirst. She looked in his eyes for the suspected thirst. He stared down at her legs and was shocked to see them smooth, pretty enough to flirt by themselves. Here she was seventy or more. Her back was slightly humped, her chest low and heavy. The young legs were an anomaly, tight in their hose.

She dressed well. Much better than he, though he did not care. She'd put him in designer dungarees. He had several too expensive turtlenecks from Atlanta because of his tattoo. He wore a better coat than he'd ever had at the height of his money. Maybe clothes were her bad habit. She dressed way above the town, her blouses in warm hues like the breasts of birds. Her pumps were girlishly simple. The girl who'd held his arm in the hall saw Hadley in the Chrysler once and said she looked stamped by Vassar or Smith. But Edgar knew she'd had only three years at a women's college as undistinguished as the one he now attended—private, small, arrogant, and mediocre. From Northwestern to here was a damned other free fall of its own. Still, three years of college for a woman in the Depression wasn't bad. His aunt had a certain sneering polish to her. As for himself, he had flogged into the "program" with minimal credits and letters of recommendation from three drug/alcohol counselors who almost had to approve of him. The big letter, though, he'd touched from a senile prof who had been a high horse in urban ethnic studies. The quality of his dementia was that he cheered thunderously everybody he came in contact with. A hoary, religiously approving idiot in atonement for all the years he'd sternly drawn the line, perhaps. Edgar sucked up to the emeritus, who favored the phrase "my poor children!" He'd never even taught Edgar. But he had a letter from the famous old man and could have had his clothes and car. The faculty here were impressed to the point of envy.

Edgar looked bent, used and ill. In short, perfect, "one of ours" among the faculty, young and old. Even his former "rough time" with drugs and drink worked for him, and his jazz name was never forgotten. Those narcoleptic from two glasses of wine could hardly believe he was alive and were glad he'd got through to bring forth more good things. They trusted him more than he did.

Gradually, though, Edgar did get better. He took to running on the track in the hot sun and at night he slept like a babe. His cough disappeared and his ulcer was cured—he became near lotused-out by well-being. The people around him were good and nothing was ruined by irony, except for Auntie Hadley. He could shake hands and mean it. Little beautiful things. But watch your pious little disease, Edgar, the counselor's voice had warned. It'll leap in good times.

Edgar unearthed his notes on the bums. With an appalling gloom he found them well written, though barely legible. They were dangerous, like his horns. He was another man, then, in his whiskey insight. How long could he go on being a mute fraud among these good people? Well, he'd practically whispered to the chairman that he was going to write about bums for his thesis—whether Chicagoan, Russian, or Southern, he didn't know yet. But were bums all right as a subject? The chairman thought it excellent. Think of the therapy for Edgar, too. This was his life's inevitable opus, wasting nothing. Hardly any of the profs had experience with a big city. The man was so happy, Edgar felt even more guilty. He did not want to write about bums any more than he wanted to play trombone. This was not how he would be significant.

In the spring the social sciences party was held on the ground floor of a Victorian bed-and-breakfast hotel made over by two bored doctors' wives who became livelier in the role of perennial hostesses. Both of the wives were flirts, sexually attractive but chaste, fired by their Perdido Bay suntans. They danced their narrow waists, merry calves, and clapping sandals over the swank oak-plank hallways and up to the "boudoirs" above. There Edgar dreamed he might surprise them with the salty fluids of his mouth: desire was grinding awfully on him now, the gates thrown open by his health. He'd have to watch it. The wives served wine and cheese on silver trays worth more than the annual salaries of most La Grange faculty. One wife when asked about her husband shouted, "Oh, that dumb old bum!" Edgar hoped the man would die soon from overwork so she could kneel in front of him with money in hand, dragging on his jeans—holy smoke. Quit. She would find Edgar "darned alive!" He'd show her deep, rare animal need.

Could he awaken her senses, perhaps in a shack by the railroad, with only a naked lightbulb and a soiled mattress on which she struggled rump up? Bum's dream, sot's hope. He was waylaid, beyond himself. The faculty men around Sally had looks of civilized attraction, he noticed. She seemed nothing but a pleasant ornament of a rousing spring day, something to break up shoptalk. Oh, Snooky, Snooky.

Edgar's aunt was at the party, too, hopefully lost in a blockade of deaf people. She'd insisted on coming. He did not know what she expected from the event. Maybe to spy on him, the fraud.

Great hell—Auntie Hadley was six feet away, under the archway, staring straight at him. For how long? He'd been caught in point-blank lust for married Sally. The old woman bored into him with distaste. In his hand he held a glass of nothing, a lemon-lime drink at which he now sipped, mortified. He pretended an aesthetic view of the premises. Whom did she expect, Plato? Since she was not mixing, not having a good time, what exactly did she want? To stalk the territory until she found something appreciably awful, like him?

He slouched away to the cheese. What she liked best, he thought, were fools in authority. Maybe she'd find a dean and nail his moronism for Edgar later. While he was tracking décolletage and secondarily a man who could be a chum like Parton or Smith, anybody but another recovering chemical fraud stuffed with sincerity, their happiness right from the manual, he glanced over the crowd toward Hadley. She was holding her wine glass like a hatchet. Some old cowboy bum wisdom he'd once heard—"Small-breasted women are mean"—could not apply to her with her low great ones. No fury like a woman scorned: by her own parents, seeing their ugly duckling have no reprieve over time; by boys and men making rude comments; beaten back into her shell, sad little ducky, left to suffer among the natural beauties of Savannah; sad in the playroom with her gorgeous dolls, maybe beheading them, and her toy villages, setting them on fire. He was trying to achieve sympathy.

"You saw that lady?" came a girl's voice below. It was the grad student who had touched him in the hall. He liked her looks, all fresh faced in her green party chemise, above the mode of faculty wives and her peers, who were deliberately nondescript. "She dresses so well. Must be somebody. An older Jackie Kennedy, except for the hump and the dog-ugly face."

The girl was naughty but risking it, touching Edgar's arm again for the first time in months, eyes bubbling, needing discipline.

"Ow, I'm sorry. Real rude. I'm half drunk."

"It's my aunt. My landlady, too. She's making things easier for me here."

"Truly sorry. Let me tell you something better. My friend knows two deaf-mutes who were looking at Pres Reagan one day on television. They began laughing like crazy. Friend asked them what it was. 'He's lying!' they signaled. They knew."

As for décolletage, this girl Emma Dean was well fixed. Either that or boosted. Her cleavage practically spoke to him and he was positive she knew it. It made him happy.

"I work with the deaf. Lifelong dissertation there, Edgar boy. They know many secret things we don't."

"I believe you."

"I know some of your secrets, too. I'm a busybody, probably *bound* for sociology, and I can see that you're not too happy here, believing it's beneath you and not Northwestern. You know too much about music and life, and worst of all, poor you, fame. You've got an honest, seasoned face. But with your slump and the hair in your face, you're so . . . morose. Like you're expecting defeat any second . . . Hate me, then. I've been improving the world since I was a little tapper."

"No. You seem kind." He straightened up and pulled back his forelock. "I've hardly been ynng," he lied, spying her every other day, wishing.

"You looked drunk. That's why I came over and embarrassed myself. I'm drunk. My glasses are all fogged up, too." She was even more friendly when she took them off. "Do you expect a lot from yourself?"

"Maybe just the rote stuff, for a while."

"My parents were nothing. Daddy at the dry cleaners his whole life, and mother had to work—white domestic help. Imagine that in La Grange. We'd drive past all the great white mansions and spreading magnolias. I wanted to be somebody. Even now, I'm not going to be just . . . sociology. They're not going to be able to study me, class me. Hey, I was a virgin till I was twenty-five. You heard of that lately? Not because I was any holy-roly, either. I knew I'd enjoy sexual intercourse with the right person. My orgasms come very easy and I cry out like a panther. But . . ."

Her lips were dry and she stopped. She licked them and took a breath. Edgar noticed her eyes were moist. She was almost crying.

"Get me some more wine, please."

He got it posthaste, hoping she wouldn't use up her drunkenness on somebody else. He hadn't been near a woman in five years.

"I'm all ears."

"See," she wept a little. "We lived in a brick bunker on a bare yard at the edge of town. There were eight of us with about the money and room for two. I wore my brother's awful brown shoes in ninth grade when it really, really mattered."

Edgar guided her to the big front porch. Good, nobody else was around. It was a wonderful bluish-yellow and green here in midspring. They sat on the steps facing east. She wouldn't say anything. He was afraid she would go off in a sick fog.

"What about those doctors' wives that run this place?" he asked.

"Society cows looking for an audience anywhere. I'm so direct today."

"I don't mind. I like you. You look good."

"How did *you* fail? Were you poor?"

"Fail?"

"You're here, I mean. You don't have any money. Nobody really means to be in sociology, do they? You're older. You look *delayed* or off track—I can tell. I can spot true success a mile off."

"Fail, really . . ."

"See, if my mother and father hadn't had to, if they hadn't . . . they got married when she was *fourteen*. My mother was beautiful and at forty she looks as old as your aunt. But they just had to . . . couple, see, they're blind as swamp rabbits. Two of my brothers are deaf, but they kept on keeping on. I was sick one day at school my senior year and walked home. We hardly ever had a working car. I walked in and tried to get on my pallet before I threw up again, and from their room I suddenly heard this ruckus. I couldn't bear it. It was noon and he was home from the cleaners. They were in there mating, cursing each other, awful curses. I went out to the front yard and vomited, all dizzy, then looked up. Right on the road in front drove these rich boys in my class who were out for a restaurant lunch. They were hanging out the windows laughing at me. I never told that to anybody, Edgar."

"Oh, no. Awful. You poor girl."

Edgar took her hand. She had long fragile fingers with a class ring from Emory on one. It was still a teenager's hand.

"Nine months from then I had a new baby sister. Mama all crumpled up and thin and lined. But I had a bright inner life and I went away on scholarship. Made A's in almost everything, and Atlanta hardened me up."

The party inside seemed a dim fraud, with Emma and her feather-light hands out here.

"I won't tell you his name, but I had an affair with a married man—a wealthy important senator in Atlanta. The upshot was it ruined my life. He and his wife 'reconciled' and they named me a call girl he'd only seen a couple times during their marital stress. He'd promised me marriage, of course, but I never asked for it or wanted it. I took some money and shut up. My pop cursed me. My mother just died. They had principles, you know. But I gave him all the money for the four kids still at home."

"Rough."

"You might ask somebody in Atlanta who the senator was. Not me."

"I believe you."

"The man would put me naked in a silver Norwegian fox coat and work me over good, half a day at a time. He took poppers. We frolicked up where you could see all Atlanta. I liked him. We played backgammon. He cried when he lost me."

"Were you 'somebody' then?"

"No. You know what I was—mainly dumb."

"You don't hear many people being truly 'ruined' anymore."

Now there was another voice behind them and above. Edgar quailed.

"That was very nice, Edgar. Perfectly stranded, and I barely knew a soul." His aunt stood peeved, he guessed, though her voice had some teasing in it, maybe in deference to Emma. He and Emma rose.

"Aunt Hadley, this is Emma Dean, one of my . . . colleagues in the department."

"Can anyone tell me, please, what sociology *is?* I've asked four or five times and got the silliest stares."

Clearly she did not want an answer. Emma smiled, blinking her eyes dry.

"You've a lovely suit!" said Emma.

The old woman did not acknowledge the comment.

"I guess I've had enough 'higher education' for a day. Are you done?"

"Yes, ma'am. We'll go then?"

Edgar was forlorn and felt infantile. The old woman demoted everyone, he knew. Suddenly he wished that he had vast wealth.

"I'll ride home with you. My home, I mean," said Emma. "I don't even have a car, Edgar. Can you believe it?"

"Oh, the poverty-stricken bohemian student is rather a tradition, isn't it?" Hadley said, bright with scorn.

"Then I'm very traditional, ma'am."

"But you go to honky-tonks."

"Ma'am?"

"Your dress. Those see-through shoes."

"Would these be like what the 'flappers' wore in your day?" Emma remained kind, without strain.

"'In my day'? I'm not dead, young lady. Surprisingly, I believe I'm still alive enough to pay all the bills."

They were quiet going to the car, calmly elegant like the old lady. Edgar noticed with some horror that Emma promptly opened the front door and sat down. Auntie Hadley just stood there, flaming. Edgar froze, with gloom and awkwardness. She knocked his hand away when he tried to help her in. They rode a piece in hard silence until Emma instructed him as to where she lived, sounding drunk. It was way out south of town on a tarry country road, Edgar found out slowly. When he finally got there and drove into the "park" it became clear she lived in a long redwood mobile home in a group of pines. There was a man sitting barefoot on wooden steps at the front door.

"That's Michael the Math Monster. He's deaf," laughed Emma.

"You have a husband?" asked Hadley.

"No, just a friend. Another grad goob. Shares the rent."

"And all the fun, I'd imagine."

Edgar was vilely impotent. Emma did not seem so attractive and remarkable anymore as she hit her leg ("Ow! Gee!") getting out. She was common and messy. He winced when she stumbled in the pine straw. His aunt would not be missing a stroke. Emma had become the thing Hadley knew her to be. But it was not Emma. He wasn't himself either around this poison. A gutless lackey at thirty-five, losing worth by the minute.

How many people become what they seem to be to harridans and wags? He was furious as he drove. Then he recalled his aunt was still in the back seat.

"Wouldn't you like to ride up front?"

"Might as well continue on back here. They'll think I'm domestic help or some retarded person not let near the wheel."

"I'd be taken more for the chauffeur. Here I am with tie and suit."

"Eyes on the road. You drive like an old man from Nester Switch. Slow, but dangerous."

"Don't want to ruffle you."

"You and those mummies I saw at the party couldn't ruffle me if you tried. You tell me what sociology is and why it is necessary they draw salary."

"It is the study of people in groups—money, trends, codes, idols, taboos." With his rage still hot, he wanted to focus on *her* case, but subtly, subtly. "Class distinction, or sometimes just ordinary meanness."

She was quiet until they almost got to her big shaded Tudor redoubt. He wanted two quarts of Manhattans just for starters.

"In other words, nosy parasites without a life of their own," she said.

"All kinds, great and low like anywhere. Could I ask you"—
Edgar flipped by money, the room, the car, the stamps, clothes—
"has there been anything . . . unusually *terrible* in your life?"

"What? Why no!" He noticed in the rearview mirror that
when she scowled she was twice as ugly. "You're not using me to
study. You stick with the bums."

A man twelve years in prison wouldn't take a rim job from
you, he thought.

But he tried to set things back to the ordinary, crabbed as it
was. He parked out front. He'd run for supper. Hadley liked Chinese food, Mexican, or something from the deli. She liked cream and
pickled herring best, curious for an old Protestant woman. Edgar
wondered if some Jew in Savannah had given her a kind word once,
maybe he'd even loved her. Auntie's wild loss.

"Well phooey," she said, out before he could help. "You were
supposed to drive into the garage. There should be something in
there for you by now. It's something that looked good for you. I had
some advice."

Edgar walked to the garage. What would need a garage—
lawn mower, weed eater, leaf blower? Something meek and janitorial.

When he nicked on the light, he could hardly reckon on it.
It was a showroom-new, cream-colored BMW motorcycle. He was
knocked dumber when he recalled what they cost. The keys were in
it and he had to get on and drive, ho neighbors! But first he must see
his aunt.

She was at her Manhattan, watching the television news.

"Thank you. What does it . . . mean?" That she projects I'll
kill myself. But a new one wasn't required. He'd almost done it on
that piece of rolling bones an era ago.

"I thought about you lumbering in to park that Chrysler on
campus. Not really fit. I'm told these motorcycles are 'hot' with your
young professionals."

"I'm staggered. Thanks again."

"Get *on* the thing. Drive it, Edgar."

"Yes, I will."

"It must be a great fight, staying sober."

He was trying to see something of his father's face in Auntie Hadley's: a long-nosed projection of the nostrils, a gathering of the lips into a plump rabbit bite. Another animal was present, too, in the forehead and eyes: a monkey. Some breed rarefied by spite and terror, squawling from a nook in a rain forest. But his father's face was pleasantly usual, as in one of those old ads of a bus driver inviting you aboard, happy hills and vales ahead.

"Frankly, boy, I wish you were more interesting." She studied him back. "Your father really didn't give you much to shoot for, did he?" Could the troll guess he was thinking of his father? His regular face. His father was deferential, almost unctuous, and uncritical. He was all right, was his father, Oliver. He should see him soon.

His father was a newspaperman—no, that was too strong a word—whose regular column in the local paper was, essentially, one timid paragraph of introduction to a reprinted item of obscure history. The articles illustrated that people of the past were much like ourselves. He had little money, few other interests except choir, and viewed himself as a meek servant of the Big Picture. His only small vanity was in seeing his articles reprinted elsewhere every now and then. Edgar knew that outside the small-town antiquarian South, a larger newspaper would have pulled the trapdoor on his father and his monkish library work. His father had wanted to be a history teacher but could not face the classroom. In the forties, in fact, a huge bully of a student, smelling out his fear, beat him up. Hadley had dutifully reported this to Edgar when he was newly in the house. He was also informed that Sue, Edgar's mother, had always made more than her husband, doing the books of shops around town. She was a CPA. They were faithful moderate Methodists. His father— he hated this—sang in the church choir. He did not like him forming the big prayerful O's with his mouth, his eyes on the director, a sissy. The BMW was coming with a great tax. He felt murderous. He should have known.

"When men were realler, they drank for good reasons. Look at Grant and Churchill with their great wars. Look at Poe and Faulkner and Jack London and their masterpieces. Now you've got a national curse of drugs and drink, millions of nobodies who never once had a great day or a fine thought. This puny *selfism,* uff! It seems to me you became a drunkard just for lack of something to do. Just a miserable fad. No direction, no strong legs under you." She was building.

"Don't you want to add 'no intestinal fortitude'?" Edgar said helpfully, blazing inside.

"Now your proposed treatise or whatever, *Bums of.* Name your poison. Why, Lord, that's less a topic than a confession of *kin.* You want to go to school and still wallow with the wretched? Where's the merit? With your history, it seems you'd seek something higher for your interest. You'd have got a snootful of bums in the Depression. It took a Roosevelt and a world war to get them off the streets."

"I suppose"—this was the limit—"you labored greatly for your fortune and all was perfect with your marriages." Her first husband, by what Edgar knew, amassed his wealth in lumber and chickens by deliberate long hours away from her. The second, before he went willfully deaf, was something of a bonds genius. He built this vast house—for her, why?—then fled to a single basement room where he did woodwork with loud tools.

"You're a spiteful young person. And not very young. I was not idle. I guided their affairs, if you want to know. I had *presence* and spirit. Both your uncles had weak hearts and not very much will. I don't know why God matched me with such invalids, but that was what I got. I'm not the prettiest thing on the block."

Her voice had quieted to something like a lament. He wondered how deeply she believed herself. What was the truth? Maybe he was the last of her invalids. Maybe she must have them. When was she going to die?

"Well, about supper."

"I'm no good for supper now, thank you. Go ride your present. Ride it, please, with one thing in mind: your talent. I've read your letters, of course, and I saw your notes, scrambled as they are. You can write. You have seen trouble. You have conquered a great flaw. Now, Edgar, nobody has known it, but I have diaries. I have jotted histories of my time. I believe there would be a discerning audience for it. And you can write it."

"Write what?"

"My life. My life and times."

He turned and went to the motorcycle, still in his suit, drenched with perspiration and stinking of acrimony. The BMW seemed a nasty, irrelevant toy. A mighty vision shot to hell. But when he got it going down the streets, big beam out front, sweet cut grass smells flowing by, the wind whipping, he began to giggle. There it was: her patronage, her life as done by Edgar who could write no more at all. He drove on to Emma's. Why not?

He felt rangy, and much better. In the summer his work in the classroom went well. He knew many of the answers and seemed to have the good questions too. His more rural peers gave him some reverence. Some of them were hardly more cosmopolitan than the rube who sang about Kansas City in the musical *Oklahoma!*

Even better, Emma Dean seemed to be going for him. He recalled Snooky and tracked the difference. This time he had to do almost nothing. It was a rapid impassioning with young Emma—was she twenty-seven? But there was an unhappy strangeness to it on her part. She wanted him near, but it seemed she wanted him mournfully. The affair was making her sad. But Emma persisted: she bought him things, and slyly hinted at the times when Michael the Math Monster, who was deaf, would be out of the mobile home. She told him mysteries about the deaf and what they knew. What that permanent silence gave them—some claimed to hear music from heaven, or right from the brain.

One night in mid-June she was impatient and gloomy, yet suddenly she pulled off her dress. This "courting" could not go on forever—they weren't infants. She did cry out like a panther, bless her. Edgar was very happy, but she wept. She wouldn't tell him why, and he could only tenderly guess, remembering her history. He knew things would get better, more natural. Most stunning, though, was the certain knowledge she would be his last woman. The truth banged him with an enormous bright weight—at last things were in motion. He was very lucky to have her. And this time he would not destroy.

For Emma he improved *his* history, sometimes believing it. After the collapse of the band he said he'd become a long meditator. It did not necessarily mean failure. It was a long wait with a nobler design. He had shed material wants willingly and sought different, wholer, more authentic company. These phases were not unknown to many great men, not that he was great. But he felt a mission, and had for a long time.

The term *mission*, in regard to Auntie Hadley's request, still made him giggle, then snarl. He began writing even worse at school. He had never answered her. This was a petty and vile act, but it bought him his first taste of power in her petty and vile world. The only token in her land was cowardly muteness. Wasn't it cowardly, after all, to nag and bite like she did? Wasn't it the life choice of a nit? He pretended to be hurt by her comments against him and his family for much longer than he actually was. She was watching him cautiously now, and keeping her mouth shut more. It wouldn't do to offend the *author,* for nit's sake. Giggle. But he was not rotten enough to tell Emma about it. All in all, he couldn't get away from pity for his aunt.

"Let's go riding on the bike, you behind, Emma."

"But I'm afraid."

"You won't be. And let me suggest something—take off your underpants and wear a dress instead."

"Excuse me."

"Please do it. Women find a whole new world, I hear."

"Well, I'm all for that."

She was game, and by Lake Tornado, she was hugging him with delight, bountiful sighs going in his ear. He was sly. Nature was with him. She liked that he'd had a wife and was experienced. She told him he was a new man, all bronzed and straight, on the motorcycle. They would have times, good times. Yelling back, he assured her—*the* best time, he shouted. Ah, he was all gone for her now.

They'd told him at the ward, just hang on, hang on. Good things would come, eternal things. It was a law of recovery, tested millions of times.

Take it at the flood, then, Edgar Alien Po' Boy, which is what Emma now called him. Her love name. Oh, the wimmens, the wimmens. Their world—holy smoke!—and how he'd missed the light hands, the sly codes in the whole little city—its own language—they set up around you. The unexpected, priceless gifts, good nowhere but the city of love. "Give me some sugar," she said. How long since he'd heard that. Despite her Emory degree, summa cum laude, Emma stayed more the congenial truck-stop waitress, the charity that most got near him. Maybe because of her many brothers she understood the good-natured cuffing that men did and the brawny highway troubles behind them. She was a pal, a corker, a skit, handed to him. Pale fire burning through it all. With her, Edgar found, in some discomfort, that he could write better, he could wax forth. But she was always a bit sad, though she worked diligently with her deaf people in the institution south of Atlanta. It was not an unworthy mission—here we were—to alleviate suffering: find its cause, cut it off, and kill it, as General Powell said he'd intended with the Iraqi army in Kuwait. Emma was a great cheerleader of the war. Her patriotism was caught up. Democracy, freedom! Protection of our sand brothers. The tattoo on his throat—Emma'd never seen it, they made love with her glasses off—caused him no end of grief. For he felt Southern now: proud and brave with no irony or cynicism. Leave that to the hag in the Tudor dungeon.

Yet Emma stayed sad.

There was something in her he could not yet touch.

Nobody had said of this mission that the good things wouldn't be tough to get. He was with her a great deal. Good Michael the Math Monster, attuned quickly in his deafness, stayed out of the mobile home for long tracts of time. Edgar halfway moved in, while he worried about the feelings (and money) of his aunt.

After, at last, the long honest letter to his parents, Edgar shook with relief. They would go to Athens. It was time, and Emma agreed. He was gratified by her presence. He still did not feel worthy to meet them alone. Emma, a prize, would tell them he stood tall. A weak and dim man could not have her. A dim and weak man could not handle the BMW with this intelligent brunette frightened on the backseat. Deliberately he drove right into the racing ring-road fury of Atlanta traffic, cocky and weaving at seventy-five plus, envied. Emma almost died, a happy leech on his back. It was the city of her "ruin," but she laughed at it, another whole venue. A woman's shouts of pleasure could knock down buildings.

Athens had grown, of course. The university took in forty-five thousand now. Edgar got solemn when they rode into his block. He hadn't remembered his house as this unprosperous. It was stained from tree sap. The yard was shaggy. All this dereliction was unlike his father in the old times. Inside it smelled like used lives—corpus smells in the homes of the meek, hard to believe of one's people. His own smell was in there somewhere, he reckoned. But the chicory coffee his mother drank constantly—a special blend from the French Market in New Orleans—was sweet nostalgia. She'd cooked a raisin-apple pie for them, too.

For his advent, Edgar's folks—Oliver and Sue—had dressed up. His father wore a tie and the gray strands of his hair were nursed back. His mother had on a blue churchy dress. She had a lot of hair, but it was white, a grief to Edgar. What did he expect though? Athens was out there, doing better than they were, that was all. His dad moved slowly with arthritis of the feet. His mother seemed resolute on showing off her younger health, bouncing a little with her coffee cup.

It went much better than he'd hoped. A taste of the coffee—like a swat—filled him with a glow. They said he looked wonderful, all grown and mature, maybe taller. He almost forgot Emma. Out back with his father, they laughed about his aunt. Edgar played her as a more minor crank than she was and spoke of "paying her off when I head out on my own." On horn or in academe, his father wanted to know. Not the horn, Edgar said. His dad didn't understand: why couldn't Edgar recover it all? He was still young. What a gift, what years! Edgar turned and saw Emma with her coffee, not glad, eavesdropping from behind the kitchen door. The backyard was bleak, rutted with water drainage.

When he left, despite the small melancholy, Edgar felt fixed and relieved.

Emma did not. She didn't speak on the motorcycle all the way back. In Atlanta, he thought he heard her crying through the wind.

He was attentive and wanted to help. But it was a cruel night for Emma. She claimed her back hurt and he could tell she wanted him to go. She'd been hurt and made sad all over again; she didn't even try to smile. There was maybe even something like hate in her eyes. Well, Edgar Alien Po' Boy's out of here, he said. This got nothing from her. The mobile home looked glum, newly desperate, not the lake cabin it had seemed before.

At his aunt's he sat unbending from his trip snags. After a while he felt there was something different about his plush garret. Then he saw—how could he have missed them? Stacked neat and high on his desk were handsome purplish leather-bound books. There were two stacks, each two feet up—her diaries and "jottings." They made him angry. They were arrogantly under lock and key, but with the keys out for him to jump in and have a go. Hadley was away somewhere. He let go an uncommon obscenity. Then he went straight to bed.

At breakfast she was on him before he could dart to class an hour early. Quietly, more like a human being, she began.

"Edgar, one thing I notice about your graduate studies: you don't really do that much. You've time for all kinds of things. I've seen your motorcycle at Emma Dean's . . . place, more than a few times."

He resented this, and braced. But she wasn't her old self. He frankly liked her pleading.

"You, if you could just do a *bit* of work every day, say two hours, on our book. You could make your own notes and start the outline, almost idly. Do the readings. I'm offering you treasured, secret views of a heart and mind that has been through crucial times. You never knew, for instance, that *I* had my day with music, did you? Not your noisy success, not your . . . bubble. My time was milder and private as girls were taught. Why, I'd play an afternoon triumph of Chopin, there would be Father, sneaking in to listen in the hall. He'd have tears running down his cheeks. Too, I did dollwork, their porcelain faces showing history and nationality when there was no world consciousness in Georgia at all. They're still in the attic for you to see. And I will be constantly available for you to consult. I've bought a new tape recorder, which is of course yours after our interviews are done. I've completed an outline. We can compare outlines once—"

The horror! as Edgar Alien Po' Boy might have written, grabbed him.

"I was no mean student, nephew, but in composition I couldn't quite express myself, though I was excellent in elocution. Ethical elocution—I was the star there. My first husband dragged me from college. There was heartbreak. Big moments in the sun were probably waiting for me! But love, love, was the order of the day. Edgar, I'm not going to live forever, I wouldn't think."

Was that a frightened giggle, a voice from a little girl in her horse-drawn carriage?

"Academic people, I've noticed, will delay things *forever*. Why, I sent some things to the press at Athens years ago. It took a year to get them back, and with a *beastly* note, beastly."

Edgar became, though sickened, interested in the long confession. Here was a sick glee, close to a great pop of vodka in a rushing airplane.

"In Savannah, old Savannah!, there were gay times. Homosexuals *won't* steal that term! There were lanterns on the levee indeed. I was good with horses. What a picture, I on my roan Sweetheart on the way to third grade in the city! Horses were thought elegant, a whole culture gone with the wind! Stephen Crane wrote *The Red Badge of Courage* in ten days, I believe. Not that you, with all our source material—seventy-three years! But Edgar, you are falling *behind*. I won't watch you do that again! You've a degree from one of our great universities."

"I'll read and form an opinion," said Edgar flatly with ire.

"Further, it would be all right, I would allow, to have Miss Dean stay here with you. You can have a larger room—Hank's, with his special woodwork, and a television, too, and his Victrola, unused since his deafness. I'm no prude. I can modernize. I don't want you at that trailer. A man needs pleasure, but in the right place. I'll put in the large couch with a fold-out. We'll get right to it. Shelley had *his* muse."

"Didn't she write *Frankenstein*?"

You couldn't get to the old thing anymore. She just faded away.

That night, Emma still in grief, he sat his horn cases on his desk next to the books. He didn't know quite what he was doing. Both things made him sick. He stared a long time, judging the contest.

At the end of the summer after two major exams, essay-type, the chairman called him in. Edgar liked him. No great achiever either in the classroom or in research (though there was a rumored thin book, *When God Was a Boy,* they said), Schmidt cheered the worthy and had no envy. He said Edgar looked good, but there was a problem.

"Your prose style. Your writing. We don't see that kind much. I agree academe needs shaking, but there is a sort of . . . grunt-talk, a primitive getting-there. Seems almost to cause you . . . pain. And some to the reader. Now I am a Hemingway fan, a Raymond Carver *zealot,* but are you trying something *new,* dimensional, I don't know, would this fit the bums' world, is that what?"

"No, sir. I'm not trying anything that I'm aware of."

"This is your best?"

"I'm looking for an awakening, I guess. In the old days at Northwestern, though, I could write better."

"Then we'll just root for you. I appreciate your honesty. We want to get life and expression together. Isn't that the whole point?"

"Sure."

"The example of pain into flowers, ho?"

Edgar nodded.

"Because very soon it's thesis time for you. There are outside readers."

Peets Lambert and his band came into town, out from seeming nowhere. Lambert was still alive. Someone called Edgar from the college and said Lambert had left tickets for him in the chapel where they'd play. The student coordinator later said Lambert was very cordial and, whoa, eighty-five years old. It had been almost twenty years since Edgar first played with the band. Lambert remembered him well and wanted to chat after the concert. The student, who knew Edgar, said Lambert wanted to know everything about him and had even driven by his aunt's house, but had found nobody home the previous afternoon.

Edgar, Emma and Auntie Hadley went together. Emma thought it would be cruel not to invite her. She'd love big band swing. This would be quite the sentimental evening for everybody! Obscurely, Emma had gotten happy again.

And swing it was. Snooky wasn't there, nor anybody near her age. Lambert had brought back some of his old friends including

Woodrow and settled for what he could get on the nostalgia circuit—
hence La Grange. By far he was the leading ancient, but several in
the band were close. They had a bad singer, and no one looked particularly happy in their black suits. The playing was sloppy and sometimes verged on the funereal. But Lambert hammed and was hip,
very, like a confident ghost pawing at the band. Surprisingly, Edgar
sat through it calmly. It *was* a sort of music, and he did not hate it,
he was not made ill. To his left, he saw his aunt looked very pleased.
Her eyes seemed to be swooning back in her biography. The band
played a Charleston, capping with the bad singer, the only leaping
youth in the band. The students who were there—not many—liked
it, they were charmed.

So when the band was breaking up, Edgar and Emma went
backstage, which barely existed. There was Lambert, alone, un-
mobbed, smoking a cigarette but looking guilty, same as years ago.
The old cancer thinness was on him, his face speckled and translu-
cent on its skull. He lit up when he saw Edgar.

"I know you, my 'boner. Oops, sorry little lady!" His naughty
hipness was imperishable, sealed with him. He wasn't missing a
thing with those eyes. Edgar wondered if his hearing, however, had
dimmed.

He drew Edgar in, slipped into an undervoice—old collab-
orators—a few feet away from Emma, who was not really shut out.
Lambert smiled over Edgar's shoulders, always a dog for the wimmens. He told Edgar about Snooky, mother of two in Dallas. Parton
Peavey had cleaned up and as everybody knew was a "rich old man,
nearing the big four-oh." Edgar was downed a little by how much
they had aged.

"You guys didn't know, but I invested for all of you, us, the
cats, way back then. Young people, all they thought of was their axes.
So there's a piece of your salary you never saw. So, beautiful, it's
come to, da-dum, something big and tidy."

Edgar jumped, very alert. He planned suddenly: cash in one
bundle back to his aunt. A made man, he'd get his own place and fix
up his parents' house. He would buy an island, where? Emma would
continue to work among the native deaf and he, what? He'd come
out with a large thing from his meditative years.

"After what I did for you, I know you'll sign it back to me. Parton Peavey, Smith, Snooky, no problem, they all did. You can see that I and the band, we needs the bread. Verily."

Edgar, first raised, now bumped the wretched bum's pavement.

"How much was it?"

"Near sixty thousand apiece. A hundred, near, for our legend Peavey. Isn't that great? I brought the pen. You know what I did for you?"

Edgar signed three lines as Lambert held out the stock transfer.

"The band goes on. I can afford a casket." Lambert winked. "Good young people making the band go on. Woodrow takes it when I'm planted. Your funds, Big Thunder Hounds Foundation, huh? Not even really for me, get it? Look at me."

"Yes, sir."

"And I saw that house where you live yesterday. Not gone with the wind, ho? The wind has come back and put you in a castle. Edgar, Edgar, I'm hating this, but could you spare me a little? A couple thou. What I did for you when you were a baby, remember. Times are rough. You can see. I'd never have seen you, chicken and peas La Grange, man—"

"I don't have any money."

"House-poor, huh? But a little scratch—the things I did for you—you cost me, the bus . . ."

Edgar moved away. Lambert was in a fit of his own virtue. Stooped and angry, Edgar caught Emma's arm and they ran to where his aunt was waiting in the foyer, caught in the act of giving the snoot to a couple of ladies peeking who (Edgar wished) spit at Lambert's Wall Street Crash music.

"What's this rushing?" his aunt wanted to know. They were in the car before Emma told her.

"Edgar has just lost a great deal of money he didn't know he had."

Emma's work with the deaf must have given her some kind of ears, Edgar grieved.

"Oh, yes. The music's wonderful for a while. But your musicians are notorious bankrupts," said his aunt.

"They're just 'bubbles,' aren't they?" He smashed at her.
"Exactly what I said. My generation always knew that."

By Christmas break, things had changed only for Emma. She had blitzed through her work and was taking the master's. Her thesis on the deaf was heralded and would be published, with the help of her major professor, her major herald. Edgar didn't know she was this good. She even got a small advance—one thousand—from publishers in New York, and was hounded instantly for it by her father, from the school of You Owe. All eight of his children owed him for their lifelong hard times. Emma gave him seven hundred.

They remained passionate, but she would not move to Hadley's house. Edgar was glad. They did make love, though, on the sofa a few times. She opened his horn cases one morning and peered at the freckled and scarred instruments a long time. They seemed to make her angry. Without a word, she left the house and drove away in the Japanese wreck she'd bought.

He was baffled by her sadness, which was turning more into anger nowadays. She would clam up and sometimes beat her fists on whatever was near, including once, his thighs. She had a television and watched the war news through January. She liked to turn up the speech of the generals and said she had a crush on Powell.

The terrible day he went into the trailer, February was ending with a big blow that made the pines *whoo* and shiver, spooky, warning the homes on wheels beneath them. There had been, during the morning, a burst water main up the road, catching the whole trailer park without water. Emma had been busy cleaning with Lysol, and was outraged by the stoppage. She was in a torrent when he entered, with good news, he thought. Inspired by her, he was well into a book about Chicago bums. He could write again, and what he had was so good that the chairman was trying to get him a large grant to revisit his old haunts. It would be enough to take Emma with him. It was not a bad city at all. Away from the South, she might be happier— holy smoke, why shouldn't she? She'd never left it. There was her depression, itself.

Edgar sat on the sprung bunk she slept on, petting her. He told her about bums.

For many years, he and female drunks had simply wound up together. He had a place. They just appeared in it, no memory of having got there, isolated by the blazing nimbus of alcohol. The woman might even be sober, some pitying angel on the spoor of a heartbroken man. You could not be awful enough for some women: they were stirred by emaciation, destitution, whiskey whiskers, bus fumes. For other women you could not get foreign enough. Witness Clem, the acned Iranian sot, always with a beauty queen. Some black women were greatly attracted to downed white men. What wild loyalties he'd seen when he'd been sober enough to notice. You had Commies, capitalists (ruined, but adhering), even monarchists, in bumhood. Take away the sickness, he had loved a good deal of the life. He even missed being insane, sometimes. The world matched his dreams some days. Something, a small good thing, almost always turned up. He missed making the nut of drink every day. He missed the raddled adventures. There always was a focus: securing the next high, defending the hoard of liquor money, but with chivalry; getting through the day without murder; being a world citizen, voting and passionate, about the headlines off some fat cat's newspaper. What about the exploratory raptures of one's own liquored mind? The drunkard, or bum, was not wasting his mind all the time. He was going deeper in than others: great lore, buzzing insights. The conversation frequently was above the university. Some few bums were *renuncios*. They had given up the regular world on purpose, and could explain why in long wonderful stories, each one distinct, bravely of no category or school. He'd also met deaf bums, of course. He knew more about them than she'd thought. He knew the blind, too—what stories he could tell about Rasta Paul!

Emma listened closely, having stopped her tears long ago. She seemed avidly sympathetic, her pretty mouth open, her dress falling off her shoulders like a flushed senorita's, carelessly revealing those breasts that shot warmth through his manhood. Her eyes met his, and it was off with her spectacles and dress, on the bunk in a minute.

Hang in, all good things will come, Edgar remembered. Even his reverie about Sally, the doctor's wife, lived out long and more on that dirty mattress, a single lightbulb shaking over it. Never had Emma been this carnal. She threw herself into long rituals of defilement, yes. Begged him to take her back there, as never before, and then she was on him with her mouth lest he finish without her tasting it all. She hurled back and forth, then out with her legs, voracious. The panther cry came, rose and fell, rose again. Then she suddenly cast him off, screaming no, no, no, no, no! Immediately she began to cry. She reached and put her spectacles back on, peering first at his naked chest, then at his throat.

"What the *hell* does that tattoo mean? I never saw that! There's a war on. Are you for that monster we're fighting?! Our generals, our airmen—they're men, and you, you don't have . . . *moxie, moxie*—that's it! Your aunt keeps you! Peets Lambert kept you! You ungrateful *bitch!* You're *gothic,* Edgar!"

This was terror. She wouldn't quit.

"You won't even play the horns—your natural God-given ticket! No, crowds get to you, weak bitch! Memory gets you! You drag me to your pitiful parents, and I saw the nowhere, the awful never, of you all. But I had to be there to prop you up! Your significant thing, your meditated thing, I've screwed, sucked, let you . . . You've even got gray, waiting, on somebody else's motorcycle!"

And, before the dish came at him,

"Now your bums, your magical romantic bums. The deaf don't *have* a choice, Mister Chicago. And let me tell you something else. After this book, the deaf aren't going to *be* my life. I've done them, I'm tired. I'm too *selfish,* if you've got to know! It's *my* time. I can't help it. I want healthy people, and rich, traveling people, happy *doing* kings and princes. But I had to love *you.* Love you, I *know,* more than you do me! How could you?"

She kneeled and brought up a bowl of Lysol and threw it in Edgar's face. The pain was so horrible, the act so sudden, that he simply laid out his arms and rocked, before his hands came up on their own and dragged at his eyes. He was conscious of her running back and forth in the trailer. But there was no water, not there or in any trailer around them. It was a long, long time before she had him, naked, in her Toyota wreck. Something went wrong with it, though, and it stopped. He was blind. He was probably good and blind before she, having raced around desperately for ditch water, opened the radiator for its fluid and came to him with a few drops of it, sprinkling some on his eyes. It tasted like antifreeze.

When he left the hospital ten days later, he had only a speck of vision, low in his left eye.

Emma had never left him, and implied her remaining life in this act.

"I'll never leave you, Edgar," she crooned, over and over.

She never discussed anything with Auntie Hadley or him. She would be there at the house with him forever, or wherever, she said. Emma had real power in her guilt. The aunt might be flabbergasted, but Edgar couldn't see things like that now. He never heard an incautious opinion from his aunt anymore. Emma said, indeed, that the woman was being sweet, real sweet. He could hear them in conference. They seemed to be agreeing about almost everything. Emma allowed the aunt to buy her clothes. She described them to Edgar, meekly delighted. All he could see were the new Paris shoes.

Her love for him, he felt, went on past the penitential, which he, manly, protested many times. She swore it was not so, not in the least. Horrible as it was, throwing Lysol at him had been an act that told her where she belonged. He could not know how much she loved him. That thing about kings and princes was just the last of her daydreamy youth shouting itself out.

Edgar asked for his valved Bach trombone. It didn't really taste like whiskey at all. He practiced it awhile. Blind men had come forth beautifully in jazz. His aunt's hand was on his shoulder, appreciative.

One day his parents came with a present of Lambert's latest swing record, a minor hit. They said it brought back memories. Edgar loved them desperately, and he could hear the kind Emma celebrating his progress as they left, meaning to visit often. It was all delightful, but the horn itself was no go. It was as if he'd never touched one. There was weakness in his chest, not from the healed sternum, but something more. He just couldn't. He cried a little. It was mainly for Emma, anyway. He didn't want her to see him cry. In fact, he was glad he was no good.

He'd gotten the grant. Emma was ready to lead him in Chicago, back to the old haunts, anywhere. Handicaps very often increased being, she said. Such people were called the "differently abled" nowadays.

Edgar had never wanted to go back to Chicago. That wasn't his item, his thing.

Once, a month blind and just sitting there, seeing if he could read a long speck in one of Hadley's diaries, he came across something from 1931: "I . . . am . . . made . . . all . . . different . . . I . . . can't . . . enjoy . . . anything . . . God . . . you . . . my . . . husband . . . pokes . . . at . . . me . . . I . . . am . . . angry . . . feel . . . there . . . is . . . a . . . dangerous . . . snake . . . down . . . there . . . not . . . him . . . me . . . before . . . he . . . got . . . there . . . God . . . help . . . me."

Hadley made a movement. She was next to him, on a wooden chair. Emma was away. Auntie Hadley started whispering about Milton and that "Argentina man," and Helen Keller's triumphant books.

"Milton was years preparing for his life's work—what a paradise regained for us all, Edgar. His daughters served him and took his dictation. I can have all this *brailled* for you. You could then dictate and Emma would surely help. She is *all* you. You are luckier than your ugly aunt, in many ways."

"Actually, the blind can write," said Edgar suddenly.

"A whole new world. 'They also serve who stand and wait.' But you wouldn't have to wait anymore."

Edgar grinned. She'd not seen him grin. He knew something deep and merry, the exact ticket.

"Your physical needs are all covered. Then there's my will, after I . . . and a big sum for the book. And all the instruments, of course, for composition."

"Do something for me, Auntie. Would you put Lambert's record on the Victrola so we can listen together? The past, swing, times forgotten."

She played it and sat, not a squeak.

God, the band was wretched, and yet they'd come round again with a hit. You never knew.

He screwed up his mouth when it was done, tongue against his teeth, watching Hadley's foot bounce to this *merde*, holy smoke!

He told her there would be a declaration when Emma came back. He wanted a gathering. This was a big moment for him.

Emma sat, a Manhattan like Hadley's in her hand, at six-thirty that evening. They told him it was snowing out even though it was early April—so very rare and lovely and ghostly quiet. The town was filling up and mute. A beloved merchants' calamity thrilling the young at heart.

"All right, let's get started. A real book knows everything. Let's clear the air in two ways. First, Auntie Hadley, to get modern, when did you first know you were a *shit?* Was it a sudden revelation, what? When did it arrive that you were and would be, *awful?* Next, we of the addicted *must* write letters of amends to everybody alive. Maybe even to the dead. I want to hear that pen scratching near me while I'm at my work, sweetie. This needn't take forever, though the sheer amount of paper will be staggering."

There was silence before she acquiesced. Did he hear something moist and flowing from her?

"Emma, dear." He himself began crying. "I release you body and soul. Don't need no cellmate, not even no lovin', till the old opus is done. Think it over then. Have at the kings and princes."

Why was he so happy, so profoundly, almost, delirious?

Loud and bright and full of jazz, *Rat-Face Confesses*—that would be the title of their book.

Scandale d'Estime

THEY WERE DESTROYING A THEATER IN KOSCIUSKO, AND MY FATHER bought the bricks. He had made a good deal. He asked me and a buddy of mine to live there a while in a hotel to stack the unbroken bricks for him and load them on a truck.

We were, my buddy and I, probably seventeen. We read *Downbeat* magazine and knew a few Dylan Thomas poems, which seemed to us as good as poetry could get. Horace was the better reader and memorized poems whole. There was a small college in our town, and we knew some of the younger faculty who had left in despair and irony over the puritan expectations of it. As they had been able to talk about upwards of three books, we considered them great poetic souls. I wish there were a good term for the zeal we felt for these older hip brethren, which included one stylish lady named Annibell: *cats* almost got it, when the Beats and jazzers established themselves. Those who got the joke and continued on with their private music. A personal groove.

Now and then there was a question of what we should do with the new women in our heads. You might go out with some local girl, but she was not really there, she was not the real faraway city woman in your cat head. You might kiss her and moil around—but she was, you knew, fifth string, a drear substitute for the musical woman in a black long-sleeve sweater you had in your mind on the seashore of the East—the gray, head-hurting East, very European to my mind, where you thought so much and the culture labored so heavy on you your head hurt. The beauty and the wisdom of this woman—uttered along the seashore in weary sighs—was a steady dream, and I woke with it, pathetically, to attack a world fouled by the gloomy usual. I yearned to talk and grope with a woman who was exhausted by the world and would find me a "droll" challenge. She would be somewhat older. She either sighed, or mumbled pure music. I had no interest in the young freshness of girls at all.

Every brick I unearthed from the dust and chalky mortar, cleaning it off with a steel brush and wet flannel rag—which made my hands red and sliced with little lines all over—became part of the house I was building in my mind for this woman. New York Slim they would call her. The house would be on the seashore, where you could look out the window and sigh in a big way. For her, even a special sighing room.

The old hotel we stayed in had rail balconies on the inside floors where you could lean and look down into not much of a lobby, your feet on a gone tan carpet.

It felt good to be tired and cut up at the end of the day, just showered and looking down at the lobby with your hair slick. You felt you were a working man. I had a red kerchief tied around my neck like a European working man, all shot with working blood. A whole new energy came through you. This was before I began to drink and smoke, and I would not feel like this, clean and worthy and nicely used in the bones, for many more times, for a great long while. The only problem was that there was absolutely nothing to do. The town might have been named for a Polish patriot who led American troops in the Revolutionary War, but the glory just mocked you in a town where shops slammed shut at five to prevent any history whatsoever beyond twilight. We had no car and had read all the magazines backward. There was a bare courtesy light bulb at the bus station, and we actually went to stand beneath it, hoping to invite life. But nothing. A man who hated to move ran a restaurant up the way and we soon got tired of his distress. Nobody even played checkers there. Gloomy John Birch literature would fall off the checkout counter, and there were flags bleached to pink and purple in a bottle on it too, seeming to represent a whole other nasty little country.

I leaned and watched the lobby for New York Slim to walk in, lost in Kosciusko, Miss., and looking for me. I would look at my watch and curse fate, giving her just a few more minutes. Then I would curse her and tell her I was through. Natalie Wood, or more probably her cousin from the South, Lee Wood, would come instead. I had seen *West Side Story* that year, and Natalie was slowly replacing New York Slim. When New York Slim did finally get here, there would be hard words, tears, and it would be tough to tell her she had lost everything—the brick house on the seashore, the sighing room, my drollness, everything—and that I was giving it all over to one of the Miss Woods. There was nothing I could do about it I'd say, it was an *affaire de coeur,* sorry. The fact is I was going mildly insane. I peered harder into the lobby. All you saw was a solitary whiskered gruff man, probably retired, not even reading a magazine, but looking straight ahead in a sort of shocked anger that put some fear into you. He was not the denizen of an interesting passionate play by T. Williams, as you might hope, but a horrified sufferer of age bound to a colorless tunnel, as if his stare were tied in a knot at the end of it. His face was spotted red, from waiting, I thought. Someday he would just disappear into the wallpaper, which also had red spots in it. Though he'd been without applicants for a long time, in my mind I made him into a smoldering corrupter of the young. We never said a word to him.

In my own town a man named Harold, old enough to be a teacher, was attending the college. Harold, who lived in an attic apartment, was balding and already a man with a heavy if not lengthy past. He had been drafted during the Korean War but had not gone over there with the army until the truce was signed, so that his adventures in the East, for which he had made a lurid album he showed me, were all done in peacetime. The photographs showed a bunch of men in fatigues hanging around in squads, the usual thing, but then there was a whole woman section too. Harold was still in love with these Asian women—I believe they were Japanese—from around where he was stationed. But I had never met a man in love this way, this very meticulous strange way. One of the women had her legs

open, and Harold had pasted a straw flat on the photograph running off the picture to the margin and a small photo of his own face.
The straw went from her private parts into his very mouth. He had
written *More, More, More!* in the margin. I had seen a few pictures of
naked women, but this one drew me back again and again, especially
when Harold was out of the room, because I had never seen a woman
so seriously and happily showing herself. A dark riot of nerves came
over me when I saw her face, so agreeable to the camera. Harold
was a very thin man with white hairy forearms, just weak sticks, and
narrow in the chest, also hairy above his shirt opening. It must have
been a time when American GIs were overwhelmingly popular over
there. Harold did not seem like a man who could support this weird
Asiatic "love," yet there were other women—none of them whores,
he pointed out—who had loved him, and were also photographed
coiled around Harold. Some were full naked or not, and some were
playing with each other, happy. Their eyes were all for Harold, who
gleamed brightly into the camera, younger and more prosperous
than now, a bitter student on the GI Bill.

Harold was a smoker of those short cork-tipped but unfil-
tered Kools. He wore black high-top sneakers, decades before they
were necessary, with irony, for artistics everywhere. The startling
denominator in Harold was that he was capable of great passions
high and low. I saw him stare at the woman on the street below his
place, an abandoned woman I found out later, who walked the bricks
smoking a long cigarette in a holder. I've never seen so much smoke
come out of a person. She would walk slowly along in the regular fog
of a ghostly cinema, staring ruefully at the brick streets. She was the
daughter of a town scion, a remarkable chemistry prof who was also
the mayor, and lived with him on the other side of the block. But her
lot was lonesome and bereft. She was one of those women who'd
had a single lifetime catastrophe and never recovered, beautiful for
the tragedies of T. Williams but now almost unheard of, when everybody joins something and gets well.

"She needs me," Harold spoke, watching her with deep concern. "That woman needs my love, and here I am selfishly with-
holding it from her." But Harold, I thought, she's the *mother* of one
of my classmates—she's very, very old. Harold went on condemning

himself for not stepping out to the curb and offering his "love" to her. Her son, my elder contemporary, was a person of almost toxic brilliance, scowling and reviling any collection of people in every room I ever saw him in. Another friend later explained that the woman died of a heart attack in that same house, with her son, then an MD, attending. Or rather, more just technically witnessing, as my friend had it, using chilly terms like *infarction* and *fibrillate*. Then she was gone—*bam*, he had said, as he struck his palm with a fist. I saw the wide and high Victorian house as a place of almost epic coldness, a hint of sulphur in the rooms. Harold stayed at the sill, hanging in the window between thought and act, the shadow on a film always in my head, like a ghost on a negative.

Harold found most learning at the college "morbid" and would declaim hotly how desperately much he did not want to know zoology, Old Testament and history. But he was here exploring the "possibles and necessaries," vaguely of the arts, "doomed to Southern history." "Oh God, yes I must *read* it, the obituaries of everybody I despise." He had a personal contempt for anybody who had ever made a public dent in anything. Fame and battles bored him—all species of dementia. Harold despised so much, you felt very lucky for his friendship. What he liked best were small, troubled people. His passion for the Asian women seemed conditional, almost, on the enormous trouble they had known. Harold attended every play, concert, reading, art opening, and recital at the college and in the adjoining capital city, and found almost everything "unbearably poignant." He was all for the arts, the more obscure the better. His friends, besides me and two other pals with their "maturity of vision," he'd call it, were all girls of forlorn mark. Too fat, too nervous, too skinny, too scattered for talk in this world's language. These he would play bridge with in the college grill. If your back was to them and you didn't know, you'd have thought they were all girls. Harold loved low gossip and considered scandal the only evidence of true existence on this morbid plain. His voice would go girlish too, more girlish sometimes than that frequent effeminacy you heard from mama- and maid-raised boys. The college was a harbor for great sissies. You'd turn around and see all the hair on his pale, skinny arms and think, well golly, that's Harold, old veteran Harold. The full Harold to me, though, would be him looking down at that abandoned wife, on the old brick street, afternoon after afternoon, hating himself for all his "wretched hesitations," saying she needed him, and that he was a cad not to "venture unto her, take her hand." Wretched hesitation, Harold said, is what embalms our lives, and that was what age demanded of you more and more, to get less and less life. But he was passionately involved in all the troubles of the odd girls he escorted to the grill, and they had a clique around him. It never occurred to me that Harold was sleeping with them, but an older guy much later told me that most assuredly he was. I could think of Harold then, a teacher of history, with another album of his women, and I could see these troubled girls, naked and happy—Harold's harem, holding out against this "morbid waterless plain," as he called the environs.

A few scandals at the college made Harold beam and emerge from his habitual state, which was, I think I can say, a kind of expectant gloom. A luster came on him when it was clear the speech and drama teacher—who had kept one of his male protégés, a prominent sissy, in lust bondage—had gone down to scandal, and packed up, leaving in the night. Harold's pale hairy arms flailed out and back, delighted, up to the neck in it. "Oh, the truth and beauty of a wrecked life, nothing touches it!" he went, imagining the moment-by-moment excruciations of the discovered pederast. The drama master, driving lonely and flushed in his car back to North Carolina. Then there was the milder, but somehow more "evocative" disclosure regarding the tall Ichabodish French teacher, a curiously removed (how! they learned) man, who drove a giant old blue Cadillac that seemed even larger than Detroit intended. This timid man oozed about in something between a hearse and a cigarette boat. His exposure came about when his landlord opened his rooms one holiday. Everywhere in the room were Kleenexes and castaway plastic bags from the cleaners. He would touch nothing in the room without a Kleenex. He had his socks and underwear dry-cleaned, and wore them straight from the bags. Unused clothes were stacked in their bags in the corner. Kleenex was all over the bedsheets. He could not touch the telephone, doorknob, faucet, or even his own toothbrush without them. Kleenex boxes towered in all nooks and closets. In his diary, there was a last sobbing entry: "Night and day,

I detect moisture around my body. Must act." He was, this French prof, comprehensively germophobic, and the strange order of his disorder howled from the room. Probably this was not even a scandal, but in this small Baptist town with the landlord so loud about it, the professor too was reduced, and soon prowled away in shame. Harold relished this. The perfection of it almost silenced him, a silly eye-shut dream on his face. "The perfection, the perfection, of this." Every worthy life would have a scandal, Harold said. There was a central public catastrophe in the life of every person of value. The dead sheep, the masses, who lived fearful of scandal (though feeding off it in nasty little ecstasies) were their own death verdict. "Prepare, prepare, little man, for your own explosion," he told me sincerely. "I am trying to be worth a scandal myself." Oscar Wilde enchanted him, and Fatty Arbuckle, but not Mae West, who had worn scandal like a gown and made a teasing whole career of it.

I once was sent over to the college by my English teacher to pick up a tape recorder, and was making as long a trip out of it as I could, when I passed a class and saw Harold in the back row, looking down at his desk in silent rage, not as if baffled but as if understanding too much, and personally offended. But this was less noticeable than what he wore. I had simply caught him out of his house in the act of being Harold, gritting his teeth, twirling his pencil, hissing. He had on an old-fashioned ribbed undershirt, some floppy gray-green pants, and some sort of executive shoes, I think banker's wingtips, with white tube workman's socks. His hair curled out everywhere from his pale skin. At this college they were stern on dress code. But they left Harold alone, I saw. He did look piercing and untouchable, his Korean near-veteranship a class of its own. They did love the Christian soldier, which he was not, but he had absolute freedom nonetheless as a lance corporal of Section 8. I was very happy for him. He had real dignity in his undershirt of the kind big-city Italians and serious white trash wore. The best thing was that he was unconscious of being out of line at all. It was hard to imagine Harold charging in the vanguard, or even hiding in a frozen hole, against the Communists in Korea, with his ascetic thinness, his hairy arms and chest, thrown against some garlicky horde and their bugles. Harold was not a coward, I'm sure, but I saw another thing suddenly about him, this partisan of Wilde and Errol Flynn: Harold was maybe doomed to no scandal of his own at all. He was too open, too egregious (a word I assure you I didn't know then) to have one, especially there in his undershirt in the fifties. But he wanted one so badly, and one for all his friends like me. He fed wistfully on the few scraps thrown his way in our dull society.

When the symphony director and several doctors and lawyers were tracked down and filmed by city police in the old city auditorium —usually a venue for wrestling—preening in women's underwear and swapping spit, Harold howled "Impeccable!" He hoped, he wanted so, for them all to be driven to the city limits sign and hurled out in shame down a notch of high weeds, their red panties up between their white buttocks. An M.D. was exposed in a zealous ring of coprophiliacs, sharing photographs at parties centering on soiled diapers. "There is a god! God is red!" In Harold's senior year, here came a lawyer exposed for teen pornography, hauling girls over state lines. Again Harold trembled, but there was always a bit of sadness that he himself was not cut down and hauled off—he loved most the phrase "spirited away"—for some dreadful irredeemable disclosure.

Harold never worried himself about the life *after* scandal. He indicated that he was, in fact, carrying on lugubriously after a lurid bomb in his past (not *the* bomb, but a bomb), but I think he was playing me false, for the first time. He wanted it so much, and lived from one minor scandal to the next, but as I say, I never expected him to be blindsided by disclosure after I saw him that day when I was seventeen. I got the sudden sense of Harold as finished, even though he was shy of thirty, too transparent and happy in his sins. He would never get the *scandale d'estime* he so wanted. I had even thought that Harold wanted badly to be gay—queer, we said then—but could not bring it off. He was a theater queer around me sometimes, but you knew he couldn't cross over the line, it wasn't made for him, or he for it.

Harold was one of the few around who knew about the existence of Samuel Beckett, and he hailed the man, perfectly ordered in his obliquity for Harold—an Irishman close to Joyce, veteran of the French underground, who lived in Paris, wrote in French, and had absolutely no hope. Drama couldn't get any better than *Waiting for Godot,* whose French title he would call out now and then like a charm, appropriate to nothing at hand I could see. Harold felt *Godot* was written in "direct spiritual telepathy" to veterans of Korea. He skipped nicely over the fact he never fought the war and I could agree that he was a telepathic cousin to them, because Harold was not, whatsoever, a phony. I was always struck by the fact he felt so sore and deep about particular people, and I felt dwarfish in my humanity, compared with him. Harold had seen *Godot* in Cambridge, and when it began playing in the South he drove his squat-rocket, mange-spotted ocher Studebaker far and wide to cities and college campuses to view it again. He would do the same for *West Side Story,* which he regarded as the highest achievement in musicals, ever. He saw the movie a number of times. Sometimes he'd take one or more of the odd girls with him, and once he asked me. He intended to drive all the way to Shreveport to see it again. He said I would see the kind of girl I wanted to marry in Natalie Wood and would hear the music of one of America's few uncontested geniuses, Leonard Bernstein. Then we would dip back to see a production of *Godot* in Baton Rouge, which, he warned, I was not really old enough for but needed because even a dunce could tell it was "necessary" for any sensate member of the twentieth century.

My mother was not enchanted. She was not happy about my trip with Harold, and much unhappier when she saw him, balding and with one of those cork-tipped Kools in the side of his mouth, behind the wheel of that car. I was a little embarrassed myself, because my folks put high stock in a nice car, and Mother was very sincere about appearances. I had told her Harold had ulcers, though I don't know how it came up. But when she said "He shouldn't smoke with those ulcers," I could tell she was much concerned by more than that. Neither was Harold throwing any charm her way. He never had the automatic smarm and gush in the kit of most Southern men at introduction. I knew he was too experienced for that, but Mother didn't like that he was a Korean near-vet, this old, just now going to college, and my friend. I waited for him to light up with just a bit of the rote charm, but he wouldn't. He looked bored and impatient, thinking probably she owed him thanks for taking this probationary brat off her hands for a weekend. I was conscious that she thought he might be queer, so I just told her outright he wasn't.

"Harold has *many* women," I said, picking up my bag. She looked at me more suspiciously than ever. I just piled in, we left, and I was unsettled five ways as this rolling mutant of the V-2 went off simpering with its weak engine. Harold said nothing to cheer me up. Then he finally spoke, across the bridge after Vicksburg.

"Your father's a very lucky man."

"You know him?"

"No, fool. Your mother's fine, A-plus fine. I'd die for her. A woman like that loved me, I'd cut off an arm."

Again, Harold seemed to be talking way beyond his years, and I believe now he must have thought of himself as extremely old. But it was the first time I realized my mother was a well-dressed, finely put together woman, and I began looking at her anew after that. Harold sat so wordlessly in silhouette in the car—I wondered if he was stunned and *putting the make on her.* With my *mother.* What impeccable depravity, as he might have said.

I had a little dance combo at the high school. Harold had come to see us, and he bragged on my trumpet playing, many notes and very fast, but, unfortunately, no soul. Soul might come to me if I was patient, he said. It could happen to Southern boys, look at Elvis, and he went on to call Roy Orbison much better than Elvis. You must hear *that* voice, he said, but he failed to get it on the lousy scratching radio. What came in almost solid was a special kind of Studebaker music, mournful like somebody calling over another lost radio. He predicted men like that were going to make horns obsolete shortly, and Harold was dead right. By the time I finished college, nobody wanted to hear anything but guitar and voice. Even pianos were lucky to get a chip in here and there. I was destroyed by the absolute triumph of the greasers, the very class I and my cronies pointedly abhorred. Maybe there is no class hatred like the small towner with airs against unabashed white trash.

He was right about Natalie Wood. I had seen her once in *Rebel Without a Cause* but ignored her in favor of Dean. In *West Side Story,* though, as she was dancing and singing, and especially when she performed "Somewhere" amidst the gang horror of New York, I teared up and wanted her more than anything before in my life. She was *it,* tripled. Please wouldn't she wait until I got famous and rich, and got some more height? Harold stood there, forever, as the credits rolled at the end. He seemed to be memorizing the name of every member who'd even carried a mop in the studio. I was smitten, looking down at the floor I was so charged, and still riding on that New York music.

We went to Baton Rouge to sleep at a Holiday Inn—very new and seeming swankier then—but on the way down Harold said maybe he should tell me this was a Negro production of *Godot* we were going to the next night.

"You're kidding. This Beckett wrote for Negroes?"

"Grow up. He wrote for *man*, little man."

"Oh. Well, sure."

You would not believe how condescending and polite I was in that audience of Negroes in suits. The play was riveting and strange to me, and I thought maybe I was one of the few not getting it, just here and there a dose of sense. Nobody laughed, and I don't know at all about the quality of the production. But it was a quiet smiling scandal that we were here at all, and I was glad to hear Harold's earnest sighs now and again when a point of confusion and futility—I got that—was made. I felt very allied to the culture-hip scene. We were not going to put up with any racists once we were outside the theater either, me and my Negro friends, hearkening in our suits— goddamnit, *let* there be trouble. Our very class and righteousness would blow them away.

Out in the foyer, digging the crowd with Harold, I felt very promoted in my suit and Ivy League haircut, only I wanted a goatee very badly. Harold had pulled off to a wall for a smoke. I also wanted to say something on the mark.

"Way out, very. But really, how many of them you think really got it, Hare?"

He was disgusted, eyes closed in smoke.

"You tit. You little tits go right from blind ignorance to cynicism, never feeling a damned thing."

"No, no, I feel. Miles Davis is my man."

I was rescued by the appearance of the first great public faggot I'd ever witnessed. This black thing, tall and skinny as a drum major, was leading a trio of admirers out of the auditorium, hands curling and thrown out from his chest, squealing like a mule on fire, and dressed in something mauve and body-fit with a red necktie on it.

I smiled across the way at Harold, who had distanced himself, checked the near-empty theater, and began doing the pantomime I had learned off Ray Wiley, a worldly child of the army base who claimed to have encountered many queers. I wet both forefingers, smoothed my eyebrows with them, and formed my mouth in an O with my lips covering the hole, then held my arms out as if in a flying tackle. We conceived of queers as sort of helpless roving linebackers apt to dive on you and bury their faces in your loins. Wiley told many happy stories about how these men were discovered in their act in army lounges and stomped senseless. You could also use burning naphtha to rout them.

"What in hell?" Harold hissed, flicking eyes around the precincts like a spy.

He came over and grabbed my arm very strongly for such a skinny creature. Harold wore a formless blue serge suit with a clip-on green tie on his flat collar like a salesman at a funeral. I don't believe he owned a button-down. He had on those heavy black executive shoes too. I noticed him red-eyed. He'd been crying quietly about *Godot*. Just as I'd wept tinnily for Natalie Wood.

"Behave, fool. You're not in your own pathetic little country. Something wonderful has happened here, and you're totally unmarked by it."

"No. I'm *marked*, Hare. Truly marked, I swear. It was all there, man, straight on."

"That and *Our Town* are the dramas of the century. Now you've seen both of them, thanks to me. What do you get from them? Zero. Out here queer-baiting. My God, you remind me of all those wry husbands dragged to the theater by their wives. Not a snowball's chance in hell."

"Look, man, I *got* something from it, all right? I only wish Natalie Wood was in it."

Harold had pushed too far and I went sullen, out to his hopelessly square car, which looked even more like the grounded rocket of a very confused small nation. I thought about how stern old Harold was a great hypocrite, really, him with his album and glue-on straw from mouth to girl. The Studebaker left the campus with its weak hissing. He wouldn't let it go.

"You're not even up to sophomoric yet, is your trouble, cat. Cats *know* things, they *sense* things. Young men like Elvis have left you light years behind."

I got a thicker skin of the sullen around me. Oh yeah? What about your Asian women, the trolls you cultivate now? I wanted to say. What great sense was in that? And, and . . . Harold did not wear his heart on his sleeve. He wore it on his forehead, throbbing away at you. I had a mother to scold me already, thank you.

"If you were worthy, I'd take you out for a drink, a liqueur. That's what your mother *expects* me to do, teach you to drink," he suddenly said, picking up on the very mother thought in my head, flicking me, chums again, on the suit sleeve. "I'm sorry for growling, cat. Really."

"Likoor? Liquor?"

On Harold's patient directions, the amused bartender at the Holiday Inn made us a sort of booze snow cone with crème de menthe. I guess I was so healthy and unpolluted, I felt it immediately, my first drink, or suck. I lit up like a pink sponge. All the world seemed at my feet, and I could barely stand the joy of *Godot*, Natalie Wood, and Harold in it at the same time. Even the city name, Baton Rouge, was vastly hip. Red stick, red stick. Very way out. Life was a long wonderful thing. It was so good you expected some official to show up and cancel it.

I tried to impress Harold with scandals I knew of myself, and told him about a shooting on a town square down south. A man had killed two policemen with a shotgun and gone home to threaten his own family, whereupon his oldest son ran him against a house with a truck and killed his own father with a .22, nine shots, the father yelling "Oh my God!" over and over. At the end, the son threw the pistol on the ground and said, "Daddy, why'd you make me do it? You knew I loved you."

"No, no. That's . . . just baroque misery. So beastly obvious. Nothing but low, mean, stunned feelings result. Nothing is left but the mourners. It's the province of our bard up at Oxford. Nobody throbs in shame, derided worldwide. Scandal *pierces*, is *poignant*, *pi-quant, resonant.* If I could reorder that sad thing they call a state fair . . . You see, scandal is obsession, essence! Instead of the freak show, I'd have the heroes of scandal caged up while folks filed by to review them."

"Review them? Then what?"

"Why, throw rotten fruit, eggs and excrement at them!" Harold gave that long girlish neigh that grabbed his throat after some of his insights, and too many heads turned in the Holiday Inn bar. He didn't care.

"Scandal is *delicious,* little man. All we are is obsession and pain. That is *all* humans are. And when these wild things go public, and are met with howls, they ring out the only honest history we have! They are *unbearable!* Magnificent! Wicked! You read where the pathetic object goes off to psychiatric care or some phony drinking hospital, or a dull jail, but that's only for the public, slamming the door shut on them. What they really are is raving on the heath, little man, in their honest unbearable humanity!"

So, in months afterward, I tried to achieve soul, or stand in the path of it so it would come to me. And I thought deeply about what I could do, what I had, who I was, to possibly rave on the heath someday. I wanted very much a rare, perhaps even dark, thing with a woman—Natalie Wood or her cousin, after I'd sent New York Slim off begging. My imagination could do nothing else for me, otherwise.

Harold sort of faded at the little college. I got tired of him, and at midyear a real Korean vet appeared as a late student on campus. He was much *like* Harold, they said, and Harold was very annoyed at being somewhat displaced and duplicated. The other fellow went crazy in a motel over in Jackson one night. Harold was called over by a local pastor to help minister to him. He didn't like this role at all, although he did what he could. The man had true awful memories of Chosin Reservoir and was not poetic at all in his breakdown, also very real. Harold, you could tell, was fairly sorry to help him get back on his feet, and considered his insanity banal. I'd never seen Harold this ungenerous before, but I guess he was threatened by this man at the tiny college, where he used to hold forth among his desperate harem in the grill. He began giving "all of his entity" to a new large buxom girl with red cheeks who played clarinet in the orchestra, and

I quit seeing much of him. He swore she was the one, an honest life's passion. He was glad the waiting was over. I saw them at the drugstore together once. Harold was even paler and thinner and a good deal shorter than the girl. Drained by love, I guess. She had big calves and a very long lap, and seemed completely conquered by him. He was soon to graduate and become a high school teacher in a town north in the state that I didn't think held much promise for scandal. He went off with no good-bye, the girl with him.

I just remembered that before he left I at last hit the mark on scandal for him, and he saw I was coming around.

"Okay, give me a worthy scandal, little man." I was taller than Harold.

"This way. General MacArthur is discovered hunching a sheep just minutes after his 'Old Soldiers Never Die, They Just Fade Away' speech to a grateful Congress."

"Finally. Perfect. Discovered by one of Truman's aides, some nervous square from Missouri."

The wild horsey shout.

My parents were much relieved, I detected, when Harold was finally away. The age, the dress, his bewildering pull, never set right for them, and my mother was disturbed when I told her he had found her attractive.

Now I was being a fine lad with my pal Horace, but not too fine, pulling out the bricks from the theater razement by honest sweat and toil, bored insane and almost to bed in Kosciusko. I looked down at the lobby desk from the balcony a long long time, but nobody came. It was just the old man sitting the night in the same chair, full speed ahead with his tangled stare, a silent movie of *Godot* even further gone into real life. Just to get a rise from him I spoke out the French title, like Harold loved to: "*En Attendant Godot!*" a little above normal speaking voice.

This worried the man, and he turned his head slowly around, then cocked it back at me, whose face denied anything had made a noise at all. He seemed very worried, even alarmed. Then for no good cause at all, I did my queer pantomime, slicking my eyebrows, running my tongue back and forth, my eyes big and avid, arms out as if to dive down on him. I was suddenly very angry at him for not being a woman. He was looking backward straight up at me. His arms began moving and a low rush of language I did not understand muttered from him.

I felt so good and healthy and showered, but I was using up all my potential here. My manhood was being sucked away by a dead town. My pal Horace opened the door of our room. He'd taken a nap to prepare himself for a real sleep in a minute, and gave a grogged palsy smile, feeling good too, with his body worked. I kept up the queer routine, which he always thought was a howl. He mimicked drop-kicking a homo in the groin. Horace was a bass player and quite a scholar, much better at books than I was. We passed much time mimicking the stone-dumb and depraved creatures of our state, especially the governor, who had recently suggested setting off large nuclear devices to blow open a canal way from the Tennessee River to Mobile.

"Come here. I want you to listen," he said.

"Listen?"

"Come here."

He took me to the window, which was open to the lukewarm Kosciusko evening, and told me not to look down, just listen.

At first I heard what I took to be just somebody mumbling on the sidewalk beneath us. Then a harmonica started up, very softly, lonely as a midnight highway dog. It was the blues, with no audience, for no money. For all my musical life, I'd never heard the blues erupt solitary and isolated like this. When the harmonica stopped, the voice went very high and strained in its grief—you couldn't really tell whether it was a man or a woman.

"Let's . . ."

"Don't look down," said Horace.

"What? Why not?"

"Let's don't find out who it is. You don't want to know, do you?"

I saw his point. Horace had a copy of *Swann's Way* on the bed beside where he was sleeping and he was deep.

Kosciusko was a better town than we thought, if it afforded this tune at ten in the night. Maybe it was a man just released from jail, or maybe a woman just off a bus somewhere. Horace was right on, it was best not to know the source of this eerie, moaning thing. You couldn't quite make out the words, but it had the blackstrap moan in it all right. The harmonica trailed in again, sweet and with a bit of terror in it. I grabbed the song. It was all mine. I heard something when the voice started and I could tell Horace had not caught it. *Buddy, could you spare a future? This can't be life.* Then it just stopped and did not come back, like something swallowed up in a storm drain. I didn't hear any steps going away. I looked over to shake my head, smiling, but Horace had already gone back to sleep.

I went out, closed the door, to see what more I could get from the balcony rail. Sometimes you see something that seems made for you, like a good fishing hole, and you won't leave it although the hours prove there's nothing there. The old man was still at his post, along with the gone tan carpet, the gone desk clerk, serried cubbyholes in a rack behind. But then, I could hardly believe it, feet in ladies' sandals appeared, and a stretch of nice tan leg, black short-cut hair in bangs with a few strands of gray in it, and I could not question: a black long-sleeve slightly unseasonal sweater, bosoms small but prominent, and like great lamps in this stag-dark tedium. It was New York Slim, about ten years older than I had guessed her. I was back to New York Slim, instantly unfaithful to Natalie Wood, Natalie was nothing, this woman and I already having had two years of history in the head, you can't deny old lovers. I couldn't see all her face, but from the cut to the profile you knew she was at least summer chicken going into fall maybe. She talked to the old man, but he did not rise like an Old South gent should. Then she came up the stairs and saw me, kept going but slower, and the age in her face wasn't too much—not quite in my mother's era—with the muscles in her face making lines that matched those in her legs, drawing tight in strands as she took the last two steps. She did not look of this place at all. Then she smiled but at the same time shook her head, as if she knew something about me besides the fact I was nothing but a boy and felt that very much as I looked into her eyes—what color?—and sensed deep events decades long. Also, she was easy here, maybe she lived here, because without checking in she opened the door two away

from ours and went in. I was so happy and tormented I looked at the
last of her foot going in the closing door many times over, gathered
to the rail like a great sinner at the bar.

I checked quickly, very quietly, to see if Horace was still
asleep. Ever since the music out on the street I knew something was
being made for me, only me, unshareable. It might have been her
singing, though already I knew it wasn't, no, but the singer could be
an agent of telepathy as Harold believed in. Sure. The set of her was
foreign here, I was certain of that. I had nothing to say. But Harold,
now Harold would just go up to somebody and talk if he wanted
to. With women he told me he just went right up and said I think we
should be friends and probably sleep together, and it worked, he was
right in with them. I went to her door and knocked, an enormous
chill all over my body. It took a while. I thought I heard her say inside *not yet*. I knocked again. She opened the door barefooted with a
bottle in her hand, a little clear one not for booze, and she was about
to say something but I wasn't who she thought.

"I feel I ought to know you," I said. "You ring a bell."

"You don't know me. And I don't want to know anybody else
now, especially not anybody decent and young." She took a pull on
the bottle, and she seemed a little drunk.

"I'm not so decent as all that."

"He thinks you are a Communist. He forgot to say you're
only a boy. Why'd you scare him?"

"That old man down there? I was just clearing my throat.
Stretching."

"He said you had symbolic gestures."

"Oh. He's a sick one, you know."

"Yes he is. A very sick one."

"Could we just talk? We've been working bricks and it gets
lonesome. We've been at it now a week."

She pulled from the bottle again and I could smell something
familiar from it, not booze, something we'd had in the house. The
label had microscopic print.

"Come in, oh Mister Communist Police. Arrest me if you
must, but I will never break. I will never tell."

"I'm no Communist. Don't kid. Say, you've been living here."

"I doubt it," she said. Not only was she blurred in speech but the speech wasn't quite American. I knew it.

"I go away, I come back. I go away, I come back," she continued.

Besides some domestic things on the dresser, there was a bicycle raised on a jack to its axle. You could pedal and go nowhere. I pointed this out, asking if something was wrong with it. You never, also, saw a woman her age on a bike where I come from.

"I go nowhere on that one." Beside the bike were tall black-laced boots, looking serious and military, but they seemed her size. She sat and slumped to one arm on the bed, pulling from the tiny bottle again.

"What's that?"

"Happy medicine for nervous bad women." I saw it was paregoric, the stuff prescribed on ice for nausea. I didn't know about the opium in it then.

"Your voice."

"Canadian. Quebec. World citizen. You all sound like the nickras down here. Who taught who to talk? This man I paid out of jail today down over Lexington, he hates the nickras too, but I ask him why does he talk like them then?"

"What was he in for?"

"Throwing things in the night. Fireworks."

"Disturbing the peace?"

"More keeping. Believes. Depends on what you believe. But dumb to get caught. More of the white trash. *Lumpen*."

On the dresser were several long steely pins. I went over and picked one up. They were too long for hairdos. It was extremely sharp on the end.

"Medical," she said. "Look but don't touch, if you please. Acupuncture, for relief. Go ahead. The man out of jail didn't believe in them either."

I wondered if she was practicing some kind of voodoo surgery. Those signs you see along the road in the country, on the outskirts of town. SISTER GRACE, PALMS. You sometimes feel your blood go darker, and I was feeling it here, more excited than disapproving. This world was fetched in fresh just for me, but I could never tell

Horace. I was greedy for all her details. She was European, ageless, a brunette Marlene Dietrich with those long legs.

It was then I saw a Klan robe, a green rounded cross on the left breast, all white otherwise. It had a small ladies' hood, cut to fashion for her, or so it seemed. The closet door was half open and she didn't mind my seeing. It all was like stumbling into an alien person's attic. My people hated the Klan, and I did too, I thought. But there is an undeniable romance, maybe adventure, to hating a whole race of people: it had its sway. Recently in Bay St. Louis, I had left a beautiful girlfriend to go to New Orleans. I did not get much of anywhere with her, but she'd talked affectionately with me. As I was leaving, she said, truly caring for me, I thought, "Oh George, do watch out for the nigguhs in New Orleans. They're all loose and free over there and they'll just do anything." She had seemed lovely in her need to be protected from the dark hordes. I was taken very warmly by this problem, and went off like a knight of the streets, full of romantic charge, with something to prove. I'd been at the closet door overlong. The hanger next over held a great length of dog chain with bracelets at both ends. I supposed she wore this around her waist, like medieval women in the "Prince Valiant" comic strip.

When I turned to her, she could see my face was different, even though her eyes were blurred and she looked ready to sleep.

"I told you thas too bad. You're decent. I'm not, young boy."

"But not really—"

"Don't tell me. I know decent from the other look. I can sort them. You've got that decent polish on you. You are decent, and you will just go to sleep with fairy plums in your head, not like me."

"That's not a church choir gown. I know that. Still—"

"You have to go. Somebody is coming. You don't want to see him."

"The man from jail? What's he . . . It's late. Why's he coming?"

"Why to frig me, I'd imagine. Out of here, Tom Sawyer with your neckerchief. Put all those nice muscles to bed."

She was right that I didn't want to see the man. I closed the door with my head flaming, confused. But I was not disgusted. I wanted to save her. You could see she was too good for anybody around here. Forces were martialed against her.

I couldn't go into my room. I put my hand on the knob of the room next to hers. It was unlocked. The room inside was made up, unused. I crept in and waited, dark in my head, forcing myself toward love of her. Even the muscle lines in her face would go away if I loved her right.

I lay on the bed without moving a spring. Then I crept to check for a hole in the wall. There was none. But I edged up the window so as to listen around.

Not five minutes passed before there were steps on the stairs, very slow and dramatic, you knew it in the rickety floor. He went over the carpet and opened her door without saying anything. She knew him all too well. Nothing, not even muffled, came through then. I lay half sick waiting for sounds of protest and struggle, and when they failed to occur, I knew the drug was used to smother her will. Mute things were proceeding as in a film so bad I might have written it myself.

But through the window I heard the clink of, yes, it had to be that dog chain, and then soon with it, at first unaccountable, but there was no mistaking it, the whir of the bicycle being pumped and clanking just a little. This went on a long, severe time. Through the window this was quite clear. I was thinking of creeping out there, but then the man's voice said short things, low and anxious, while the bicycle kept up. It was moaning, pathetic, but fearful at the same time. At first I thought it was the woman. Only her voice, in a dismayed faint gasp was heard then, and this was unbearable. It seemed as though she was afraid that he would hit her. He moaned shortly again, but not in sex: it sounded like encouragement in another language. The whirring slowed, and I heard his big steps, the knocks going through the carpet in my room. I waited and waited, waiting for bedsprings and weeping, but I never heard them. The silence became deader than quiet, and then *Now here it is!* the man said very plainly. But there had passed an enormous amount of time. Only my head was racing, flushed, ahead of the seconds.

Then I heard nothing for so long I fell off asleep very deep into the night, close to dawn, I think. I woke when the light came in gray and went back to our room. I stared at the ceiling, and that day at the bricks, a moron's job, I was worthless. Horace wanted to know what had me all blown. We'd eaten in the hotel dining room, but we were the only ones there. He wanted to know what I was watching for, what was ailing. I kept going back to the hotel all day, telling him I had a bad stomach. I was really letting him down on the work. The old man still sat there, but once, for the first time, he was gone. I couldn't tell if anybody else was around. So I knocked on her door, worn out and shucking my labor.

She was having a nap and was fresher than last night, no blur to her, and in a homey wrap. She didn't mind at all I was there. I asked if I could get her anything. She said well indeed I could get her two Coca-Colas with ice. I was so fast at this, down to the dining room, troubling the one harried fat lady—though she was doing nothing else—and back, it had to be a record for service. She'd brushed her hair (I mattered, she cared) and her face was not so tired.

"I have the feeling you could use a friend, miss." I had rehearsed that all day.

She put her head down, then sat. I was sure she was crying. Her eyes blinked pink at the rims when she lifted up, and I was gone for her, out of my depth. The other Coke wasn't for me, though. She poured from a new paregoric bottle on the dresser into one glass and added Coke, storing the other one. Then she drank.

"Much better. It gets hard alone. This is a clean drink. All this is very clean. With your Tennessee whiskey it gets sloppy and all ragged. This is dry-cleaned magic. Not so bad."

"I guess the nerves never leave you."

"Never. I had a husband and you aren't like him at all. But it's the youth, the age in it, nearly the same. You get to me, neighbor. It's clean, the look. Washed and pure in the blood, that lucky color. I've had it." For the first time, she smiled. Her teeth were not that bad, a maturer gold was all. My dentist could brighten them right up.

"Tell me. Why did you yell *waiting* down to him last night? He thought you knew all about him. He was very disturbed."

"That old man." I was struck cold and wretched. "*Him?* You waited for *him* last night? I don't believe it."

Not only that but the man was her father-in-law, and French. Her husband had been killed with the French Legion at Dien Bien Phu in 1954. The Communists did it. The father had lived in Saigon, wanting to be close to his son with the war on. She was Canadian French, going to school there. It was ballroom and ballet dancing, her whole life, until the war went bad. She'd not been married very long when Edouard was killed. His father had lost twice now from the "other side." He had been Vichy, was imprisoned after the war, but got out still vocal against Communists and Jews. France was inhospitable to him, so he went to Indochina, and made much money in rubber and tires. After the death of her husband she was lost and absolutely poor. Her parents had left for Canada. She did not think of the old man at all. She began dancing naked in a special club, full of opium and not knowing whether she liked it or not. The old man came in with some friends, he too in awful despair. He did not know where she was, nor did he know it was "Baby Doll"—her husband's nickname for her— dancing. He watched her on the stage and she soothed his grief long before he knew who she was. He'd only seen her a few times. He went up to her afterwards, she in her silk cape and big shoes, stage-dancing whore shoes. They fell into each other weeping. But he was gone for her in no father-in-law way, and she had nothing. So he took her to Quebec where her parents guessed what was going on; she would not marry him nor did he seem to want it. Her parents told her to die in hell and never speak their name. The way he was about Communists and Jews and now *nickras*, the way he sent out very angry and offensive literature, got him shunned again but noticed by a visitor from the South in the States. There was much work to be done here after the *Brown* decision, integration, the last order breaking down in the last great power, and he would be most welcome down here, he and his money and organization. People were listening up. The public was for them, only the forms against. She did nothing but be his and run as a bag woman here and there at a necessary point. She could not stand the trash at the Klan rallies, and she never wore the gown or hood outside the room. As for the *nickras*, they were fine primitives and she felt sorry for them; some of the men were beautiful with their smiles and shoulders, and they were happy until the Jews and Communists *ageetated theem*. She had never met a Jew, but the *Communeests*, without a god they both could not bear a healthy white race, it was an abomination to them, and they owned entertainment, much of government, bragging always about how smart they were because they did not have hearts. Or guts. I mustn't think too badly of the old man. Everything was wrong with him. Bowels, liver, arthritis, skin cancers, ulcers, psoriasis, piles. There was always a good room for her. This is the worst one she'd ever had. It was she I should think badly about. She was telling me all this because I was young, something was going to happen soon, and she had no church, nor any friends. Witness Albert, the father-in-law, he had all *theeeese tings eell* and he took no pain medicine, compared to weak her, Felice, who had nothing really wrong and did not do much but whore for her kin. He was so unhealthy it didn't take but once a month or so now. It took him that long to recover. It took him forever to . . . befit himself, a longer riding of the bicycle naked in the robe with the hood on, wearing the black boots, and racing with the skirt of it tied up, the chain from her wrist to his wrist on the bed, his face buried in half a watermelon, but peeping like a child at her pumping nether parts. She giggled. Something from his youth, she couldn't know. I was not a man yet and I shouldn't smile. One day odd things might overcome me in my despair, if I ever had despair. Sometimes she thought he was doing it to his own youth, or his son, or he and his son together, at the end long long long silence, his having got with her but demanding her to ride still until it was finished and he a dead ruin. It had crossed her mind he might die, and in ingratitude she had driven the bike faster and faster, hoping to bring on the classic champion's death to him, but she didn't know if his will was in order, she'd gotten that mean. But really there was a way of not even being there and responding that a man couldn't know. Women got married and lived their whole lives doing that, absent and wild and pleasing all at once.

She'd finished two Cokes and the blur was on again. At one point I thought she was breaking down and crying, but I cannot remember at what point. There was sweat on her forehead, and her lips moving, I could swear she'd become younger and younger as her cheeks stretched, then got older at the end, the paregoric driving a hotter, duller black to her eyes.

"I need a bath. Sometimes seven or eight a day," she said dully. "Don't forget to be my friend, boy. I think I've done something to your youth. You don't look so decent now." She waved for me to go.

This had taken a long while, and when I went by the room, Horace was in it, asking what in hell was going on, the day was done.

I told him a person down the way had some medicine for me and that we had chatted while I got better.

At breakfast the next day, Horace and I were still the only ones in the dining room, and feeling obliged for detaining the help, I claimed stomach distress that was not completely a lie. I was too excited and too heavy in her story, like a walking boy museum, hebephrenic and bitten at the scalp and loins. I was up the stairs before I realized I had passed the old man, who was back in the chair, with a black suit on. I knocked and she met me in the door on her way out. She drew me in and shut the door.

"He's down there, isn't he?"

"Yes," I said, all nerves.

"Albert is very jealous. You have to watch it. It's the worst thing about him. We're going out to see my dog in the country. A man gave me a Weimaraner dog, a real lovey. When Albert gets bad he threatens to kill it."

"No. He's a monster."

"In jealousy, yes."

She was dressed in an innocent-looking country outfit, printed skirt and baby blue blouse. The little bow in her hair turned my heart around. Next she put on a raincoat I thought marked for French espionage. I was simply riveted to my stuttering place in awe.

"Visit me when you can, but be careful. Tonight he's away."

"Oh yes. I'm your friend. I'm hanging tough."

That afternoon I worked twice as hard, owing it to Horace from yesterday. I was in the bricks so smoothly I might have been made for them. The sweat was pouring off me. I stood up and untied the kerchief to swab off. Horace was looking across the street.

"That old man, he's watching you."

He stood in front of the Baptist church across the road, hat in hand, and not looking at me as meanly as I had expected. He was standing just in front of the bricked marquee, with its message or sermon of the week: JESUS WEPT. COME AND GATHER. He was simply studying me mildly, almost kind in his face of red spots and raked-down short gray hair. He was younger too, up and about on the pavements, the chair a whole other life dismissed with some strength.

I mopped through to my eyes and peeked. *His face buried in half a watermelon but peeking every now and then,* I thought. My shirt was off and I felt small, a grimy peon.

"I believe he's looking at your mighty build," said Horace. "Must be the village queer. Let's set him on fire."

It is quite mature, I thought, to know everything and say nothing. I had not practiced this much in my life, and felt myself almost plump with rough wisdom, as the old man walked on.

I told Horace I was not wanting any supper that night, stomach knotted and butterflied. But I was her prized friend, heavy on the aftershave, the shave itself a ludicrous solemn wipe of the blade through foam. He went down to the John Birch diner with his *Swann's Way* in hand, to give the shiftless owner more grief.

She was not right. Something had happened. There were five new bottles of paregoric on the dresser next to the long needles, the brush and the hand mirror. She stared at me with her mouth pinched and her eyes wary with fear and sadness. What is it? I wanted to know. You can tell me, in my last clean shirt, a blue one to match her blouse, telepathy.

"He took me to the field, the fence, and the dog was not there anymore. But he wanted me to look at the vacant field where it had been, I know it. The man in the house wasn't our friend anymore, either, Albert told me, angry. He was a busybody, a turncoat, maybe a fellow traveler or a Jew."

"You think he killed them both?"

"I don't know. We go on a while and then there's always some kind of rage or treachery."

"Why don't I take that Klan outfit and shove it up his ass for him?"

"No," she said quickly, head swung up to glare and then dissolve, back into her bewildered tortured beauty.

"But you have no real home and an awful life. I could get money. My father is well-off. By the end of this week I'll have two hundred."

"Very, very sweet. Hand me my dream bottle."

I did, and went and fetched her two Cokes, lightning across the face of the piggish, unknowing woman alone in the dining room.

"You're Peter Pan," she smiled. "I think you remind Albert of his son."

"Your husband."

"He wasn't so much older when we met. He liked my legs, even my poverty."

"So do I, Felice." It was rich and almost too heavy on my tongue.

"All I can do is drag youth down to indecentness."

"No. You care. You're in a trap. There's a whole other world. There's movies, and music, and poems, and fishing in a private place with cypresses in the water. You with me. You can't tell. Time—"

"Oh, please shut up. I told you I didn't need to know anybody else. I'm just sailing along the current in the rain gutter, a piece of nothing, nobody can touch me without drowning."

I thought that was the most beautiful thing I'd ever heard.

I was just on the edge of breaking into song with that great anthem of blind Christian affirmation of the fifties, "I Believe." All jazz, Beatism, cattism had fallen away. By God, I was in Harold's world, women with troubles, a spell of swooning charity on me.

"You've forgotten I'm your friend," I told her.

"Well, that's something. To know you're not alone. A part of me must have that."

I knew she was about to say a thing so sincere and poignant, from that bleak experienced face of hers, that it would be a sign for our parting, and she did.

"Even in hell the real part of me can carry that young face of you with me, friend George."

I left the room all moist and on the verge of going ugly in the face with sorrow and joy.

I was wanting to be a broader man when next we met, so I picked up Horace's Proust and began reading it that night while he went down to the bus station to see if the magazines had changed. The great champion of sensitivity and time, in his cork-lined room, allergic to noise, claimed my pal. This thicket of nerves I could not broach, however, most likely because I had my own, clawing over the pages in competition. But it was still of great use in the room, because it was French, I thought as I tossed it away.

Horace came in with a great smile. I was on the bed dreaming high and valiant stuff. He looked behind him down the hall.

"Well, *somebody's* having a good time here. Did you know there was a *woman* down the way? And she must be *all* woman. They hadn't shut the transom. She couldn't get enough from some guy. Oh Bertie, Bertie, deeper, deeper!" I changed from the smile of my good dreams to a face that must have been stone fury.

"You couldn't have heard that. That's from a dirty comic book."

"I tell you. And get this, what she was moaning when I left: *Churn butter churn! Churn butter churn!* Old Bertie whamming away."

He couldn't have made this up.

"Your kind go from blind ignorance straight to cynicism. You don't feel, you don't know."

"Hey, George, you quoting Marcel? I'm not cynical at all. She was having a hell of a time."

Her language, an image from French dairy cow country—my good horror. How could this thing be? Albert was using the dog against her. He was forcing the paregoric down her, making her sick and blabbering.

"Now, man. You ought to see your face. What's eating you?"

Horace was tall, too wise, knowing nothing. I hated him.

I couldn't go see her that night. It was a bitter, bitter evening. Horace wanted to go down to the lobby and lie in wait so we could check out the woman when she came by. I told him that was a horrible sophomoric idea. Why? he asked, getting fed up with me. He said we might have found a lady with a profession here. He was ready to do a Chinese dwarf.

"Let's leave it like the harmonica player," I said, stonily.

"That isn't the same at all."

"Leave it."

"You don't tell me, all right? You're not the duke of Kosciusko."

He went down and I was happy he came back without seeing her.

The next morning was Sunday. Horace called himself a free-thinking Baptist. He'd brought a suit and he went out to that church down the way. I was apostate, but very glad he wasn't. I checked the rail, being stealthy. That bastard Albert was in the chair, staring tiredly, having forced her twice this week. I was praying for an artery to snap in his face and vowed direct revenge if it didn't. The man must be stomped and dragged off in a net. I could see venom popped up in his cheeks, spotting them red.

"Hey you," I called, not very loud.

He twisted his head back, trying to find me.

"*En Attendant Godot? En Attendant?*"

He got up, shaken, and I watched the top of his head, gray hair brushed forward Roman, leave for the street.

When I knocked on the door and waited, I heard something clink inside. She came to the door in nothing but a house wrap, wet from the bath.

"Friend George." Her eyes were very dull. She was on the stuff, her conscience awful.

When I went in she'd already gone back to the tub. I sat on the bed and heard her stir the water. Then I heard the clink again. For the longest time she said nothing.

"You ought to watch your transom. My friend heard you really having a good time last night."

There was no reply at all.

"I thought wrong. You don't need a friend so much as . . . somebody to betray."

Nothing. You heard water sounds, just a little.

I studied the bed and carpet and dresser—all she had and was, as far as I knew. A hotel was a stupid and desperate place to live, I suddenly thought. And rotation from one to another, having her bicycle and robe and boots and chain everywhere, up the stairs dutifully with them again and again, setting up like carnival gypsies except with less dignity and no good at all even to yokels with a quarter. But I was being unfair to her, and caught myself up again. Because I cherished her, nothing could budge me.

"I so need a friend now. It's the end of things," she said in a little, faint voice. "Come in here and sit. There's a curtain between us. Oh!" I thought she gasped and I hurried in, face blushing and dying to help. The curtain was closed, all right, the brown shadow of her behind it sitting in the water. "Oh!" I thought she said again.

Around the front gathered edge of the curtain near the faucets the dog chain lay out on the floor with one of its bracelets open, the rest of the chain in the tub with Felice.

"Put it on your wrist, my pal," she said tinnily, almost sighing it.

So I did and snapped it on. I would be a gypsy too. I'd be the panting boy in the wings, waiting until her act was over and the others had had their fill of her. Until we made our move. This charity and long-suffering had never even nearly come near me before. *I'm just sailing along the current in the rain gutter, a piece of nothing, nobody can touch me without drowning.* The steel of the cuff was very serious and required a key for release, I noticed.

"You will be with me down down down oh! There's a way to do it in the liver they said brings it there quick but oh! no no no." This was all so faint and not recollected until a long while afterwards.

"Felice! Are you okay? I'm buckled on the chain with you."

"Something's not right, and I've used the last one." Her voice was faint, dimming like a small girl going to sleep, her breath wet on the pillow.

"Everything will be all right. Everything. I know you're under horrible pressure. I'm reading Proust, drawing closer to your world. The *French* Proust."

There would be no way for me not to view a lot of her with the chain binding us, I reckoned. This would be an unearthly familiarity. The die would be cast. The new world would begin right then, and I felt actual waves of a kind of happy nausea.

"Oh oh oh oh ohh! Not right."

This voice did not rise in friendship or passion. She was very sick and I knew something was wrong, unpretended and real.

"I'm not dying the right way, George."

I got up, thinking, and pulled the chain to the door. I couldn't look at what I wanted without pulling her a little, with a splash from the tub. I finally had my eyes just past the jamb and looked on the dresser. The paregoric bottles were there, three empty, but where the long acupuncture needles always were was empty space. It was too catastrophic a thing to even consider; but I knew she had them.

"Felice, I'm opening the curtain!"

She was lying over with her head forward, drugged, on the shower plunger between the faucets. Her hands were down on her stomach. The tub water was pink around it with three streams of blood. She'd pushed them in the right side where the liver was, I found out. *Oriental, Oriental,* I remember thinking over and over, trying to call the dread something.

I got in the tub with her and lifted her. You think you are one muscled champion until you try to lift a wet naked woman dead-haul. It can barely be done, and I thought she was already dead, so that in this fear I finally did it and we both fell over together, confused in the chain, off the tiles into the carpet of the room. My nose was flat in it and it smelled like the dusty feet of a horde. She was whimpering. When I saw the heads of the needles, puffed out with blue and darker skin, with a near-black blood dripping out like spread fingers, I almost went under.

I looked for a phone, but we had no phone in these rooms. Her legs began moving although her face looked dead. I drew up and whirled my head around looking. I reached the robe on the hanger and dragged it off, then threw it over her and put my arms under hers, tugging and pleading with her.

With as much ease as I could I got her out on the stoop and she began walking a little, saying *oh oh oh.* We went down the stairs very slowly. When we got toward the bottom, I raised up and there Albert was staring at us from his black suit, his eyes seeming beyond a known emotion. I gasped at him to phone help, she was dying. Some others behind Albert stood there, but I barely noticed even their shoes. I settled her on the last stair then sat myself, un-wrapping the chain around us both and getting some free length to my wrist. Then I saw she was revealed and I pulled the robe together on her.

She had a great deal of blood in her lap and on the side of the robe, up level with the circled cross of the Klan.

"This is *my* affair," said Albert. "Let her go."

"It is *not.* I'm with her now. Can't you see? *I'm* her future now!"

"No you ain't, son," said my father, who'd come up with Horace, the both of them in suits.

He'd come up to bring us some treats from Mother and had intercepted Horace coming in from church. My father had a cigarette in his mouth, but it had almost fallen out of his sidelips and hung there while he stared with an open mouth at the bloody woman in the Klan robe. He looked so damned distinguished and in charge I felt dimmed out and pushed back to about age ten, staring at the handcuff of the dog chain on my wrist. Horace was holding the sack of goodies and seemed exactly the son he deserved.

I didn't see Harold again until almost twenty years later. I was in a very bad band playing at cocktail hour for peanuts and for a convention of educators in San Antonio, Texas. I had been fired from my regular job for drinking, and before that I had been jailed and nuthoused for setting fire to my estranged wife's lawn, which blew up her lawn mower. In the band I was desperate and would have been throbbing in shame but I was still drunk enough to ignore it and was majoring on the theme Whim of Fortune, and I believe trying to attach myself to a woman of such low estate that the two of us would destroy ourselves in spontaneous combustion at an impossible diving speed. But I had clarity enough to see Harold walk out of the milling pack of cocktailers in the ballroom and come right up to the bandstand, natty in a good slim blazer, and stare at me with an even brotherly smile.

He had heard about my troubles, and commiserated, seeming the picture of sobriety and successful wisdom to me. His hair was all gray, but his posture had improved, and his baldness was distinguished, even at the ears all around. Something terribly healthy was going on in his life and I envied him. I hadn't felt decent in three years.

"Oh, no. I'm *not* nice, my friend, not at all. I'm just *ordinary* as potatoes."

"Aw Harold. I doubt it."

"That was the last gasp of riot, in school when you knew me. That was the whole wad."

"You didn't reach your juicy scandal, the great one?"

"Never. My head simply turned around and I got old. I just wasn't even looking that way anymore. All I had was divorce—very usual—and my memories. It's like I knew you'd be here. C'mon up to the room. I'll show you something. Pathetic, and I can't leave it alone."

"Telepathy, Harold. Remember?"

I dragged my horn case along with him to the elevator. Harold began attacking the stupefying hopelessness of his students. I had grown enough to know only a good teacher could assault them this meticulously, and that he adored them. He was reading a paper on mild innovations in the classroom here at the convention. Many of his students had won national honors. He was still at the same obscure little school.

In the room he pulled out his albums—the one with the Asian women, and then another one with photographs of all his college girls in total surrender, bare, and all of them very happy about it, Harold beaming among them. The effect was more of an arcane archaeological find where a race of drab and ungainly women were frozen in postures of ritual fulfillment. How could he get them to be so glad about it, *all* of them? I wondered. Only the last album was very sexy. There were pictures of that big woman he married, from clothed to very unclothed, to inside her, many angles. In these the woman seemed cruel and proud, with threatening smiles, dominating the photographer himself, and triumphant in a near-fascist way.

"See, I'm not nice. I've got to keep them. Look again, caress them."

Given the times, none of this was very scandalous, and you had to reimagine the fifties to get very disturbed. They were curios, and Harold did seem pathetic, hanging on to them, and having them along to assist his biography, which nobody was ever going to write.

"I'm a sad old man," he smiled.

"I had a great scandal, I think," I told him.

"Well. Word gets around. It must have been rough."

I stared at him. It must have been blankly.

"Not those. Those are nothing. Those were mere absolutely typical drunkenness, right on schedule," I at last admitted to somebody.

Then I tried, and failed, with boorish pauses and needless lies, to tell him about Felice.

She lived, but just barely. All three needles had found the liver, and others had died with a third of the same wounds. I understand she was yellow and even black all over for weeks. A newsman called our home. I had been identified as "a youth" in their local small paper. My father took the call and politely told him that I really had nothing further to add and was trying to get on with my life. The newsman himself was very understanding and polite. My father wasn't, not to me. He had a name in town. Above all things, he despised scandal.

My love for Felice went on belligerently, sullenly, for a month. It was all I had that was undiscussable and untouchable, and it pulled me through, wondering about her and the difference I might have made in her life. I would see her in other hotels, and there she behaved much like a nun of the old tales, looking out a drab window with a bar of light on her face, and you saw a tear under her eye for remembrance of wholesome youth and true love and what could have been. I tried to rave on the heath but was too conscious of the real fact that I was just bawling like a brat.

"But Harold, Harold!" I took the sleeve of his blazer, shaking it. "I was real then. I throbbed, buddy. I did throb."

Harold was stunned.

"That woman got *you*. But she needed *me*," he said.

★ ★

Hey, Have You Got a Cig, the Time, the News, My Face?

★ ★

HIS DREAMS WERE NOT GOOD. E. DAN ROSS HAD CONSTANT NIGHT-mares, but lately they had run at him deep and loud, almost begging him. He was afraid his son would kill his second wife. Ross often wanted to kill his own wife, Newt's mother, but he was always talking himself out of it, talking himself back into love for her. This had been going on for thirty-two years. E. Dan Ross did not consider his marriage at all exceptional. But he was afraid his son had inherited a more desperate fire.

Newt had been fired from the state cow college where he taught composition and poetry. Newt was a poet. But a friend of Ross's had called from the campus and told him he thought Newt, alas, had a drinking problem. He was not released for only the scandal of sleeping with a student named Ivy Pilgrim. There was his temper and the other thing, drink. Newt was thirty. He took many things very seriously, but in a stupid, inappropriate way, Ross thought. There were many examples of this through the years. Now, for example, he had married this Ivy Pilgrim. This was his second wife.

The marriage should not have taken place. Newt was unable to swim rightly in his life and times. The girl was not pregnant, neither was she rich. If she had made up that name, by the way, Ross might kill her himself. He could imagine a hypersensitive dirt-town twit leeching onto his boy. Newt's poetry had won several awards, including two national ones, and his two books had been seriously reviewed in New York papers, and by one in England.

Ross did not have to do all the imagining. Newt had sent him a photograph a month ago. It was taken in front of their quarters in the college town, where they remained, Newt having been reduced in scandal, the girl having been promoted, Ross figured. Ross was a writer himself. He was proud of Newt. Now he was driving to see him from Point Clear, Alabama, a gorgeous village on the eastern shore of Mobile Bay. Ross and his wife lived on a goodly spread along the beach. He worked in a room on the pier with the brown water practically lapping around his legs. It was a fecund and soul-washed place, he felt. He drove a black Buick Riviera, his fifth, with a new two-seater fiberglass boat trailing behind. It was deliberately two-seater. There would be no room for the girl when they went out to try the bass and bream.

He saw ahead to them: the girl would be negligent, a soft puff of skin above her blue jeans, woolly "earth sandals" on her feet, and a fading light in her eyes, under which lay slight bags from beer and marijuana and Valium when she could get it. Newt's eyes would be red and there would be a scowl on him. He will be humming a low and nervous song. He will be filthy and misclothed, like an Englishman. His hands will be soft and dirty around the fingernails. He'll look like a deserter on the lam. This is the mode affected by retarded bohemians around campus. Cats would slink underfoot in their home. Cats go with really sorry people. If anybody smokes, Newt and Ivy will make a point of never emptying the ashtray, probably a coffee can, crammed and stinking with cigarettes. Somebody will have sores on the leg or a very bad bruise somewhere. They will have a guitar which nobody can play worth spit. A third of a bottle of whiskey is somewhere, probably under the sink. They'll be collecting cash from the penny bowl in order to make a trip to the liquor store. This is the big decision of the day. Old cat food would lie in a bowl, crusted. Shoes and socks would be left out. Wherever they go to school or teach it is greatly lousy, unspeakably and harmfully wrong. This was his son and his wife, holding down the block among their awful neighbors in a smirking conspiracy of sorriness; a tract of rental houses with muddy, unfixed motorcycles and bicycles around. Somebody's kid would sit obscene-mouthed on a porch.

E. Dan Ross, a successful biographer, glib to the point of hackery (he prided himself on this), came near a real monologue in his head: your son is thirty and you see the honors he has won in poetry become like cheap trinkets won at a fair and now you know it has not been a good bargain. A bit of even immortal expression should not make this necessary. It should have brought him a better woman and a better home. Your son has been fired in scandal from a bad school. Newt must prevail, have a "story." These poets are oh, yes, insistent on their troubled biography. The fact is that more clichés are attached to the life of a "real" writer than to that of a hack. Every one of them had practically memorized the bios of their idols and thought something was wrong if they paid the light bill on time. When I talk to my son, Ross thought, it is comfortable for both of us to pretend that I am a hack and he the flaming original; it gives us defined places for discussion, though I have poetry in my veins and he knows it, as I know damned well he is no real alcoholic. The truth is, Newt would drink himself into a problem just for the required "life." Nobody in our family ever had problems with the bottle. It is that head of his. He did not know how to do life, he did not know how to cut the crap and work hard. He did not know that doomed love would wreck his work if he played around with it too much. There is cruelty in the heart of those who love like this. There is a mean selfishness that goes along with being so deplorable. You will say what of the life of the spirit, what has material dress to do with the innerness, the deep habits of the soul, blabba rabba. Beware of occasions that call for a change of clothing, take no heed for the morrow, Thoreau and Jesus, sure, but Newt has no mighty spiritual side that Ross has seen. Newt's talent, and it is a talent I admit, is milking the sadness out of damned near everything. Isolating it, wording it into precise howls and gasping protests.

Newt swam in melancholy, he was all finned out for tragedy, right out of the nineteenth century, à la Ruskin, wasn't it? Look deep enough into the heart of things and you will see something you're not inclined to laugh at. Yeah, gimme tragedy or give me nothing. My heart is bitter and it's mine, that's why I eat it. He would squeeze the sadness out of this Buick Riviera convertible like it was a bright black sponge. Ross agreed that his son should win the awards—he was good, good, good—but he could make you look back and be sorry for having had a fine time somewhere. You would stand convicted in the court of the real for having had a blast at Club Med, or for seeing the hopefulness at a christening. Ross had been offered university jobs paying four times what his son made, condo included. But Newt's readers—what, seventy worldwide?—rejoiced in the banal horror of that. They were, doubtless, whiskered Philip Larkinophiles in shiny rayon pants, their necrotic women consorts sighing through yellow teeth. The job Newt had thrown away, his allegiance to the girl for whom he had thrown it all away, had paralyzed him. There *must* be love; it has to have been all worthwhile. Ross took an inner wager on Newt's having a pigtail. He now sang with a punkish band. Odds were that he had not only a pigtail but some cheap pointless jewelry too around his wrist, like a shoelace.

Ross intended to talk his son out of this Ivy Pilgrim. A second brief marriage would go right into the vita of a modern poet just like an ingredient on a beer can. No problem there. Lately his son had written "No poems" in every letter, almost proudly, it seemed to Ross. But this was more likely a cry beneath a great mistake. In the backseat of the car were a CD player and a superior piece of leather Samsonite oversize luggage, filled with CDs. It was not a wedding gift. It was to remind Newt, who might be stunned and captured in this dreadful cow-college burg, that there were other waters. Sometimes the young simply forgot that. The suitcase was straight-out for him to leave with. Ross was near wealthy and read Robert Lowell too, goddamnit. And "The Love Song of J. Alfred Prufrock" was his favorite poem. Had poetry done any better in this century? No. There were inklings here and there, Ross thought, that his boy was better than Eliot, if you take away the self-prescribed phoenix around his neck, this thing with women. Newt had a son from his first wife, a college beauty who had supported his melancholy. Already Newt was at odds with his seven-year-old son, who was happy and liked sports and war toys. He cursed his ex-wife and raised her into an evil planetary queen, since she sold real estate and had remarried a muscled man who had three aerobic salons. But Ross recalled the time when this woman was the source of Newt's poems, when it was she and Newt against the world, a raving dungeon teasing the eternally thirsty and famished.

This little Ivy Pilgrim had to be a loser and Newt would kill her one day. He had threatened his last wife several times and had shot a hunting arrow into his estranged house. Ross projected seeing Newt in the newspaper, jailed and disconsolate, Ivy Pilgrim's corpse featured in his bio, Newt not remembering much, doomed forever. Then bent on suicide. Or a life of atonement, perhaps evangelism. Or teaching prison poetry workshops, a regular venue for worthless poets nowadays.

Everett Dan Ross (given, not a pen name; how he despised writers who changed their names for whatever reason!) could see Ivy Pilgrim in the desolate house. Hangdog and clouded, nothing to say for herself. It made him furious. He predicted her inertia, a feckless, heavy tagalong. The bad skin would tell you she was a vegetarian. At best she would be working a desk out of a welfare office someday. Or "involved" in an estate settlement (meticulous leeching of the scorned dead). One always appreciated those who gave attention to one's son, but she would have a sickening deed to him, conscious that they were a bright scandal at this dump of a college ("Oh yes, they don't know what to do with us!") in the Romantic vein. When the truth was, nobody cared much. They might as well have been a couple of eloped hamsters. She was a squatter, a morbid lump, understanding nothing, burying him with her sex. She'd favor the states of "laid back" and "mellow," as if threatened crucially by their opposites.

Ross, through life, had experienced unsafe moments. He knew where Newt's melancholy came from. It was not being sued by that true hack whose biography Ross had done. It wasn't Ross's fault the man was too lazy to read the book before it came out, anyway, though Ross had rather surprised himself by his own honesty, bursting out here at age fifty-two—why? Nor was it the matter of the air rifle that always rode close to him. Nor was it a panic of age and certain realizations, for instance that he was not a good lover even when he loved his wife, Nabby. He knew what was correct, that wives liked long tenderness and caressing. But he was apt to drive himself over her, and afterward he could not help despising her as he piled into sleep for escape. She deserved better. Maybe his homicidal thoughts about her were a part of the whole long-running thing. The flashes of his murderous thoughts when she paused too long getting ready to go out, when she was rude to slow or mistaken service personnel, when she threw out something perfectly fine in the trash, just because she was tired of it or was having some fit of tidiness; even more, when she wanted to talk about them, their "relationship," their love. She wondered why they were married and worse, she spoke this aloud, bombing the ease of the day, exploding his work, pitching him into a rage of choice over weapons (Ross chose the wire, the garrote, yes!). Didn't she know that millions thought this and could shut up about it? Why study it if you weren't going to *do* anything? She did not have the courage to walk out the door. *He* did, though, along with the near ability to exterminate her. She also called his work "our work" and saw herself as the woman behind the man, etc., merely out of cherished dumb truism. But none of these things, and maybe not even melancholy, could be classified as the true unsafe moments.

Especially since his forties, some old scene he'd visited, made his compromises with, even dwelled with, appeared ineffably sad. Something beyond futility or hopelessness. It was an enormous more-than-melancholy that something had ever existed at all, that it kept taking the trouble to have day and eyesight on it. He felt that one of them—he or it—must act to destroy. He would look at an aged quarter—piece of change—and think this. Or he would look at an oft-seen woman the same way. One of them, he reasoned, should perish. He didn't know whether this was only mortality, the sheer weariness of repetition working him down, calling to him, or whether it was insanity. The quarter would do nothing but keep making its rounds as it had since it was minted, it would not change, would always be just the quarter. The woman, after the billions of women before her, still prevailed on the eyesight, still clutched her space, still sought relief from her pain, still stuffed her hunger. He himself woke up each morning as if required. The quarter flatly demands use. The woman shakes out her neurons and puts her feet on the floor. His clients insisted their stories be told. He was never out of work. Yet he would stare at them in the unsafe moments and want the two of them to hurl together and wrestle and explode. His very work. Maybe that was why he'd queered that last bio. The unsafe moments were winning.

Ross's Buick Riviera, black with spoked wheel covers, was much like the transport of a cinematic contract killer; or of a pimp; or of a black slumlord. There was something mean, heartless and smug in the car. In it he could feel what he was, his life. Writing up someone else's life was rather like killing them; rather like selling them; rather like renting something exorbitant to them. It was a car of secrets, a car of nearly garish bad taste (white leather upholstery), a car of penetrating swank; a car owned by somebody who might have struck somebody else once or twice in a bar or at a country club. It was such a car in which a man who would dye his gray hair might sit, though Ross didn't do this.

He kept himself going with quinine and Kool cigarettes. All his life he had been sleepy. There was nothing natural about barely anything he did or had ever done. At home with his wife he was restless. In his writing room on the pier he was angry and impatient as often as he was lulled by the brown tide. Sleeping, he dreamed nightmares constantly. He would awaken, relieved greatly, but within minutes he was despising the fact that his eyes were open and the day was proceeding. It was necessary to give himself several knocks for consciousness. His natural mood was refractory. He'd not had many other women, mainly for this reason and for the reason that an affair made him feel morbidly common, even when the woman displayed attraction much past that of his wife, who was in her late forties and going to crepey skin, bless her.

It could be that his profession was more dangerous than he'd thought. Now he could arrange his notes and tapes and, well, *dispense* with somebody's entire lifetime in a matter of two months' real work. His mind outlined them, they were his, and he wrote them out with hardly any trouble at all. The dangerous fact, one of them, was that the books were more interesting than they were. There was always a great lie in supposing any life was significant at all, really. And one anointed that lie with a further arrangement into prevarication—that the life had a form and a point. E. Dan Ross feared that knowing so many biographies, *originating* them, had doomed his capacity to love. All he had left was comprehension. He might have become that sad monster of the eighties.

Certainly he had feelings, he was no cold fish. But many prolific authors he'd met were, undeniably. They were not great humanists, neither were they caretakers of the soul. Some were simply addicted to writing, victims of inner logorrhea. A logorrheic was a painful thing to watch: they simply could not stop observing, never seeing much, really. They had no lives at all. In a special way they were rude and dumb, and misused life awfully. This was pointed out by a friend who played golf with him and a famous, almost indecently prolific, author. The author was no good at golf, confident but awkward, and bent down in a retarded way at the ball. His friend had told Ross when the author was away from them: "He's not even here, the bastard. Really, he has no imagination and no intelligence much. This golf game, or something about this afternoon, I'll give you five to one it appears straightaway in one of his stories or books." His friend was right. They both saw it published: a certain old man who played in kilts, detailed by the author. That old man in kilts was the only thing he'd gotten from the game. Then the case of the tiny emaciated female writer, with always a queer smell on her—mop water, runaway mildew?—who did everything out of the house quickly, nipping at "reality" like a bird on a window ledge. She'd see an auto race or a boxing match and flee instantly back to her quarters to write it up. She was in a condition of essential echolalia was all, goofy and inept in public. Thinking these things, E. Dan Ross felt uncharitable, but feared he'd lost his love for humanity, and might be bound on becoming a zombie or twit. Something about wrapping up a life like a dead fish in newspaper; something about lives as mere lengthened death certificates, hung on cold toes at the morgue; like tossing in the first shovelful of soil on a casket, knocking on the last period. "Full stop," said the British. Exactly.

Ross also frightened himself in the matter of his maturity. Perhaps he didn't believe in maturity. When did it ever happen? When would he, a nondrinker, ever get fully sober? Were others greatly soberer and more "grown" than he? He kept an air rifle in his car, very secretly, hardly ever using it. But here and then he could not help himself. He would find himself in a delicious advantage, usually in city traffic, at night, and shoot some innocent person in the leg or buttocks; once, a policeman in the head. Everett Dan Ross was fifty-two years old and he knew sixty would make no difference. He would still love this and have to do it. The idea of striking someone innocent, with impunity, unprovoked, was the delicious thing—the compelling drug. He adored looking straight ahead through the windshield while in his periphery a person howled, baffled and outraged, feet away from him on the sidewalk or in an intersection, coming smugly out of a bank just seconds earlier, looking all tidy and made as people do after arranging money. His air rifle—a Daisy of the old school with a wooden stock and a leather thong off its breech ring—would already be put away, snapped into a secret compartment he had made in the car door which even his wife knew nothing about. Everett Dan Ross knew that he was likely headed for jail or criminal embarrassment, but he could not help it. Every new town beckoned him and he was lifted even higher than by the quinine in preparation. It was ecstasy. He was helpless. The further curious thing was that there was no hate in this, either, and no specific spite. The anonymity of the act threw him into a pleasure field, bigger than that of sexual completion, as if his brain itself were pinched to climax. There would follow, inevitably, shame and horror. Why was he not—he questioned himself—setting up the vain clients of his biographies, his fake autobiographies, some of whom he truly detested? Instead of these innocents? They could be saints, it did not matter. He *had* to witness, and exactly in that aloof peripheral way, the indignity of nameless pedestrians. He favored no creed, no generation, no style, no race. But he would not shoot an animal, never. That act seemed intolerably cruel to him.

Assuredly his books raised the image of those he wrote about. Ross had developed the talent long ago of composing significance into any life. He had done gangsters, missionaries, musicians, politicians, philanthropists, athletes, even other old writers. He could put an aura on a beggar. Then with the air rifle, he would shoot complete innocents to see them dwindle. He would swear off for months but then he would come back to it.

It had happened often that Ross was more interesting than his subjects. He was certainly not as vain. Writing his own autobiography would not have occurred to him. But there was a vain and vulgar motive in everybody he depicted: *look at me,* basically. The ones who insisted on prefaces disclaiming this howling fact made him especially contemptuous. It was not hilarious anymore, this "many friends have beseeched me to put down in writing," etc. Blab, blook, blep. It was astounding to Ross to find not one of his biographees conscious of this dusty ritual in their own case. *Their* lives were exempt from the usual flagrant exhibitions of the others. His last chore on a porcine Ohio hack writer—the suer, as Ross called him—a sentimental old fraud who'd authored one decent book a century ago when he was alive, then rode like a barnacle the esteem of the famous who suffered him the rest of his life, dropping names like frantic anchors in a storm of hackism and banality. Ross had to pretend blithe unconsciousness to the fact that the man "was ready for his story to be told," and had sent friends to Ross to "entice you to sit down with shy, modest X." Ross also had to watch the man get drunk about seventy times and blubber about his "deep personal losses," his "time-stolen buddies." The depth of his friendship with them increased in proportion to their wealth and fame. Ross kept a bland face while the obvious brayed like a jackass in the room. The amazing fact was that the man had lived his entire life out of the vocabulary and sensibility of his one decent book. There seemed to be no other words for existence since 1968, no epithets for reality outside the ones he'd bandaged on it twenty years ago. He'd written his own bible. Most of all he adored himself as a boy, and wept often now about his weeping then. Ross gutted through, and one night, as it always did, the hook fell out to him gleaming—the point of the biography: history as a changeless drunken hulk, endlessly redundant; God himself as a grinding hack The sainthood of no surprises. The Dead Sea. This truth he sedulously ignored, of course—or thought he had—and whipped out a tome of mild hagiography. This was his fifteenth book and sold better than the others, perhaps because it celebrated the failure of promise and made the universal good old boys and girls very comfortable. The hack was a Beam-soaked country song.

The fact that Ross himself was a sort of scheduled hack did not alarm him. There weren't many hacks of his kind, and that pleased him. He dared the world to give him a life he could not make

significant on paper and earn some money with. So didn't this indi-
cate the dull surprise that nobody was significant? Or was it the great
Christian view—every man a king? Ross had no idea, and no inten-
tion of following up on the truth. Years ago he had found that truth
and the whole matter of the examined life were overrated, highly.
There were preposterous differences in values among the lives he
had thrown himself into. Even in sensual pleasure, there was wide
variance. He himself thought there was no food served anywhere
worth more than ten dollars. No woman on earth was worth more
than fifty, if you meant bed per night. Others thought differently,
obviously. The young diva who put pebbles in her butt and clutched
them with her sphincter (she insisted he include this)—well, it was
simply something. It made borderline depraved people feel better
when they read it. Also, when would the discussion about love ever
quit? He could be deeply in love with most of the women in every
fashion magazine he'd ever flipped through. The women would have
to talk themselves *out* of his love, stumble or pick their noses. Usually
he did not love Nabby, his wife, but given an hour and a fresh situation he could talk himself into adoring her.

What he loved was his son.

What was love but lack of judgment?

So if God judged, he was not love, eh?

This sort of stuff was the curse of the thinking class. You went
away to college and came back with such as that to nag your sleep
till you dropped.

Best to shut up and live.

Best to shoot anonymous innocent citizens with an air rifle
and shut up about it. The delicious thing was that the stricken howled
and bore the indignity as best they could, never to have an answer.
He saw them questing through the decades for the source of that
moment. He saw them dying with the mystery of it. Through the
years the stricken had looked up at the top of buildings, sideways to
the alleys, and directly at passersby. Once he had looked directly at a
policeman, beebeed, rubbing his head and saying something. Twice
people had looked deeply at Ross and his car—another year, another
Riviera—but Ross was feigning, of course, sincere drivership. What a
rush, joy nearly pouring from his eyes!

In Newt's neighborhood his car was blocked briefly by some children playing touch football on the broken pavement. They came around and admired his car and the two-seater boat towed behind as he pulled in between dusty motorcycles in front of a dark green cottage, his son's. Already he wanted away from it, on some calm pond with the singing electric motor easing the two of them into cool lily-padded coves, a curtain of cattails behind their manly conversation. They had not fished together in ages. Newt used to adore this beyond all things. Ross had prepared his cynicism, but he had prepared his love even more. The roving happy intelligence on the face of little Newt, age eleven, shot with beauty from a dying Southern sun as he lifted the great orange and blue shellcracker out of the green with his bowed cane pole—there was your boy, a poet already. He'd said he had a new friend, this fish, and not a stupid meal. He'd stroked it, then released it. You didn't see that much in the bloody Southern young, respect for a mere damned fish. He'd known barbers to mount one that size, chew and spit over it for decades.

They seemed to have matched Ross's care in his presents with (planned?) carelessness about his arrival. This sort of thing had happened many times to Ross in the homes of celebrities, even in the midst of his projects with them. Somebody would let him in without even false hospitality: "Ah, here is the pest with his notes again," they might as well have said, surprised he was at the front door instead of the back, where the fellow with their goddamn mountain water delivered.

The girl indicated somebody sitting there in overalls who was not Newt, a big oaf named Bim, he thought she said. Yes, there always had to be some worthless slug dear to them all for God knew what reasons hanging about murdering time. Bim wore shower shoes. He did not get up or extend a hand. Ross badly wanted his cynicism not to rise again, and made small talk. The man had a stud in his nose. He dressed like this because the school *was* a cow college, Ross guessed. It was hip to enforce this, not deny it, as with Ivy League wear, etc.

"So where do you hail from, Bim?"

"Earth," said the man.

Drive that motherfucking stud through the rest of your nose, coolster, thought Ross. Ross looked straight at Bim with such bleak amazed hatred that the man rose and left the house as if driven by pain. Ross stood six feet high and still had his muscles, though he sometimes forgot. There wasn't much nonsense in him, and those who liked him loved this. The others didn't. He might seem capable of patient chilly murder.

"I don't know what you did, but thanks," said Ivy Pilgrim. "He's in Newt's band and thinks he has a title to that chair. Can't bear him."

"Bimmer has a fine sensitivity. Hello, Dad." Newt had entered from the back. There were only four rooms. "Where'd Bimmer go?"

Newt did not have a ponytail. He had cut off almost all his hair and was red in the face around his beard. He wore gold-rim glasses set back into his black whiskers, and his dark eyes glinted as always. His head looked white and abused, as just shoved into jail. The boy had looked a great deal like D. H. Lawrence since puberty. Here was the young Lawrence convicted and scraped by Philistines. But he didn't seem drunk. That was good.

"I don't believe Bimmer liked me," said Ross.

"He moves with the wind," sighed his son.

"Mainly he sits in the chair," said Ivy Pilgrim.

Ross looked her over. She was better than the photograph, an elfin beauty from this profile. And she wasn't afraid of Newt.

"You have the most beautiful hair I've seen on a man about forever. That salt and pepper gets me every time," she said to Ross.

"Thank you, Ivy." Watch it, old man, Ross thought. Other profile suggests a kitten, woo you silly.

"What instrument does Bimmer play?" he asked.

"Civil Defense siren, bongos, sticks," said Newt seriously.

"So you're in earnest about this band?"

"I've never been more serious about anything in my life." Since Newt was twenty, Ross was wary of asking him any questions at all. He'd get the wild black glare of bothered pain.

Who could tell what this meant? Though with his bald head it seemed goony and desperate.

Ross was parched from the road. He sat in Bimmer's chair, big and tweedy. The place was not so bad and was fairly clean. There were absolutely no books around. He wondered if there were a drink around. He'd planned to share some iced beer with Newt, by way of coaching him toward moderation, recovering what a man could be—healthy in a beer advertisement. He was throwing himself into the breech, having lost the taste for the stuff years ago.

"I'm either going to sing or go into the marines," said Newt. Was he able to sit still? He was verging in and out of his chair. *Akathisia,* inability to sit, Ross recalled from somewhere. It was a startling thing when one's own went ahead and accumulated neuroses quite without your help. Ross looked at the girl, who'd come in with a welcome ginger ale, Dr. Brown's.

"Newt remembered you liked this," she said.

This was an act that endeared both of them to him. At last, a touch of kindness from the boy, though announced by his wife.

"Well, I need a splash with mine," said Newt. He went to the kitchen and out came the Rebel Yell, a handsome jug of bourbon nearly full. However, this was histrionic, Ross was sure. Newt did not look like he needed the drink. He had affected the attitude that a man of his crisis could not acknowledge ginger ale alone. Ross, having thought more than usual on the way up to Auburn and presiding too much as father to this moment, sincerely wanted to relax and say to hell with it. He wasn't letting anybody live. The marines, singing? So what? Give some ease. He himself had been a marine, sort of.

Where was it written in stone, this generational dispute? Are fathers always supposed to wander around bemused and dense about their young? Wasn't it true old Ross himself had nailed the young diva, weeping runt, with her heavy musical titties bobbling, right in the back door? While Nabby, loyal at home—source of Newt right in front of him   was shaking her mirror so a younger face would spill out on it? Not very swell, really, and his guilt did not assuage this banal treachery. Old, old Ross, up the heinie of America's busty prodigy. Awful, might as well be some tottering thing with a white belt and toupee, pot, swinging around Hilton Head. What a fiend for one of Newt's poems, but really beneath the high contempt of them.

"So how's the poetry making, anyway, sport?"

Newt was tragic and blasé at once, if possible, gulping down the bourbon and ginger.

"Nothing. It's the light. Light's not right."

"But you're not a painter, Newton. What light?"

"He means in his *brain*," explained Ivy.

"My love for Ivy has killed the light."

Newt had to give himself his own review, this seriously? Good gad. Save some for the epitaph.

"I like it that way," Newt added hurriedly, but just as direly.

Ivy seemed upset and guilty, yearning toward Ross for help. "I didn't want to be any sort of killer."

He liked this girl. She had almost not to say another thing in her favor. *She* had the pigtail, pleasant down the nice scoop of her back.

"Well, can't we open the shroud a little here, Newton? Look outside and see if you can see a little hope. Maybe some future memories, son."

Newt shuffled to the door and looked at the car and boat a whole minute, too long. Ivy got Ross another Dr. Brown's. The last thing Ross might say in a hospital room someday in the future, nurse turning out of the room: "Nice legs." Good for little Ivy. Would it never stop? Ross had long suspected, maybe stupidly but as good as any genius, through life and his biographies, that women with good legs were happy and sane. Leg man as philosopher. Well, Nabby's seemed to persuade mostly joy out of the day, didn't they? Even given the sullen, jagged life he sometimes showed her. Get out of my skin and look, he thought: Was I ever as, oh, *difficult* as Newt myself? Probably, right after he'd fired himself from the war, though he hid it in Chase's house in San Pedro.

"So what do you see, Newt?"

"No wonder Bimmer left," said Newt.

"Now, can you explain that?"

"Bimmer's father is a man of . . . merchandise."

Hold off, *hang fire*, with Henry James. Ross cut himself off. With a new enormous filtered Kool lit—stay with these and you've got at most twenty-five years, likely; we don't have a clumsy century of discord to work it out, Newt, for heaven's sake—he thought, Don't give me that *merchandise* crapola, young man. I bred you in Nabby. You know very well my beach house and all of it could burn up and not impress me a great deal, never did. Let's take off the gloves, then. *I* came here.

"Is that why your man Bimmer dresses like a laid-off plough-boy? Missing the fields and horse shit over to the back forty?"

Newt smiled. Maybe this was the real turf, here we were. The smile was nice, at last, but why did he have to destroy his head? His son's hair was black and beautiful like his used to be.

"So let me declare myself and your mother finally. The quick wedding, there wasn't any time for presents much."

Ivy went with him to the Riviera. She saw the CD player inside and gave a gasp of pleasure. It was the piece of luggage full of CDs she wound up with.

"This wonderful suitcase. I'll bet you want us to get out of this dump p.d.q.?"

Ross felt very mean for his previous plans for the bag.

"Where are *you* from, Ivy?"

"Grand Bay, close to Bayou La Batre. Right across the bay from you. The poor side, I guess. But I loved it. And I'm not broke."

"Fine. Very fine." Unnecessary, but necessary, on the other hand. She'd won him.

"So there we are. Boat, motor, the player. And *voilà!* (Ross opened the bag, nearly a trunk). Some late wedding music."

"Must be fifty discs there!" cheered Ivy.

"Thought you and I might break in the boat and pursue the finny tribe this afternoon," said Ross, brightly.

Christmas in May, he was feeling, was really an excellent idea. Look down, son.

Newt barely glanced into the suitcase.

"Fishing? That's pretty off the point, Dad."

"Oh, Newton!" Ivy jumped right on him.

"What's . . ." Don't, Ross. He was going to ask what *was* the point, you bald little bastard?

"I've promised the kids I'd play some touch with them. Just about to go out there. Then there's the band tonight. You can come with Ivy if you want."

"Newt takes the band very seriously," said Ivy. This seemed to be a helpful truth for both the men. Ross forgot Newt's rudeness. Or did he *know?* What part of loony Berryman or Lowell had he researched? Newt glanced at Ivy dangerously. This brought Ross's nightmares right up, howling. This was the feared thing. His son seemed to want to beat on this strange idiot who'd just opened her mouth.

Ross couldn't bear it. He went out with a fresh Kool and the remains of the ginger ale and stood in the yard near his sleek Buick, gazing through some cypresses to a man-provoked swamp behind the hideous cinder blocks of an enormous grocery, some kind of weeds native only to the rear of mall buildings, ripping up through overflowed mortar on the ground.

Here he was back in "life," shit, man with twenty-five years to go, wearing a many-pocketed safari shirt next to a pimp's car. What did an old American man *wear* rightly, anyway? Fifty-two *was* old. Cut the hopeful magazine protests. You spent half your time just trying not to look like a fool. What intense *shopping*. Hell, shouldn't he have on a blazer, get real in a gray Volvo? Disconnection and funk, out here with his killer Kool, pouting like a wallflower; son inside wrecking the afternoon with bald intensity. Back to his nightmares, the latest most especially: Ross, as an adult, was attending classes in elementary school, somehow repeating, but bardlike, vastly appreciated at the school by one and all for some reason, king of the hill, strolling with the children, glib, but why? The school was paying him a salary while he was doing what? But at the school gate he was in a convertible with two girls, and two men—one of them Newt—jumped in the car and rammed long metal tongs through the skulls of the girls. Their screams were horrible, the blood and bone were all over Ross. Then policemen appeared and drove metal tongs through the skulls of Newt and the other man. The screams of Newt were unbearable, loud! He'd awakened, panting. Ross almost wept, looking at the back of that grocery now. But it was a dry rehearsal, with only a frown and closed eyes.

Ivy touched him on the arm. "Sometimes you've just got to ignore him. I'll go fishing with you. Please, I'd love to. And I love everything you brought. Thank your wife, Nabby, for me."

Marriage was a good cause, thought Ross. On a given day chances were one of you might be human. Was D. H. Lawrence a rude bastard, even into his thirties?

He saw the kids gather and Newt go out as the giant weird quarterback. The day was marked for gloom but he was going to have something good out of it. He did not want to watch his son play football. But thanks, Lord, for providing him with the dread image: Newt had once embarrassed him playing football with young kids.

He was home from graduate school—Greensboro—at Christmas. He was invited over to an old classmate's house in Daphne. Ross came later to have a toddy with the boy's father. It was another big modest beach house with a screened porch all the way across the back. They took their hot rums out to the old wooden lounges and watched Newt and his friend quarterback a touch game with his friend's nephews and nieces, ages five to twelve. Ross was pleased his boy cared about sports at all. It was a stirring late December day, cool and perfect for neighborhood touch, under the Spanish moss and between the hedges. But then Ross saw his contemporary staring harder out there and when Ross noticed, things were not nice. Newt was hogging the play and playing too rough, much too rough. He smashed the girl granddaughter of this man into the hedge. She didn't cry, but she hung out of the game, rubbing her arms. Then Newt fired a pass into the stomach of a boy child that blew him down into the oyster-shell driveway. The kid was cut up but returned. Newt's friend implored him and the children were talking about him, but he remained odd, yes, and driven. Ross was looking at something he deeply despised seeing. He did not want to think about the other examples. They called the game. The children came up on the porch hurt and amazed, but gamely saying nothing around Ross. They were tough, good children, no whiners. In the car home, he said to Newt, "Son, you were a mite fierce out there. Just kids, *kids.*" Newt waited a while and came back, too gravely: "You want me to smile all day like a waitress?"

This *fierceness,* off the point, that was it.

So they drove around and Ivy, who did not change from her short skirt and flowered blouse to go fishing, directed him through town to pick up Newt's bounced checks—this tavern, that grocery, the phone company. Ross didn't mind. He'd expected financial distress and had brought some money. With some irony of kinship he'd brought up a fairly big check from Louisiana State University Press to sign over to Newt. This concern had published Newt's books. Ross had just picked up a nice bit of change from a piece of his they were anthologizing. Christ, though, the kid might make something out of it. But not a kid. He was thirty. Newt's sister Ann was twenty-eight, married in Orlando, straight and clean as a javelin, thanks. Ivy Pilgrim (her real name) wanted to know all about Ann and Nabby. Then they did go fishing.

Auburn had some lovely shaded holes for fishing in the country. Erase the school, and it was a sweet dream of nature. Ross, a Tuscaloosa man, could never quite eliminate his prejudice that Auburn U should have really never occurred, especially now that it had fired his boy. There had been some cancerous accident among the livestock and chicken droppings years ago, and, well, football arose and paid the buildings to stay there and spread. These farm boys, still confused, had five different animal mascots, trying to get the whole barnyard zoo in. Ivy was amused by these old jokes, bless her, though he really didn't mean them. She was in architecture, hanging tough. How could Newt have attracted *her*? he thought, instantly remorseful.

She thought Newt would return to his poems soon. Improbably, she *understood* his books and wanted him to move on to—pray for rain!—some *gladness*, bless him. The poetry had won her over, but as a way of life it sucked wind.

"Newt is proud of you and he wants to be glad," she said.

"Honestly?"

"Honestly."

Once he had been to an inspirational seminar with one of his clients. The speaker was a man who had been through unbearable, unlucky, unavoidable horror. He told the crowd he intended never ever to have another bad day. He just wouldn't. He was going to force every day to be a good day. Ross was heeding the man now. He was glad he'd remembered. He concentrated on Ivy, who was a good fisherman. She had sporting grace. They caught several bluegills and one large bass. There was never any question but that she'd clean them and put them in the freezer, since Ross was buying her supper.

"I suppose, though, Newt is casting around for other work?"

"It's the band, the band, the band. He writes for it, he sings. He says everything he's ever wanted to say is in the band."

Ross had noted the late gloomy competency in American music, ever a listener in his Riviera. Electricity had opened the doors to every uncharming hobbyist in every wretched burg, even in Ohio. You could not find a dusthole without its guitar man, big eyes on the Big Time beyond the flyspecked window, drooling, intent on being wild, wild, wild. America, unable to leave its guitar alone, teenager with his dick: "Look here, I've got one too." He saw Newt, late-coming thirty, in the tuning hordes, and it depressed him mightily. As witness the millions of drips in "computers" now. Yeah, toothless grizzled lay-about in the Mildewville Café: "Yep, my boy used to cornhole bus exhausts, he's now in computers." Look down at a modern hotel lobby, three quarters of them were in "computers," asking the desk clerk if the sun was shining. His daughter's husband, a gruesome Mormon yuppie, was "in computers." Then Ross's ears harked to the Riviera speakers—something new, acoustic, a protolesbian with a message. Give people a chance, Ross corrected himself: you were a G-22, Intelligence, with the marines in the worst war ever, by *choice*, dim bulb in forehead. Whole squad smoked by mortars because of you, put them on the wrong beach. A gloomy competency would have been refreshing, ask their mothers. I could have stayed home and just been shitty, like the singer Donovan, hurting only music.

Back at home, she showered while Ross set up the CD player with its amazing resonant speaker boxes. What a sound they had here with Miles Davis. She heard it while the water ran. Ross was excited too. In his fresh shirt, blazer, trousers and wingtips, he emerged from his own shower, opened the mirror door of the medicine chest to check Newton's drugs, and caught Ivy Pilgrim sitting naked on her bed, arms around her breasts, sadly abject and staring at the floor. Ross looked on, lengthening the accident. This is my daughter, my daughter, he thought, proud of her. The brave little thing.

There was a great misery she was not sharing with him. Doomed or blessed—he couldn't know—he froze at the mirror until she looked over at him in the reflection and saw him in his own grief. Ross felt through the centuries for all chipper wives having to meet their in-laws. Holy damn, the strain. She was such a little lady, revealed. He smiled at her and she seemed to catch his gratitude instantly. Oops, slam the mirror. Nice there was nothing ugly here. I won't have a bad day, I won't. This was the best of it, and later he thanked the highway rushing in front of him for it.

• • •

The place was a converted warehouse rank with college vomit, beer in AstroTurf, a disinfectant thrown contemptuously over it. The spirit of everywhere: spend your money, thanks, fuck you. Chicken-yard hippies, already stunned by beer, living for somebody right out of suburban nullity like them, "twisted" on his guitar stroking: "He don't *give* a damn." Couple of them so skinny they looked bent over by the weight of their cocks. Ivy had quit beaming. Since the mirror there had been an honest despair between them.

Newt and his truly miserable band came on, tuning forever as the talentless grim do. Ross was sorry he was so experienced, old. He could look at the face and bald pate of the drummer, comprehending instantly his dope years and pubic sorriness, pushed on till damned near forty, no better on drums than any medical doctor on a given Sunday afternoon with the guys. Then came Bimmer, a snob in overalls, fooling with his microphone like some goon on an airport PA system. Then a short bassman so ugly he *had* to go public. The sax man could play, but he was like some required afterthought in a dismal riot of geeks. Then there was a skinny man near seven feet tall who just danced, male go-go. What an appalling idea. Then Newt, not contented with the damage he'd done on backup guitar, began singing. He was drunk and fierce, of course. The point seemed to be anger that music was ever invented. It was one of the ugliest episodes Ross had ever witnessed. He smiled weakly at poor Ivy, who was not even tapping her foot. She looked injured.

At the stage, Ross saw the chicken-yard hippies and a couple of their gruesome painted hags, hateful deaf little twats who might have once made the long trip to Birmingham. They loved Newt and egged him on. This was true revolt. Ross wondered why the band had bothered to tune.

He had had dreadful insights too, too often nowadays, waking up in a faraway hotel with his work sitting there, waiting for him to limn another life. The whole race was numb and bad, walking on thin skin over a cesspool. Democracy and Christianity were all wrong: nobody much was worth a shit. And almost everybody was going to the doctor.

"Professional help" for Newt flashed across his mind, but he kicked it away, seeing another long line, hordes, at the mental health clinic, bright-eyed group addicts who couldn't find better work waiting inside. Ross had known a few. One, a pudgy solipsist from Memphis, had no other point to his life except the fact he had quit cigarettes. A worthless loquacious busybody, he'd never had a day of honest labor in his life. What did he do? He "house sat" for people. But the fellow could talk about "life" all day.

Then things really got mean.

Newt, between sets, red-eyed, hoarse, angrily drunk, drew up a chair ten feet away from Ivy and his father, muttering something and bearing on them like some poleaxed diagnostician. Ross at last made out that Newt was disgusted by his blazer, his shoes, his "rehearsal to be above this place."

"This place is the whole world, sad Ross-daddy. You won't even open your eyes. There's nowhere else to go but here! No gas, no wheels, no—" He almost vomited. Then he walked his chair over to them, still in it, heaving like a cripple. He was right in their faces, sweat all over him.

"Good-looking pair, you two. Did you get an old touch of her, Pops?" He reached around and placed his hand over Ivy's right breast. "But I tell you. Might as well not try. You can't make Ivy *come*, no sir. She ain't gon come for you. Might as well be humping a rock, Rosser!"

Crazy, mean, unfinished, he laid his head on the table between them. The sweat coming out of his prickly head made Ross almost gag. Then he rose up. His eyes were black, mad. He couldn't evict the words, seemed to be almost choking.

Ross handed over the endorsed check and stood to leave.

"What are you going to do for work, son?"

"S'all that bitch outside says. Job, job, job."

"Well, bounced checks, bounced checks, bounced checks is not your sweetest path either." He hated Newt. An image of Newt, literally booted out the window by an Auburn official, rose up and pleased him.

"Shut up, you old fuck," said Newt. "Get home to Mama. And remember, remember . . ."

"What? Be decent, goddamnit."

"Let the big dog eat. Always fill up with supreme."

Ross looked with pity at Ivy. Given the tragedy, he could not even offer to drive her home.

Outside the turn at the Old Spanish Fort, Ross knew he would lie to Nabby. All was well in Auburn. Save Nabby, God, he asked. She was a fine golfer, in trim, but all those days in the sun had suddenly assaulted her. Almost overnight, she was wrinkled and the skin of her underchin had folds. The mirror scared her and made her very sad. Ross, for all his desk work and Kools, and without significant exercise, was a man near commercially handsome, though not vain. There was something wrong with the picture of a pretty fifty-two-year-old fellow in a Riviera, anyway. In the mirror, he often saw the jerk who'd got eleven young men mortared over there—a surviving untouched dandy. A quality in all of Ross apologized and begged people to look elsewhere.

Newt, by the way, had married somebody much like his mother. Small, bosomy, with slender legs agreeable in the calf. Probably he wouldn't kill Ivy. Ross would make a good day of this one, be damned. It was only midnight. Nabby was up.

He caressed her, desperate and pitiful, wishing long sorrowful love into her. She cried out, delighted. As if, Ross thought, he were putting a whole new son in Nabby and she was making him now, with deep pleasure.

Newt had left some books in the house a while back. Ross wanted to see what made his son. He picked up the thing by Kundera with the unburdening thesis that life is an experiment only run once. We get no second run, unlike experience of every other regard. Everything mistaken and foul is forever there and that is you, the mouse cannot start the maze again; once, even missing the bull's-eye by miles, is all you got. It is unique and hugely unfair. No wonder the look you see on most people—wary, deflected, puzzled—"What the hell is happening?" Guy at a restaurant, gets out of his car and creeps in as on the surface of the moon. Ross liked this and stopped reading. There would be no Newt ever again, and whatever he'd left out, fathering the boy, it was just botched forever, having had the single run. Forgiven, too, like a lab assistant first day on the job. And then Ann, not a waver, twice as content as Ross was, almost alarmingly happy. She was the one run too. He could call Ann this instant and experience such mutual love it almost made him choke. There was the greedy Mormon, her husband, but so what? You didn't pick her bedmate out of a catalog.

The old hack suing E. Dan Ross backed off, unable to face the prospect of any further revelations on himself the trial might bring. He called up Ross himself, moaning. He was a wreck, but a man of honor too, a First Amendment champion after all. Ross, who'd never even hired a lawyer, felt sorry for what the erupting truth had brought to both of them. He feared for his future credit with clients. But the hack was invited on television, in view of his new explosion of hackery, a photo album valentine to every celebrity he'd let a fart off near. He became a wealthy man, able to buy a chauffeur who took him far and wide, smelling up the privacy of others.

For months they did not hear from Newt, only two cards from Ivy thanking them for boat, motor, luggage and Newt. This sounded good. Around Christmas they got a letter from Newt. He was in the state asylum in Tuscaloosa, drying out and "regaining health and reason." The marriage was all over. He was smashed with contrition. There'd been too many things he'd done to Ivy, unforgivable, though she'd wanted to hang in right till the last. What last nastiness he had done was, after her badgering, he'd written her a poem of such devastating spite there was no recovery. It was a "sinful, horrible thing." Now he still loved her. She'd been a jewel. He was a pig, but at least looking up and out now. He pleaded with them not to visit him. Later, out, when he was better. He still had health insurance from the school and needed nothing.

. . . And Dad, the boat and motor was wonderful. Bimmer stole it, though. He proved to be no real friend at all. I ran after him down the highway outside the city limits with a tire tool in my hand. They say I was raving, my true friends, and they brought me up here. True. I was raving. No more "they said." Please forgive me. I'm already much better.

Love, Newton

Nabby and he held hands for an hour. Nabby began praying aloud for Newt and then blamed the "foreigners at Auburn and all that dreadful radioactivity from the science department." Ross was incredulous. Nabby was going nuts in sympathy. Have a good day, Ross, have a good day. He walked out to the pier, into his writing room, and trembled. For no reason he cursed the Bay of Mobile, even the happy crabs out there. What could a man take?

Then, next week, another blow lowered him. Chase's wife called and told him Chase was dead. He'd taken a pistol over to Long Beach, threatened his ex-wife, and was killed in a shoot-out with the police. God have mercy. Chase was a policeman himself.

Ross recalled the street, the long steep hill down to Paseo del Mar from Chase's house, with thick adobe walls around it. Ross had needed the walls. He was badly messed up and stayed that way a month, having fired himself from the war, G-22, all that, after he misdirected the Seals to a hot beach and got them mortared. Chase met him in a bar and they stayed soaked for five weeks. Chase was a one-liner maniac. All of life had a filthy pun or stinger. Ross thought it was all for him and appreciated it. But when he got better and wouldn't drink anymore, Chase kept it up. Ross needn't have been there at all, really, he found out. Chase became angry when Ross quit laughing. Not only were the jokes not funny anymore, Ross knew he was witnessing a dire malady. Chase kept hitting the beer and telling Ross repeatedly about his ex-wife, whom he loved still even though married to Bernice, a quiet thin Englishwoman, almost not there at all but very strong for Chase, it seemed to Everett D. Ross, before he was E. Dan Ross. Ross heard of vague trouble with the woman in Long Beach and the law. But Chase was selfless and mainly responsible for Ross's recovery, giving him all he needed and more. Chase had also adopted a poor street kid, a friend of his daughter's. He was like that. He would opt for stress and then holler in fits about it. When Ross told him he was leaving, taking his rearranged name with him back to Mobile where his wife waited, hoping for his well-being, Chase went into a rage and attacked him for ingratitude, malingering, and—what was it?— "betrayal." Not of the Seals. Of Chase. It was never clear and Chase apologized, back into the rapid-fire one-liners. Chase was very strange, but Ross had not thought he was deranged. The shoot-out sounded like, certainly, suicide, near the mother of his children. Too, too much. A man Ross's age, calling happily to the ships at sea around LA Harbor over his ham set. Raving puns and punchers.

The very next day he heard that a classmate of his, the class joker, had shot himself dead in a bathtub in San Francisco. Wanted to make no mess. Something about money and his father's turning his back on him. Ross could not work. He stayed in his pier room rolling up paper from his new biography—of an old sort of holy cowboy in San Antonio. Talked to animals, birds, such as that. Four wives, twelve children. The balls of paper lay in a string like popcorn on the meager tide, going around the ocean to California where the dead friends were. Ross thought of the men not only as dead but as dead fathers. Children: smaller them, offspring of grown pranksters, gag addicts. Ross thought of his air rifle. His classmate, last Ross had seen of him, right before he went over to Vietnam, was in the National Guard. He did something hazy for athletic teams around Chicago, where Ross last saw him. It didn't take much time. His real life work was theft and happy cynicism about others. Bridge could level anybody with mordant wit. He'd kept Ross and others howling through their passionate high school years. Once, on a lake beach in late April, a class party where some of the girls were in their bathing suits sunning themselves, first time out this spring, Bridge had passed a couple of lookers and stopped, appreciative, right in front of them: "Very, very nice. Up to morgue white, those tans." The boys howled, the girls frowned, mortified. Given everything by his psychiatrist parents, Bridge still stole, regularly. Ross heard he'd been kicked out of the university for stealing a football player's watch from a locker. Bridge was an equipment man. He deeply relished equipment, and ran at the edge of athletic teams, the aristocracy in Southern schools. In Chicago, he'd taken Ross up to his attic. Here was a pretty scary thing: Bridge had stolen from his unit a Browning .30-caliber machine gun and live ammo and enough gear to dress a store dummy, stolen somewhere else; he had set the dummy behind the machine gun among a number of sandbags (the labor!) so that the machine gun aimed right at the arriving visitor. Ross jumped back when the light was turned on. Bridge, Bridge. Used to wear three pairs of socks to make his legs look bigger. Used Man Tan so he was brown in midwinter. Children, money and booze. Maybe great unrepayable debt at the end.

Ross knew he was of the age to begin losing friends to death. But more profound was the fact that he was not the first to go. Fools, some thirty of them from his big high school in Mobile, had gone over to Asia and none of them was seriously scratched or demented on return. It was a merry and lusty school, mental health or illness practically unheard of. What was his month of breakdown? Nothing. What was he doing, balling up the hard work and watching it float off? Nothing.

His son in a nut ward, Nabby collapsing, he took down a straight large glass of tequila and peered strongly across the bay to where Ivy Pilgrim had grown up. Did she have to be all disappeared from Newt, forever? A smart young woman, very sexy, plenty tough, endowed, couldn't cure him. He missed her. Ross, frankly, was glad Newton didn't want him at the asylum. But he sat down and wrote him a long letter, encouraging his strengths. The tequila gave him some peace. He took another half glass. His friend, Andy the pelican, walked into the room and Ross began talking to him, wanting to know his adventures before he opened a can of tuna for him.

He confessed his grief and confusion to the pelican. The absurd creature, flying bag, talked back to him: "Tell me. It's rough all over, pard. Lost my whole family in Hurricane Fred." One thing about the sea, thought Ross, sneering toward it, it doesn't care. Almost beautiful in that act. Maybe we should all try it.

Next thing they heard, Newt was visiting his sister in Orlando. She and her husband lent their condo at New Smyrna Beach to him. He was sunning and "refining his health" at pool and oceanside. He was working on poems and didn't know how he felt about them. Walker, Ann's husband, came by frequently and chatted. He liked Walker a lot. He wasn't going to impose on them forever. The world was "over there" and he knew it. Ross and Nabby's music was helping, thanks. Especially Bach. Had they ever listened to the Tabernacle Choir? Glorious. Newt said that he wanted "excruciatingly to walk in the Way." Grats extreme too for the money. He was just beginning his life and would be reimbursing everybody soon.

"Truly, though, people, I like being poor and I am going to get used to it."

Ross had written himself neutral. He rewrote what he had thrown to sea, it didn't matter, there it was all back and the life of the saintly cowboy wrote itself. He wrote twenty pages one night, nonstop, and recollected that he could not remember what he had said. When he read the pages, however, they were perfect. The words had gone along by themselves. Ross seemed not to have mattered at all. His mind, his heart, his belly were not engaged. Entailed was a long episode of murder, rape, and the burning alive of a prized horse. A short herd of people were killed, the cowboy wounded in the throat. It was some of Ross's best writing, but he had not particularly cared. Even hacks sometimes cared, he knew. This business was too alike to the computer goons he despised. Ross was bleak. He'd just gotten too damned good at his stuff. He was expendable. Nothing but the habitual circuitry was required.

Otherwise, it was a good year. Nabby did not say any more insane things. But she badly wanted a face-lift. Felt sure she was falling apart and would not show herself near sunlight. Back in her room the ointments overblew the air. She kept herself in goo and almost quit golf. They had had separate rooms since Newt went to the asylum. She felt ugly. Ross felt for her deeply. This emotion was a constant tender sorrow and that was what he had instead of the eruptions of love and homicidal urges. It was much better, this not too sad little flow. Their love life was much better, in truth. A sort of easy tidal cheer came over Ross, fifty-three. He was appreciating his years and the pleasant gravitation toward death. It had a sweet daze to it. He could look at his tomb and smile, white flag up in calm surrender.

Why not a face-lift, and why not love? Things were falling together even though he was a disattached man. He rushed to finish the book before the old cowboy died. Blink, there it was. The old man's children read it to him and he liked it very much. They told Ross his eyes, like a robin's eggs, brightened. He blessed the author. He had never thought his life made any sense. He had never meant to be famous or read about. He wished he could read. By far he was the most pleasant subject Ross had ever worked with.

Nabby, fresher at the neck though a little pinched at the eyes after her face-lift, wanted the children to visit over Thanksgiving and have a family portrait made. They'd not heard much from either of them lately. Newt was teaching night classes at a community college in Orlando. He had his own place.

But when Ann called he could hear his daughter was not right. Something had happened. The upshot was Newt had converted to Mormonism, very zealously, and had simply walked out of town and his job and his apartment, without a word to anyone. Nobody knew where he was. He had destroyed all his poetry two months before. He left everything he owned.

Ross could see his wife, blank in her new face, holding the phone as if it were a wounded animal. She cradled it and stroked it. Ross had never seen an act like that. Ann's voice continued but her mother listened at the end, when Ross took the phone, as if death were speaking to her directly. Ann's husband, Walker, came on and detailed the same version.

"What do Mormons, new Mormons, do?" asked Ross.

"There's no place, like a Mecca, if that's what you mean," said Walker.

"I mean how should they act?"

"It's inside, Ross. They affirm. They attend. They practice. They study. A great deal of study."

"What *did*, damn it, Mormonism—or *you*—do to Newton?"

"He wasn't raving. It's not charismatic."

"Would he be in some fucking airport selling flowers?"

Walker hung up. His reverent tongue was well known. All told, he was a Boy Scout with a hard-on for wealth; the boy so good he was out of order. He wouldn't even drink a Coke. Caffeine, you know. When Ross lit a Kool, Walker looked at him with great pity. Ross hated him now, smug and square-jawed, wearing a crew cut. He saw him dripping with a mass of tentacles attached to him, dragging poor Newton into the creed, "elders" spiriting him away. The cult around Howard Hughes, letting him dwindle into a freak while they waited on his money. Clean-cut international voodoo. Blacks and Indians were the tribes of Satan, weren't they? Ross always rooted against BYU when they played football on television. Sure. Hardworking, clean-limbed boys next door. Just one tiny thing or three: we swallow swords, eat snakes, and ride around on bicycles bothering people for two years. Nabby lay on her bed with her new face turned into the pillow. Ross petted her, but his anger drove him out to the pier again, where for a long time he searched the far shore for the image of his lost daughter-in-law, Ivy, naked and in grief, hugging her breasts.

So. The colleges wouldn't have him anymore. There goes that option. He had a great future behind him, did Newt.

"Destroyed his poems." Right out of early Technicolor. Have mercy on us. What kind of new Newton did we have now? Fig Newton, Fucked Newton. He tried hard again not to detest his boy. He tried to picture him helpless. Mormons probably specialized in weak depressed poets. Promise him multiple wives, a new bicycle. But more accurately Ross detested Newton for the sane cheer of his letters. What a con man, cashing Ross's ardent checks. Venal politician. Ross could hit him in the face.

From Ann he had heard that Ivy was at home with her father, who was sick and might die. They'd cut a leg off him just lately. Ross wanted to take the form of Andy the pelican and fly over there to her.

This did not feel like his home right now. He did not like Nabby collapsing again, especially with her expensive new face. He reviewed his grudges against her. Five years ago, at the death of his father—an ancient man beloved by everyone except Nabby, who thought he was an awful chauvinist who loved to be adored too much: true—she had not shed a tear until later in the car when she told Ross some woman had alluded slyly to her sun wrinkles. She began cursing and crying for herself, his father barely in the ground, Ross almost drove the Riviera off the road. He said not a word all the way home from Florida. Nabby, jealous of the dead man who'd upstaged her own dear plight; the funeral a mere formality while huge issues like sun wrinkles were being battled.

Feeling stranded, he'd driven over to Bayou La Batre four days later. He didn't call ahead. The Pilgrims lived just off Route 90 in a little town called Grand Bay. A healthy piece of change from the old cowboy's book had just arrived. He was anxious to spend money on something worthwhile. How impoverished were the Pilgrims?

The mother had been a surprise. He'd not told Nabby about it, for the first time in his life with her.

Their home was neat. On the front were new cypress boards, unpainted. The house was large and the yard was almost grassless, car ruts to one side, where he parked behind a jeep with an Auburn sticker on the rear window. Over here you got a sense of poor Catholics, almost a third world, some of them Cajun and Slavic and Creole. He'd always loved this country. Most of your good food came from these people; your music, your bonhomie, your sparkling black-eyed nymphs. Upland, the Protestants had no culture. If anything, they were a restraint on all culture, especially as it touched on joy. He thought of Newton, now even odder than they were, beyond them, in a culture of how much crap can you swallow, unblinking, and remain upright. Close by was the great shipyard at Pascagoula, where Ivy's father had worked. You threw a crab net in the water and thought of submarines the length of football fields close under you, moving out with fearsome nukes aboard. Almost a staggering anomaly, these things launched out of the mumbling-dumb state of Mississippi.

Ivy and one of her brothers, also a painter at Ingalls, met him at the door. They were very gracious, though mournful. It didn't look like their father was going to make it. An hour from now they would go back to the hospital in Mobile. Surprising himself, Ross asked if he might go with them, drive them. They thought this was curious, but would welcome a ride in his Riviera, which the brother thought was the "sporting end." He had a coastal brogue. Ivy had got rid of hers. Maybe it would not go with a career in architecture. Ivy looked radiant in sorrow. When he mentioned Newt, the brother left for the back of the house, where it smelled like Zatarain's spices and coffee.

"I've heard a few things, none of them very happy. I'm afraid I don't love him anymore, if you wanted to know that," she said.

The finality hurt Ross, but he'd expected it. He did not love the boy much either.

"He was in the shipyards 'witnessing.' My brothers saw him. Some security guys took him out of the yard. He had a bicycle. He told my brother he was going to places around large bodies of water."

"Did he have 'literature'?"

"The Book of Mormon? No, he didn't. You'd know that Newt would be his own kind of Mormon or anything. He'd stretch it."

Ross recalled his hideous singing.

"Did you ever think of Newt's age?" she asked him.

Ross went into a terrible cigarette cough and near-retching, reddening his face. Father of Newt, he felt very ugly in front of her; a perpetrator.

"His age. Thirty-one. Jesus Christ was crucified at age thirty-three. A Mormon is a missionary, all the males, for two years." Ivy revealed this much in the manner of a weary scientist. The evidence was in: cancel the future.

"You figured that out, Ivy. Do you . . . How . . . Would you like him dead?"

"Oh *no,* Dan!" She was shy of using his first name, but this brought her closer to him. "A friend of mine from Jackson, big party girl, said she saw him at the Barnett Reservoir north of the city. He was 'witnessing' outside a rock-and-roll club and some drunk broke his ribs. The ambulance came but he wouldn't get in."

"He rode a bike to Jackson, Mississippi?"

"I suppose so. Don't they have to?"

At the hospital he was useless, pointless, and ashamed of his good clothes, a pompous bandage on his distress. He smoked too much. He looked for a Book of Mormon in the waiting room. One of the nurses told him no flatly and looked at him with humor when he asked if there were one around. An alien to their faith, he was being persecuted anyway. The world was broken and mean.

The only good thing about the trip was the sincere good-bye hug from Ivy in her yard. She was on him quickly with arms tight around his neck, not chipper anymore, and she cried for her father, him and Newt, too, all at once. The strength of it told him he would probably never see her again. So long, daughter. I will not have a bad day, will not. He crashed into early night.

In Mobile, on Broadway beneath one of the grandfather live oaks "bearded with Spanish moss"—as a hack would write—Ross beheld a preacher, a raver, with a boom box hollering gospel music beside him on the sidewalk. He was witnessing through the din, screaming. Heavy metal would be met on its own terms. Three of the curious peered on. It was a long red light. Ross unsnapped the chamber, lower left, where his air rifle was hidden. He badly needed to shoot. But for that reason, he did not. He saw it was in there oiled, heavy with ammo, *semper fidelis,* a part of his dreams.

The next option was to buy a tramp and hump her silly. Make a lifelong friend of her. Nice to have a dive to dip into, young Tootsie lighting up in her whore gaud. Calamity Jane. Long time, no see, my beacon. Miserable bar folks withering around their high-minded big-time copulation. Relieve himself of wads, send her to South Alabama U, suckology. Nabby bouncing dimes off her face back home, considering a mirror on the ceiling and her own water tower of ointment.

He cruised home, shaking his head. He was having another bad day, and the clock was up on legs, running.

The next day he set out for Jackson, got as far as Hattiesburg, saw a bicycle shop, hundreds of bikes out front, sparkling spokes and fenders under the especially hired muttering-dumb Mississippi sun, and grew nauseated by chaos. Too many. He'd never find Newt, going on one mission from one large body to the next. He feared his own wrath if he found him. Two more years of life for him, if you listened to Ivy, who might know him better than Ross. Newt's conversion still struck him as elaborately pretended, another riot of fierceness. In Salt Lake City, he would have turned Methodist. What was he "witnessing"—what was his hairy face saying? He wouldn't sustain. He was a damned lyric poet, good hell, having a crucifixion a day, maybe even broken ribs, but chicken when the nails and the hill hove into view.

They did not know where he was for nearly a year. Minor grief awoke Ross every morning. Nabby almost shut down conversation. Some days he woke up among his usual things, felt he had nothing but money and stuff, was crammed, pukey with possessions—its, those, thingness, haveness. One night in April he tore up a transistor radio. Nothing but swill came out of it, and he always expected to hear something horrible about Newton. He dropped his head and wanted to burn his home. The men he'd got mortared called to him in nightmares, as they had not ever before. The tequila, nothing, would help.

The murdered men begged him to write their "stories, our stories." Their heads came out on long sprouts from a single enormous hacked and blasted trunk. He got to where he feared the bed and slept on the couch under a large picture of him and Nabby and the kids, ages ago. Everybody was grinning properly, but Ross looked for precocious lunacy in the eyes of young Newt, or some religious cast, some grim trance. He fell asleep searching for it.

What was religion, why was he loath to approach it on its own terms? You adopted it, is what you did, and you met with others you supposed felt as you did, and you took a god together, somebody you could complain to and have commiserate. Not an unnatural thing one bit, though inimical to the other half of your nature, which denied as regularly as your pulse out of the evidence of everyday life. For instance the fact that God was away, ancient and vague at his best. Also there was the question of the bully. Ross had never been a bully. Better that he had been, perhaps. He had never struck a man in a bar or country club. Ross's mother was a religious woman, aided in her widowhood by church friends and priest, who actually seemed to care. He had never bullied her. Rather the reverse. She'd used the scriptures to push him around, guiltify him. There was no appeal to a woman with two millennia of religion behind her. Ross suddenly thought of the children Newt played football with, or *at*, hurting them, oppressing them. A thin guy, *he* was the bully, as with his little wives. A lifelong bully? Bullying the happiness out of life. Bullying his parents—a year and a half without a word.

When Ross was in his twenties, he went to Nabby's family reunion up in Indiana. Most of her relatives were fine, scratchy hill people, amused by the twentieth century, amused by their new gadgets like weed eaters, dishwashers and color televisions. They were rough, princely Southern Americans. Ross thought of Crockett and Bowie, Travis, the men at the Alamo. But then the pastor of the clan came on board, late. It was Nabby's uncle, against tobacco, coffee, makeup, short dresses, "jungle music" and swearing. Stillness fell over the clan. The heart went out of the party. That son of a bitch was striding around, quoting the prophets, and men put away their smokes, women gathered inward, somebody poured out the coffee, and he was having a great time, having paralyzed everybody before he fell on his chicken. So here was Newt? Indiana preacher's genes busting out, raiding the gladness of others.

They received a letter, finally, from Newton, who was not too far from them, eight hours away in Mississippi. He was superintendent of a boys' "training school" and taught English. The school had a storm-wire fence around it, barbed wire on top, armed guards, and dogs for both dope and pursuit at the ready. Tough cases went there. Sometimes they escaped out to the county and beyond to create hell. Parents had given up, courts had thrown in the towel and placed them here, the last resort. Occasionally there were killings, knifings, breakages; and constant sodomy. A good many of the boys were simply in "training" to be lifelong convicts, of course. Much of their conversation was earnest comparison of penal situations in exotic places, their benefits and liabilities. Many boys were planning their careers from one joint to another as they aged, actually setting up retirement plans in the better prisons they considered beds of roses. A good half of them never wanted outside again. The clientele was interracial, international and a bane to the county, which was always crying out for more protection and harsher penitence. Newt wrote that he had to whip boys and knock them down sometimes, but that "a calm voice turneth away anger," and he was diligently practicing his calmness. He was married yet again. His wife was pregnant. She was plain and tall, a Mennonite and recovering heroin addict, healthy and doing very well. This love was honest and not dreamy. Newt apologized for much and sent over twelve poems.

They were extraordinary, going places glad and hellish he'd never approached before.

Ross cried tears of gratitude. His hands shook as he reread the poems: such true hard-won love, such precise vision, such sane accuracy—a sanity so calm it was beyond what most men called sanity. He raised his face and looked over Dauphin Island to the west, taken. Nabby trembled the entire day, delirious and already planning Christmas three months ahead. Newt was bringing his wife over to meet them and visit a week, if they would have him. He invited Ross to visit him at the school as soon as he could get over. His voice on the phone when Ross called seemed a miracle of quiet strength. He made long, patient sentences such as Ross had never heard from him before. Ross would leave that night.

His brand-new navy blue Riviera sat in the shell drive. It was a sweet corsair, meant for a great mission: nothing better than the health and love of the prodigal son. Bring out the horns and tambourines. Poor Ann. There was no competition. All she was now was nice, poor Ann. He wanted to pick up his wealth in one gesture and dump it on Newton.

Outside Raymond, Mississippi, he pushed the hot nose of his chariot into a warm midmorning full of nits, mosquitoes, gnats and flying beetles. His windshield was a mess. Ross was going silly. He felt for the bugs and their colonies. Almost Schweitzer was he, hair snowier, fond, fond of all that crept and flogged.

They were very stern at the gate, sincere cannons on their hips, thorough check of the interior, slow suspicious drawls rolled out of the lard they ate to get here. While they repeated the cautions three or four times—about stopping the car (don't) and watching his wallet ("hard eye if I's yoo") and staying some lengths away from everybody, they acted as if Newt were a great creature on the hill ("Mister Ross he funk nare boot cup, nard").

Ross had not been searched thoroughly since the war, when at the hospital they feared briefly for his suicide, and in a strange way he felt flattered by these crackers taking the time around his own domain. Only when he was driving up to Newt's house did he go cold, as splashed with alcohol. They'd missed the air rifle, which he had forgotten was there. Then he fell back, silly. It was an *air* rifle only. There would have been no trouble, only shy explanation about its presence and the snap compartment, where there should have been, if he were mature he supposed, a sawed-off pump for danger on the road. The times they were a-changing, all the merciless ghouls prowling for you out there, no problem. A shotgun would be easier to explain than a Daisy. Over here was the *home* of the peacemakers racked across the rear windshield, handy to the driver. Could always be a fawn or doe out of season to shoot, Roy Bob. Over here they considered anybody not in the training school fair gubernatorial timber.

So this was Newt's new job, new home, new Newt. He'd not said how long he'd been here. A job like this, wouldn't it take a while to qualify? But this was the Magnolia State. He'd probably beaten out somebody who'd killed only two people, his mother and father; little spot on his résumé.

Some boys were walking around freely, gawking at his car. This must be how a woman felt, men "undressing her with their eyes," as that Ohio tub of guts might "inscribe." Those kids would probably tear this car down in fifteen minutes. My God, they had skill-shops here to give them their degrees in it. Ross noticed that almost every boy, whether gaunt or swaybacked, chubby or delicate, had on expensive high-top sneakers. Crack and high-tops were probably the school mascots. But he saw more security men than boys outside. He'd glanced at the Rules for Visitors booklet: no sunglasses, no overcoats, no mingling with the student body. Do not give cigarettes or lighters if requested. Your auto was not supposed to have a smoked glass windshield or windows, but they had let him through because he was the father of "Mister Ross."

At Newt's WPA-constructed house, like the house of a ranger in a state park—boards and fieldstone—Ross hugged his son at the door, getting a timid but then longer hug back. His wife was still getting ready. They had just finished a late-morning breakfast. There had been trouble last night. Three boys cut the wire and escaped, APBs were issued, the dogs went out, and they were brought back before they even reached Raymond, where they were going to set fire to something.

Ross was thinking about the appearance of Newt's pregnant wife. Why had he thought it necessary to describe her as "plain" in his letter, even if she was? It was something too deliberate, if you worried the matter. Revenge? Against Ivy, his first wife, his mother? Ross's handsome world scorned? He hoped not.

She, Dianne, was very tall, taller than Newt by three inches and close to Ross's height. She sat at the dining room table, very long and big-stomached, about seven months along. Her father had run this place before Newton. He was retiring and Newton, well, was right there, ready, willing, able—and with (she placed her hand over Newton's at the salt and pepper shakers) the touch of the poet.

Ross did not want to ask his boy the wrong questions and run him away. He was gingerly courteous—to the point of shallowness, he realized, and hated this. It made him feel weak and bullied and this couldn't go on long. But Newt was forthright.

"Not just the broken ribs over at the reservoir, Dad. I was saying my thing at Tishomingo, on the boat dock, and her" (he smiled over at Dianne, who looked fine although a bit gawky—old romantic history a-kindling) "boyfriend, this tattooed, ponytailed 'ice' addict, stabbed me with a knife right in the heart."

"You're not telling me—"

"Right *in* the heart. But Dianne knew, she was once a nurse and still will be when she gets her license back. She wouldn't let me or anybody pull it out. The knife itself was like a stopper on the blood."

"That's true," said Dianne. "He went all the way to the hospital with it still in him and you could see it pumping up and down with Newton's heart. They helicoptered him to Memphis."

"She followed me in a car, without her boyfriend." Newt giggled. "She was strung out, violently sick herself, but drove all the way over, couple hundred miles."

"The love got me through, don't you see, Mr. Ross? I was already in love with him, like a flash. It pulled me through the heroin, the withdrawal. I sat out there in that waiting room, sick as a dog. But there is a God, there is one."

"Or love. Or both, sure," said Ross. "He stuck you for being a Mormon, Newt?"

Newt still smiled at his father. He looked much older, used, but his grown-out hair was long, like a saint's or our Lord's, thought Ross. Now the spectacles gentled him and he seemed wise and traveled, much like his new poems.

"Pa, don't you know me? I was Mormon, I was Jew, I was Christ, I was Socrates, I was John the Baptist, I was Hart Crane, Keats, Rimbaud. I was everything tragic. I'm still outcast, but I'm almost sane."

His son giggled and it was not nervous or the giggle of a madman. It was just an American giggle, a man's giggle—"What the hell is going on?"—full-blooded and wary.

"You love these boys? I suppose they're helping you back to . . . helping you as . . ."

"Hell no, I don't love them. I hate these bastards. It might not be all their fault, but they're detestable vermin and utter shits, for the main part. I love, well, five. The rest . . . What you find most often is they've been spoiled, not deprived. Like me. Nobody lasts long here. They try to love but it gets them in a few months. Dianne's father lasted, but he's the meanest, toughest son of a bitch I've ever met."

Dianne assented, laughing again, about this paternal monster, just a solid fact. The laugh surely lit up that plain face nicely.

"Come eat with me in the big hall and I'll show you something," said Newt.

"Is this a bad question? What are you going to do? Stay here *because* you hate it?"

"No. I'll do my best. But I'm in fair shape for a job up at Fayetteville. They've seen my new work and I guess they like post-insane poets at Arkansas. Actually, a lot of folks like you a lot when you straighten out a little. The world's a lot better than I thought it was."

Ross considered.

"Newt, do you believe in Christ?"

"Absolutely. Everything but the cross. That never had anything to do with my 'antisocial' activity. I'll still holler for Jesus."

"I love you, boy."

"I know it. Last month I finally knew it. Didn't take me forever, is all I can say."

"Thanks for that."

"There's some repaying to do."

"Already done. The new poems."

Dianne wept a little for joy. This was greatly corny, but it was magnificent.

In the big hall, eating at the head table among the boys, Ross got a drop-jaws look at real "antisocial" manners. Guards were swarming everywhere, but the boys, some of them large and dangerous, nearly tore the place apart. They threw peas, meat, rolls, just to get primed. Two huge blacks jumped on each other jabbing away with plastic knives. A half grapefruit sailed right by the heads of Ross and Newt. It had been pegged with such velocity that it knocked down the great clock on the wall behind them. Whoever had done it, they never knew. He was eating mildly among them, slick, cool, anonymous, wildly innocent, successful. Right from that you could

get the general tenor. Unbelievable. Newt and he were exiting when
a stout boy about Newt's height broke line and tackled him, then
jumped up and kicked him with his huge black military-looking
high-tops. Newt scrambled up, but was well hurt before the guards
cornered the boy, who'd never stopped cursing violently, screaming,
the whole time. With their truncheons the guards beat the shit out
of the kid and kept it up when he was handcuffed and down, maybe
unconscious. None of the other boys seemed to think it was unusual.
They neither cheered nor booed.

Newt wanted him to sleep over so they could go fishing early
the next day. He knew a place that was white perch and bass heaven.
Dianne insisted, so he did.

They did fairly well on the fish, again in a pond so dark green
and gorgeous you could forget the training school and human horror
everywhere.

"I guess, like I heard anyway, you went to bodies of water because, well, because what?" Ross asked.

"Because in the South, I figured, the men who change the
world mostly go fishing?" He laughed at his father with the fly rod
in his hands, so sincere. "They want *out* of this goddamned place."

Next morning he left them cheerfully, driving out, but then,
as he neared the gate, he circled back—out on his own hook, cautious in the car with smoked windows. He had seen what he wanted,
set it up, had found his nest. There was a place in the parking lot for
officials and staff that the Riviera nestled into, uniform in the ranks
of autos and pickups, as you might see in a big grocery lot. Behind
his smoked window he was unseen. Sixty feet away was the entrance
to a shop or snack bar. Anyway, a lot of the boys were gathered there,
allowed to smoke.

Ross unsnapped the compartment and withdrew the Daisy.
My, it had been months, years. Thin, tall, lumpy, sneering, bent,
happy, morose, black, white, Indian. It didn't matter. He rolled the
window down just a tad, backing up so the barrel wasn't outside the
window.

He began popping the boys singly, aiming for the back of their
necks and, if lucky, an ear. That was about the best pain he could in-
flict. A boy leapt up, howling, holding his wound. He got another

right on the tit. Did he roar, drop his cigarette, stomp and threaten the others? Yes. He popped another in the back of the head, a hipster with tattooed arms mimicking sodomy. Many of them were questioning, protesting, searching the trees in the sky and other inmates.

Ross rolled up the window and watched them through the one-way glass.

That's it, lads. Start asking some big questions like me, you little nits. You haven't even started yet.

★ ★

1993-1996
High Lonesome

★ ★

Get Some Young

SINCE HE HAD RETURNED FROM KOREA HE AND HIS WIFE LIVED IN MU-
tual disregard, which turned three times a month into animal passion
then diminished on the sharp incline to hatred, at last collecting in
time into silent equal fatigue. His face was ordinarily rimmed with a
short white beard and his lips frozen like those of a perch, such a face
as you see in shut-ins and winos. But he did not drink much anymore, he simply often forgot his face as he did that of his wife in the
blue house behind his store. He felt clever in his beard and believed
that his true expressions were hidden.

Years ago when he was a leader of the Scouts he had cut way
down on his drink. It seemed he could not lead the Scouts without going through their outings almost full drunk. He would get
too angry at particular boys. Then in a hollow while they ran ahead
planting pine trees one afternoon he was thrust by his upper bosom
into heavy painful sobs. He could not stand them anymore and he
quit the Scouts and the bonded whiskey at the same time. Now and
then he would snatch a dram and return to such ecstasy as was painful and barbed with sorrow when it left.

This man Tuck last year stood behind the counter heedless of
his forty-first birthday when two lazy white girls came in and raised
their T-shirts then ran away. He worried they had mocked him in
his own store and only in a smaller way was he certain he was still

desirable and they could not help it, minxes. But at last he was more aggrieved over this than usual and he felt stuffed as with hot meat breaking forth unsewed at the seams. Yes girls, but through his life he had been stricken by young men too and became ruinously angry at them for teasing him with their existence. It was not clear whether he wished to ingest them or exterminate them or yet again, wear their bodies as a younger self, all former prospects delivered to him again. They would come in his life and then suddenly leave, would they, would they now? Particular Scouts, three of them, had seemed to know their own charms very well and worked him like a gasping servant in their behalf. Or so it had felt, mad wrath at the last, the whiskey put behind him.

The five boys played in the Mendenhall pool room for a few hours, very seriously, like international sportsmen in a castle over a bog, then they went out on the sidewalks mimicking the denizens of this gritty burg who stood and ambled about like escaped cattle terrified of sudden movements from any quarter. The boys were from the large city some miles north. When they failed at buying beer even with the big hairy Walthall acting like Peter Gunn they didn't much care anyway because they had the peach wine set by growing more alcoholic per second. Still, they smoked and a couple of them swore long histrionic oaths in order to shake up a meek druggist. Then they got in the blue Chevrolet Bel Air and drove toward their camp on the beach of the Strong River. They had big hearts and somehow even more confidence because there were guns in the car. They hoped some big-nosed crimp-eyed seed would follow them but none did. Before the bridge road took them to the water they stopped at the store for their legitimate country food. They had been here many times but they were all some bigger now. They did not know the name of the man in there and did not want to know it.

Bean, Arden Pal, Lester Silk, Walthall, and Swanly were famous to one another. None of them had any particular money or any special girl. Swanly, the last in the store, was almost too good-looking, like a Dutch angel, and the others felt they were handsome too in his company as the owner of a pet of great beauty might feel, smug in his association. But Swanly was not vain and moved easily about, graceful as a tennis player from the era of Woodrow Wilson, though he had never played the game.

From behind the cash register on his barstool Tuck from his hidden whitened fuzzy face watched Swanly without pause. On his fourth turn up the aisle Swanly noticed this again and knew certainly there was something wrong.

Mister, you think I'd steal from you?

What are you talking about?

You taking a picture of me?

I was noticing you've grown some from last summer.

You'd better give me some cigarettes now so we can stamp that out.

The other boys giggled.

I'm just a friendly man in a friendly store, said Tuck.

The smothered joy of hearing this kept the rest of them shaking the whole remaining twenty minutes they roamed the aisles. They got Viennas, sardines, Pall Malls, Winstons, Roi-Tans, raisins; tamales in the can, chili and beans, peanut butter, hoop and rat cheese, bologna, salami, white bread, mustard, mayonnaise, Nehi, root beer, Orange Crush; carrots, potatoes, celery, sirloin, Beech-Nut, a trotline, chicken livers, chocolate and vanilla MoonPies, four pairs of hunting socks, batteries, kitchen matches. On the porch Swanly gave Walthall the cigarettes because he did not smoke.

Swanly was a prescient boy. He hated that their youth might end. He saw the foul gloom of job and woman ahead, all the toting and fetching, all the counting of diminished joys like sheep with plague; the arrival of beard hair, headaches, the numerous hospital trips, the taxes owed and the further debts, the mean and ungrateful children, the washed and waxen dead grown thin and like bad fish heaved into the outer dark. He had felt his own beauty drawn from him in the first eruption of sperm, an accident in the bed of an aunt by marriage whose smell of gardenia remained wild and deep in the pillow. Swanly went about angry and frightened and much saddened him.

Walthall lived on some acreage out from the city on a farm going quarter speed with peach and pecan trees and a few head of cattle. Already he had made his own peach brandy. Already he had played viola with high seriousness. Already he had been deep with a "woman" in Nashville and he wrote poems about her in the manner of E. A. Poe at his least in bonging rhymes. In every poem he expired in some way and he wanted the "woman" to watch this. Already he could have a small beard if he wanted, and he did, and he wanted a beret too. He had found while visiting relatives around the community of Rodney a bound flock of letters in an abandoned house, highly erotic missiles cast forth by a swooning inmate of Whitfield, the state asylum, to whatever zestfully obliging woman once lived there. These he would read to the others once they were outside town limits and then put solemnly away in a satchel where he also kept his poetry. A year ago Walthall was in a college play, a small atmospheric part but requiring much dramatic amplitude even on the streets thereafter. Walthall bought an ancient Jaguar sedan for nothing, and when it ran, smelling like Britain on the skids or the glove of a soiled duke, Walthall sat in it aggressive in his leisure as he drove about subdivisions at night looking in windows for naked people. Walthall was large but not athletic and his best piece of acting was collapsing altogether as if struck by a deer rifle from somewhere. For Walthall reckoned he had many enemies, many more than even knew of his existence.

Swanly was at some odds with Walthall's style. He would not be instructed in ways of the adult world, he did not like talking sex. Swanly was cowlicked and blithe in his boy ways and he meant to stay that way. He was hesitant even to learn new words. Of all the boys, Swanly most feared and loathed Negroes. He had watched the Negro young precocious in their cursing and dancing and he abhorred this. The only role he saw fit in maturity was that of a blond German cavalry captain. Among Walthall's recondite possessions, he coveted only the German gear from both world wars. Swanly would practice with a monocle and cigarette and swagger stick. It was not that he opposed those of alien races so much but that he aspired to the ideal of the Nordic horseman with silver spurs whom he had never seen. The voices of Nat King Cole and Johnny Mathis pleased him greatly. On the other hand he was careful never to eat certain foods he viewed as negroid, such as Raisinets at the movies. There was a special earnest purity about him.

The boys had been to Florida two years ago in the 1954 Bel Air owned by the brother of Arden Pal. They were stopped in Perry by a kind patrolman who thought they looked like runaway youth. But his phone call to Pal's home put it right. They went rightly on their way to the sea but for a while everybody but Swanly was depressed they were taken for children. It took them many cigarettes and filthy songs to get their confidence back. Uh found your high school ring in muh baby's twat, sang Walthall with the radio. You are muh cuntshine, muh only cuntshine, they sang to another tune. From shore to shore AM teenage castrati sang about this angel or that, chapels and heaven. It was a most spiritual time. But Swanly stared fixedly out the window at the encroaching palms, disputing the sunset with his beauty, his blond hair a crown over his forehead. He felt bred out of a golden mare with a saber in his hand, hair shocked back in stride with the wind. Other days he felt ugly, out of an ass, and the loud and vulgar world too soon pinched his face.

The little river rushed between the milky bluffs like cola. Pal dug into a clay bank for a sleeping grotto, his tarp over it. He placed three pictures of draped bohemian women from the magazine *Esquire* on the hard clay walls and under them he placed his flute case, pistol, and Mossberg carbine with telescope mounted there beside two candles in holes, depicting high adventure and desire, the grave necessities of men.

The short one called Lester Silk was newly arrived to the group. He was the veteran army brat of several far-flung bases. Now his retired father was going to seed through smoke and ceaseless hoisting on his own petard of Falstaff beers. Silk knew much of weapons and spoke often of those of the strange sex, men and women, who had preyed the perimeters of his youth. These stories were vile and wonderful to the others yet all the while they felt that Silk carried death in him in some old way. He was not nice. Others recalled him as only the short boy, big nose and fixed leer—nothing else. His beard was well on and he seemed ten years beyond the rest.

Bean's father, a salesman, had fallen asleep on a highway cut through a bayou and driven off into the water. The police called from Louisiana that night. All of the boys were at the funeral. Right after it Bean took his shotgun out hunting meadowlarks. The daughter of his maid was at the house with her mother helping with the funeral buffet. She was Bean's age. She told Bean it didn't seem nice him going hunting directly after his father's funeral. He told her she was only a darkie and to shut up, he made all the rules now. Her feelings were hurt and her mother hugged her, crying, as they watched young Bean go off over the hill to the pine meadows with his chubby black mutt Spike. Bean was very thin now. He had a bad complexion. He ran not on any team but only around town and the gravel roads through the woods. Almost every hour out of school he ran, looking ahead in forlorn agony and saying nothing to anybody. He was the Runner, the boy with a grim frown. When he ran he had wicked ideas on girls. They were always slaves and hostages. His word could free them or cause them to go against all things sacred. Or he would leave them. Don't leave, don't leave. I'll do anything. But I must go. After the death of his father he began going to the police station when he was through with his run. He begged to go along on a call. He hoped somebody would be shot. He wished he lived in a larger city where there was more crime. When he got a wife he would protect her and then she would owe him a great deal. Against all that was sacred he would prevail on her, he might be forced to tie her up in red underwear and attach a yoke to her. Bean was vigilant about his home and his guns were loaded. He regarded trespass as a dire offense and studied the tire marks and footprints neighbor and stranger made on the verge of his lawn. Bean's dog was as hair-triggered as he was, ruffing and flinching around the house like a creature beset by trespass at all stations. Both of them protected Bean's mother to distraction. She hauled him to and fro to doctors for his skin and in the waiting room thin Bean would rise to oppose whoever might cross his mother. Of all the boys, Bean most loved Swanly.

Three boys, Bean among them, waded out into a gravel pool now, a pool that moved heavy in its circumference but was still and deep in its center like a woman in the very act of conception. The water moved past them into a deep pit of sand under the bridge and then under the bluffs on either side, terra-cotta besieged by black roots. An ageless hermit bothersome to no one lived in some kind of tin house on the bank down the way a half mile and they intended to worry him. It was their fourth trip to the Strong and something was urgent now as they had to make plans. They were not at peace and were hungry for an act before the age of school job money and wife. The bittersweet Swanly named it school job money whore, and felt ahead of him the awful tenure in which a man shuffles up and down the lanes of a great morgue. Swanly's father was a failure except for Swanly himself who was beautiful past the genes of either parent. He worshiped Swanly, idolized him, and heeded him, all he said. He watched the smooth lad live life in his walk, talk, and long silent tours in the bathtub. He believed in Swanly as he did not himself or in his wife. It was Swanly's impression there was no real such thing as maturity, no, people simply began acting like grown-ups, the world a farce of playing house. Swanly of all the others most wanted an act, standing there to his waist in the black water.

The storekeeper Tuck knew for twenty years about the clothesline strung from the shed at the rear of the yard of the house behind the store. The T-bar stood at the near end with high clover at its base. Yet that night two weeks ago. His throat still hurt and had a red welt across it. He ran through his lawn and necked himself on the wire. Blind in the dark in a fury. What was it? All right. He had given himself up to age but although he did not like her he thought his wife would hold out against it. After all she was ten years younger. But he saw she was growing old in the shoulders and under the eyes, all of a sudden. That might cause pity, but like the awful old she had begun clutching things, having her things, this time a box of Red Hots she wouldn't share, clutching it to her titties, this owning things more and more, small things and big, when he saw that he took a run across the yard, hard on baked mud, apoplectic, and the wire brought him down, a cutlass out of the dark. Now he was both angry and puny, riven and welted and all kind of ointment sticky at his shirt collar. It was intolerable especially now he'd seen the youth, oh wrath of loss, fair gone sprite. His very voice was bruised, the wound deep to the thorax.

Swanly, out in the river in old red shorts, was not a spoiled child. His father intended to spoil him but Swanly would not accept special privileges. He did not prevail by his looks or by his pocket money, a lot at hand always compared with the money of his partners, and he was not soft in any way so far that they knew. He could work, had worked, and he gave himself chores. He went to church occasionally, sitting down and eyed blissfully by many girls, many much older than Swanly. Even to his sluttish pill-addicted mother he was kind, even when she had some pharmaceutical cousin over on the occasion of his father being on the road. He even let himself be used as an adornment of her, with his mild temper and sad charm. She would say he would at any moment be kidnapped by Hollywood. And always he would disappear conveniently to her and the cousin as if he had never been there at all except as the ghost in the picture she kept.

Walthall with his German Mauser was naked in the pool. He had more hair than the others and on his chin the outline of a goatee. On his head was a dusty black beret and his eyes were set downriver at a broad and friendly horizon. But he would go in the navy. There was no money for college right away. His impressions were quicker and deeper than those of the others. By the time he knew something, it was in his roots as a passion. He led all aspirants in passion for music, weapons, girls, books, drinking, and wrestling, where operatic goons in mode just short of drag queens grappled in the city auditorium. Walthall, an actor, felt the act near too. He was a connoisseur and this act would be most delicious. He called the hermit's name.

Sunballs! Sunballs! Hefting the Mauser, Lester Silk just behind him a foot shorter and like a wet rat with his big nose. Swanly stood in patient beatitude but with an itch on, Arden Pal and Bean away at the bluff. You been wantin' it, Sunballs! Been beggin' for it, called Silk.

Come get some! cried Bean, at that distance to Walthall a threatening hood ornament.

None could be heard very far in the noise of the river.

Tuck, who had followed in his car, did hear them from the bridge.

What could they want with that wretch Sunballs? he imagined.

He was not without envy of the hermit. What a mighty wound to the balls it must take to be like that, that hiding shuffling thing, harmless and beholden to no man. Without woman, without friend, without the asking of lucre, without all but butt-bare necessity. Haunt of the possum, coon, and crane, down there. Old Testament specters with birds all over them eating honey out of roadkill. Too good for men. Sunballs was not that old, either. But he was suddenly angry at the man. Above the fray, absent, out, was he? Well.

Tuck knelt beneath a cluster of poison sumac on the rim of the bluff. He saw the three naked in the water. There was Swanly in the pool, the blond hair, the tanned skin. Who dared give a south Mississippi pissant youth such powerful flow and comeliness? Already Tuck in his long depressed thinking knew the boy had no good father, his home would stink of distress. He had known his type in the Scouts, always something deep-warped at home with them, beauty thrown up out of manure like. The mother might be beautiful but this lad had gone early and now she was a tramp needed worship by any old bunch of rags around a pecker. A boy like that you had to take it slow but not that much was needed to replace the pa, in his dim criminal weakness. You had to show them strength then wait until possibly that day, that hour, that hazy fog of moment when thought required act, the kind hand of Tuck in an instant of transfer to all nexus below the navel, no more to be denied than those rapids they're hollering down, nice lips on the boy too.

You had to show them something, then be patient.

They hated Sunballs? I could thrash Sunballs. I can bury him, he thought. I am their man.

Tuck was angered against the hermit now but sickened too. The line of pain over his thorax he attributed now directly to the hermit. The hermit was confusion.

I am a vampire I am a vampire, Tuck said aloud. They shook me out of my nest and I can't be responsible for what might happen.

He knew the boy would be back at his store.

The storekeeper's sons were grown and fattish and ugly They married and didn't even leave the community, were just up the road there nearly together. They both of them loved life and the parts hereabouts and he could not forgive them for it.

The boy would know something was waiting for him. It would take time but the something was nearly here. There had been warmth in their exchange, not all yet unpromising.

That night in another heat his wife spoke back to him. You ain't wanted it like this in a long time. What's come over you? Now you be kindly be gentle you care for what you want, silly fool.

As he spent himself he thought, Once after Korea there was a chance for me. I had some fine stories about Pusan, Inchon, and Seoul, not all of them lies. That I once vomited on a gook in person. Fear of my own prisoner in the frozen open field there, not contempt as I did explain. But still. There was some money, higher education maybe, big house in downtown Hawaii. But I had to put it all down that hole, he said pulling back from the heat of his spouse. The fever comes on you, you gasp like a man run out of the sea by stingrays. Fore you know it you got her spread around you like a tree and fat kids. You married a tree with a nest in it blown and rained on every which way. You a part of the tree too with your arms out legs out roots down ain't going nowhere really even in an automobile on some rare break to Florida, no you just a rolling tree.

But you get some scot-free thief of time like Sunballs, he thinks he don't have to pay the toll. You know somebody else somewhere is paying it for him, though. This person rooted in his tree sweats the toll for Sunballs never you doubt it. That wretch with that joker's name eases in the store wanting to know whether he's paying sales tax, why is this bit of bait up two cents from last time? Like maybe I ought to take care of it for him. Like he's a double agent don't belong to no country. Times twenty million you got the welfare army, biggest thing ever invaded this USA, say gimme the money, the ham, the cheese, the car, the moon, worse than Sherman's march. The babysitting, the hospital, throw in a smoking Buick, and bad on gas mileage if you please. Thanks very much kiss my ass. Army leech out this country white and clay-dry like those bluffs over that river down there. Pass a man with an honest store and friendly like me, what you see is a man sucked dry, the suckee toting dat barge. The suckers drive by thirteen to the Buick like a sponge laughing at you with all its mouths, got that music too, mouths big from sucking the national tit sing it out like some banshee rat speared in the jungle.

Tuck had got himself in a sleepy wrath but was too tired to carry it out and would require a good short sleep, never any long ones anymore, like your old self don't want to miss any daylight, to lift himself and resume. That Swanly they called him, so fresh he couldn't even handle a Pall Mall.

There he was, the boy back alone like Tuck knew he would be. Something had happened between them. No wonder you kept climbing out of bed with this thing in the world this happy thing all might have come to.

It ain't pondering or chatting or wishing it's only the act, from dog to man to star all nature either exploding or getting ready to.

Tuck had seen a lot of him in the pool, the move of him. This one would not play sports. There was a lean sun-browned languor to him more apt for man than boy games. It went on beyond what some thick coach could put to use.

A sacred trust prevailing from their luck together would drive them beyond all judgment, man and adolescent boy against every ugly thing in that world, which would mean nothing anymore. He would look at fresh prospects again the same as when he the young warrior returned to these shores in '53. It would not matter how leeched and discommoded he had been for three decades. Put aside, step to joy.

You boys getting on all right sleeping over there? Tuck asked Swanly.

Where'd you hear we slept anywhere? The boy sccmed in a trance between the aisles, the cans around him assorted junk of lowly needs. His hair was out of place from river, wind, and sand. Smears of bracken were on his pants knees, endearing him almost too much to Tuck. My dead little boyhood, Tuck almost sobbed.

I mean is nature being kind to you.

The boy half looked at him, panting a bit, solemn and bothered.

Are you in the drama club, young man?

Swanly sighed.

You sell acting lessons here at the store?

Good. Very quick. Somebody like you would be.

You don't know me at all.

Fourth year you've been at the river. I've sort of watched you grow at the store here, in a way. This time just a little sad, or mad. We got troubles?

We. Swanly peeked straight at him then quickly away.

When I was a little guy, Tuck spoke in his mind, I held two marbles in my hand just the blue-green like his eyes. It was across the road under those chinaberries and us tykes had packed the clay down in a near perfect circle. Shot all day looking at those pretty agates. Too good to play with. My fist was all sweaty around them. I'd almost driven them through my palm. The beauty of the balls. There inside my flesh. Such things drive you to a church you never heard of before, worship them.

I have no troubles, the boy said. No we either. No troubles.

You came back to the real world.

I thought I was in it.

You've come back all alone.

Outside there's a sign that says store, mister.

Down at the river pirates playhouse, you all.

Where you get your reality anyway? said the boy. Gas oil tobacco bacon hooks?

You know, wives can really be the gate of hell. They got that stare. They want to lock you down, get some partner to stoop down to that tiny peephole look at all the little shit with them. If you can forgive my language, ladies.

So you would be standing there 'mongst the Chesterfields seeing all the big?

Tuck did not take this badly. He liked the wit.

I might be. Some of us see the big things behind all the puny.

The hermit Sunballs appeared within the moment, the screen door slamming behind him like a shot. He walked on filthy gym shoes of one aspect with the soil of his wanderings, ripped up like the roots of it. You would not see such annealed textures at the ankles of a farmer, not this color of city gutters back long past. All of him the color of putty almost, as your eyes rose. The clothes vaporish like bus exhaust. The fingers whiter in the air like a potter's but he had no work and you knew this instantly. He held a red net sack for oranges, empty. It was not known why he had an interesting name like Sunballs. You would guess the one who had named him was the cleverer. Nothing in him vouched for parts solar. More perhaps of a star gray and dead or old bait or of a sex organ on the drowned. Hair thicket of red rust on gray atop him.

He pored over the tin tops in the manner of a devout scholar. The boy watched him in fury. It was the final waste product of all maturity he saw, a creature fired-out full molded by the world, the completed grown-up.

Whereas with an equal fury the storekeeper saw the man as the final insult to duty: friendless, wifeless, jobless, motherless, stateless, and not even black. He could not bear the nervous hands of the creature over his goods, arrogant discriminating moocher. He loathed the man so much a pain came in his head and his heartbeat had thrown a sweat on him. The presence of the boy broke open all gates and he loathed in particular with a hatred he had seldom known, certainly never in Korea, where people wearing gym shoes and smelling of garlic shot at him. Another mouth, Tuck thought, seeking picking choosing. He don't benefit nobody's day. Squandered every chance of his white skin, down in his river hole. Mocks even a healthy muskrat in personal hygiene. Not native to nothing. Hordes of them, Tuck imagined, pouring across the borders of the realm from bumland. His progeny lice with high attitudes.

Tuck saw the revulsion of the boy.

You ten cents higher than the store in Pinola, spoke Sunballs. His voice was shallow and thin as if he had worn it down screaming. A wreckage of teeth added a whistle at the end.

Tuck was invested by red blindness.

But Swanly spoke first. I warn you. Don't come near me. I can't be responsible, you.

The hermit whispered a breeze off rags where feral beings had swarmed. Ere be a kind of storeman take his neighbor by the short hairs like they got you dead in an airport and charges for water next thing you know.

What did you say? demanded the storekeeper coming around the register. You say neighbor and airport? You never even crossed through an airport I bet, you filthy mouthbroom.

Sunballs stood back from the beauty of Swanly but was not afraid of the anger of Tuck. He was too taken with this startling pretty boy.

Oh yes, my man, airport I have been in and the airplane crash is why I am here.

He pointed at the oiled floor swept clean by the wife who was now coming in from the rear in attendance to the loud voices, so rare in this shop, where the savage quiet reigned almost perpetual both sides of the mutual gloom, the weary armistice, then the hate and lust and panting. Only lately had her own beauty ebbed and not truly very much. She was younger with long muscular legs and dressed like a well-kept city woman in beach shorts. Her hair was brunette and chopped shortish and she had the skin of a Mexican. Her lips were pulled together in a purse someone might mistake for delight by their expression, not petulance. Her name was Bernadette and when Tuck saw her he flamed with nostalgia, not love. Brought back to his own hard tanned youth returned from the Orient on a ship in San Diego. Swanly looked over to her, and the two of them, boy and married woman, in the presence of the gasping hermit, fell in love.

What's wrong out here? she asked gently, her eyes never off the boy.

Said they can have it if that's what's there in the modern world, continued Sunballs. It was a good job I had too, I'm no liar. They was treating me special flying me to Kalamazoo, Michigan, on a Constellation. We was set upon by them flight stewards, grown men in matching suits, but they was these beatniks underneath, worse, these flight stewards, called, they attended themselves, it didn't matter men women or children, they was all homos all the time looking in a mirror at each other, didn't stir none atall for nobody else in their abomination once the airplane began crashing. It took forever rolling back and forth downward near like a corkscrew but we known it was plowing into ground directly. These two funny fellows you know, why when we wrecked all up with several dead up front and screaming, why they was in the back in the rear hull a-humpin' each other their eyes closed 'blivious to the crash they trying to get one last 'bomination in and we unlatched ourselves, stood up in the hulk and they still goin' at it, there's your modern world I say, two smoky old queers availing theyselve and the captain come back with half a burnt face say what the hell we got. Ever damn thing about it a crime against nature. No money no Kalamazoo never bring me back in, damn them, yes I seen it what it come down to in your modern world.

Tuck watched Swanly and his wife in long locked estimation of each other, the words of the hermit flying over like faraway geese.

People is going over to the other side of everything, I say, and it all roots out from the evil of price, the cost of everything being so goddamned high. Nothing ain't a tenth its value and a man's soul knows it's true.

What? Tuck said, down from his rage and confused by everybody. You ain't flapped on like this in the seven years you been prowling round.

Sunballs would not stop. Old man Bunch Lewis up north in the state, he run a store and has a hunchback. The hermit spoke with relish, struck loquacious by the act of love proceeding almost visibly between the boy and the wife, each to each, the female lips moving without words. It behooved him, he thought, to announce himself a wry soldier of the world.

Fellow come in seen Lewis behind the counter with a ten-dollar shirt in his hands. Said Lewis, What's that on your back? Lewis got all fierce, he say, You know it's a hump I'm a humpback you son of a bitch. Fellow say, Well I thought it might be your ass, everything else in this store so high. What he say.

Neither the storekeeper nor his wife had ever heard the first word of wit from this man.

The hermit put a hand to his rushy wad of hair as if to groom it. The plain common man even in this humble state can't afford no clothes where you got the Bunch Lewises a'preying on them, see. After this appeal he paused, shot out for a time, years perhaps.

This isn't a plain common boy here, though, is he, son? Bernadette said, as if her voice had fled out and she powerless. The question called out of her in a faint tone between mother love and bald lechery. Is it real? Has this boy escaped out of a theater somewheres? demanded the hermit. His eyes were on the legs of the wife, her feet set in fashion huaraches like a jazz siren between the great wars.

You never even looked at my wife before, said Tuck. Pissmouth.

Hush everybody. You getting the air dirty, said Bernadette.

Her own boys were hammy and homely and she wandered in a moment of conception, giving birth to Swanly all over again as he stood there, a pained ecstasy in the walls of her womb. He was what she had intended by everything female about her and she knew hardly any woman ever chanced to see such a glorious boy.

Tuck was looking at her afresh and he was shocked. Why my wife, she's a right holy wonder, she is, he thought. Or is she just somebody I've not ever seen now?

Out of the south Mississippi fifth-grown pines, the rabbit-weed, the smaller oaks and hickories, the white clay and the coon-toed bracken, she felt away on palisades over a sea of sweetening terror.

She said something nobody caught. Swanly in shyness and because he could not hold his feelings edged away with a can of sardines and bottle of milk unpaid for, but he was not conscious of this.

I am redeemed, she said again, even more softly.

Sunballs left with a few goods unpaid for and he was very conscious of this. Tuck stared at him directly as he went out the door but saw little. It must have been the hermit felt something was owed for his narration.

The wife walked to the screen and looked out carefully.

You stay away from that boy, she called, and they heard her.

When Tuck was alone behind the register again he sensed himself alien to all around him and his aisles seemed a fantastic dump of road offal brought in by a stranger.

He was in the cold retreat from Chosin marching backwards, gooks in the hills who'd packed in artillery by donkey. You could smell the garlic coming off them at a half mile but my sweet cock that was my living room compared to this now, he thought.

All the fat on him, the small bags under his eyes, the hint of rung at his belt he summoned out of himself. He must renew his person. Some moments would come and he could do this simply by want. Tuck felt himself grow leaner and handsomer.

Walthall had wanted the peach wine to become brandy but alas. He brought his viola to the river camp and Pal his bass flute, two instruments unrecognized by anybody in his school, his city, and they played them passing strange with less artistry than vengeance sitting opposed on a sunken petrified log like an immense crocodile forced up by saurian times, in the first rush of small rapids out of the pool. This river in this place transported them to Germany or the

Rockies or New England, anywhere but here, and the other boys, especially the hearkening beatific Swanly, listened, confident paralyzed hipsters, to the alien strains of these two mates, set there in great parlor anguish swooning like people in berets near death.

Bean, the sternest and most religious of them all, set his gun on his knees, feeling a lyric militancy and praying for an enemy. Like the others, this boy was no drinking man but unlike them he did not drink the wine from the fruit jars. For the others, the wine went down like a ruined orchard, acid to the heart, where a ball of furred heat made them reminiscent of serious acts never acted, women never had.

The wine began dominating and the boys were willing slaves. When the music paused Lester Silk, son of the decaying army man who never made anything but fun of poetry and grabbed his scrotum and acted the fairy whenever it occurred at school, said, I believe in years to come I will meet a pale woman from Texas who plays clarinet in the symphony. Then we shall dally, there will be a rupture over my drinking, she'll tear up my pictures and for penance over the freedoms she allowed me she will go off to the nun mountains in a faraway state and be killed accidentally by masked gunmen. Forever afterward I will whup my lap mournfully in her memory.

Somebody must die when you hear that music out here, I feel it, said Swanly, cool-butted and naked in the little rapids but full hot with the peach wine after five swallows.

Walthall, stopping the viola, wore a necklace of twine and long mail-order Mauser shells. He exclaimed, Send not to ask for when the bell tolls. I refuse to mourn the death by fire of a child's Christmas on Fern Hill. Do not go gently in my sullen craft, up yours. He raised the fruit jar from his rock.

All that separates me from Leslie Caron must die, said Arden Pal. He held his flute up like a saber, baroque over the flat rocks and frothing tea of the rapids. Pal was a gangling youth of superfluous IQ already experiencing vile depressions. His brain made him feel constantly wicked but he relieved himself through botany and manic dilettantism.

Like a piece of languid Attic statuary Swanly lay out with a sudden whole nudeness under the shallow water. He might have been something caught in the forest and detained for study, like a white deer missing its ilk, because he was sad and in love and greatly confused.

Bernadette cooked two chickens, made a salad, then Irish Cream cookies, for the boys' health, she said, for their wretched motherless pirates' diets, and Tuck drove her down to the bridge with it all in a basket. Catastrophic on both sides of the washboard gravel was the erosion where ditches of white limesoil had been clawed into deep small canyons by heavy rains, then swerved into the bogs in wild fingers. Tuck pretended he was confused as to where the boys might be in camp and guessed loudly while pulling off before the bridge into the same place he had been earlier. Ah, he said, the back of their car, Hinds County, I recognize it.

But he said he would wait and that was perfect by Bernadette. Then he followed her, tree to tree, at a distance. Bernadette came to the head of the bluff and he saw her pause, then freeze, cradling the food basket covered in blue cloth with white flowers printed on. Through a nearer gully he saw what she saw.

Hairy Walthall, at the viola with his root floating in the rills, might have seemed father to Swanly, who was hung out like a beige flag in the shallows. She could not see Arden Pal but she heard the deep weird flute. Swanly moved as a liquid one with the river, the bed around him slick tobacco shale, and Bernadette saw all this through a haze of inept but solemn chamber music. She did not know it was inept and a wave of terrible exhilaration overcame her.

Tuck looked on at the boys from his own vantage, stroking the wound to his throat.

The hermit Sunballs was across the river before them in a bower of wild muscadine, prostrate and gripping the lip of the bluff. He owned a telescope, which he was now using. He viewed all of Swanly he could. The others were of no concern. For a while Tuck and his wife could not see him, flat to the earth and the color of organic decay. None of them for that matter would have recognized their own forms rapt and helpless to the quick, each with their soul drawn out through their eyes, beside themselves, stricken into painful silence.

It was habitual with Pal as he played the flute, however, that his eyes went everywhere. He was unsure at first then he thought he had invoked ghosts by his music, the ancient river dead roused from their Civil War ghoulments by the first flute since in these parts. He was startled by this for the seconds the thought lasted then he was frightened because they were on both bluffs and he mistook the telescope pushed out of the vines for a weapon. Perhaps they were the law, but next he knew they were not, seeing one was a woman.

They're watching you, Swanly!

The boys, except Swanly, came out of the water and thrashed back to the camp incensed and indignant. Pal pointed his flute at the telescope, which receded. Then the hermit's face came briefly into the frame of vine leaves. He could not tear himself away.

Swanly stood wobbling in the shallows, his hand to the slick shale rock, then at last stood up revealed and fierce in his nakedness. He swayed on the slick rocks, outraged, screaming. Then he vomited.

Keep your eyes off me! Keep away! he bawled upwards at the hermit, who then disappeared.

Pal pointed upwards to the right. They watched too, Swanly! But Swanly didn't seem to understand this.

Walthall fired his Mauser twice in the air and the blasts made rocking echoes down the river beach to beach.

Bernadette and Tuck melted back onto the rooted path in the high cane and the woman came cautiously with her basket, trailed fifty yards behind by her husband who was trembling and homicidal toward the hermit. Also he knew the boy loved his wife more than him. The boy's nakedness to him had had no definition but was a long beige flag of taunting and every fine feeling of his seemed mocked and whored by the presence of the hermit. Tuck felt himself only a raving appendage to the event, a thing tacked on to the crisis of his wife.

Yoo hoo! Oh bad bad boys. I've got a treat for you, called Bernadette. All wet in their pants they stared up to the woman clearing the cane above them, their beds spread below her. Their sanctuary ruined. Only Swanly knew who she was.

Oh no, is it a woman of the church? said Walthall.

There will always be a woman around to wreck things, said Pal.

No, she's all right, Swanly intervened, though he was still sick. He came up from the shore roots and struggled into his shorts slowly. He seemed paralyzed and somewhere not with them, an odd sleepiness on him. Be nice, all of you, he added.

Big Mama Busybod, said Walthall. Courtesy of the Southern regions.

Out in the sun they saw she was not a bad-looking case though she seemed arrested by a spiritual idea and did not care her hair was blowing everywhere like a proper woman of the '50s would.

Her husband came behind, mincing over the stone beach. She turned.

I heard the shots, he said.

Fools. Eat, said Bernadette. But she remained startled by Swanly and could not turn her face long from him.

Tuck didn't understand it, but his jaw began flapping. You boys ever bait a trotline with soap? Yes Ivory soap. Tuck pointed under the bridge where their line was set on the near willow. Tuck was not convinced he even existed now outside the river of want he poured toward Swanly. He was not interested in what he continued to say, like something in a storekeeper's costume activated by a pull-string and thrust into a playhouse by a child. Fish began biting on the substances of modern industry in the '40s, boys. Why they're like contemporary men they ain't even that hungry just more curious. Or a woman. They get curious and then the bait eats them, huh.

Yes sir, said Walthall, annoyed.

Tuck kept on in despondent sagery then trailed off as the boys ate and he next simply sat down on a beach boulder and stared away from them into the late bower of Sunballs across the river.

When he twisted to look he was astounded by the extent of bosom his wife was visiting on Swanly. She was bared like some tropical hula but not. Swanly ate his chicken kneeling in front of her with his bare smooth chest slightly burned red and of such an agreeable shape he seemed made to fly through night winds like the avatar on the bow of a ship. That hussy had dropped her shawl down and Tuck noticed more of her in truth, her mothersome cleavage, than he had in years, faintly freckled and still not a bad revelation. Not in years atop her.

It was eleven years ago when he had pursued illicit love with another woman. This was when his boys were small and cute. He could not get over how happy he was and blameless and blessed-feeling, as if in the garden before the fall. She was a young woman with practical headquarters in the Jackson Country Club, a thing he felt giant pride about, her sitting there in a swimsuit nursing a Tom Collins, high-heeled beach shoes on her feet, talking about storms how she loved them. Now she was a fat woman and his children were fat men and it was not their fatness that depressed him so much as it was watching visible time on them, the horrible millions of minutes collected and evident, the murdered idle thousands of hours, his time more than theirs in their change. They had an unfortunate disease where you saw everything the minute you saw them, the awful feckless waiting, the lack of promise, the bulk of despair. The woman had been attracted to him through his handsome little boys and she would excite him by exclaiming, Oh what wonderful seed you have. He stayed up like a happy lighthouse with rotating beam. She had no children, never would, but she whispered to him he might break her will if he didn't stop being so good. All the while he had loved Bernadette too, even more, was that possible? The woman didn't mind. What kind of man am I? Tuck thought. Was time working every perversion it had on him, were there many like him? He felt multiplied in arms and legs, a spider feeling eight ways, he was going into the insect kingdom. Oh yes, lost to the rest.

He loved his boys but my God they were like old uncles, older than him, mellow and knee-slapping around a campfire. He loved his wife, but no he didn't, it was an embattled apathy each morning goaded into mere courtesy, that was what, and he felt wild as a prophet mocking an army of the righteous below him at the gate.

Now isn't that better? his wife said to the boys, who had fed themselves with hesitation before they fell to trough like swine.

You're too thoughtful of us, ma'am, said Swanly.

I'm Bernadette, she said.

You are desperate, thought Tuck. I sort of like it. Hanging all out there, little Mama.

Was it how you like it? she said only to the boy.

My mother never cooked for me like that.

Ah.

Nobody ever has.

Oh. What's wrong?

That hermit, you know. He saw me without anything on.

She could see he was still trembling, warm as it was.

I know how it is. She looked more deeply into his eyes. Believe me.

What is it? said Tuck, coming up.

This boy's been spied on by that creature Sunballs.

Tuck leaned in to Swanly. The boy was evilly shaken like a maiden thing out of the last century. He was all boy but between genders, hurt deep to his modesty. Tuck was greatly curious and fluttered-up. All execrable minutes, all time regained. I would live backwards in time until I took the shape of the boy myself. My own boyself was eat up by the gooks and then this strolling wench, my boyself was hostaged by her, sucking him out to her right in front of me, all over again as with me. Woman's thing stays hungry, it don't diminish, it's always something. A need machine, old beard lost its teeth harping on like a holy fool in the desert. They're always with themselves having sex with themselves, two lips forever kissing each other down there and they got no other subject. Even so, I feel love for her all over again.

Lester Silk, Bean, and Pal studied this trio isolated there where the water on rills avid over pebbles made a laughing noise. Walthall raised his viola and spread his arms out like a crucified musician and he stood there in silence evoking God knows what but Arden Pal asked the others what was going on.

Wake up and smell the clue, whispered Silk. Walthall wants the woman and our strange boy Swanly's already got her.

Swanly's okay, Silk. He's not strange.

Maybe not till now.

Leave him alone, said Bean. Swanly's a right guy. He has been through some things that's all. Ask me.

You mean a dead daddy like you?

I'd say you look hard enough, a dead both, but he wouldn't admit it. Bean intended to loom there in his acuity for a moment, looking into the breech of his gun which he had opened with the lever. It was a rare lever-action shotgun, 20-gauge. Bean worshiped shells and bullets. Ask me, he's a full orphan.

They blending with him, said Arden Pal. They watched us naked too. She didn't jump back in the bushes like a standard woman when I caught her.

Swanly came over getting his shirt.

She's giving me something. I'm feeling poorly, he said.

The rest did not speak and the three, Tuck, Bernadette, and Swanly, walked up the shallow bluff and into the woods.

Silk sighed. I don't quite believe I ever seen nothing like that. Old store boy there looks like somebody up to the eight count.

Walthall, who had actually had a sort of girl, since with stubborn farm boy will he would penetrate nearly anything sentient, was defeated viola and all. Lord my right one for mature love like that. No more did he heed the calling of his music and he was sore in gloom.

Bean could not sit still and he walked here and there rolling two double-aught buckshot shells in his palm, looking upward to the spying bower of the hermit, but no offending eye there now, as he would love.

They closed the store as Swanly began talking. She went to the house and got something for his belly and some nerve pills too and diet pills as well. Bernadette was fond of both diet and nerve pills, and sometimes her husband was too, quite positively. Some mornings they were the only promise he could fetch in and he protected his thefts of single pills from his wife's cabinet with grim slyness. In narcosis she was fond of him and in amphetamine zeal he returned affection to her which she mistook for actual interest. The doctor in Magee was a firm believer in Dexamyl as panacea and gave her anything she wanted. The pain of wanting in her foreign eyes got next to him. In a fog of charity he saw her as a lovely spy in the alien pines. He saw a lot of women and few men who weren't in the act of bleeding as they spoke, where they stood. The pharmacist was more a partisan of Demerol and John Birch and his prices were high since arsenals were expensive. His constant letters to Senator McCarthy, in his decline, almost consumed his other passions for living, such as they were. But the pharmacist liked Bernadette too, and when she left, detained as long as he could prolong the difficulty of her prescription, he went in the back room where a mechanic's calendar with a picture of a woman lying cross-legged in a dropped halter on the hood of a Buick was nailed to the wall and laid hand to himself. One night the doctor and the pharmacist met in this room and began howling like wolves in lonely ardor. Bernadette's name was mentioned many times, then they would howl again. They wore female underwear but were not sodomites. Both enjoyed urban connections and their pity for Bernadette in her aging beauty out in the river boonies was painful without limit; and thus in the proper lingerie they acted it out.

Swanly, after the pills, began admitting to the peach wine as if it were a mortal offense. Bernadette caught his spirit. They adjourned to the house where he could lie comfortably with her Oriental shawl over him.

We don't have strong drink here. Not much. She looked to Tuck. You don't have to drink to have a full experience.

Tuck said, No, not drink. Hardly.

No. I'm having fun just talking. Talking to you is fine. Because I haven't been much of a talker. That's good medicine. My tongue feels all light.

Talk on, child. She gave Swanly another pill.

Tuck went to relieve himself and through the window he saw the clothesline over the green clover and he speculated that through time simple household things might turn on you in a riot of overwhelming redundancy. He had heard of a man whose long dear companion, a buckskin cat, had walked between his legs one night and tripped and killed him as he went down headfirst onto a commode. Cheered that this was not him he went back to listen to the boy.

But after all you wouldn't have just anybody look at you all bared. Surely not that awful person, Bernadette was saying. I'd not let him see me for heaven's sake.

It seems he ought to pay. I feel tortured and all muddy. I can't forget it.

Just talk it out, that's best. It seems there's always a monster about, doesn't it?

I feel I could talk all afternoon into the night.

We aren't going anywhere.

We aren't going anywhere, added Tuck.

I'm feeling all close to you if that's all right.

Some people are sent to us. We have been waiting all our lives for somebody and don't even know it.

Older ones are here to teach and guide the young, Tuck said.

Bernadette glanced at Tuck then looked again. He had come back with his hair combed and he had shaved. He was so soft in the face she felt something new for him. In this trinity already a pact was sealed and they could no more be like others. There was a tingling and a higher light around them. A flood of goodwill took her as if they had been hurled upon a foreign shore, all fresh. The boy savior, child, and paramour at once. Swanly spoke on, it hardly mattered what he said. Each word a pleasant weight on her bosom.

Walthall and the rest stared into the fire sighing, three of them having their separate weather, their separate fundament, in peach wine. Pal could swallow no more and heaved out an arc of puke luminous over the fire, crying, Thar she blows, my dear youth. This act was witnessed like a miracle by the others.

God in heaven, this stuff was so good for a while, said Silk.

Fools, said Bean.

Bean don't drink because he daddy daid, said Walthall. So sad, so sad, so gone, so Beat.

Yeh. It might make him cry, said Pal.

Or act human, said Silk.

Let it alone. Bean had stood unmoved by their inebriation for two hours, caressing his 20-gauge horse gun.

Teenage love, teenage heart. My face broke out the other night but I'm in love wit yewwww! sang Walthall.

What you think Swanly's doing, asked Pal.

Teenage suckface. Dark night of the suck.

They are carrying him away, far far away, Silk declared.

Or him them.

Having a bit of transversion, them old boy and girl.

You mean travesty. Something stinketh, I tell you.

We know.

The hermit made Swanly all sick. We should put a stop to his mischief, said Bean all sober.

That person saw the peepee full out of ourn good friend ourn little buddy.

This isn't to laugh about. Swanly's deep and he's a hurting man.

Boy, said Pal. He once told me every adult had a helpless urge to smother the young so they could keep company with the dead, which were themselves.

You'd have to love seeing small animals suffer to hurt Swanly. The boy's damn near an angel. I swear he ain't even rightly one of us, said Silk. Bean did not care for Silk, who had only joined them lately. But Silk redeemed himself, saying, Christ I'm just murky. Swanly's deep.

You know what, Walthall spoke, I felt sorry for all three of them when they left here. Yes the woman is aged but fine, but it was like a six-legged crippled thing.

So it was, said Pal. I declare nothing happy is going on wherever they are.

Whosoever you are, be that person with all your might. Time goes by faster than we thought. It is a thief so quiet. You must let yourself be loved and you must love, parts of you that never loved must open and love. You must announce yourself in all particulars so you can have yourself.

Tuck going on at dawn. Bernadette was surprised again by him. Another man, fluent, had risen in his place. She was in her pink sleeping gown but the others wore their day clothes and were not sleepy.

Listen, the birds are singing for us out there and it's a morning, a real morning, Bernadette said. A true morning out of all the rest of the mornings.

By noon they were hoarse and languid and commended themselves into a trance wherein all wore bedsheets and naked underneath they moved about the enormous bed like adepts in a rite. The question was asked of Swanly by Tuck whether he would care to examine their lovely Bernadette since he had never seen a woman and Swanly said yes and Bernadette lay back opening the sheet and then spreading herself so Swanly saw a woman as he had never seen her for a long while and she only a little shy and the boy smiled wearily assenting to her glory and was pulled inward through love and death and constant birth gleefully repeated by the universe. Then husband and wife embraced with the boy between them on the edge of the bed, none of them recalling how they were there but all talk ceased and they were as those ignorant animals amongst the fruit of Eden just hours before the thunder.

Long into the afternoon they awoke with no shame and only the shyness of new dogs in a palace and then an abashed hunger for the whole ritual again set like a graven image in all their dreams. The boy had been told things and he felt very elegant, a crowned orphan now orphan no more. Bernadette, touched in all places, felt dear and coveted. All meanness had been driven from Tuck and he was blank in an ecstasy of separate parts like a creature torn to bits at the edge of a sea. Around them were their scattered clothes, the confetti of delirium. They embraced and were suspended in a bulb of void delicate as a drop of water.

Sunballs came around the store since it was closed and he wore a large knife on his belt in a scabbard with fringe on it and boots in white leather and high to the knee, which he had without quite knowing their use rescued out of a country lane near the bridge, the jetsam of a large majorette seduced in a car he had been watching all night. At the feet he looked blindingly clean as in a lodge ceremony. He walked quickly as if appointed and late. He looked in one window of the blue house, holding the sill, before he came to the second and beheld them all naked gathering and ungathering in languor, unconscious in their innocence. He watched a goodly while, his hands formally at his side, bewitched like a pole-axed angel. Then he commenced rutting on the scabbard of his knife grabbed desperately to his loins but immediately also to call out scolding as somebody who had walked up on murder.

Cursed and stunned Tuck and Bernadette snatched the covering but Swanly sat peering at the fiend outside until overcome by grief and then nausea. His nudity was then like one dead, cut down from joy. Still, he was too handsome, and Sunballs could not quit his watching while Swanly retched himself sore.

He might well be dying, thought Sunballs, and this fascinated him, these last heavings of beauty. He began to shake and squalled even louder. There was such a clamor from the two adults he awoke to himself and hastened back to the road and into the eroded ditch unbraked until he reached his burrow. Under his bluff the river fled deep and black with a sheen of new tar, and the hermit emerged once on his filthy terrace to stand over it in conversation with his erection, his puny calves in the white boots.

The boys labored with oaths down the bedrocks of the river. All was wretched and foul since waking under the peach wine, which they now condemned, angry at daylight itself. Only Bean was ready to the task. They went through a bend in silence and approached water with no beach. They paused for a while then flung in and waded cold to their chests. Bean, the only one armed, carried the cavalry shotgun above his head.

I claim this land for the Queen of Spain, Bean said. God for a hermit to shoot. My kingdom for a hermit. Then he went underwater but the shotgun stayed up and dry, waggled about.

When he came up he saw the hermit leering down from his porch on the bluff. Bean, choked and bellicose, thought he heard Sunballs laughing at him. He levered in a round and without hesitation would have shot the man out of his white boots had this person not been snatched backwards by Tuck. All of them saw the arm come around his neck and the female boots striding backwards in air, then dust in vacant air, the top of a rust hut behind it. A stuffed holler went off the bluff and scattered down the pebble easements westerly and into the cypresses on either side. Then there was silence.

He was grabbed by something, said Walthall, something just took Sunballs away.

By hell, I thought he was shot before I pulled the trigger, swore Bean. Bean had horrified himself. The horse gun in his hand was loathsome.

Don't hit me no more in the eye! a voice cried from above.

Then there were shouts from both men and much stomping on the terrace.

Tuck shrieked out, his voice like a great bird driving past. They heard then the hysterical voice of Swanly baying like a woman. The boys were spooked but drawn. They went to finding a path upwards even through the wine sickness.

Swanly, he ain't right and that's him, said Pal.

Well somebody's either humping or killing somebody.

We charging up there like we know what to do about it.

I could've killed him, said Bean, dazed still. Damn you Swanly. For you, damn you.

Then they were up the fifty feet or more and lost in cane through which they heard groans and sobs. They turned to this and crashed through and to the man they were afraid. At the edge of the brake, they drew directly upon a bin buried three-quarters in the top of the bluff, this house once a duck blind. In front of it from the beaten clay porch they heard sounds and they pressed around to them like harried pilgrims anxious for bad tidings. They saw the river below open up in a wide bend deep and strong through a passage of reigning boulders on either side and then just beside them where they had almost overwalked them, Bernadette and Swanly together on the ground, Swanly across her lap and the woman with her breasts again nearly out of their yoke in a condition of the Pietà, but Swanly red and mad in the face, both of them covered with dust as if they had rolled through a desert together. This put more fear in them than would have a ghoul, and they looked quickly away where Tuck sat holding his slashed stomach, beside him the hermit spread with outstretched boots, swatted down as from some pagan cavalry. Sunballs covered his eyes with his hands.

They thought in those seconds that Tuck had done himself in. The big hunting knife was still in his hand and he gazed over the river as if dying screnely. But this was only exhaustion and he looked up at them unsurprised and baleful as if nothing more could shock him.

I can't see, moaned Sunballs. He never stopped hitting my eyes.

Good, good, spoke Tuck. I'm not sorry. Cut your tongue out next, tie you up in a boat down that river. See how you spy on those sharks in the Gulf of Mexico.

I ain't the trouble, moaned the hermit. You got big sons wouldn't think so either.

Nothing stands between me and that tongue, keep wagging it.

Them ole boys of yours could sorely be enlightened.

Sunballs moved his hands and the boys viewed the eyes bruised like a swollen burglar's mask, the red grief of pounded meat in the sockets. The fingers of both Tuck's hands were mud red and fresher around the knife handle. But Tuck was spent, a mere chattering head, and the hermit in his agony rolled over and stared blind into his own vomit. His wadded hair was white flecked by it and the boys didn't look any more at him.

It was Swanly they loved and could not bear to see. He was not the bright shadow of their childhoods anymore, he was not the boy of almost candescent complexion, he was not the pal haunting in the remove of his beauty, slim and clean in his limbs. This beauty had been a strange thing. It had always brought on some distress and then infinite kindness in others and then sadness too. But none of them were cherubs any longer and they knew all this and hated it, seeing him now across the woman's lap, her breasts over his twisted face. Eden in the bed of Eros, all Edenwide all lost. He was neither child, boy, nor man, and he was dreadful. Bean could barely carry on and knelt before him in idiocy. Walthall was enraged, big hairy Walthall, viola torn to bits inside him. He could not forgive he was ever obliged to see this.

We're taking our friend with us.

You old can have each other, said Bean. He had forgot the shotgun in his hand.

Bury each other. Take your time.

The woman looked up, her face flocked with dust.

We're not nasty. We were good people.

Sure. Hag.

Come on away, Bean, Pal directed him.

Bring Swanly up. Hold him, somebody, help me. Walthall was large and clumsy. He could not see the way to handle Swanly.

Bernadette began to lick the dust from Swanly's cheeks.

There ain't nothing only a tiny light, and a round dark, sighed Sunballs. It ain't none improved.

We are bad. Tuck spoke. Damn us, damn it all.

Silk and Pal raised Swanly up and although he was very sick he could walk. There was an expression simian wasted on his face, blind to those who took him now, blind to the shred of clothes remaining to him, his shorts low on his hips.

They kept along the gravel shoulder the mile back to their camp. Bean with the handsome gun, relic of swaggering days in someone else's life. He seemed deputized and angry, walking Swanly among the others. Sometimes Swanly fell from under him completely, his legs surrendered, while they pulled him on, no person speaking.

In the halls of his school thenceforward Swanly was wolfish in his glare and often dirty. In a year no one was talking to him at all. The exile seemed to make him smile but as if at others inside himself he knew better than them.

His mother, refractory until this change in her son, withdrew into silent lesbian despair with another of her spirit then next into a church and out of this world, where her husband continued to make his inardent struggles.

Some fourteen years later, big Walthall, rich but sad, took a sudden turn off the regular highway on the way to a Florida vacation. He was struck by a nostalgia he could not account for, like a bole of overweening sad energy between his eyes. He drove right up to the store and later he swore to Bean and Pal that although Tuck had died, an almost unrecognizable and clearly mad old woman hummed, nearly toothless, behind the cash register. She was wearing Swanly's old jersey, what was left of it, and the vision was so awful he fled almost immediately and was not right in Boca Raton nor much better when he came back home.

When Walthall inquired about the whereabouts of Swanly the woman began to scream without pause.

A Creature in the Bay of St. Louis

WE WERE OUT EARLY IN THE BROWN WATER, THE LIGHT STILL GRAY AND wet.

My cousin Woody and I were wading on an oyster shell reef in the bay. We had cheap bait-casting rods and reels with black cotton line at the end of which were a small bell weight and a croaker hook. We used peeled shrimp for bait. Sometimes you might get a speckled trout or flounder but more likely you would catch the croaker. A large one weighed a half pound. When caught and pulled in the fish made a metallic croaking sound. It is one of the rare fish who talk to you about their plight when they are landed. My aunt fried them crispy, covered in cornmeal, and they were delicious, especially with lemon juice and ketchup.

A good place to fish was near the pilings of the Saint Stanislaus school pier. The pier gate was locked but you could wade to the pilings and the oyster shell reef. Up the bluff above us on the town road was a fish market and the Star Theater, where we saw movies.

Many cats, soft and friendly and plump, would gather around the edges of the fish market and when you went to the movies you would walk past three or four of them that would ease against your leg as if asking to go to the movie with you. The cats were very social.

In their prosperity they seemed to have organized into a watching society of leisure and culture. Nobody yelled at them because this was a very small coastal town where everybody knew each other. Italians, Slavs, French, Negroes, Methodists, Baptists, and Catholics. You did not want to insult the cat's owner by rudeness. Some of the cats would tire of the market offerings and come down the bluff to watch you fish, patiently waiting for their share of your take or hunting the edges of the weak surf for dead crabs and fish. You would be pulling in your fish, catch it, and when you looked ashore the cats were alert suddenly. They were wise. It took a hard case not to leave them one good fish for supper.

That night as you went into an Abbott and Costello movie, which cost a dime, that same cat you had fed might rub against your leg and you felt sorry it couldn't go into the movie house with you. You might be feeling comical when you came out and saw the same cat waiting with conviction as if there were something in there it wanted very much, and you threw a jujube down to it on the sidewalk. A jujube was a pellet of chewing candy the quality of vulcanized rubber. You chewed several during the movie and you had a wonderful syrup of licorice, strawberry, and lime in your mouth. But the cat would look down at the jujube then up at you as if you were insane, and you felt badly for betraying this serious creature and hated that you were mean and thoughtless. That is the kind of conscience you had in Bay St. Louis, Mississippi, where you were always close to folks and creatures.

This morning we had already had a good trip as the sun began coming out. The croakers swam in a burlap sack tied to a piling and underwater. The sacks were free at the grocery and people called them croaker sacks. When you lifted the sack to put another croaker in you heard that froggy metal noise in a chorus, quite loud, and you saw the cats on shore hearken to it too. We would have them with french-fried potatoes, fat tomato slices from my uncle's garden, and a large piece of deep sweet watermelon for supper.

It made a young boy feel good having the weight of all these fish in the dripping sack when you lifted it, knowing you had provided for a large family and maybe even neighbors at supper. You felt to be a small hero of some distinction, and ahead of you was that mile walk through the neighborhood lanes where adults would pay attention to your catch and salute you. The fishing rod on your shoulder, you had done some solid bartering with the sea, you were not to be trifled with.

The only dangerous thing in the bay was a stingaree, with its poisonous barbed hook of a tail. This ray would lie flat covered over by sand like a flounder. We waded barefoot in swimming trunks and almost always in a morning's fishing you stepped on something that moved under your foot and you felt the squirm in every inch of your body before it got off from you. These could be stingarees. There were terrible legends about them, always a story from summers ago when a stingaree had whipped its tail into the calf of some unfortunate girl or boy and buried the vile hook deep in the flesh. The child came dragging out of the water with this twenty-pound brownish-black monster the size of a garbage can lid attached to his leg, thrashing and sucking with its awful mouth. Then the child's leg grew black and swelled hugely and they had to amputate it, and that child was in the attic of some dark house on the edge of town, never the same again and pale like a thing that never saw light, then eventually the child turned into half-stingaree and they took it away to an institution for special cases. So you believed all this most positively and when a being squirmed under your foot you were likely to walk on water out of there. We should never forget that when frightened a child can fly short distances too.

The high tide was receding with the sun clear up and smoking in the east over Biloxi, the sky reddening, and the croakers were not biting so well anymore. But each new fish would give more pride to the sack and I was greedy for a few more since I didn't get to fish in saltwater much. I lived four hours north in a big house with a clean lawn, a maid, and yardmen, but it was landlocked and grim when you compared it to this place of my cousin's. Much later I learned his family was nearly poor, but this was laughable even when I heard it, because it was heaven: the movie house right where you fished and the society of cats, and my uncle's house with the huge watermelons lying on the linoleum under the television with startling shows like "Lights Out!" from the New Orleans station. We didn't even have a television station yet where I lived.

I kept casting and wading out deeper toward an old creosoted pole in the water where I thought a much bigger croaker or even a flounder might be waiting. My cousin was tired and red-burnt from yesterday in the sun, so he went to swim under the diving board of the Catholic high school a hundred yards away. They had dredged a pool. Otherwise the sea was very shallow a long ways out. But now I was almost up to my chest, near the barnacled pole where a big boat could tie up. I kept casting and casting, almost praying toward the deep water around the pole for a big fish. The lead and shrimp would plunk and tumble into a dark hole, I thought, where a special giant fish was lurking, something too big for the croaker shallows.

My grandmother had caught a seven-pound flounder from the seawall years ago and she was still honored for it, my uncle retelling the tale about her whooping out, afraid but happy, the pole bent double. I wanted to have a story like that about me. The fish made Mama Hannah so happy, my older cousin said, that he saw her dancing to a band on television by herself when everybody else was asleep. Soon—I couldn't bear to think about it—in a couple of days they would drive me over to Gulfport and put me on a bus for home, and in my sorrow there waited a dry redbrick school within bitter tasting distance. But even that would be sweetened by a great fish and its story.

It took place in no more than half a minute, I'd guess, but it had the lengthy rapture and terror of a whole tale. Something bit and then was jerking, small but solidly, then it was too big, and I began moving in the water and grabbing the butt of the rod again because what was on had taken it out of my hands. When I caught the rod up, I was moving toward the barnacled pole with the tide slopping on it, and that was the only noise around. I went in to my neck in a muddier scoop in the bottom, and then under my feet something moved. I knew it was a giant stingaree instantly. Hard skin on a squirming plate of flesh. I was sorely terrified but was pulled even past this and could do nothing, now up to my chin and the stiff little pole bent violently double. I was dragged through the mud and I knew the being when it surfaced would be bigger than me and with much more muscle. Then, like something underwater since Europe, seven or eight huge purpoises surfaced, blowing water in a loud group explosion out of their enormous heads, and I was just shot all over with light and nerves because they were only twenty feet from me and I connected them, the ray, and what was on my hook into a horrible combination beast that children who waded too far would be dragged out by and crushed and drowned.

The thing pulled with heavier tugs like a truck going up its gears. The water suddenly rushed into my face and into my nose, I could see only brown with the bottom of the sun shining through it.

I was gone, gone, and I thought of the cats watching onshore and I said good-bye cat friends, good-bye Cousin Woody, good-bye young life, I am only a little boy and I'm not letting go of this pole, it is not even mine, it's my uncle's. Good-bye school, good-bye Mother and Daddy, don't weep for me, it is a thing in the water cave of my destiny. Yes, I thought all these things in detail while drowning and being pulled rushing through the water, but the sand came up under my feet and the line went slack, the end of the rod was broken off and hanging on the line. When I cranked in the line I saw the hook, a thick silver one, was straightened. The vacancy in the air where there was no fish was an awful thing like surgery in the pit of my stomach. I convinced myself that I had almost had him.

When I stood in the water on solid sand, I began crying. I tried to stop but when I got close to Woody I burst out again. He wanted to know what happened but I did not tell him the truth. Instead I told him I had stepped on an enormous ray and its hook had sliced me.

No.

Yes. I went into briefer sobs.

When we checked my legs there was a slice from an oyster shell, a fairly deep one I'd got while being pulled by the creature. I refused treatment and I was respected for my close call the rest of the day. I even worked in the lie more and said furthermore it didn't much matter to me if I was taken off to the asylum for stingaree children, that was just the breaks. My cousin and the rest of them looked at me anew and with concern but I was acting funny and they must have been baffled.

It wasn't until I was back in the dreaded schoolroom that I could even talk about the fish, and then my teacher doubted it, and she in goodwill with a smile told my father, congratulating me on my imagination. My father thought that was rich, but then I told him the same story, the creature so heavy like a truck, the school of porpoises, and he said That's enough. You didn't mention this when you came back.

No, and neither did I mention the two cats when I walked back to shore with Woody and the broken rod. They had watched all the time, and I knew it, because the both of them stared at me with big solemn eyes, a lot of light in them, and it was with these beings of fur then that I entrusted my confidences, and they knew I would be back to catch the big one, the singular monster, on that line going tight into the cave in the water, something thrashing on the end, celebrated above by porpoises.

I never knew what kind of fish it was, but I would return and return to it the rest of my life, and the cats would be waiting to witness me and share my honor.

Two Gone Over

I was in North Dakota around the SAC base in March. The wind blew hard across the beet fields and the tarmac, wherever it was. I had done my duty in Grand Forks and we talked in a bar. She and her girlfriend were both in cowboy boots. The woman I was interested in had very excellent calves. Her face was high cheekboned with huge eyes like china marbles. Her forehead was touched around by brown bangs that made my stomach ache. She was a Florida beauty, Tallahassee, just a slight quarter inch heavy with winter flesh, that's all, a slight quarter inch.

I told her she was the one who broke my heart in high school and made me cry on my pillow. She was the type. Little Anthony and the Imperials sang about her. I loved Little Anthony because he could gasp so good, he wrung it all.

Later, when I was alone with her, she said she wasn't really that type. She was a simple Southern girl, but her father was Satan. We were in those couples apartments near the SAC base. The apartment was similar to rooms I had down South when I was first a bachelor, divorced. But they were even smaller and poorer, with a feeling of transience, little attempt at decoration.

My home woman and I had become, I think, old friends more kindly than passionate. In fact she was still married although long separated. We had hung together in a vast common loneliness

346

almost like love. I liked to see her onstage in a gown playing her flute in the orchestra, very well. She had a doctorate from Boston University, which I understand is something.

She had lent me some money in a humiliating emergency, and now in Grand Forks I had a check in my pocket. I could repay her and I felt square, decent, and very American all of a sudden, as when you leave a gym with your hair seriously combed, wet, and walk into the cool evening. The earth is glad to see you.

The girl from Tallahassee was only twenty-four. I was forty-two.

She showed me album after album of B-52s in the air and on the ground. Her husband had wanted to be a fighter pilot but had not come up to the mark when he left Colorado Springs, the academy. I didn't mean to be ugly but I thought this was boring, the sky and the bombers, the ground and the bombers, the squad and the bombers. I might have said this. But she thought they were beautiful and told me so again and again. She was divorcing her husband, who was in the air now, but she thought the B-52s were exquisite. She wanted something beautiful in her life, these pictures, and I should not have commented at all, especially since her father was the Devil and she did not have him either.

After the tour through the photos I told her I ought to go back.

This is not turning out like I wanted it to, she said.

Well, this is your home, your married home. I couldn't possibly do anything here, don't you understand? Their married bed, and besides the husband might come in from an aborted mission. She could understand that, couldn't she? I couldn't have her here.

But—looking back—maybe her point was to have it here, right here. Don't be fast, be slow, she insisted. Right in the middle of the B-52 pictures. However, we drove in her car back to the motel. Crying cold black wind outside, all over Dakota.

I knew it would be like this, I could imagine, she said when we were in my room. She was downcast. I felt sorry for her. My clothes were strewn around. I didn't care for the look either, although I had never planned on much in this town. I wanted her in an almost crippling way now. It seemed more urgent with the black wind out there. Don't be fast, please. Just don't be fast, all right? she asked me.

You have other experiences?

No, only with my husband Nicholas. Now you.

By this time I was flooded with gratitude. I was little but a token offered in her satisfaction. I did not quite understand this. I did not want to be greedy. Her face all this while was never ironic, always sincere. She had set about this evening with conviction. I could hardly believe it, but we were becoming friends, and I found this very arousing.

I'm a little old for you, I guess.

No. What, forty-five?

Only forty-two. She thought I was even older and it seemed not to matter in the least. I may have been in my last blaze of attraction, whatever it was. But I could hardly believe my fortune. I began feeling sorry for her husband. Nicholas, she said, not Nick. Lumbering around the sky, obsolete.

In my memory, she was at school and in airports, peeling me with her eyes, just a few seconds, then turning and gone on her belly-dropping legs, off to better zones. She was the girls I could never have, in one. Then too I was having the air force and all the frigid black wind of the Dakota night, all that black wind between the places you have left behind that don't want you anymore.

All over America from shore to shore such lovely women as this marry too soon because somebody wants them too much. They are wanted so much they can't deny the hunger. The loves are too hungry and quick, the men fall on them and ravish them and use up the love almost instantly. They must eat every part. Then nothing is left, only two husks with their manners and they are just sitting there together glum and naked in the hats of their choice, not another word to say, not a drop left to give. Nature is through with them for a long while, and they begin friction over nothing, except that each feels cheated, always cheated, cheated every minute. Somebody once told me, as a thought in consolation, when you see a beautiful woman, always remember: somebody is tired of her. Like most advice this is probably true and absolutely useless except to the wise dead. The dead sit around us in their great hats, nude, yammering away nevertheless.

I have felt of consequence to the universe only while drunk or at the moment of orgasm. These are lies too, I know, but good ones, an inkling. Maybe next for me is prayer, but with her I was praying only not to be too fast. She had drunk three wines at her apartment while going through the photos, I nothing for a long while now. Now she was lying naked on the bed, heavy breasts with dark exhuberant paps, her head propped on one arm, facing me under her pixie-cut hair with her high cheekbones, cheerful even though we were not lying on the B-52 pictures.

I was thinking of all that black wind outside the motel window, with her lying in the wind, only her. I saw nothing else in the room, just her and black rushing air around her. It was wonderful, this picture, but with an edge of terror too, an image come alive out of regular life. The wind was screaming and her husband's big plane, the size of a football field, was screaming through and breaking up.

When I was with her I did not have her so much as melt twice inside. My word, I became a woman in her, is what it felt like. All the excitement, the hard passion from her place to here—I was sighing as if penetrated and then wrung out. Never in my life before, nothing like this. I would tell only you this, pal. I have nothing to boast about, nothing to leer at, I promise. No, there was hardly any pride. She was all the power, every minute of lost lechery in my life, a sucking dream in a black wind.

But when she left the room, she still smiled as if she were my friend, everything was lovely. I felt unsatisfying, my spine was vapor. She had admired my body, but I was the chew toy of a dog, pal, a sad man. I had wanted too much, I think, waited too long. I had dragged her back to the motel. This was wrong. So was her apartment wrong. There was no good place, there was no right place for us.

In the airplane home to Memphis I tried to raise myself, have my esteem back. For a few minutes I would recall her beauty and then boast inside, but this went away fast. Then I tried to attach a profound narrative to myself.

My uncle, a laughing athletic monument of a man, had mysteriously gone down in his B-26 while chasing Rommel in North Africa. For years my mother waited for news of her brother. In my infant memory I recalled her crying for him, didn't I? His widow was a delta beauty who remarried an important man, maybe a college president. I would see the two of them pictured in the paper. She stayed fine looking for at least thirty years. I admit to strange family thoughts about her. At fifteen I imagined that one day she would call me up and have me over to show me the ropes, in honor of my uncle's memory. All this was fitting for his nephew, perhaps even decreed in the Old Testament. They were twenty-three when my uncle disappeared. The woman of Grand Forks was twenty-four. She acted as if all this were inevitable. Witness our easy, instant friendship. Said I must see the bombers, must see how beautiful they were. We would have toiled in the photographs of the bombers. This was a profound narrative.

But it wouldn't stick, although I tried. I wanted badly to be a part of weeping history but the ghosts in this thing would not line up. Every now and then I would catch myself in a gasp, even a sob. Something was overcoming me, a kind of weak shame.

Life went on with my woman back home, but not for long. She left teaching at the college for banking, which was the profession of her father, a grim man in a characterless brick town on a hill in east Texas. I went around town dopey. The words *fill me, fill me* came to my lips constantly without my will. This would have been frightening but I was not that alert. I saw her play flute with the Tupelo Symphony a last time when an old man—once a master, I guess—was featured at the piano in a Gershwin concert. Either my ears had gone totally out or the man was simply possessed and awful. He thrashed on the keys way too loud and without sense. The audience sat there as if everything were sweet and ordained, but couldn't they hear that this old man in tails was awful? He might not even be the musician they invited. He might be someone deranged, an understudy who had killed the master and was now mocking him. Was I the only one appalled? I kept listening, then I suddenly saw him naked in a tall hat. A nude hatted monster, banging down with closed fists. Nobody around me reacted, of course. It was a sorry thing, and again, I would have been frightened, but I was dull as if doped.

Finally I could not stand this feeling anymore and went on a bender, after a year without a drink. I dragged the woman away from her commencement duties and took her to a reservoir in the north-eastern corner of the state near Tombigbee. I imagined the woodsy rocks and bluffs with a cold stream down the middle. We never found this, a place I thought very necessary, very much an emergency. The cool wet rocks and mountain laurel with fish to catch. I conceived of our eating fish and living off the land, a rebaptism of ourselves. My fishing rods lay helter-skelter in the back of the car. But there was no proper place, then the moment was gone and I was just a fool. We stayed in a motel with thin pseudowood walls owned by Pakistanis, the poor woman exhausted, her last loyalty expired. I couldn't sleep well, and when I did I dreamed a number of the tall naked dead in extravagant hats, standing about like cattle.

Within the month, the woman got an abortion as I waited in the car. It was early on. I think I cared more than she did. She had never had children and didn't want any. Then, out in Texas while she worked in her father's bank beginning her new future, she met a blond man of new interest. I wrote to her but she didn't write back. I smelled something wrong and went on another bender, using every room in my house, a huge rented country estate—modest to be sure—to have pretentious toddies in. I was intent on finding the safe and happy mix. No sick loonies this time, surely not.

In the midst of this the girl in North Dakota called and said her divorce from Nicholas was accomplished. She was headed back South and would drop by on her way to Florida. This was good, I was happy. There may be something serious here. I smiled in my mansion under the oaks, my dogs racing around the yard beneath the giant magnolia. Christ, I was baronial, you couldn't stop me, man of many parts, hear, old son?

When she came in the house I was in a Confederate cavalry hat. I have no clear idea why, except I had become also a pilot. I could not refuse the conviction I was a fighter pilot. The hat gave me a certain authority, I felt. The passion of my race ran high in me. I talked in this vein while she sat and watched. She had lost weight and was all sun browned and lithe. I spoke directly into her black eyes, unconstrained, possessed. She seemed charmed and amazed. My powers wanted out of me. I could not hold them back.

I had a long drink in the kitchen, staring out at my rented orchard. The future looked bright now with missy in the house. Yes, there would be great carrying on. When I returned she was gone.

My nephew walked through.

Who was that? That was the best-looking woman I've seen in my life. Now she's just up and gone. Didn't even get her name.

Old son, you fool. Don't you understand she'll be back? She has no choice, I told him.

I got a letter from her in Florida. Who *are* you? she began.

It couldn't have occurred to me then, and didn't for another year, that I must have been, in my cavalry hat, a lunatic older version of the very man she had left behind in the air force. Even days after she left I could not quit being a pilot. I woke up in the mode.

Then the other collapse of that summer. A butchy wife and her namby husband, lawyers, bought the rented estate right out from under me. I had to pile my belongings into a two-story hovel next to a plowed field, an instant reversal from baron to sharecropper. My nephew had to drag me out of a bar where I was attempting to buy a coed with a roll of hundreds. My ex-woman was driving around town with her new smiling blond Texas boyfriend. She had changed the locks of her doors. I lost my driver's license. I went broke. I could not eat, I went to the doc for depression. I was a wraith. Once, after some business in San Diego, as a passenger from the Memphis airport to home I was arrested for drunken riding. I have a clear memory of the dream I had those few hours in jail. The naked dead, all in hats and a foot taller than I, were in the jail cell. They said nothing. But they were mute with decision, letting their height speak.

The woman from Tallahassee wrote about her affairs. Living near her father who was Satan. Becoming adjusted to freedom. She was easy and friendly as if nothing had happened. However, I thought I detected a patronizing tone. She took me for a common fool, I decided. I drove to the home of my ex-woman. When she came out in the yard I promised her that in the future evil would come upon her. Or perhaps we could get married, I added.

At the end of a bender I have, like thousands of others, been stricken with righteousness. I wanted to have discussions with the naked dead but I could not dream them back. At the gate of an air force base near Columbus, Mississippi, I was thrown out by APs after certain demonstrations. I claimed to have friends on the base, imperative that they see me. I drove following a contrail in the sky to New Orleans, got out of my car dropping money, and was mugged before I could let out I was in the secret ground air force they had better stand wide for. The mugging did not make much of an impression on me. Unlike other drunks, I remember almost everything. Only the humiliation is left out, until later it leaps and is unbearable.

I turned toward Florida, seeking Tyndall air base beyond Panama City. I would have a chat with the pals there who didn't know me yet, perhaps even her ex-husband down on a mission, then on to Tallahassee where I would explain to the woman I was not a fool. No, I was in control, in vast control. But first I took a turn into Magnolia Springs on the eastern shore of Mobile Bay, where an old student of mine lived.

We talked a while. His parents were in the back, visiting, but he did not want me to meet them. Then he asked me to go, please. So I took my bottles and left in a huff. It seemed to me the world was certainly turning rude here lately, a lamentable sign of the times, those times you read about. Oh I was high into my righteousness, and just out near some swamp and palmettos I went way off into it and attempted to set fire to my car, which would not fly and was really hot on my feet. I threw matches into it, a '73 MG convertible. Then somebody stopped my arm. He put out the little rug fire I'd started. He was the son of a strange nearby family who fed me for three days. I could not decide whether they were white or colored.

They didn't pay much attention to me and did not speak much, but I thought I caught a foreign brogue, not creole, when they did. They ate rice and collards. This brought my health back in little angry fragments. One morning I was suddenly very sober, just very frail. They didn't mind how much I ate because they had their eye on my car over there out of sight. Then my old student came back and told me he was taking me home. I never gave them the car but I gave them the keys and was ashamed to return a week later. My student took a look around my cottage, then took a U-turn back the long trip. I still did not understand I had been gently but seriously kicked out of his county, 350 miles far.

My old girlfriend married the Texan. In the fall I got a call from my nephew who had heard from a musician that she was killed in a robbery of her bank in Jacksonville, Florida. Killed by crack people. She was no doubt in her smart executive suit, all bright and cheerful. New leaf, new man. She was not good with people, she once told me. Maybe a bit of a snob. I understand the new breed of crack killer is much concerned with respect. Something in her eyes, maybe. Maybe nothing at all, she was white and too lovely. She was there. I thought of her father, the dour banker on that hill in the east Texas town, her tiny thin mother. One of their daughters was a lesbian psychiatrist and the other was now dead from banking. He hustled peas in the Depression and now he was in modern life, on the hill there with the wind blowing the last of his hair.

Nevertheless, it is said we are predators, eyes forward, and we go on towards the hunt, as if nobody had eaten it all before us. As if just around the corner is the really fine feed, the really true woman, the world that will call us son. Somebody is missing to our left but we only sniff deeper, it must be there, there.

I was doing this in the aisle of a small local grocery when I turned a row and was shocked chilly, down to the bones of my hands, nearly crippled from a swat of cold nerves into my thighs and scalp. It was a very tall man all naked, in a large hat. He had a long gray country face I was certain I knew, a man confined somewhere too long.

The crown of the hat was above the top shelf of cans. He was turning my way to look but I did not want him to look at me. Then I noticed he was in a bleached pink set of long underwear, not naked, but the possibility was so close it was jolting. He opened his mouth. I ran away with my hands and groceries in my ears, with his lips twisting up there over me.

I went out in the street with the groceries still in my hands. Nobody called me back. I was well home before I was aware I had them, still locked in my fingers. I had no excuse for running out with them, for running away, nothing manly anyway. My act could not be explained. I was ill and ashamed, and jerking with breaths.

Next day I got a letter from the woman—now twenty-five—in Tallahassee. My hands still shook a little and my breathing came hard. I was without sleep because I didn't want to dream.

She wrote that things were not going very well. She lived with her mother, but Satan, her father, lived close by. Not going well. Too close, this man. As if he could move away but not very far. It felt like forever. It hurt to discuss certain things.

She asked me to forgive *her.* She had visited me with her winter pounds shed and with a dark suntan so as to hurt me, in her vanity. To make my mouth water. But yet I was her friend and this could no longer go unconfessed. She had wanted to change and ruin me for a while, with her beauty. It was an unfortunate trait. Her father had accused her of it all her life, but only now she was truly adult could she admit she enjoyed inflicting pain this way, always had. Her mother, a beauty, was fast losing her looks and was always in a state, afraid to go out with anybody new. She and her mother spent the days simply keeping a watch on each other. They had begun going to church together. Even there, they knew the great Satan was in one of the cars in the parking lot, watching them.

You must never write about me, she wrote. *You think I am special but I am not. I am to be forgotten, do you understand. We have had a bad house, wherever I am is a bad room.*

A week later I won an award from the governor. My old parents were there glowing in the mansion. I was in a suit, now a goodly time healthy, but in my short acceptance speech I was conscious of sneering ironic people somewhere in the crowd. When I looked at the rear rank of those standing I did see three hats way above the rest and flashes of beige skin. I may have broken all forms for modesty, unwilled actually, but from a diminished heart, and held my work in an esteem equal to that of a scratching worm drowned in ink and flung against a tombstone. Through all this too I confess I was coming on to the governor's wife—helplessly, God—and finished in a burst of meekness coupled with hideous inappropriate lust. I could hear the laughter and was led away.

I was looking at the plaque and stroking myself a couple days later as the phone rang. A voice I could not remember began. At once I could feel the black wind of North Dakota between us on the lines. She was a friend of the Florida girl. I had not seen her since I chatted with them at that bar near the Minnesota line. She was clear for a while but then started sobbing and stalling. Her friend. Our friend.

You were kind to her, she said. Always she mentioned your kindness. What?

In Tallahassee the father had run her over in her own living room and killed her. The car came in through the bay window and crushed her as she sat on the couch in her bikini swimsuit. Her mother, also in a swimsuit, was broken up badly but would survive. Abruptly after the collision, the father, still in the driver's seat, put a pistol to his ear and destroyed himself. The women were having lunch after sunning. He must have known all their moves. You are a good person, the woman said—a scrap of memory through the black air of days and days ago—and I had to tell a good person. Somebody who knew her.

I am not a good person, I told her. This is too awful.

Do you believe in God?

Foxhole Christian. When all else is lost.

Nothing else was said and she hung up.

I was suddenly something fresh to her, a way I did not know. Then she was destroyed by a monster I had never believed in, who was true. My pity was so confused I could not accept I was even worthy of having it, for weeks. Or worthy of her, or my former girlfriend.

It is true now that, years later and desperately married (to the daughter of a World War II pilot named Angel), whenever a flute plays I have the woman sweet in my ears and think of our laughter. Wherever I see a headline beauty I brag quietly: come on, I had better, with a sad smile, I'd imagine, that fine appreciation of ourselves when we have bittersweetness right on time.

I have not had that many women, is the truth, and this, pal, I know seems crammed with serial romance and grief, but I'm not quite through, and you will understand me at last as more that poor man on the east Texas hill with the wind in his last hairs, too thick in modern life, too thick in dream, too sad for years now. Maybe the girl in North Dakota mistook my sadness for kindness; defeat for gentleness. I look at an old photograph of myself at eight when I was just a boy and his dog under a cowboy hat. I was looking at the world across the cornfield, all ready to touch it all under the shade of my tall Hoot Gibson. Now I understand I have been witness to the worst fifty years in the history of the world. A tragedy that might make Caligula weep in commiseration. And I have had, you know, a relatively pampered life, although you see me puffing away on my smoke like a leathered vet, a tough cookie.

I used to be a considerable tennis player. So in my health I took it up again and got the game back quickly. I just had a tough time giving a damn about the score. Once I was playing with a friend and noticed a very tall pale woman through the fence on another court. She had her back to me. I saw she struck the ball with authority and grace. I wanted her within seconds of seeing her. I needed her. I had never had a tall woman, blonde, and I was already in my mind rocking with her in great abandon like a dying cannibal. The nourishment would be endless, so generous.

My friend and I played well. We sat down exhausted in that fine chill of Southern twilight that heaven might be. I looked to my right and somehow, in the flesh, the tall pale woman was sitting between us. You never see that kind of European paleness in women on a Southern tennis court. I was amazed at her musculature, like strands of soft wire. Then I saw the hat. She had been wearing a big unusual hat that must have given her seven feet in height. She was looking toward my friend. I had never seen her face. When she turned I looked away and in great fear I stared through the woods. I wanted her more than ever but I would not see her face. I heard her voice, though, just the once up close.

I believe I've got something you want.

I grabbed my bag and got in my car and was almost home before I remembered my friend had no ride home, a long way. But I couldn't go back and I almost threw up.

He called me, however.

Man, the woman was fast on you. What the devil, did you *see* all of her, fool? I'm much the better-looking, but all she gave me was a pouting ride home.

Who is she?

Somebody's relative. Can't remember. Too busy stealing looks. That's quite a drink of water, long and cool, old son. You never knew her?

Never set eyes on her.

You're an uncommon fool. And sober.

She has been around town now for a couple of years. I see parts of her here and there, but I walk or drive right away. I don't intend to see her face because I know I've already seen it. When we touch one of us will die and be in the other's dreams.

I am not insane. My affairs are composed in vicious sobriety. I did not see my tennis partner either for several months. Then he called at the end of the summer.

You don't play anymore?

A few times, other places.

The tall one was back on the courts the other day. I swear, fool, she's like something from the heart of winter in a foreign land. Same old story full of wolves where you'd stumble into a woman lying in the woods. I'm going to use a word. *Alabaster.*

I swallowed. You mean living or dead?

I'm not sure, mister.

Wolves.

I wonder, when she dies, likely by violence, will she be named like the lesser creatures in that story? Certain people believe all are given names when we die, not at birth.

The creature goes to heaven very baffled.

My God, what was all that about? it asks.

God says: Well, you were a wolf.

I see, says the wolf.

I wonder will it be that simple for her, or for me.

Drummer Down

H<small>E HAD NEVER LIKED THE YOUNG DANCING</small> A<small>STAIRE, ALL GREEDY AND</small> certain. But now he was watching an old ghost thriller, and he liked Astaire old, pasted against the wall of mortality—dry, scared, maybe faintly alcoholic. This was a man. He pitied him. Everything good had pity in it, it seemed to Smith, now fifty and a man of some modest fashion himself. Even as a drunkard he had been a bit of a dandy. It was midnight when he turned off the set. He had begun thinking sadly about his friend Drum again, the man whose clothes were a crying shame. Drum two summers ago had exchanged his .22 for a pistol of a large bore, one that was efficient. In his bathtub in a trailer home on the outskirts of that large town in Alabama, he had put the barrel in his mouth. He had counted off the days on his calendar a full month ahead of the event of his suicide, and on the date of it he had written "Bye Bye Drum." The note he left was not original. It was a vile poem off the bathroom wall, vintage World War II. He had destroyed his unpublished manuscripts and given away all his other art and had otherwise put his affairs in order, with directions he was to be cremated and there was to be no ceremony.

But two young friends had organized a ceremony for themselves. Many had loved and needed Drum. They had pleaded over the phone for Smith, of all people, to gather with them, but the town was such a valley of the shadow to Smith, with an air choked by rotten

359

cherries and whiskey, he did not go. He felt cowardly and selfish, because it was ceremonies of pity that most moved him now, but he could not take his part. He asked his sons to appear at the ceremony for him. They wore suits and went to the funeral home and stood with a mournful group of people in wretched cheap dark clothes, and stood quietly for an hour before they discovered it was a rite for another person.

Smith did not like arithmetic or its portents, but he recalled Drum at his death was sixty-six, twice the age of Christ at Golgotha. With Drum this was relevant, and overbore the vile poem. Drum had been a successful carpenter several years previous.

But in Smith's class ten years before the end, Drum was fifty-six and looked much like Charles Bronson. Big flat nose and thin eyes with a blue nickel gleam in them; three marriages behind him, and two sons by an opera singer far away in Germany. He held a degree in aeronautical engineering from UCLA. He could fix anything, and with stern joyful passion. He had written six unpublished novels. He served in the army in Panama in the years just after the world war, which he would have been a bit young for. Smith stole glances at Drum while he taught, or tried to, with his marriage and grip on things going to pieces. He tried to understand why this old man was in his class, whether he was a fool or a genius. There were indications both ways.

As in Smith's progress toward the condition of a common drunkard.

Smith wanted to be both lost and found, an impossibility. He was nearly begging to be insane. He saw this fellow of great persuasive ugliness, with his small airy voice and his sighs; the weariness about him, even with his blocky good build and the forearms of a carpenter. He was popular in class even these short weeks into the semester. Drummond was his last name. He pleased the girls around him. He was avuncular and selfless in his comments, with a beam of patient affection in his eyes. Somehow he scared Smith, Drum holding his smile, the flattened great bags under his eyes from rough living and failure. He spoke often of "love" and "quest." He prefaced many things he said with "I am a Christian," sadly, as if he were in some dreadful losers' club.

Paul Smith looked at the table in front of him and had a brief collapse.

"I'm sorry." He put his hands down flat. There seemed to be a whole bleak country in front of his eyes, the ten hills of his fingers on the desert floor of linoleum, speckled by gray lakes, all dry. "I'm sorry to be confusing. Things aren't going well at home. Bear with me."

Drum befriended him. He seemed to be just all at once there, his hand on Smith's shoulder and the grave twinkle in his eyes. The little smile of a prophet on his lips. Two of the very attractive girls from the class, right behind him, were looking concerned. Maybe they liked Smith. He didn't know. He couldn't get a read on much at all these days. Arrogance punctuated by bouts of heartbreaking sentiment had come on Smith since the publication of his last book, which was hailed by major critics and bought by a few hundred people.

He didn't want to be arrogant, but he was experiencing a gathering distaste for almost everybody. He would nowadays mumble and shout a few things in anguish that seemed loud and eternal, then call class. To others that might seem derelict, but many of his students grandly appreciated the quick hits and release, right in the manner of a punk lecture. Punk was all the rage that year, and in his class was a lame girl wearing a long sash with sleigh bells on it, so that when she wallowed along in the hall on big stomping crutches, a holy riot ensued. She wore enormous eyeglasses but was otherwise dressed and cut punk, wearing a hedge of waxed hair atop her tubular head. She was the punkest of them all, a movement unto herself. Smith noticed that Drum was very kind to her and cheered her various getups every class meeting. The girl was unceasingly profane too. This seemed to interest Drum even more. He grinned and applauded her, this funny Christian Drum.

Nevertheless, she had gone to the chairwoman about Smith's asthmatic style. She loved his hungover explosions, but complained that he cut them too short and she was not getting her money's worth. Smith was incredulous. It was his first experience with a vocal minority, the angry disabled woman. Angel B. was very serious about her writing—very bad—and viewed it as her only salvation. He was not imparting the secrets of the art to her. She must know everything, no holding back. All this with a punk's greediness and nearly solid blue language, the bells shaking. Smith noted that he made no complaint about the bells. Smith planned to kill her and insist on one of her prettier banalities for her headstone, so that she could be mocked for centuries. But this man Drum loved her even as the talentless bitch she was. How could he be here offering to help Smith?

"What can we do, Paul?" Drum was whispering and uncle-ish. The two girls nodded their wishes to help too. Smith looked them over. He was already half in love with the taller one, pretty with lean shanks, who looked like she was right then slipping into a bathtub with Nietzsche, that lovely caution about her. The other was pre-Raphaelite, a mass of curly hair around a pale face very oval, the hair coiled up on her cheeks and separating for the full lips.

"We could drink," said Smith, dying for a taste. He was imagining a long telescope of whiskey and soda through which to view these newcomers to his pain. He liked people waving like liquid images, hands reaching toward him.

At home the end was near. His wife, just out of the tub, would cover her breasts with her arms as she went to her drawers in their bedroom. Smith watched, alarmed and in grief. No old times anymore. She meant, These are for something else, somewhere else down the road. He had hoped to hang on to ambivalence just a little bit longer. He wanted her more than ever. He said unforgettable, brutal things to her. His mouth seemed to have its own rude life. Here he was, no closer to her than a ghoul gazing through a knothole to her toilet, the hole rimmed with slobber, in their own big smart house.

They all went to the Romeo Bar on the university strip. Smith saw Drum drive up with the girls in a bleached mustard Toyota with a bee drawn on it at the factory. Smith thought it was an art statement, but it was not. Drum was poor.

He wore unironed clothes, things deeply cheap, dead and lumpy even off the rack at bargain barns, and the color of harmful chemicals, underneath them sneakers with Velcro snaps instead of shoestrings. The clothes of folks from a broken mobile home, as a pal of Smith's had described them. Drum at fifty-six lived upstairs in a small frame house of asbestos siding. In the lower story lived his mother, whom he called the Cobra. The brand of his smokes was Filter Cigarettes. His beer was white cans labeled Beer.

Nothing surprised Drum, and the girls were rapt as Smith poured forth. He was a bothered half-man, worn out by the loss of heart and music of the soul.

Drum agreed about the times, entirely. "There should be only a radio in every home, issuing bulletins on the war. The war of good against evil. That's all the news we need," he said, directing the bar air like a maestro. "But all they give us is facts, numbers, times. Enough of this and nobody cares about the war anymore. Why, all television addresses is the busybody in everybody!

"We're born to kill each other. First thing in the morning we take something to numb us, then parachute into the sordid zones of reality. Layers of dead skin on us, layers!" he finished.

Everything surprised the girls. They seemed to adore being confidantes in Drum's presence. They were anxious to become writers and have sorrows of their own. The grave male details of Smith's distress the girls thought exquisite. That through a knothole looking at her toilet thing was beautiful, said the pre-Raphaelite Minny.

Later, they all stayed over at Smith's green hovel by the railroad tracks he'd rented as his writing place, a heartbreaking first move toward divorce. Minny took ether and began talking about her enormous clitoris, a thing that kept her in nerves and panic every waking hour. Pepper passed out before she could recall any true sorrow. Drum went back in the kitchen with some of Smith's stories. He had on half-glasses bought at a drugstore, and Smith saw him foggily as a god: Charles Bronson as a kitchen god. Smith retired with Minny.

Then in the morning his wife knocked on the door. Smith answered in a leather overcoat, nude underneath. He was stunned by drink and ether, and his wife's presence simply put a sharpness on his wrecked eyesight. Behind him in a bedsheet sat Minny in front of a drum set. She was sitting there smiling at Smith's palomino-haired wife. It was her first scandal, she told them later.

His wife said something about divorce papers, and Smith slapped her. She rammed the door shut.

"Oh, how Old World!" Minny cried. She dropped the sheet and rose naked and curly like something from a fountain. Already Smith was tired of her. He loved Pepper, the lean beauty who could not get her sorrow out, asleep in the rear room.

"That's no good, Paul. You shouldn't hit." Drum had awoken and come out. His big fingers were around a fresh cold beer. "Oh, I hit my second wife. She thrived on it. Some women like hitting, they work for it. But it's a bad thing. A man of your sensitivity, with that sad little child in you, *you* won't survive, is what I'm saying."

"I love the sad child!" said Minny.

"But it makes an end to things at least. You need to end things, Paul. Purgatory is much rougher than hell. Well I know. You've got to wish them well, and be off. Wish them well in love, hope they have good orgasms."

"My God!" Smith could not imagine this charity.

Sometime later in the week Smith asked Drum how he'd lost three wives.

"Because I was a failure, man!" Drum seemed delighted. "I wrote and wrote and couldn't get published. I quit all my jobs. I'd had it with facts, the aeronautics industry. Working plans to fly in a *coal mine,* baby! The heart, Paul, the heart, that's where it is."

On the last of his GI bill the man was taking ceramics, photography, sculpture, and Smith's writing class.

"I *pride* myself on being a dilettante! I am looking for accidental successes. Heart accidents. I want to slip down and fall into something wonderful!"

As for Drum's physical heart, there was a bad thing running in his family. His father and two older brothers had gone out early with coronaries, and he himself took nitroglycerin tablets to ward off angina.

Even Smith's punk band excited Drum. Anything declamatory of the heart moved him. He was very often their only audience. He applauded and commended, through their vileness. They switched instruments, versatile in absence of talent. It didn't matter.

"*Everything* must be explored! Nothing left untouched!" Drum shouted, slugging down his cheap beer, smoking his generics.

They played their own "Yeast Infection Blues" and a filthy cover of George Jones's "He Stopped Loving Her Today." The regular guitarist was a vicious harelip pursued all over town for bad checks. The singer was a round man with dense eyeglasses and a squint who sold term papers to fraternity boys. They called him the Reverend. The bass man was a boy who never wore shoes, hardly bathed, and in appearance approached the late Confederate veterans around Appomattox—gaunt, hang-necked, and smutty. Drum absorbed them all. They were his children, junior alcoholics to Smith. Sometimes he'd dance with Minny or Pepper. They shook the little green house and the police came. Perfect.

Smith poured Southern Comfort in a Pepsi can in order to make it through his lectures, which seemed a crucifixion. The crippled girl Angel B. seemed satisfied, liberated more thoroughly and writing even worse. As for his own heart, Smith wanted to get rid of it. He missed his wife terribly. The thing pounded as if it were an enormous fish in him. He was barred from his old home. The band was angry over his lack of endurance on the drums. One night Drum brought him over some chicken soup, vitamin B, and gluconate. He was worried.

"Look at you. Look at this room," he said.

Smith's SS overcoat was spattered with white paint. He had painted everything instead of cleaning. He had painted even Minny's dog. It was under the table licking itself. He had nailed bedsheets to the floor. The novel he was writing was strewn out in copies all over the musical instruments. He and the band were singing his novel. The children from his first marriage were not allowed to visit him anymore. He had been fired at the college. Bare inside his overcoat, with a Maltese cross made by Drum hanging from a chain around his neck, he had grown so thin that his wedding band had fallen off somewhere. He was now almost pure spirit, as Minny called him.

"We need your big heart, Paul. The forces of good need you. Technique and facts and indifference are out there winning. Money is winning, mere form and the tightasses are winning. Commerce is making the town uglier and uglier. We Christians need you. You're giving over to low anger and spite, drinking away your talent. An old bad thing coiled in the dust, that's not you."

Smith poured the remainder of a jar of cherries into a mug half filled with Southern Comfort. The overcoming taste would remind Smith forever of his last days in this town.

Drum had made the mug. On it was an ugly face with a cigarette in its lip. It was one of the forms of "Sarge," an old army drunk Drum had known in Panama. The man had been only in his thirties, like Smith, but already grotesque. He would line up for review every morning, everything wrong with his uniform, but with a tiny smile and ruined goggle-eyes, maimed in every inch by the night before. He'd been busted from sergeant four times.

Later Smith fought with the band and threw them out. Minny ran out of Valium. Now living was almost impossible without constant fornication. People with police records began showing up in the house. Some played musical instruments or sang, then stole the equipment. One night while he was plying Minny, who poured out high spiritual sighs, he had to have a drink. On his way to the kitchen, he caught a thief in the house. The man sprinted out the back window as Smith pulled his father's antique shotgun off the wall. Then out came Minny, screaming for him please to not shoot anybody.

In the morning he accused her and her dog, who had remained silent, of setting him up. He put the cur in her arms and kicked them both out. Then he fell out in a sleep of a few hours. When he woke up it was midafternoon, and he knew something was gone. The antique shotgun was not on the wall. He stumbled to his kitchen and pulled a hunting knife out of his drawer. He intended to cut Minny's pre-Raphaelite hair off and drag her down the railroad tracks by her ankles. In a swimsuit and his serious coat he went out to the tracks. He seemed to remember her other place was near the tracks somewhere down there. So he walked and walked and then he was in a black section of town, there in his overcoat with lion-tamer boots on, holding the large saw of his knife, in the hottest summer on record. In the overcoat he was drenched, just an arm with the pounding awful fish of his heart inside him. A black teenager, tall, came out of one of the houses and asked him what he was doing with that knife out here, his mama didn't like it.

"Hunting woman."

"You sit down in that tree shade." Smith gave him the knife. "How much you take for that coat? I can get that paint off it."

"I'll sell you the coat if you'll call a number for me. I don't feel good. I'm not all right. Here's some money. Please get me some liquor too." He gave his wallet to the boy.

"You wait."

When Drum at last came out across the tracks and knelt beside him, Smith had terrible shakes, and could not pass out like he wanted to.

"You think you're drunk, kiddo? Shit, this is nothing. I was drunker. And I was drunker *alone.*" Drum laughed.

Smith sold the black boy his coat for fifty dollars and got back his wallet. Then Smith stared into his wallet.

"Drum? I got exactly the same in my wallet. That boy bought my coat with my own money."

"Forget it. It was a horrible coat. A chump's coat. A pretender's coat. It was the coat of a man with a small dry heart."

"It was?"

Smith was out of money now, but he was waiting for a *Reader's Digest* sweepstakes check very seriously. His unopened mail was a foot high, but none of it was the right envelope. Then a letter came offering him some work in Hollywood. He took it around town, running up tabs with credit on it. Some people still liked Smith. One night late he came in from drinking and misplacing his car. He felt there was something new in the place. Yes, there it was. On the kitchen table. The kitchen had been cleaned. But on the table was the final version of "Sarge," the life-size ceramic head of the grinning old drunk, the butt of a real Pall Mall hanging from his lips. Drum, a year in labor on it, had given it to Paul Smith. There was a short note underneath it: "All yours. Go with Sarge." Smith did not know it then, but this was as far as Drum would ever go in the arts. At first it made Smith afraid. He thought it was an insult. But then he knew it wasn't. He laid his head down and wept. He had lost everything. He did not deserve this friend.

About three in the morning, into the last of his cheap wine, he heard a car in his drive and some bells at his door. It was Angel B., the punk crippled girl. She settled inside with her crutches and her bells on what was left of a wicker armchair.

"I know I can't write, but you are a great man. I can get your job back for you. I know some things on the person fired you, some of them taped. This would destroy her."

It seemed a plausible and satisfactory thing to Smith.

"I might not can write but I want a piece of a great man to remember. Would you dim the lights?"

He recalled the revulsion, but with an enormous pity overcoming it. In his final despair, the last anguished thrust and hold, he tried to mean actual love. He wanted to be a heavy soft trophy to her. The bells jangled faintly every now and then before he accomplished the end of his dream. Smith stroked Angel's mohawk, grown high and soft. Then she was businesslike getting her clothes and crutches back together. She was leaving immediately. Smith suggested they at least have a wine together.

"No. I'm drinking with Morris, the Reverend. He's out there waiting. We've got a tough morning tomorrow. We're going down to the station and I'm putting rape charges on him."

"He's driving you? What, pleading guilty?"

"No, innocent. We're still close. But I know what I know."

She waddled out to the old Mustang. Morris waited in it like a pet. His dense glasses were full of moonlight.

A week later Drum drove him to the airport.

"I think that was it, Drummer. Pit bottom. And I can still taste her." Smith was trying to get a long march out of sips of Southern Comfort.

"It probably wasn't, sport. You get to go to California, stomping grounds of all *my* failures. Be patient, Paul. Nobody gets well quick, not with what you've got."

He remembered Drum taking his luggage. The man wore a shapeless blue-green jumpsuit with plastic sandals on his feet. The porter was a diplomat, compared.

Smith was not a success as a screenwriter. After he destroyed two typewriters, he spent a month in a hospital, where they talked about the same little child inside that Drum had often mentioned. Smith was befriended by a kind genius of a director, one of his heroes. The man gave him money that put him right with his child support, but Smith was unable to compose anything worthy for him, for all his effort. The bright healthy weather and opulence mocked him. He could not get past stupid good feelings. His work was entirely made up and false. There was no saving it by pure language. He could not work sober and was greatly frightened by this fact. He was failing right along with the old Drummer. He had to take another teaching job in the Midwest. It was a prestigious place, but Smith felt dumb and small.

He kept up with Drum through the years left. The Drummer was making a lot of money as a carpenter in house construction. He wrote to Smith that he could have, if he were not a Christian, any number of miserable lonely housewives. The Cobra, his quarrelsome mother, died. He moved out to a big mobile home on the outskirts of town, near Cottondale. He attended the high school graduation of Smith's son. He took and sent over a photograph of the boy in his gown receiving his diploma. He gave Smith's children presents at Christmas. Many times he took them fishing.

Three years ago, Smith had bitten the bullet and visited Drum in his trailer. Drum had had a heart attack six months previous. He told Smith he could hold in pain, but this was too much. He drove himself to the hospital. Uninsured, he paid out a ghastly amount. The trailer was all he could afford now. A preacher had become his landlord. Smith offered to lend him some money. Drum refused.

"Oh no. We don't want money to get into this, baby. Somehow things go rotten with money between friends. Believe me. This thing we have is too beautiful."

The streets of the town were a long heart attack themselves to Smith. Everything felt like sorrow and confusion, and tasted like Southern Comfort with cherry juice poured in—a revulsion of the tongue that had never left him. He felt the town itself was mean and fatal, each street a channel of stunned horror. He feared for Drum's health. How could he carry on here?

He met Drum's woman, a handsome lady of Greek descent. Drum was wild for her. She stayed over the night in their larger bedroom at the other end of the trailer. When she left, Smith told Drum he was very happy for him.

"I worried you'd turned queer," Smith kidded him.

"You ought to hear her moan, boy. I'm bringing happiness to that one."

Now Smith saddened, and his teeth cut into his tight underlip. Drum all those years without a woman, the uncle to everybody, in the background, cheering them on; urging them on to the great accidents of art and love. Drum the Drummer. Keeping the panic out, keeping the big heart in. He had convinced Smith he was worth something. He had convinced others that Smith was rare. Many days in California Smith had nothing else to take him through the blank stupid days.

"I'm living on borrowed time, man. Nothing is unimportant. Every minute is a jewel. Every stroke of pussy, every nail in the board."

He had lived that way every minute Smith had known him. That seemed very clear now. He looked at his friend and a shock passed through him. Drum was old, with wisps of gray hair combed back. He was pale, his eyes wet. The strong arms gestured and the mouth moved, but Smith heard nothing. Then the voice, like a whisper almost, came back. What was he saying? The vision had overcome everything.

It occurred to Smith later that success did not interest Drum. When Smith told him of some publishing luck and gave him a book, the man just nodded. You could see the boredom, almost distaste, freeze his eyes. He was not jealous. It simply didn't matter.

Near the end he had broken off relations with the Greek woman. His oldest son had come back from Germany to live with him, but he could not live with anybody. He asked him to leave the trailer.

And then the poem when they found him:

Here I sit all brokenhearted.
Paid a nickel to shit,
And only farted.

A common piece of trash off a bathroom wall, a punkish anonymity.

How could he? Why not even a try at high personal salute? The way he had believed in work, the big heart, the war.

Smith was angry a long time that Drum had left nothing else.

The waiting on borrowed time, the misery of his heart yearning like a bomb, the bad starving blood going through his veins. Smith could understand the suicide. Who was good for endless lingering, a permanent bad seat and bad magazine at the doctor's office? And with heaven looming right over there, right next to you salvation and peace, what Christian could hold out any longer?

Yes, but the poem.

So common, so punk, so lost in democracy, like an old condom.

The wretched clothes, beneath and beyond style, the style of everybody waiting intolerable lengths of time in an emergency room. Clothes the head of Sarge belonged on, the smile of ruin on his lips. Here, sir. All accounted for.

Uncle
High Lonesome

★ ★ ★ ★ ★ ★ ★ ★ ★ ★ ★ ★ ★ ★ ★ ★ ★ ★

THEY WERE COMING TOWARD ME—THIS WAS 1949—ON THEIR HORSES
with their guns, dressed in leather and wool and canvas and with different sporting hats, my father and his brothers, led by my uncle on
these his hunting lands, several hundred acres called Tanglewood still
dense in hardwoods but also opened by many meadows, as a young
boy would imagine from cavalry movies. The meadows were thick
with fall cornstalks, and the quail and doves were plenty. So were
the squirrels in the woods where I had been let off to hunt at a stand
with a thermos of chocolate and my 20-gauge double. At nine years
old I felt very worthy for a change, even though I was a bad hunter.

But something had gone wrong. My father had put me down
in a place they were hunting toward. Their guns were coming my
way. Between me and them I knew there were several coveys of quail
to ground, frozen in front of the dogs, two setters and a pointer, who
were now all stiffening into the point. My uncle came up first. This
was my namesake, Peter Howard, married but childless at forty-five.
I was not much concerned. I'd seen, on another hunt, the black men
who stalked for my uncle flatten to the ground during the shooting,
it was no big thing. In fact I was excited to be receiving fire, real
gunfire, behind my tree. We had played this against Germans and

371

Japanese back home in my neighborhood. But now I would be a veteran. Nobody could touch me at war.

My uncle came up alone on his horse while the others were still hacking through the overhang behind him. He was quite a picture. On a big red horse, he wore a yellow plaid corduroy vest with watch chain across, over a blue broadcloth shirt. On his bald head was a smoky brown fedora. He propped up an engraved 16-gauge double in his left hand and bridled with his right, caressing the horse with his thighs, over polo boots a high-gloss tan. An unlit pipe was fixed between his teeth. There was no doubting the man had a sort of savage grace, though I noticed later in the decade remaining to his life that he could also look, with his ears out, a bit common, like a Russian in the gate of the last Cold War mob; thick in the shoulders and stocky with a belligerence like Krushchev's. Maybe peasant nobility is what they were, my people. Uncle Peter Howard watched the dogs with a pleasant smile now, with the sun on his face at midmorning. I had a long vision of him. He seemed, there on the horse, patient and generous with his time and his lands, waiting to flush the quail for his brothers. I saw him as a permanent idea, always handy to reverie: the man who could do things.

In the face he looked much like—I found out later—the criminal writer Jean Genet, merry and Byzantine in the darks of his eyes. Shorter and stockier than the others and bald, like none of them, he loved to gamble. When he was dead I discovered that he also was a killer and not a valiant one. Of the brothers he was the most successful and the darkest. The distinct rings under my eyes in middle age came directly from him, and God knows too my religious acquaintance with whiskey.

The others, together, came up on their horses, ready at the gun. They were a handsome clan. I was happy to see them approach this way, champion enemy cavalry, gun barrels toward me, a vantage not many children in their protected childhoods would be privileged to have. I knew I was watching something rare, seen as God saw it, and I was warm in my ears, almost flushed. My uncle Peter tossed a stick over into a stalk pile and the quail came out with that fearsome helicopter bluttering always bigger than you are prepared for. The guns tore the air. You could see sound waves and feathers in a space of dense blue-gray smoke. I'd got behind my big tree. The shot ripped through all the leaves around. This I adored.

Then I stepped out into the clearing, walked toward the horses, and said hello.

My uncle Peter saw me first, and he blanched in reaction to my presence in the shooting zone. He nearly fell from his horse, like a man visited by a spirit-ghoul. He waddled over on his glossy boots and knelt in front of me, holding my shoulders.

"Boy? Boy? Where'd you come from? You were *there?*"

"Pete, son?" called my father, climbing down mystified. "Why didn't you call out? You could've, we could've. . . ."

My uncle hugged me to him urgently, but I couldn't see the great concern. The tree I was behind was wide and thick; I was a hunter, not a fool. But my uncle was badly shaken, and he began taking it out on my father. Maybe he was trembling, I guess now, from having almost shot yet another person.

"Couldn't you keep up with where your own boy was?"

"I couldn't know we'd hunt this far. I've seen you lost yourself out here."

An older cousin of mine had had his calf partially blown away in a hunting accident years ago, out squirrel hunting with his brother. Even the hint of danger would bring their wives to their throats. Also, I personally had had a rough time near death, though I hadn't counted up. My brother had nearly cut my head off with a sling blade when I walked up behind as a toddler, but a scar on the chin was all I had. A car had run me down as I crossed the street in first grade. Teaching me to swim the old way, my pa had watched me drown, almost, in the ocean off a pier he'd thrown me.

But this skit I had planned, it was no trouble. I wanted them to fire my way, and it had been a satisfactory experience, being in the zone of fire.

I felt for my father, who was I suppose a good enough man. But he was a bumbler, an infant at a number of tasks, although he was a stellar salesman. He had no grace, even though nicely dressed and handsome, black hair straight back, with always a good car and a far traveler in it around the United States, Mexico, and Canada. His real profession was a lifetime courting in awe of the North

American continent—its people, its birds, animals, and fish. I've never met such a humble pilgrim of his own country as my father, who had the reverence of a Whitman and Sandburg together without having read either of the gentlemen. But a father's humility did not cut much ice with this son, although I enjoyed all the trips with him and Mother.

From that day on my uncle took more regard of me. He took me up, really, as his own, and it annoyed my turkey-throated aunt when I visited, which was often. We lived only an hour and a half away, and my uncle might call me up just to hear a baseball game on the radio with him as he drove his truck around the plantation one afternoon. On this vast place were all his skills and loves, and they all made money: a creosote post factory, turkey and chicken houses, cattle, a Big Dutchman farm machinery dealership; his black help in their gray weathered wrinkled houses; his lakes full of bass, crappie, bluegills, catfish, ducks and geese, where happy customer/friends from about the county were let fish and sport, in the spirit of constant merry obligation each to each that runs the rural South. Also there was a bevy of kin forever swarming toward the goodies, till you felt almost endlessly redundant in ugly distant cousins. Uncle Peter had a scratchy well-deep voice in which he offered free advice to almost everybody except his wife. And he would demand a hug with it and be on you with those black grinding whiskered cheeks before you could grab the truck door. He was big and clumsy with love, and over all a bit imperial; short like Napoleon, he did a hell of a lot of just . . . surveying. Stopping the truck and eyeballing what he owned as if it were a new army at rest across the way now, then with just the flick of his hand he'd . . . turn up the radio for the St. Louis Cardinals, the South's team then because the only broadcast around. I loved his high chesty grunts when one of his favorites would homer. He'd grip the steering wheel and howl in reverential delight: "Musial! Stan the Man!" I was no fan, a baseball dolt, but I got into it with my uncle.

Had I known the whole truth of where he had come from, I would have been even more impressed by his height and width of plenty. I mean not only from the degrading grunting Depression, beneath broke, but before that to what must have been the most evil hangover there is, in a jail cell with no nightmare but the actual murder of a human being in your mind, the marks of the chair legs he ground in your face all over you, and the crashing truth of your sorriness in gambling and drink so loud in your head they might be practicing the trapdoor for the noose over and over right outside the door. That night. From there. Before the family got to the jurors. Before the circuit judge showed up to agree that the victim was an unknown quantity from *out of town*. Before they convicted the victim of not being from here. Before Peter himself might have agreed on his own reasonable innocence and smiled into a faint light of the dawn, just a little rent down on any future at all. That was a far trip, and he must have enjoyed it all every time we stopped and he, like Napoleon, surveyed.

He taught me to fish, to hunt, to handle dogs, and horses, to feed poultry. Then, one day, to stand watch at the post factory over a grown black man while he left in a truck for two hours. But this I highly resented.

"I want to see if this nigger can count. You tell me," he said, right in front of the man, who was stacking posts from the vat with no expression at all. He had heard but he didn't look at me yet, and I was afraid of when he would.

Such were the times that Peter Howard was hardly unusual in his treatment of black help around the farm. He healed their rifts, brought the men cartons of cigarettes. He got them medical treatment and extended credit even to children who had run away to Chicago. Sometimes he would sock a man in the jaw. I don't believe the etiquette then allowed the man to hit back. In his kitchen his favorite joot, habitual, was to say to a guest in front of their maid Elizabeth: "Lord knows, I do hate a nigger!" This brought huge guffaws from Elizabeth, and Peter was known widely as a hilarious crusty man, good to his toes. But I never thought this was funny, and I wanted my uncle to stop including me in this bullying niggerism, maybe go call a big white man a nigger.

While he was gone those two hours in the truck I figured on how mean an act this was to both me and the man stacking the fence poles. I never even looked his way. I was boiling mad and embarrassed and could not decide what the man, my uncle, *wanted* from this episode. Was he training me to be a leader of men? Was he squeezing this man, some special enemy, the last excruciating turn possible, by use of a mere skinny white boy, but superior kin, wearing his same name? I couldn't find an answer with a thing decent in it. I began hating Uncle Peter. When he came back I did not answer him when he wanted to tally my figure with the black man's. I said nothing at all. He looked at me in a slightly blurred way, his eyes like glowing knots in a pig's face, I thought. He had on his nice fedora but his face was spreading and reddening, almost as in a fiend movie. Too, I smelled something in the car as from an emergency room I'd been in when I was hit by that car, waking up to this smell.

"Wharoof? Did you ever answer? Didja gimme the number?"

"Have you been in an accident somewhere, Uncle Peter?"

"No. Let me tell you. I have no problem. I know you might've heard things. This"—he lifted out a pint bottle of vodka, Smirnoff—"is just another one of God's gifts, you understand? We can use it, or we can abuse it. It is a gift to man in his lonesomeness." To illustrate he lifted it, uncapped it, turned it up, and up came enormous bubbles from the lip as in an old water cooler seriously engaged. He took down more than half of the liquor. The man could drink in cowboy style, quite awesomely. I'd never heard a word about this talent before.

"I'm fessin' up. I'm a bad man. I was using you out here as an alibi for having a drink down the road there, so's your aunt wouldn't know. She has the wrong idea about it. But she knew I wouldn't drink with you along."

"You could drink right here in front of me. I wouldn't tell, anyway."

"Well. I'm glad to know it. It got to my conscience and I came back to make my peace with you about it. Everything between you and me's on the up and up, pardner."

"You mean you didn't need me counting those poles at all?"

"Oh yes I did. It was a real job. It wasn't any Roosevelt make-work."

"Don't you consider that man over there has any feelings, what you said right in front of him?"

"What's wrong with shame, boy? Didn't you ever learn by it? You're tender and timid like your pop, you can't help it. But you're all right too."

"Anybody ever shame you real bad, Uncle Peter?"

He looked over, his jowls even redder and gone all dark and lax, gathered up by his furious eyes. "Maybe," he said. An honest answer would have been, had he come out with it all: "Once. And I killed him." I wonder how much of that event was in his mind as he looked at me sourly and said, "Maybe."

He feared my aunt, I knew it, and let me off at the house, driving off by himself while I gathered my stuff and waited for my folks to pick me up. I heard later that he did not return home for three weeks. For months, even a year, he would not drink, not touch a drop, then he would have a nip and disappear. Uncle Peter was a binge drinker. Still, I blamed my aunt, a fastidious and abrasive country woman with a previous marriage. It was a tragedy she could give him no children and I had to stand in as his line in the family. She blundered here and there, saying wrong and hurtful things, a hag of unnecessary truth at family gatherings—a comment about somebody's weight, somebody's hair, somebody's lack of backbone. She was always correcting and scolding when I visited and seemed to think this was the only conversation possible between the old and young, and would have been baffled, I think, had you mentioned it as an unbearable lifetime habit. I blamed her for his drinking and his insensitivity to blacks. He was doing it to show off to her, that's what. He was drinking because he could not stand being cruel.

The next time I saw him he had made me two fishing lures, painting them by hand in his shop. These he presented me along with a whole new Shakespeare casting reel and rod. I'd never caught a fish on an artificial lure, and here with the spring nearly on we had us a mission. His lakes were full of big healthy bass. Records were broken every summer, some of them by the grinning wives and children of his customers, so obliged to Mister Peter, Squire of Lawrence County. On his lands were ponds and creeks snapping with fish almost foreign they were so remote from the roads and highways. You would ramble and bump down through a far pasture with black Angus in it, spy a stretch of water through leaves, and as you came down to it you heard the fish in a wild feeding so loud it could have been schoolchildren out for a swim. I was trembling to go out with him to one of these far ponds. It seemed forever before we could set out. Uncle Peter had real business, always, and stayed in motion constantly like a shark who is either moving or dead. Especially when he came out of a bender, paler and thinner, ashen in the face almost like a deacon. He hurled himself into penitential work. His clothes were plainer, like a sharecropper's more than the baron's, and it would be a few weeks before you'd see the watch chain, the fedora, or the nice boots—the cultured European scion among his vineyards, almost.

I did not know there were women involved in these benders, but there were. Some hussy in a motel in a bad town. I'd imagine truly deplorable harlots of both races, something so bad it took more than a bottle a day to maintain the illusion you were in the room with your own species. He went the whole hog and seemed unable to reroute the high lonesomes that came on him in other fashion. But had I known I'd have only cheered for his happiness against my aunt, whom I blamed for every misery in him.

At home my father meant very well, but he didn't know how to do things. He had no grace with utensils, tools, or equipment. We went fishing a great many times, never catching a thing after getting up at four and going long distances. I think of us now fishing with the wrong bait, at the wrong depth, at the wrong time. He could make money and drive (too slowly), but the processes of life eluded him. As a golfer he scored decently, but with an ugly chopping swing. He was near childlike with wonder when we traveled, and as to sports, girls, hobbies, and adventures my father remained somewhat of a wondering pupil throughout his life and I was left entirely to my own devices.

He had no envy of his wealthy brother's skills at all, on the other hand, only admiration. "Old Peter knows the *way* of things, doesn't he, son?" he'd cheer. It seemed perfectly all right that he himself was a dull and slow slob. I see my father and the men of his generation in their pinstripe suits and slicked-back hair, standing beside their new automobiles or another symbol of prosperity that was the occasion for the photograph, and these men I admire for accepting their own selves and their limits better, and without therapy. There's more peace in their looks, a more possessed handsomeness, even with the world war around them. You got what you saw more, I'd guess, and there was plainer language then, there had to be. My father loved his brother and truly pitied him for having no son of his own. So he lent me to him, often.

In the dullish but worthy ledger mark my father down as no problem with temper, moodiness, or whiskey, a good man of no unpleasant surprises that way. He was sixty-five years old before he caught a bass on a spinning reel with artificial bait. He died before he had the first idea how to work the remote control for the television.

At last Uncle Peter had the time to take me and himself out to a far pond, with a boat in the bed of the truck and his radio dialed to his beloved Cardinals. We drove so far the flora changed and the woods were darker, full of odd lonesome long-legged fowl like sea birds. The temperature dropped several degrees. It was much shadier back here where nobody went. Uncle Peter told me he'd seen a snapping turtle the width of a washtub out in this pond. It was a strange, ripe place, fed by springs, the water nearly as clear as in Florida lakes.

He paddled while I threw a number of times and, in my fury to have one on, messed up again and again with a backlash, a miscast, and a wrap, my lure around a limb six feet over the water next to a water moccasin who raised its head and looked at me with low interest. I jerked the line, it snapped, and the hand-painted lure of all Uncle Peter's effort was marooned in the wood. I was a wretched fool, shaking with a rush of bile.

"Take your time, little Pete. Easy does it, get a rhythm for yourself."

I tied the other lure on. It was a bowed lure that wobbled crazily on top of the water. I didn't think it had a prayer and was still angry about losing the good one, which looked exactly like a minnow. We were near the middle of the pond, but the middle was covered with dead tree stumps and the water was clear a good ways down.

A big bass hit the plug right after it touched the water on my second cast. It never gave the plug a chance to be inept. It was the first fish I'd ever hooked on artificial bait, and it was huge. It moved the boat. My arms were yanked forward, then my shoulders, as the thing wanted to tear the rod out of my palms on the way to the pond bottom. I held up and felt suddenly a dead awful weight and no movement. The bass had got off and left me hooked on a log down there, I knew. What a grand fish. I felt just dreadful until I looked down into the water when the thrashing had cleared.

The fish was still on the plug in ten feet of water. It was smart to try to wrap the line around the submerged log, but it was still hooked itself and was just sitting there breathing from the gills like some big thing in an aquarium. My uncle was kneeling over the gunwale looking at the fish on the end of the line. His fedora fell in the water. He plucked it out and looked up at me in sympathy. I recall the situation drew a tender look from him such as I'd never quite seen.

"Too bad, little Pete. There she is, and there she'll stay. It's almost torture to be able to look at your big fish like that, ain't it? Doesn't seem fair."

Uncle Peter didn't seem to enjoy looking in the water. Something was wrong, besides this odd predicament.

"No. I'm going down for it. I'm going to get the fish."

"Why, boy, you can't do that."

"Just you watch. That fish is mine."

I took off all my clothes and was in such a hurry I felt embarrassed only at the last. I was small and thin and ashamed in front of Uncle Peter, but he had something like fear or awe on his face I didn't understand.

"That fish big as you are," he said in a foreign way. "That water deep and snakey."

But I did swim down, plucked up the fish by its jaws, and came back to throw it in the boat. The plug stayed down there, visible, very yellow, as a monument to my great boyhood enterprise, and I wonder what it looks like now, forty years later.

My uncle had the fish mounted for me. It stayed in our home until I began feeling sorry for it after Peter's death, and I gave it to a barber for his shop. The fish weighed about nine pounds, the biggest I'll ever catch.

I was not the same person to my uncle after that afternoon. I did not quite understand his regard of me until my father explained something very strange. Uncle Peter was much the country squire and master of many trades, but he could not swim and he had a deathly fear of deep water. He had wanted to join the navy, mainly for its white officers' suits, but they had got him near a deep harbor somewhere in

Texas and he'd gone near psychotic. He seemed to expect great creatures to get out of the sea and come for him too and it was past reason,
just one of those odd strands in the blood about which there can be
no comment or change. Since then I've talked to several country people with the same fear, one of them an All-American linebacker. They
don't know where it came from and don't much want to discuss it.

When television appeared I was much enamored of Howdy
Doody. Some boys around the neighborhood and I began molding
puppet heads from casts you could buy at the five-and-dime. You
could have the heads of all the characters from the *Howdy* show in
plaster of paris. Then you'd put a skirt with arms on it and commence the shows onstage. We wrote whole plays, very violent and full
of weapons and traps, all in the spirit of nuclear disaster and Revelations, with Howdy, Flub-a-Dub, and Clarabell. I couldn't get over
my uncle's interest in the puppets when I brought them over and set
up the show in his workshop.

The puppets seemed to worry him like a bouncing string
would worry a cat. He looked at me as if I were magic, operating
these little people and speaking for them. He had the stare of an intense confused infant. When I'd raise my eyes to him, he'd look a bit
ashamed, as if he'd been seduced into thinking these toys were living
creatures. He watched my mouth when I spoke in a falsetto for them.

I still don't know what the hell went on with him and the
puppets, the way he watched them, then me. You'd have thought he
was staring into a world he never even considered possible, somewhere on another planet; something he'd missed out on and was
very anxious about. I noticed too that he would dress *up* a little for
the puppet shows. Once he wore his fedora and a red necktie as well.

A number of years went by when I did not see my uncle much
at all. These were my teen years when I was altogether a different person. He remained the same, and his ways killed him. I don't know if
the dead man in his past urged him toward the final DTs and heart
attack, nor will I ever know how much this crime dictated his life, but
he seemed to be attempting to destroy himself in episode after episode
when, as he would only say afterwards, the high lonesomes struck him.

The last curious scene when I recall him whole was the summer right after I turned thirteen. We were all around the beach of Bay

St. Louis, Mississippi, where we'd gathered for a six-family reunion of my father's people. The gulf here was brown, fed by the Wolf and Jordan rivers. It provided groaning tables of oysters, shrimp, flounder, crabs, and mullet. Even the poor ate very well down here, where there were Catholics, easy liquor and gambling, bingo, Cajuns, Sicilians, and Slavs. By far it was the prettiest and most exotic of the towns where any of the families lived, and my Uncle Max and Aunt Ginny were very proud showing us around their great comfortable home, with a screened porch running around three sides where all the children slept for the cool breeze from the bay. All over the house were long troughs of ice holding giant watermelons and cantaloupes and great strawberries. Something was cooking all the time. This was close to heaven, and everybody knew it. You drifted off to sleep with the tales of the aunts and uncles in your ears. What a bliss.

Most of us were on the beach or in the water when Uncle Peter went most bizarre, although for this I do have an interpretation that might be right. He had been watching me too intently, to the exclusion of others. He was too *around,* I could feel his eyes close while I was in the water swimming. He was enduring a sea change here at the sea, which he was supposed to be deathly afraid of. I believe he was turning more *urban,* or more cosmopolitan. He'd been to a Big Dutchman convention in Chicago. Somebody had convinced him to quit cigarettes, take up thin cigars, get a massage, and wear an Italian hat, a Borsalino hat, which he now wore with sunglasses and an actual designed beach towel, he and his wife sitting there in blue canvas director's chairs. He had been dry for over a year, had lost weight, and now looked somewhat like Versace, the Italian designer. If this was our state's most European town, then by God Uncle Peter would show the way, leading the charge with his Italian hat high and his beach towel waving.

He was telling all of them how he was getting rid of the bags under his eyes. He was going to take up tennis. He had bought a Jaguar sedan, hunter green. Now on the beach as he sat with the other uncles and my father, watching us kids swim, he seemed all prepared for a breakout into a new world, even if he couldn't swim, even in his pale country skin. Here he was in wild denial of his fear of the water. His wife, my aunt, seemed happier sitting there beside him. She'd been kinder lately, and I forgave her much. Maybe they had settled something at home.

I'll remember him there before the next moment, loved and honored and looking ahead to a breakout, on that little beach. He could be taken for a real man of the world, interested even in puppets, even in fine fabrics. You could see him—couldn't you?—reaching out to pet the world. Too long had he denied his force to the cosmos at large. Have me, have me, kindred, he might be calling. May my story be of use. I am meeting the ocean on its own terms. I am ready.

The New Orleans children were a foulmouthed group in general out there in the brown water of the bay. Their parents brought them over to vacation and many of the homes on the beach were owned by New Orleans natives. The kids were precocious and street-mouthed, sounding like Brooklynites really, right out of a juvenile delinquent movie. They had utter contempt for the local crackers. The girls used rubes like me and my cousins to sharpen up their tongues. And they could astound and wither you if you let them get to you. They had that mist of Catholic voodoo around them too.

Some sun-browned girl, maybe twelve, in a two-piece swimsuit, got nudged around while we were playing and started screaming at me.

"Hey cracker, eat me!"

"What?"

"Knockin' me with ya foot! Climb on this!" She gave me the finger.

You see? Already deep into sin, weathered like a slut at a bingo table, from a neighborhood that smelled like whiskey on a hot bus exhaust. I guess Uncle Peter saw the distress in my face, although I was probably a year older than the girl. He had heard her too. He began raving at her across the sand and water, waving both arms. He was beside himself, shouting at her to "Never say those things! Never ever say those things to him!"

I looked at her, and here was another complicating thing. She had breasts and a cross dangling by a chain between them and was good-looking. Uncle Peter had come up to the waterline and was looking at her too, forcing his hooked finger down for emphasis, "Don't ever!" But she leaned back to mock this old man, and she confused him and broke his effect.

Another uncle called out for him to come back, I was old enough to take care of myself, there wasn't any real problem here. But Uncle Peter hurled around and said: "There *is* a problem. There *is*."

Then he left the beach by himself and we didn't see him the rest of the reunion. I saw my aunt sitting in their bedroom with her shoulders to me, her head forward, alone, and I understood there was huge tragedy in my uncle, regardless of anything she ever did.

A couple of the brothers went out on his trail. They said he began in a saloon near the seawall in Waveland.

Could it be as simple as that my uncle saw, in his nervous rage and unnatural mood, that girl calling me down the road to sin, and he exploded? That he saw my fate coming to me in my teens, as his had, when he killed the man? Or was he needing a drink so badly that none of this mattered? I don't know. After that bender he didn't much follow up on any great concern for me. Maybe he gave up on himself.

It took seven years more. My father came and got me at my apartment in the college town and told me about his death, in a hospital over in that county. My father had white hair by then, and I remember watching his head bowed over, his arm over the shoulders of his own, their mother, my grandmother, with her own white-haired head bowed in grief no mother should bear. My grandmother repeated over and over the true fact that Peter was always "doing things, always his projects, always moving places." His hands were busy, his feet were swift, his wife was bountifully well off, forever.

A man back in the twenties came to town and started a poker game. Men gathered and drank. Peter lost his money and started a fight. The man took a chair and repeatedly ground it into his face while Peter was on the floor. Peter went out into the town, found a pistol, came back, and shot the man. The brothers went about influencing the jury, noting that the victim was trash, an out-of-towner. The judge agreed. The victim was sentenced to remain dead. Peter was let go.

I've talked to my nephew about this. For years now I have dreamed I killed somebody. The body has been hidden, but certain people know I am guilty, and they show up and I know, deep within, what they are wanting, what this is all about. My nephew was nodding the whole while I was telling him this. He has dreamed this very thing, for years.

2000s
Long, Last, Happy: New Stories

Fire Water

THE WOMEN FISHED FROM A RENTED ALUMINUM BOAT WITH THEIR
own big electric trolling motor, handled well by Dr. Haxton, a white
woman of eighty years, the same as Betty Dew. They both fished with
stout cane poles and goldfish minnows bought at the gun and tackle
store ten miles north in Holly Springs, where Betty Dew had one of
the mansions Grant spared in his first defeated assay on Vicksburg.
The old women fished studiously and in a mild ecstasy in the black-
green waters of Wall Doxey Lake here in twilight with a foggy gloom
already set. Early October. They were catching large saddle-blanket
white crappie and had four bass over three pounds. They wore straw
hats as in their youth, and they could not give up this fortunate day
yet. They violated the curfew of the state park the same as in their
youth. No sound but loud bullfrogs and tree frogs and thick crickets.
Such a day will not come the same to them again, ever. They knew
this and wore the darkening end of this Thursday like the gown of a
happy ghost.

But something was very different suddenly.

A fire seemed to be leaping around the entirety of this lake
on every verge but the sand beach and riprap around the boat ramp.

Neither woman spoke. At first the fire seemed a dream ignited by their last conversation, two moving mouths alone on the

lake, the boat tied to a lesser of the hundreds of dead cypress trunks when no fish bit for a half hour.

Both were literary women. Betty Dew had an expensive education and was an MD with a residency in pediatrics before she found she was terrified by children and parents and became an emeritus overnight. She rode a bicycle everywhere in this hill country of north Mississippi. She wrote poems, had received second place or honorable mention in half a hundred contests. She read with the young at the late-night open-mike poetry slams in the bars of Oxford.

Dr. Jo Haxton had been a neurosurgeon forty years. She was seventh in a family of nine geniuses in Greenville. She wrote quiet novels about villages of no ascertainable geography, real but hard-edged, too. Her theme was fairly constant. Small acts of kindness and charity countervened by such horror wherein nothing availed except violence by gentle persons. Perhaps inspired by the Civil War, but whose, ever? Her books were acclaimed by highbrow and middle. They sold well.

The fire caught up in all points of the compass, running, almost speaking in snaps of twigs mad orange all suddenly. But now they saw a darker high fire in and around an edifice two hundred yards south of them. It was a church here in the sticks that neither knew existed. A steeple, meager as blacks or poor whites could afford, covered by asbestos siding, which bore up for a few minutes. It was the last to fall into a heart of black and purple as the whole structure went down, wracking, gnashing what teeth were left. And briefly a crackling Japanese kind of song. Perhaps the piano was perishing. Loud spangs, then back to silence. It's when the women thought and connected in great fright. The church, temple, and mosque burnings in the north half of this state and up through Memphis. One church exploded right by one of the grand casinos in Tunica, poorest county in the USA.

These healthy and astute women, pioneers long before feminism sucked its first tit and screamed, wanted off the lake and out of the dusk very badly. Dr. Haxton untied the stern rope and turned the throttle to full 5. They looked shoreward for a tall ranger with a pistol, but the park was dead, cabins and resident warden house dark, while the ring of fire dulled, then jumped in places where it got hold of straw grass and dead willows. But the church was the main nightmare, orange now, then green and yakking with a sound like burned souls would make.

Their last conversation haunted them.

They talked about a private fire, a grand bomb of organ music, about the fire in the bottle neither of them had a taste for, not the volume that white-heated his brain and forced silence into a hill march of county citizens puny and eloquent as God on the page. Compared, they were only mild grannies with a patient lightbulb inside. Some lucky flashes somedays, Betty Dew whispered to Jo in the throes of another poem. Jo spoke back low, limpid, and kind, remembering him alive. The little man of the manor on Old Taylor Road. He seemed weary of his daily resurrection. Both of them had worked in the shadow of this statue. Faulkner. Damn the organ tones, the way he wrote like an octopus with pencils. Sullen fire ran through all his books, the organ in his head brought forth by firewater so intense he couldn't allow victrola music in the house, even when he was sealed behind his workroom door, where he lived with the falls and rises of geography beset by two-legged fires.

Or could you think all this while in this panic of curiosity, of hard-on terror? Jo wondered. When they were ten feet from the beach the two old ladies climbed as one mind out of the johnboat and walked in a foot of cold October water—to hell with the boat, the gear, the fish—to where fire wasn't. On dry land in wet sneakers they heard something huge thrash in the water behind them. Impossible. A fat beaver dropped from thirty feet couldn't make that noise. Maybe a gator, but they'd never seen one in the lake of Wall Doxey. This was not literary at all. Two women of eighty wracked by emphysemic gasping and deep chill.

Out close to the loosened boat in ten feet of lake, then coming toward them slowly in only a fathom, was the head and shoulders of a giant male who could have come from nowhere but the bottom of this black spring-fed pond with dying fires around it, the church beyond still showering sparks into the purple. Almost, I'm almost dead, Betty Dew whispered. The man was seeking them. He began the moan and the tale.

Jimmy Canarsis, seven-foot savant, was known to exist by very few. Because Jimmy, devout Christian, played the piano in the church, all day, every day, alone except Sundays and Wednesday nights, when others of the tiny flock gathered around him. He was always already there then they came. The church had caught fire and swiftly. He was surrounded by it on the bench in front of the keyboard before the flames got his attention and thus was badly burned walking out of it. Exploding cheap stained glass from the windows raked his face before he made his own door getting out the back of the church. He sensed a vacuum of the steeple high behind him taking the air from his lungs and scorching the meat that remained of them. So he walked up the beaver-sieved dam and then walked through the lake on its bottom since he could not swim. He had no fear of the water, he just could not swim it. Water is good, he thought, the way the cold springs soothed his burns and cuts. The shadowed ocher not on fire was his reckoning. Head at last out of the water he saw the two human figures, their boat floating near him. He reckoned these creatures were the arsonists so he would beat them as much as the Holy Lord would allow. It seemed like in the Old Testament you could beat on a multitude of folks but in the New, Jesus was not like your football coach screaming for you to kill somebody. Because Jimmy Canarsis had played some ball for Holly Springs in his last grade of school, either the tenth or the fourth. "But ball now, they said play it but wasn't nobody hardly playing but flatout cracking faces or attempting to chop a fellow's knees off, and the rest of them were running away. Say you were playing Byhalia and four of them was eviling on me, testicles or eyes or I've had an old farm boy with them hard hands like a Chickasaw spearhead rammed clear through past my aner. I'm going to crack these's heads until the police can come get them, but wait, these is two old women and I'm burnt to agony out of that water. Or you'd have Olive Branch or Como, their teams weren't nothing but so they was just out to prove something it didn't matter, offense or defense, all eleven of them would run straight at me and lay me out every play of the game and the coaches scream-ing at me to be tough Jimmy, these boys ain't even up to your tits, kill one and the others would just quit, and we'd be like ninety to two over them, they only wanted to tell their sons or grandchildren they once laid out a seven-foot man, so that's our family story and I'm'on go ahead and die now, tell them that's the way it was, and one that played church piano. One game the only play we had was hand off to me up the middle, over and over. The little boy quarterback never learned that one play right, he kept getting in my route down the center's back. I'm not fast or he'd of been in the hospital more than the four times he was, flattened over like a scarecrow man fell off his stick."

"We aren't that interested in your football season, you're forty or more years old. Who are you, setting these fires? Stand off us. Betty has a gun, you ugly idiot."

All three crept warily toward a low-watt bulb hung over the door to a homemade recreation vehicle the size of two outhouses. Jimmy Canarsis was in awful pain but some righteous battle was still in him. He'd been playing "A Mighty Fortress Is Our God," the Martin Luther classic, when the fire surrounded him. He was not interested in the mobile hut, and now he saw Betty Dew was holding no gun, only a long screwdriver from the tackle of their boat. He saw how thin these old women were, one short, one taller.

"This man set no fires, Jo," said Betty. "He's burned bad. Unless by his own gasoline. I know who he is. It's the Canarsis child, a savant, a pianist. He could play. He could play in the Ford Arts Center, but he won't leave the church. He can drive a car but doesn't need to, he said. His parents brought him over to my house for a medical opinion. I'd told them I'd never practiced, but they insisted I was in baby doctor school seven years and *wasn't no way you'd forgot it all and you're called doctor as we heard on it and some said a genius where they give you a award too big to get in this living room.*"

Betty detailed the case of this giant in a daze, looking past Jimmy at the tall glow of the church. The sounds of the county fire trucks, police, and ambulances were all over the night then. At last there were nineteen vehicles howling.

"It didn't take long for me to figure out the question here was financial, to get him on some concert tour. But they were not greedy. He was a big mouth to feed and he wouldn't leave the church. They were exasperated for him, even as church people. Where you'd never know a church could ever be. You've got the beavers and the hard rains. It's always been flood land."

"I don't believe it's there yet. Just the fire of it," said Jo.

"Women, I'm going back in the lake. I can't stand this no more. You talking about me like I'm a baby right in front of my face. And Dr. Dew a real doctor. The church is real and I'm real."

Jimmy acted on his words. They heard him sloshing in the water and both felt very ashamed. Ashamed in a common dream, watching the fire and hearing the men around it now five football fields away.

They had nothing but a screwdriver and a cell phone, and they were eighty, healthy but each minute brought to them personally like a tornado in the night come into their frailty, a thief before their eyes could perceive that death was a train in the window, permitting no peace. You were just old guts.

Sick Soldier at
Your Door

★ ★ ★ ★ ★ ★ ★ ★ ★ ★ ★ ★ ★ ★ ★ ★ ★

ANSE BURDEN AT YOUR SERVICE. HERE IN OXFORD I'VE FOUND SIX
soldiers from the '91 desert war with Iraq. I flew the F-18 Hornet
off the Roosevelt carrier, I believe. At the time I was loaded on Percodan and Dexedrine so maybe it was another. In the ready room we
watched ourselves bombing and missing on CNN. Nobody else in
my squadron was even nicked.

But a Stinger blew my tail off and I bailed, blown horizon-
tally into the air as the plane was corkscrewing. The ejection seat was
dead solid perfect, all it was supposed to be. I was in love with it and
was not conscious the ejection had broken my back a little. It seemed
I floated onto a beach of the Persian Gulf for no more than twenty
seconds. I must have hit the silk at an altitude of less than three hundred feet. I believe I was in shock briefly because I was sitting in a
shallow surf with black sand under me, still attached to the chute out
in front of me in deeper surf water, rising up and down like a dirty
white whale pulling gently at me with strings from its mouth.

Adrenaline, what a beauty, flowed through my shock and the
Dex and Percodan. I felt wonderful, the finest high I've ever had. I
was a child in an illuminated storybook, way off in a foreign brilliant
home. The whale pulled on me and Persia was singing to me from

across the water. And I was speaking baby talk into my radio, they said. Me down, me unhurt, me giggle, me see the spotter plane so Father will have the copter here soon.

What father? I later wondered.

I am certain it was Jesus Christ. Father, son, and brother, and most apparent of all, ghost, by all evidence. He carried a lamb under one arm and a Roman sword upraised by the other. This is how I saw him in a dream, a very hard-edged dream with red mountains behind him. Six feet tall. He was in a rough beige robe parted at the chest. Defined pectorals. Forearms lean and sinewy. I dreamt the dream that very night asleep below decks in the hospital.

Some decided it was not a Stinger missile, no SAM at all. They believe I shot my own jet out of the air. They did not court-martial me but they busted me down to lieutenant. I didn't care. I kept smiling for days even when the break in my tailbone and one of my vertebrae began a long explosion of pain.

My squadron liked me and so did the skipper and an admiral. I had built up a store of good will and beat the drug dependency forthwith. The fact was I flew twenty missions and was terrified around the third one on. Maybe it was nerves. I have nerves. They got harder and harder to hide. I was a ninny among true men.

My father died on the day of my last mission, to spook it further. The navy let me out and paid me handsomely to quit its service.

Now I come to Oxford and I am war. I've found the six other vets and am now a lay minister. My wife Brazile left me but might come back. What else did you expect? I cannot tell whether I've got the guts to minister to the other vets because of confusion among love, war, peace, and former nefarious behavior on my own part. I bought a church near the casino in Vicksburg right on a bayou. I knew the law and the law left me alone. My congregants were rough and smooth but all wanted to talk about God and each was allowed to give his own sermon until it became Babel and I made the rule that we could only talk about Christ. Several cursed me and left in their leather and denim all Prussian with medals and pins all over, out to the motorcycles and gone. The sergeant at arms of the church was a close friend. We did not truly need a sergeant at arms but the office made him feel good. He carried a baseball bat with barbed wire wrapped tightly around the sweet spot, a fine piece of crafts-manship, and he came through and brought the others back into the fold with him. After all, the bikers were just oily Prussian children with no place to go. Three of them lived with my pal Dan, of the barbed wire bat, in a cabin near a colossal junkyard. They were on heavy metal, they listened to heavy metal music, and they breathed oily heavy metal on a good wind off the yard.

After church the gambling would begin. The church was a casino and a pawnshop. Folks not even remotely connected to God, and happy Vietnamese and Chinamen, Haitians, Black Muslims, and Mexicans with the smell of road tar, all gathered to gamble and pawn.

My wife was an inattentive Roman Catholic from Morgan City, Louisiana, who flew helicopters out to the oil rigs in the Gulf when I met her. She was from the upper middle class and wanted to prove something and she did. I could never figure what delight anybody could have piloting a copter but her moxie brought me over. That and she was a rare gem of a fuck, with long legs, bouncing bosoms, and the only hair I've ever seen that was naturally black and gold.

She was as tall as I was, five feet eleven.

I'm not going to say a damned thing about 9/11, by the way. I think the innocent dead will appreciate that. When will "poets" ever realize they've long since been irrelevant after Bruce Springsteen's *The Rising*? And in all other matters by Dylan, et al.

Maybe all books must die before we form the peace.

I am war for Christ and my Brazile fled what she called outright insanity. She played the violin very well, I mean tempestuously while I entered her naked entrances from every angle possible. I wish her ears could suck. Get in there deep to her unarguable perfect pitch. I was a lucky man but I thought I had to prove something every day. I was thrown out of my war but am not comfortable with peace. Something always seemed left out of it. Like when we were kids and rigged a cannon that fired a two-inch shell of mule shit tightly wrapped in aluminum foil at the most beautiful white mansion in Natchez.

Too many books will deny their slaves the race to die in battle with the shout of victory in their ears. Otherwise you only get a cool nap in the shade and kick off with a little *ah* sound so they know to get you in the ground haste-wise before the public stink.

You dream maybe of Sam Houston whose own army ignored him and struck out to attack Santa Anna at San Jacinto. Old Sam yelled, "Gentlemen, I applaud your bravery but damn your manners," as he watched the slaughter and rode his white horse five times around the battle, getting his own licks in with no choice left.

Two regiments clash by afternoon. Gluttonous killings. Mexican drummer boys stuck in the bayou mud, half-beheaded by musket butts. Thus the birth of Texas, the birth of all states by mob slaughter.

For me, my own scribblings in my Life Book must end. Burn your books or hand them to other slaves who've lost their voices, their silence, their souls to literature, a feeble sucking religion.

What dream was I in January and February, 1991, when I made my last flyover of Baghdad? All F-18 Hornet, hardly a human creature at all. No balls, no soul, just fire, lift, drift, roll over, *bang*. The gorgeous missile tracks oranger than orange, or your hand-rolled bomb for any occasion. What a heavy leap of fire down there. You never imagine the hunched-down earthling in the streets or sand. Sheet, burnoose, and sandals, a helmet held to his dick. Look out above!

In the cockpit I was nothing but quiet screaming head, watching the immolations with small concern. I may have burned up this self and soul when I accidentally saw the burning man on the ground. My handiwork.

But somebody down there owned a vector on me. When I blew out with my already dead copilot just behind me somewhere in the air and never found, I believe I went from a mild scream to nothing, not a long trip.

Now I have the soul of an abandoned hospital. The six other Desert Storm vets, I want to invite them into it. Fill me up. But I'm a coward and a bad host in my ministry, astride this yellow Triumph Tiger, 1970 and mint, given to me by good Dan Williams.

In my journey from needy ones to other needy ones, I smile and think of Dan, who taught me how to hide things, my airplane and my last hundred thou. He knew the IRS as the gestapo and planned to attack three of the jackals who stalked him, still after money rightly devoted to Jesus.

Lt. Cmdr. to grievous joystick gambler, money changer in the temple of God, to Idiot of Christ, then lay minister, then simply four diseases all at once. Two cancers and chemo with its attendant friends neuropathy, boiling claws inside my legs, and a maddening ring ever constant in my head, half a heart and lungs blown away, three invasive surgeries, the horror of waiting waiting waiting for doctors who don't want to see you and cannot abide the idea of pain. How do I count the ways, fair pain, among the criminals and loafers of the drug, med, hospital, insurance white-collar-larceny colossus?

But will you believe this?

I am happy to just get down the road when I can, giving even unluckier muckers a ride if I can. Near death by pneumonia I had dreamed of all my pals and gals, foremost Brazile Varas Burden, the woman who will surely come back to me because she'll understand I'm no longer insane. Rather, to the contrary, serene and filled with peace that passeth understanding.

May I say this. Mark this: I do not feel saved but only born again into a parallel world where all my animals, all the girlfriends and powerful pals, the handsome infants, all of us children of a quiet green meadow with the ocean over there just beyond the trees, where we live when misery that passes understanding knocks down our last doors to come and claw us. It will always be there when no pills, no help, no release are left, only the hard wall of stupid random torture and malicious indifference. Then Christ comes if you give this kind stranger a chance. Simplicity. Ecstasy, all speech and acts converted to a fundament of rest.

Plus I'm still a handsome dude, hung like a small bear. I am faithful to my wife in our separation and she is faithful to me. Time is all, a hard matter, time and its exasperations like minutes stretched to no horizon.

Now in Oxford, drawn by the church, mosque, and tabernacle burnings from northwest Mississippi to St. Louis along the river through Memphis, I admit again I am a worm. I am organizing walking tours from blackened ruin to blackened ruin. Some of the churches were not just burned. They were bombed expertly as well. They exploded as only the hand of a specialist could bring about.

This does not harken back to the Klan burnings of the sixties, which were done by imbecilic cowards cheered on by silence from miserable governors. This is new history. You think Iraq. Vets of Iraq. I know six of them but have not a clue if the crimes are connected to any, none, or all of them.

I forgot to say, because I am a worm, that there is a fee for enrollment in these tours. I have written some articles regarding medicine in literature and have an instructorship at the university, hired on by the kind chairman of English, Joe Urgo, now at Hamilton College. My ship was continued by the next chairman, Patrick Quinn, the important Graves scholar with the hair of Mick Jagger. Dan the junkyard preacher dropped out of the sad motorcycle gang that remained behind in his cabin mourning when he went to Texas Christian for advanced knowledge of the Bible. I understand his studies were thorough and he came out completely insane though functional like most seminary students. Then there is the Choctaw Indian, Pearl Room, from Philadelphia, Ms. and the Indian casino down there, who, well, lectures on the spirituality of the Indian culture, among Choctaws and Chickasaws, the two tribes of the state.

The fee for the walking tour is 5 K.

I came to gawk, just like the rest, and am now the most experienced gawker. In my case, as leader and an invalid I ride the motorcycle and wait around the ruins preparing my lecture for the pilgrims. We have enrolled twenty pilgrims so far, mainly wealthy retirees from the Great Lakes cities who need the exercise and are crazy for Southern Culture, outside of catfish, the leading export of these precincts. Half of them are Jewish, the rest Irish and Swedes. The Swedes, you recall, gave Faulkner the Great Prize, so we start at his home Rowan Oak under the cedars in the long driveway, because cedars were the Indian funeral trees, as Pearl Room explains.

The point is to strip down, get protestant, then even more naked. Walk over scorched bricks to find your own soul. Your heart a searching dog in the rubble.

My own church down on the bayou north of Vicksburg exploded.

On a hunch I told the pilgrims that from thirty-thousand feet above you see the black dots that connected into the face of Jesus of

Nazareth. Then I found out this was true, with only a little push from the imagination.

It was a great shame my church exploded before the IRS could auction it.

But here's the worst news: my nephew Wilkes Bell is one of the arsonists. My sister, his mother, Ellen, knows nothing about this. My love for them prevents me turning him in to the law. That is a bit of a lie. I'm dazzled and exhilarated and proud of him until my best self comes back.

All the way through art school at the university he painted indifferently but the subject was always fire. The art school was totally ignored by the university, lucky for him. His teachers were alarmed by nothing since it was shit anyway, his paintings. Not even coded fire. Just fire, what fire does to whatever—beginning, middle, and end.

It is true I was licensed by this nation and the navy to burn and explode structures and the humankind near them, this aloof and with impunity. Just as whatever blew me out of my plane was licensed. Burning a church is one sorry damned thing. What hopes, prayers, and dreams, humble houses of worship that civilize and make gentle the hearts clustered to them. When you see flames eating up what kind, thoughtful hands have prepared for their deity, it is the least mirthful matter on the table. Nowhere in my soul is there even pity for such arson, not at my worst. Only the insanely religious or the pathological can bring it off. Or the other crime of long passion: revenge.

My nephew lives in the townhouse apartment in the very room the famous Eli Manning had during his college days at Ole Miss. I've chatted with this lad. Both he and his dad, Archie, remind me of Huckleberry Finn at quarterback. Loosey-goosey, they can flat fling the football, and then an *Aw shucks, wasn't* that *good,* toe in the sand. Grand boys, as are also the other two sons, Peyton and Cooper Manning. A national treasure under the miracle tree. God, I love the Harvard crimson and Yale blue of the Ole Miss Rebels. This fall under Houston Nutt we might get back to our 7–4 or even 8–3 seasons in the roughest toughest conference there is. At thirty my nephew Wilkes Bell is not a grand boy. He doesn't want to be a trust-fund baby, but he most certainly is.

I go by his apartment in the second story of a storied brick hotel now given over to overpriced clothing for swanky hunters and smooth tan daughters just a little younger than their mothers who are also smooth and tan and with sandals and legs. At the north end of the block is the famous Off Square Books. I must get the New Testament on CD to work with the young mid-age mothers in my home church, a white shingled two-story farmer's mansion with giant magnolias and thin wooden columns, a balcony from which I might one afternoon play the CD over loudspeakers with the women under me in lawn chairs and poolside wicker love seats. I can imitate the Pope. Whichever king of piety the Catholics have now. Yes, go again to Africa and preach in favor of exponential births where the sand and flies fight it out for misery. Has a pope ever held a bloated starving, dying infant in his arms speaking the last rites to it? But I rant. From the balcony I could simply raise my arms and look down. Because I hate to preach and congregations spook me. You must understand I'm no phony. Christ's Sermon on the Mount on CD and I could look at the tan cleavage, sweating in summer heat much like the Holy Lands.

And I am faithful to Brazile. I look at the cleavages and enjoy them as the women would have me do. But I'm thinking of my lovely Brazile, finally. She's a woman of mutating beauty. A fearsome beauty in wrath, a quiet madonna at peace, in joy. I have a hard time remembering her face, frankly. And lord I have other troubles.

There's my nephew Wilkes on *his* balcony, drunk, hanging over the rail in his suit like a black flag and pumping his arm in a thumb-up victory wave, then a salute. He adores me. Once said he would follow me to hell. I'm afraid my influence on him has been vicious, even if I'm straight and sober now ten years.

Suddenly on my right is the French mockery of a restaurant, 208, yes named for its address on South Lamar, where another vet of the 2003 Iraq war rises and falls as bartender and kitchen man. He's still a kid although bulked up from the army. They say he's not doing well, and you know *they say* is truer than the Bible. Went over to help schools and hospitals. Then received fire. Returned it. The poor boy is pouring out of the mold that formed him.

By Mississippi standards, Oxford is a city. Pop 30,000 counting the university of 14 K. You can get lost merely changing your haircut, your car, your bar.

Could it be that I'm losing my very heart, Brazile. Didn't I fight for her before we met in that feast for flyboys over Iraq? No. Christ the lamb, Christ the sword. Couldn't He decide? Am I worshipping at the feet of nothing but a difficult poem? But most days I have Him. All pieced out into the meek and least of us. My ruin is insufferable but god, look at the alternative: the pampered zombies of most America.

There is a groove in all roads that leads this motorcycle to needy souls at home, as if the old Triumph can't go anywhere else. Both my nephew and I are hopeless, helpless, maybe turning into souls as I speak but it feels like only fumes.

I'll die if I lose her. She keeps our dogs down in Edwards, Ms. There's barely enough of me left to be jealous of the sound handsome men who look on her when she walks the dogs in the nearby Civil War Park and Cemetery around Vicksburg. The war dead would snap awake too when they felt her and her several hounds' feet above them. But she is faithful, she told me so. My mission baffles and frightens her, that's all. Yes, laughing friends deride, oh smoke is in my eyes. I've got faith in my bones, she said, why make a pageant out of it? You're always trying to make a comeback, putting your doomed march on, the biggest kid in the Children's Crusade. I swear you want to die in some god-awful place, the nastier the better. I don't, I want to die in your arms, Brazile, I said. Wherever and whenever.

My pathway is a foggy circle back to her. I pray to the motorcycle. Please do keep me in a fog. I'm weary of light shed on myself, the sick and whining always at your door. Help. Love. Service. Find, but time always whispers *lost lost lost*. And *fool*, fool astride this smoking rocket called *Quo vadis?*

I arrived at the first house where a man on disability is breaking the seal on his first bottle of the day. He dismisses his wife to the rear quarters, but not unkindly. They seem to have an agreement that she is a speechless ghost.

Christ is difficult enough. Do we have to meet his father, too? The man sits next to an end table where the bottle and ice and Sprite in cans rest. With his iron gray hair parted and combed straight back you can guess he was an authority somewhere, old school. Black business oxfords on his feet, lanky, more master than slave by far, maybe an old god himself. Things speak to him, he said over the phone, but as with homicidal maniacs the voices are of himself as god, no outer god speaks to him. God the father whose shrieks of laughter behind that tome of law and mass homicides they call the Old Testament this reader can't doubt. Old Dad somewhere busting his ribs with glee over the misreadings of rabbis, monks, and the television preachers from the Academy for Significant Hair. Smiling charismatics trying to improve on Jesus because he's just too mad and wild. Fishermen and failures were his chums, most of them confused even when they saw him walking on water. Why did he choose men who could never understand him? Father why hast thou forsaken me? is not the utterance of a man certain of his painless ascent into heaven. It's the same cry I and billions make when wracked by undeserved pain.

I look at him in his Barcalounger in a clean white shirt. Indicates he is involved in a solemn vocation that did not brook meddlers. He looks like the deceased actor William Holden. He is watching *Animal Planet* on a big-screen TV.

"You want me to turn it off?" He lowered the volume with his remote.

"No. I love animals."

"Three years ago one of those stingrays killed that Australian man."

"Awful. But he was lucky. Happy in his work."

"You're here for Jesus, who died for these shits. Stay as long as you'll drink with me."

"I can't. Well, a very light one I'll nurse a good spell."

"Hello to mellow." He handed over a weak bourbon. My chair was new and overstuffed. I felt I was its first guest.

"Well it's *bon voyage* to this old ship. I wish there was a fresh ocean we hadn't ruined. I'm in the throes of nervous collapse, can't bear to work with people anymore. I give them work and even love for thirty years but people piss on it. They drove to a shrink with a tackle box full of wonder drugs. Hell, I'm on four of 'em. Excellent if you want to shuffle around like the living dead and eat the ass out of your kitchen. I never had a big stomach before, I was trim. I was a fine old troubleshooter for Winchester worn out by people. *People* wasn't the acceptable answer, but Dr. Meatloss signed the script for my long vacation. I was supervisor, got awards. You think I can afford this? I was handsome and some called me an intellectual. Now I couldn't stand even you, one unlucky pastor, if I wasn't well into the Beam."

He wore rimless glasses. I looked at his stomach pouch slyly. I asked him what drugs he took. A depth charge for depressive manias, I wondered he could be awake with the Beam on top.

"Tell me what people are like, Mr. Perry."

"Conrad. Conrad Perry. Rodents, but every one of 'em has studied the course Ratocracy. They're angry they're mediocre and believe you're to blame. Feel my pain. Lookit my cancerous ass."

"You're describing the school, the church, the state, the nation."

"E-mail opened the floodgates. We weren't meant to know this much about so many."

I agreed.

"I have half a college education. I was quiet and dumb then. Scared."

"I'd take that as a reasonable state for all of us."

"I'm well nigh on drunk already, Anse Burden. You have kin here?"

"No. Maybe long ago."

"All those people standing around outside. You saw them when you came in."

"No. Just me, right here alone."

"You're a minister and smoke Camel filters? I'll take one if I can."

"I set a low example. My pride is invested in cigarettes, I'm sure. Nobody tells me what to do," I admitted. "And I'm nervous as a cat on a hot tin roof coming in homes like this, Conrad."

"That's a good one. I never heard that."

"It's an old one, a play by our native son Tennessee Williams."

"What if those nasty people around the house sent you in, Anse, to finish me off?"

"You're on too much medicine, Conrad."

"I know that."

"Good grief, man, I was sent here by Christ because you're in trouble. I'm a piece of wreckage, myself. Love. I believe I'm just now learning it."

"Who called you, Pastor Burden? What a name. Pretty heavy on you, I guess some buddy or my wife called you."

"You called me."

"Did? Oh I do remember. Commonality, isn't that a word? I have a busted Harley-Davidson out back. Those men broke it. I never heard a thing. I heard you were a motorcycle man, maybe we could ride someday. Then second, your career as a flyer in the navy. I thought you could bring higher power against those dangerous idiots after me. I'm no chicken, I swear, but the two of us. See here, I'm not drinking in a bar and cursing blacks and immigrants. I already have a Jesus in me but he is tiny."

"I can't be violent anymore. But how did you get this information, Conrad?"

"Not much in this town gets past the wife. She barely speaks but she has damn near canine hearing. My nerves need a long rest. Nembutal, Percocet, oxycodone when I can get it. Got a vicious ache in my spine, center of my back. My heart pounds like it wants out. So I wash these friends down with the Beam. Then Jesus gets bigger in me, I get a beautiful floating kind of courage, like when you come out of the shower after whipping somebody in a football game.

"You could help me if you had the words, just some new words about this war. The words that would make me free again."

"You're still some kind of athlete to even be awake. I went through the Desert Storm shoot-out loaded on Percodan and amphetamines. Afterward, I stayed stoned and would've been busted out except for squadron pals and higher brass. No way no kind of hero, I assure you."

"Still, I can help *you*. In your own bosom you have nursed the pyromaniac."

I went cold. "Your wife again? What could you mean? She knows the arsonists?"

"Maybe one, who's made friends."

Perry stared at the ceiling nearly knocked out but smug enough to smile.

"What are we trading for here, Conrad? Because I am an empty and officially nobody. No connections with the law or the churches."

"If you'll have another weak one with me, I'll show you my suicide guns."

"I'll have another weak one. How many choices do you need for suicide?"

"The *quality* of my departure is still out for debate."

"I'm not drinking with you if this threat keeps up, Conrad. You'd have already blown your head off in the backyard if you'd been serious. Give my church the guns. One of the members, the sculptor, Beck, has donated over two hundred of them, historical pieces. We'll have an auction."

"On the straight?"

"The straight. Your weakness would be our strength. The odds are you and your wife Betty are stronger than this minister."

"Well, this is my church."

I walked in and saw the pistols on blue velvet, the rebel flag, the big trout he caught in Arkansas with the flyweight crawfish stuck in its lips and the nylon leader leading back to his fly rod leaned in a corner. But it was an unhappy male chamber with food and drink stains on the sofa and rug. A smell as if a fire had swept through just months ago, but there was no fireplace, no embers. Then I saw the great burned spot on the rug, stomped out by a white sneaker that still remained. Not much toil against unkempt here.

"You know the arsonists? Tell me," I asked him.

He was nodding out on me on the crumby yellow sofa. "'Sman who can't exist without being two men together. 'Sman of money, all these places, all these munitions. 'Nfaxt I thought it was you. You can get me Percodan and I would cheer you on. I'm highly in need. You can have all the pistols. Here's a sack for them."

He went to some rear shadows and wrestled out a croaker sack. You don't see this burlap much anymore. I eased the guns into the mouth of it and was fascinated by these fine instruments, pearl-handled, a silvery .38 with recessed hammer, a gun of the noir forties.

I reached in my pocket and gave him four Percocets. Chuckled for this old bird's knowing very well I was holding.

"What idiocy led you to think I'm the arsonist?"

"Exploded your own church for cover. Then a stranger to these parts, you *arrive* and the fires get widespread."

"They were already doing that."

He stood in front of me but his eyes were closed.

"Here I've been a fool thinking you wanted closer to Christ," I said.

"You're a little ungrateful. I gave the guns for Christ." Conrad wobbled and I thought I'd have to catch him.

"Please call your physician. You've got way too much head medicine already. You're asking for a coma of zero quality departure. Your wife mourning over a vegetable. You've got depression, Conrad. I don't buy the insanity. It's just your brain is carrying buckshot."

"What about the people, all that mischief around my windows?" The man opened his eyes and smiled a hopeless smile, one of false discovery after long confusion.

"Since you're not climbing the walls in terror, I think you know the answer. Take some steps toward getting well and maybe you'll feel like helping people. They need you. I believe you once did help people. Now I've got another fellow down the road in much worse shape than you."

When I said this he sat on the filthy sofa and went dead asleep. I was on the front porch making my way to my saddlebags with the sack full of pistols when I heard his wife speak very softly behind me through the screen.

"Thank you. You never know the form of the good one who comes."

"Pray, Missus Perry, I'm the good one," I asked her. I felt more like a busy malingerer.

I wonder if our Christ ever liked people. Plenty of evidence has him confused about them as well as his father, even as he loved them. He fled to the outlands when he couldn't bear healing any more of them. The press of the crowds drove him to solitary meditations many times. Who was his friend, as we know *friend*? Or did the hungry and angry time of his ministry preclude friendship. He must have faced madness to know tragedy and glory up close and both at once. Did he know only pain from word go? Our dreary march of case histories. Nevertheless, I revamped myself on the optimistic noise of the Triumph, and got along the road, a merry old cowboy dressed in his corpse.

Talk, talk, talk. Much said and nothing settled. You're not even certain of the subject anymore.

I knew an old gal and boy, married, who to anybody's knowledge had never finished a sentence they started. They didn't finish each other's sentences. They didn't even like each other. But perhaps the romance depended on the other never completing a thought.

Lastward,
Deputy James

HE HIMSELF MIGHT BE ONE OF JUST ANOTHER CONFUSED BUT ADA-
mant sect. This idea had crossed his mind, since he was certain there
was much to repay or regain from his past woes and he knew who
had burned the small church on the verge of Wall Doxey Park that
Wednesday evening. None but himself.

His wardrobe, the woman reminded him, improved past the
penitent rags he had once stolen from Goodwill warehouses. He also
quit stealing books. Formerly it just seemed he should, since he was
outcast already. Before the church, he'd not burned anything for long
months, either.

The woman he found himself with would barely leave home
except to spend $200 almost exactly each trip to Wal-Mart. She
watched television movies or she cleaned or threw out older new
things. She rarely cooked. He figured this love would not last long
but she had her good side when she was not directing scathing attacks on him or slapping him as he lay sleeping in the bed he had
bought, in the diminished hacienda he'd bought for them. After the
eruptions she was quiet a long while, which the deputy discovered
after months with her was her form of apology. Because she was

never wrong and never spoke an apology. He was to understand her moods, that was his constant homework.

Mainly she attacked him for once being a Montana deputy who refused to reattach himself at good salary to the law. She wondered where his money came from, anyway.

It was from his army savings and his father's photographic inheritance, a prudent man young as he was when death popped him. His pension from Montana and an uncle's inheritance, Old Ralph who loved him and pitied him in Toronto. But she would not leave him alone about the rest of his secret money for he was the sole source of her income now she had risen from near welfare and could throw out more old new things. She cleaned the house with the meticulous fury of a German analist, and she did enjoy dirty jokes. She was pleasant in the face, then grew pretty with expensive cosmetics. Her figure was in trim although she quarreled with her hips. She was angry about age, too. Her wrath and resentment were perfect like the work of flood or fire. No man or woman was spared.

He wondered idly sometimes why he did not kill her, but then in rare times she was good company and claimed to love him above all things in the world. She won him over, but he always knew what she was up to, which was to set him up for a sort of vicious theater where one character, himself, a bum with prospects, stands speechless while a harridan who owes everything to him attacks him up and down for not improving himself so that she could owe him even more. This debt was intolerable to her, she would never forgive him, especially now that she didn't have to appear in the workforce at all.

He would leave slapping her to somebody else even though a comprehensive bitchslapping would help her. Her lone mission was to go out into town and berate others.

Now the taste for burning had left him he was practically a saint. Outside of the church, what he had burned was just a hobby, for god's sake. He improved places by fire. He held himself in some esteem for not reattaching his talents to the law, the last career on his mind, and for doing almost nothing ardently except the secret trips. Like a great artist. His vocation was looking clean cut, now weeks away with a crop of recluse's bush all around his head and chin, and staying awake for upward of eighteen hours. Even so, he owned an exceptional facility for falling asleep dead center of one of the woman's attacks. This act calmed her and she was in awe of him.

Their house was a weathered one, old Spanish elegance as the realtors would have it, rented and tested by college men before they took it, the landlord negligent since many of the boys spirited themselves away to other quarters where mommy or granny lay waiting to spoil them and their creditors paid hard to find them. Our hero paid for a new roof and paint, white with slate trim, and a fence planted with Carolina jasmine soon thick and green, and her dogs could dig around the roots of the pecan and hickory trees safe from the highway out front. The dogs were a mix of corgi and shepherd, and he adored these oddly made creatures too. Our man, Franklin James, also paved the driveway where sat his carpentered hut with wheels, towed by a 600cc Ducati motorcycle from the seventies but in perfect repair. The hut's roof was peaked, it had a shatterproof window on either side, a smart thing as huts go. Tan and lean, he could be handsome with his beard lost. He had lived in federal and state campgrounds for nearly four years. He'd lived almost without cost, for an adventure hostile to most. He had had a bad night, only one bad experience with a small pack of motorcyclists anointed wild by themselves and carrying their own priests and witches.

He carried a nickel-plated hammerless .38 but the weapon had acquired the status of a mere hammer about the cabin, a wide enough rectangle with a small electric heater so that he slept comfortably in innocence, doom, and fatalism all three.

James was Canadian French. In the early sixties his father was killed by suspicious gunfire called random because another had died, this at a campus riot against the entry of a black man to the university. His father was a photojournalist. The shooter was never found and barely sought. The state then was in apartheid hotly and there was little sympathy for outside agitators, as his father was labeled, a meddler with no credentials in this place of fire and blood. James himself was a lieutenant in the French Legion, riding a .50-caliber machine gun in a sand jeep during Desert Storm, but this was not important.

Important was that even though the Klan had been broken by the FBI and lawsuits, they and their fellow travelers might still live and worship or preach in certain wooden churches. Such people tended to stay undriven from their soil, holy to their feet regardless of their less genial reception or the rough success of integration decades-old now in the Magnolia State. The best band in these parts was a mixed pigment group, sons of the famous Dickinson, Kimbrough, and Burnside blues/rock geniuses. But old murderers and burners muttered against them, even as they were hauled to jail lately for crimes forty years old.

His father was Anglo-French, a Parisien by way of Toronto. A good-natured lively man who wrote and shot stirring photos heralded in many news magazines in both Canada and the States. He was strong. He worked long distances from home and always came back with happy presents from these regions. Franklin James had lost him when he was fifteen.

Now he was fifty-three, an ex-sheriff's deputy from Missoula, sworn to fire anyway and also to a refinement to the precise gunman in golden years who now gained respect from his fellow churchmen and love from his teenaged grandchildren, which idea drove James near insane with rage. He would kill or find the grave of his father's murderer. He tried to live out this disease, tried to burn it out of himself, but it was fickle with mere time and would rise like a flaming snake in even sublime nature, the staggering gorges and pools of America's parks of prime natural glory. He hoped the killer played a fine fiddle and even rode on a scooter in a Shriner's fez in a parade for the Christmas blind.

His woman, in her rages, never knew how he could snap her in two if she were the murderer's niece, so her rages amused him, too. He did love her as she swore to love him. She knew nothing of his mission. He slipped ever easily into the brogue of love, that long hill-country moan that required slow action around the tongue and almost no lip opening to a song against coherence. Without her around he despised it, listening to men gossip at the barber's, the cafés in Holly Springs and Oxford. General Grant was headquartered in Holly Springs, where the antebellum mansions still stood, although in a flat of lackness frozen in brine, much like those in

Natchez, a back-lot set for zombies in a costume feed. The general had sent the drunker general, Smith, to burn Oxford three times, in reprisal for Forrest's raids on his supply lines toward Vicksburg. Now Oxford had the university and life, restaurants, nightclubs, gorgeous women on its walks hurrying to nothing, cellphoning nothing, but gladly come spring wearing nearly nothing. Five hundred lawyers and a state-of-the-art county office building and jail, along with the storied Faulknerian courthouse, the pale redbrick Art Deco city hall, and it seemed five though only two state flags flew high and wide here, one quarter of each the stars and bars of Dixie. James saw nothing but the Confederate flag and spat on the pavement until he had no spit. He cared little about the history of anywhere, but the irony of his lost father's body among all this formal law brought on a near faint of resentment. Like blood and vomit with a flag on it.

       With his new accent he led conversations among suspicious men. He did hear things but the men lied and invented so much it was a jam box of hell to get anything of substance from them. Two men claimed to know his father during his short tragic stay. Not a prayer. He heard men from the church he'd burned and surprised himself by this sympathy with them, poor country sorts looking for a new hall of fellowship. A poor giant boy savant played sacred tunes on its piano day and night all week and was burned terribly because he would not leave his instrument until the flames were on him. The injury to the boy savant was an injustice that depraved him and made him soberer in his hatred. He made daily trips to eavesdrop on the boy's condition after he left the burn ward in a Memphis hospital and came for further therapy to Oxford's Baptist one. He had meant nothing like that, nothing near it, and he hated that he had polluted his mission. He could not tell the boy or his parents his sorrow and guilt. He could tell nobody. At night he writhed as if sleeping in a coffin on a king-size bed he'd wanted, and this was mistaken by his wife Goodie Drake as amorous hunger, and she supplied him as he gave to her afraid to hurt her feelings. Neither of them was listless in bed.

       Teresa was her proper name. She bought the bed a headboard of Byzantine pattern befitting this name, and elevated it to nearly four feet on risers, then put many comforters and a phalanx of fat pillows over these. He slept in the effeminate pomp of a bed and breakfast resort. When there was too loud a fight, excruciating for a half hour while he stood silent, he slept out in the cabin, which she called his "pouting house." Be a man, she commanded him over and over. He couldn't tell her the kind of man he was. She didn't know he had received and returned much fire in Iraq with French troops. She didn't know what happened to make him an *ex*-deputy and a runaway from Missoula, Montana. He was tall and windblown like the actor Sam Shepard, she said, and she'd proclaim her love for him without once apologizing for her rages, a condition that came on like epilepsy. Another man would have left months ago.

The destruction of the guilty one would not make him right. He killed without hatred in the desert once, perhaps twice. He was in no way made right. To kill a man perhaps twenty years older than he, an *oldster in the hallowed years* as some called it, would be no more than shooting down an old rabid dog. But you had a mix of religion, Dixie patriotism, and blind hatred down here as you did in the countries of Islam. The worst of them were often old farts who could lead younger ones by the nose. Much was owed them by history and the black man. Franklin James was happy to do his part. To annul this living figment and his church with him was his dream since a boy, deprived of his papa.

His mild vocation for setting things afire had made the miserable jobs of the military happier. Standing around big fires where once were men and carefully constructed vehicles or buildings of great ingenuity for beauty and safety against all the elements, but now to no avail, no use, was not a bad assignment. Very meditative. Many a child will concentrate for hours on end to build a small town of cardboard only to stand back and incinerate it with licked big kitchen matches which sailed, smoked, then burst into flames like missiles. *He* had. But he did not run to conflagrations in Toronto when he was young or to smoldering Russian tanks in the desert, kind as they were to his eyes and gut. In Toronto, to be sure, he had made conflagrations almost beyond his will.

He was in a tank in which there was a boom box playing only three tunes. Jimi Hendrix's "Hey Joe," about shooting a woman and going down Mexico way. The Rolling Stones' "No Expectations," about death. The Beatles' "A Day In the Life," about death, or most likely. They were the best three tunes he knew, still. They moved him. Over the gun sight he and his commander saw Iraqi tank fires while the music, funeral tunes, written for the men burning against the far orange twilight horizon, played away. Neither man thought the music apt to the point, though. Some unwritten song waited but they couldn't guess what it should be. A tender symphony almost nonexistent as soon as it sounded. These days he listened to the tunes and smelled gas, cordite, and burned lamb, and saw tank carcasses against deep orange and black.

In the matter of his wife Goodie "Hey Joe" hung around his head but no song was exact to his suffering. Goodie despised lending her own possessions to him, she who took gifts from him—house, roof, bed, direct satellite TV—as a matter of natural transfer. She deepened her voice into one of a raspy carnival barker right in the microphone with loud hissing sarcasms about the low caste of his French mother and his infantile love for his murdered father. He had not described either of his parents to her. She'd had two husbands before James, and all he heard of them was their dullness and parsimony. James did not believe in Satan until a week after he married her.

Yet her beauty. She was quietly stunning in the face. Goodie, Teresa when she was kind and romantic. He would never know her. He wondered if, after his reckoning with the man who shot his papa, he'd be roused to more fury and annihilate her.

Her beauty, and she was hungry in bed. She was smart. After retirement from chief reference librarian once they were married, she used her pension to finish a college degree in Greek and Roman history. This was brave, a woman in her midforties sitting with spoiled children who drove BMWs. She called most of her professors fools and losers. She had dyslexia but memorized her way through tough biology and math classes. She dressed very well and owned a mink coat worth upward of thirty thousand. When she graduated, James took her to Paris, where she wore the coat as she believed the city demanded. He wore pressed jeans and a jacket, with suede boots. She could not bear his unconscious cowboy habits, as she called them. Once, when beauty and smarts mattered, she had been an airline stewardess. Now she found herself among lax slobs too often. A former husband had beaten her. Her attitude toward love was very rocky, very tense. Goodie seemed to like it that way. When would he ever find decent professional work? Versed in her own degree in history and art, she was decorating the house.

She did not know he had burned a Boston Whaler boat in berth at Pickwick Dam in Tennessee, or a white Cadillac Esplanade, or the church with the giant boy playing inside.

She only knew he was moody and once for four days hardly rose from his bed. Afterward he disattached his mobile cabin and rode the Ducati away to unknown parts while she cursed the motorcycle and the cabin both, standing in her driveway, the spectacle of a grease monkey, the sorry outhouse parked like a hillbilly joke in the drive. The front lawn had high cactuses, a rock garden, and a pool. Nothing like it stood near them in these rolling horse hills. The traffic on the highway beyond the entrance arch grew heavier. The house was something of a joke but Goodie meant to fix that by a high wooden fence around the grounds, and she goaded James into getting the cheap Latino labor for it. During their courtship she said his machine and abode were clever and cute. She made long protests over receiving all his gifts, rescuing her from that awful job at the library. Her vocation was a homemaker and landscaper now. She could see river birches all around the home, azaleas, roses. They needed the wooden fence for privacy and elegance. Their guests would be vetted by a Mexican in the right shirt. One day they might give a magnificent ball, people dressed to the nines, but her friends numbered two, a beautician and a gymnast.

Franklin James had no even near-friends but he studied the deep South with more care than Goodie suspected. On the matter of bad grammar, these people seemed to have taken courses in it. They took pride in being normal, dumb, and prejudiced, as if they'd won an award in these areas recently. Their voices dropped when the matter of race came up. To the man, they were close with good blacks but *true niggers ran the show too much.* Even those who lost children to cancer or car crashes believed in God. They spoke of secrets that should not be revealed. They knew crimes and killings the law could never uncover, just as it should not, because some needed killing. The murder of a bad seed who'd taken a life was ruled a suicide by the sheriff even though the instrument of his death, an axe, lay ready to hand. The men greatly admired James's motorcycle. It would spark narratives long held secret and spoken in lowered voices.

He rarely thought of his own history, but now he did. He had turned hermit and built the wheeled cabin for good reason although he felt little eccentricity in himself, as most men believe. But he was wrong, wrong, wrong. Then he was slightly racist against black people. He'd known few of them, and these few were good soldiers, good lawyers, good whores, and good garbagemen. Then a few months ago he was assaulted by the motorcyclists in the Kentucky park. Even more he was racist against white Southerners and especially those who had religion. He imagined the white-hot righteousness of the man who shot his father during the confusion of the riot, which might be the essence of the man who'd told him the story about the slain bad seed. This righteousness, biblical, hailed by the loud and cowardly brethren, kept him awake at night when he was not copulating with Goodie. He twisted, he pretended to sleep, a haggard man in the morning, when it arrived with depressing horror. The Hendrix masterpiece "Hey Joe" would replay as an anthem over and over in his head. You only had to change "old lady" to "old man." You could ride this tune through false sleep, sincere intercourse, and the solo trips he took on his motorcycle and in her Mazda with the sunroof down, CD of the sweet blue voice of Hendrix prevailing. Ride to where, where else but blowing the killer into his evil sky after all these years untouched by the depraved indifference of Southern law.

He *did* hate the Southern voice, with its presumed charm, even among its educated. The drawling masturbation of the mouth, the self-worship they knew as culture down here, and their frat-boy scions. He could shoot or burn down more than one killer with this rage.

Goodie was from California with a different voice or he couldn't bear her, but even she was affected and went into a drawling mush-mouthed countryese when she needed more charm. In the service he'd known pleasant, smart, efficient Southerners. But their voices were an agony, a ball of grub worms in the throat.

With decent representation, given the overcrowded penitentiaries, a white man could expect about seven years or even less when he killed a man in the passion of revenge. You could premeditate and kill and be out in a tenure of med school, internship, residency. He might go down Mexico way or even study medicine in the joint. The newspapers and the NRA might hail him.

He'd once heard an adage: When you read military history, read standing and count yourself as one of the dead. In a book of essays on the Civil War, James read about Burnside's stupid command in Fredericksburg as he fed regiment after regiment against Marye's Heights, where rebel troops four and five ranks deep with nine-pound muskets and rifles loaded with ball and buckshot delivered volley after volley from behind a sunken wall and reaped a slaughterhouse against blind and ignorant Federals. Such a vast murder that Lee, atop his horse on the hill, commented, "It is well that war is so terrible or we would grow fond of it." James threw the book down and sailed into a blind rage of swear words. He frightened Goodie, thinking the odd rage was directed at her. She stayed quiet for three days. Then she asked him if he was over whatever that was last Tuesday.

Now he held sway over her and heard no more scathing research of his personal clouded history or where his money was.

But he grew a new problem. He had lived in worse places than Lafayette County, Mississippi, much worse. On his sorties, people of all ages and callings were unfailingly kind to him, even when he was gruff or sarcastic. These were church people, pastors, police, riffraff, and elderly square-spitters, two Corsair pilots in the Korean War, a newspaper photographer, old blacks in Freetown, the county sheriff, old and young lawyers, and a professor who knew this Mississippi, a vertical rectangle of woe from the Gulf to the north hills, all the Indians, all the lynchings, and much about the '62 riot. He spoke to the head of the university library and received patient guidance from him in the place he'd met Goodie and asked her out. Married her in days, maybe a fortnight, the ancient measure accounting for happy and tragic collisions forevermore.

He became a better listener although half-deafened by the running hound inside him. Young black men always asked him how much he would take for his yellow Ducati. This seemed to be a form of courtesy. They could not raise two hundred for it. They knew it, he knew it. Impossible to sell, he said. Know what you mean, they agreed. Smooth, smooth, you say Italian? He feared liking these folks, yet grew easier with them.

* * *

In Montana, Missoula, he used his deputy's position to distance himself from men. In his office and patrol car he was a tyrant about silence, his conversation blunt, short, and dead-ended. Well respected though access to him was rare. Just a few years ago Montana, enormous and sparsely populated, its earth and humbling, humorless mountains stretched by horizons into beauty almost devastating to a man, was a force that drew mute isolators, some of them dangerous and armed. And free. You could drive ninety and salute an oncoming highway patrolman with a beer in your hand.

He was not a friendless man. He was close with pals in school and the Legion, who knew inside him was a big strange edifice he could give no key to. Grief is a strength after a great weakness, so he was told by his colonel once. Maybe that was Franklin James now and ever. The silence came on him when his woman quit loving him.

The Toronto of his youth was quadra-cultured, rich in art and big water, Ontario beyond the gorgeous wharf. A clean and efficient city. Safe for children to roam. His mother educated him early in two languages, her hands were soft on him. Her young beauty seemed permanent, but now he recalled only her long black hair pinned up or let down, and her mouth that kept whispering something out of shock long after his father was murdered. Possessed by disease and unaware her mouth moved while neighbors and his pals looked on, dismayed or embarrassed for her son.

He then despised his city for still carrying on and thriving, stupid as a giant horse towing a boxcar of shit. All things around him were noxious, frantic with idiocy.

He began to express himself in acts of sabotage and pointless theft and was never caught. He attended the very university where two statues were beaten headless by his sledgehammer. He was too sly. He loved himself as the professional innocent in the face of his good mother Celestine when she exclaimed about a fire-bombed city bus or his spray-painted masterpiece in the art museum. They were two against the world, but she never knew how far he took this war.

In Missoula his patrol was one through largely peaceable denizens and a few violent drunks, but once the actual Hell's Angels stayed at a bar nearly a week. One of them beat up the girlfriend of a lawyer with a cocaine habit. After a night of sleepless fury fed by powder, he shot down dead this Angel in the street. James was first to arrive, before the city police. His hand never came near his weapon, snapped down by the tongue of his holster. The lawyer was staggering on the bricks near the body and its blood, waving his pistol toward everywhere and nowhere. With contempt and quick study of those who might be dangerous to him, he disarmed the man and led him uncuffed into the front seat of his cruiser. Wide fame for his coolness and restraint attended him. But he avoided interviews. No charges were ever brought against the lawyer. The Angel got what the Angel begged for. The lawyer cleaned up and praised Franklin James all over the town and all the Northwest where his practice led him into fortune and fame. James was promoted to deputy captain. He got a letter from his married ex-girlfriend congratulating him and assuring him of her true affection. He tore it to pieces.

He already planned to leave the force when out in the brown hill sticks toward Lolo Pass he drove a dirt road in the grounds of an Aryan survivalist cult and received a .223 round through his rear window from an unseen sniper. The act was so stupid he was incredulous. But he turned the cruiser around and told his sheriff it was a stray round from a deer hunter he had arrested and seriously warned.

Two days later he drove the same road with a new rear window in the car. He eased toward the settlement without incident.

Everybody was gone from the barracks, likely into their caves and bomb shelters, two of them Hitlerian bunkers smartly constructed. With a wheeled propane flamethrower he burned down all the barracks and the cafeteria, standing for an hour like a pest exterminator in a sculpture of boredom. He quit the force a week later. Then he knew he was capable of many, many more fires. Perhaps the art-movie house still run by his old girlfriend and her family, who now came to mind as gargoyles fallen off its roof and mocking him in roars and farts. He was wired his due salary and retirement money in Toronto while he visited his dying mother. The chief sent him a note pleading for his return to the force, at more salary.

He told Goodie only enough to satisfy her nosiness about his career and money. The French army continued paying him a good monthly amount for combat pay and the RPG fragments in his calf, for which he had due decorations. His mother had seen little of him for decades but she was proud of him now, even though she could do little but cry as the lung cancer took its last course to her brain. After he buried her he went completely within himself and away from the touch or voice of man.

He found the marvelous parks where ten or twenty dollars got you hookups without another demand. You chose your favorite season and moved to it on the Ducati with the hut in tow. His mother had left him more money. He spent almost nothing. Seeking further and further deprivations became as art for him, though he stole books and wrote with a pencil between the lines of these histories. He took two Gideon Bibles on rare visits to hotels, in whose rooms he slept for two days and destroyed the telephones, just for the hell of it.

To Goodie he told a true tale of unexpected riches.

"You mean off dead soldiers?" she asked.

"Yes. They coptered some of us over to Kuwait City and northward. We overran many corpses loaded with American cash and loot of all kinds. Some priceless diamonds. I got about half the amount of priceless in order to get the money in a bank account, but at prime interest rate. You might've seen the exodus of Iraqis on the highway cut up by our air, Mercedes, and Rolls-Royces."

"I *did* see it. On teevee."

"Other French and me were in the southmost tail of it."

"A soldier of fortune."

"Definitely."

"You deserved it."

He laughed. He liked his wife, silly as she was and screwed up, wrapped all tight. Everything was appearances to her, even when there was nobody to look on or give a damn. Our *personal* environment, she said, bespoke our tone, our pride.

"I'm working even when I'm not working right now. A long-distance project to make us even happier," he said.

She nodded. "I'm hot for you, Franklin. Can I get some of that long-distance project from you right now?"

"I don't notice one thing stopping us."

He told her the next day he was fifty-four years old and that he'd been shaken by an episode in Kentucky when he realized his loneliness after four years as a vagabond in camps. The episode had brought him to Oxford and to the university library where he found her.

He was in his cabin reading and writing under his hundred-watt bulb at sunset in a Kentucky state park famous for its caverns. Came a knock on the door, not an odd event, and usually from a friendly ranger in aid to his safe and comfortable stay, say a black bear warning. From the war he was almost deaf in one ear but his right ear heard uncannily well. He found the .38 where he'd almost forgotten it in the toolbox. Strange and subconscious, because this rapping was different.

Thick woods stood fifty feet behind them when he opened the door. They were black motorcyclists. Their leader said they'd come to admire his Ducati and cabin. Like the Wise Men for the Saviour. But in leather and the minute he stepped out on the ground he knew he was in trouble. The leader said they would cut him bad with the knife in his hand and wanted everything he owned.

"Whether you dead or alive don't matter to us but it's up to you."

The other three were opening the door to his hut when he told them, Stop. He had the pistol out of his back pocket. He felt the world and nature were begging him to kill them and, despite himself, he began to cry great tears of sorrow. All of his long grief broke out in his eyes. He could barely see the men under the station halo when they obeyed and spread out in a straight packed rank as if to die as one or rush him. He was cool when the tears stopped, very close to murder. He knew he would be exonerated if the law ever found him. All his service and medals backed him. They knew he would shoot and stayed as quiet as altar boys except for agreeing with him when he robbed them, Yes sir, Yes sir. In four bags was $104 thousand in baled hundreds. They put it all and also their crack cocaine and methedrine in his hut, the latter in big plastic freezer bags. They knew he was the law but could not imagine how he'd imagined this bust.

They handed every bike key over to him and then stripped naked. He broke every spark plug he could see with his hammer, had a second thought and told them each to open the lid of their gas tanks and drop a lighted match into it. They were slow about this until he shot a round through the nearest gas tank.

When he'd got to Jackson, Tennessee, making only fifty miles per hour max, he had long since ceased being wily. He kept south into Mississippi, the very place he'd vowed never to go.

It was only when he rested in a motel in Holly Springs that he became aware of how lucky he was the black men were so befogged on their own product and he began weeping again, this time loudly, moans and rending sobs. Except for the Pakistani couple who lived in the office, no other people were in these rooms. This was a shame. He wanted others to hear him, hug him, and stay as company to his grief until it subsided.

The license tags on the motorcycles of the black motorcyclists read *Mississippi*. Once his weeping spell was over he was pleased by the idea they might find him again. He knew methedrine and carefully measured some grains into his morning coffee for the next several days. He kept a modest high putting eastward to Tishomingo and Iuka, where he bought two boxes of .38 hollow points simply because he was high. At the same Wal-Mart he bought new propane tanks. He felt free and less threatening than in ages, happy that somebody might kill him. He was not goofy, perhaps had never been, not once. James could not reckon what he was now but his dead father rose and stood inside him. He walked the earth of Tishomingo, but that chief's magic was just a part of the spirit in his arms, legs, eyes, and preternatural ears so that he walked and glided on a narrow river impervious to harm and quite happy to be a burner and a killer when he met those who begged for him to guide their fates. He'd come near this feeling in the war but it had not filled him as in this time and place.

Immediately he went to work, which came easily. A tall lank man with acne scars, native of Oxford, swore to others in a café how his motherfucking yacht was tiresome to him now and he stood to gain more from the insurance on it. Another swore he'd had to drive up from Meridian in his wife's Cadillac Esplanade, *a nigger car*, but his was in the shop. Still another with even more vodka in him was a wealthy minister built like a football linebacker. He had a televised Sunday morning sermon in his huge protestant cathedral surrounded by his wealthy congregation in Germantown, the affluent suburb of Memphis dense with white flight. This man too had a yacht on the Tennessee River. However, what called to Franklin James was this man's erotic success with a divorcée who lived just off Highway 30 between New Albany and Oxford. Her real name was Teresa but she was called Goodie. He asked the men at the table to guess why. Grins went around. The minister had a wife and several other women, whom he described in detail for the delectation of the others. The church, he declared, was actually a castle and city unto itself as in feudal times. Here was much money to be made, many wives and single women in graduate school, medicine, the arts. These were often confused and lonely souls, you could not imagine the loneliness and compliance of these lovely, soft, and wet creatures, demanding he take them in all ways granted the healthy, wild prophet of God that he was. They may laugh, but he *did* believe and was beloved like King David of the Psalms, and what memory did we have of Solomon except for his wisdom and love songs? Men of many wives, concubines, the wives of other men. The other men grew quiet beneath this sincerity, a sermon itself, unexpected among drunks in a rib house built on stilts in a womb of granite hill near Pickwick Dam.

James harked to this minister four booths away. It seemed these men formed a club that met four times a year with the seasons. Each was a singular financial wizard, were men of the lusty world, and here was their chaplain, second-team All American out of Tulane in the late eighties. He could turn pro or turn demigod, so he went to seminary at Sewanee.

James was newly bathed, soap in a cold creek, but no longer had his thick bush of a beard, so his face was both sunburned and white. He might be a bargeman or professor. He wore round tortoise prescription spectacles that changed with light. He was happy, again mildly high from methedrine granules in his iced tea. Beside his plate of rib bones lay a Gideon Bible open to his pen, the matchless Pilot Precise rolling ball. Between the lines of Acts of the Apostles he wrote down much of what this minister said.

He was not unusual here. Most likely, since it was Saturday night, a deacon on vacation preparing his lesson for Sunday school, that was all. The minister who talked and bragged could drink an entire bottle of Stolichnaya vodka with no ill effects the next day. In fact he would preach on television tomorrow, a suntanned and berobed hunk of love with just a few white strands in his black hair. James was already in church with this man at the podium on the dais before him. He was a seeker of heat and light, attentive in the pews. The good pastor was not even drunk, just savvy and loquacious, as he described the geography, portfolio, and erotics of his circuit. He did not neglect his visits to the hospitals and to the shut-ins, the ancient lunatics of the rest homes so happy to will wild portions of their nest eggs to him. He told how his congregation loved him as a sportsman casting wide for bass and sauger, loved his prosperity, his fine auto.

But you might hurt and burn, thought James happily. This bliss I ride. On the edge of things there and then reduced to ash. He had just painted his cabin slate gray. After the fires he headed to Oxford. He threw away all the powder and crack in hides and kudzu all the way from Corinth to New Albany.

The minister had called his church the Neo-Fortress Village, out of California theosophy. The others were not too drunk to take him seriously. Franklin James also took him seriously. He watched him that Sunday on his motel TV.

The die was cast. He cared nothing for his body even though it was trim and well muscled from sprints through the meadows of everywhere.

After his heated affair with Goodie, after his marriage to her, once the preacher's but available no more, he took trips to Jackson where he could stand the history of his father's killing. There was the building with the newspaper whose clarion was well nigh the voice of Goebbels in the early sixties. Obfuscators of the weak search for the assassin. Then he was at the door of the First Baptist Church, a very big one on North State where the pastor remained a silent, good German with big hair, chicken guts, who never made a stand, never a whisper, about the Klan, the killer, their Old Customs, as racists would have it. These of the Southern Baptist Church bore the most sins as good Germans in apartheid sweetly. This is where the redundant sheep of fundamentalism took a stand on nothing, except for wanting the Jews to hurry up Armageddon in the Holy Lands.

Now he had burned a small church in the wildwood and despised the fact his guilt made him kinder toward small houses of worship.

He walked the grounds of the state capitol but did not go inside. He had no doubt that half its body were grandchildren of the blood that brought down his father. James knew that the advent of television and blacks owning their own guns had done as much for defeating the Klan and status quo as all the sermons and marches of Dr. King, because I told him so. He spat on the capitol grounds as much as salivation allowed him to. His hatred grew back to its perfect fury when he thought of his mother, a priest-bound sick woman who never achieved fury, only the flattened presenility of mourning, this vivacious French lady of culture, quickest to laugh a laugh in any room, the laugh that brought tears of thanks from James, then and now in his memory. She became a dead woman he could not bear to visit. All natural love was cut and down. He was too weary of his fury now, like bricks on his head until he ran down his man, who was very much alive and, a loud churchman, a tattooed deacon of the boondocks.

Why had he begun his mission so late then? Why had he circled it so long? Why the petty necessity of marriage to Goodie and in the near future the sophisticated immolation of the great cathedral in Memphis, venue of Goodie's former lover, that pastor he had overheard in the Pickwick rib house? In which the organist died of molten pipes in avalanche.

He only half knew himself. And he could not have known the organist slept with the pastor and was thinking of suicide already.

I am still unclear whether after the first fires he appeared reincarnated as Captain Max Petraeus who began his long campaign of church arsons up and down the Mississippi Valley. He seemed too chastened for this after the woman died. He sent anonymous money to help the concert career of Jimmy Canarsis. But James's vendetta against the old tattooed man was settled also, and you'd imagine also his love of flames, for a good long while.

*   *   *

The riot and anarchy on the Ole Miss campus in 1962 has often been called the last civil war, and I was square in the thick of it as a captain of the state National Guard. All that fire and shooting, three dead by gunshot and the shooter never found, against the entrance of James Meredith, a black man. What you had was both students and the Klan, with their fellow travelers. I had boys in my own command who wanted to join the rioters. It was rot, the last of an old cancer on us.

The Nobel laureate William Faulkner died in the hot July preceding the September riots. It was good he didn't have to watch. He was a racial moderate, read *nigger lover* in these parts then, and left much of his estate to the United Negro College Fund. I mention him only to place this story on the map and call to memory, now I'm an old man, that not all of us were rot. I did understand much of Faulkner's greatest books. Personally I disliked him as a snob who with no effort at all could have been kinder to the neighbors in the village we were then. He was passing strange and spiteful to many. You had to reckon with some conceit as birthright, which made him contemptuous of the very humble folk he was celebrated for taking to his heart on the written page. You will often see pure words in a great wash of self-atonement, no people necessary to them. Like your pastors of the pulpit James despised. If masturbation had an echo, he said.

Well James found me and made me honest, without threat. It was way high time I unburdened. I sit in front of a glass of peach schnapps on my lake south of town. Prime woodlands, thick elder pines, spruces. I was privy too long to the grievous matter. Now my hands are red, not a prayer of a peaceful death, but some wonderful living behind me with the wife and daughters so fine. I served in Korea, came home almost cursed with life after being with many gut-shot fellows with snow falling on ice, temp minus 30. It was nighttime, but I knew James's man and had never divulged the true rot of him, although I brought him up on charges of cowardice. I believe I witnessed the event itself, him in a tree and raising the M1 Garand.

But there were all kinds of gasses in the air, all kinds of flares, gunshots, overturned cars burning. This done by handsome young frat boys. The man was dishonorably discharged from the army, but that was a slap on the wrist.

The town of Water Valley in Yalobusha County sixteen miles below us hired him, nevertheless, on its patrol force. One soggy night, say 1977, me and the old gang were coming back from an Ole Miss/State game that we'd won when a gust of wind like out of the Bible blew the state kicker's try for an extra point backward from the goalposts. I mean dead missed a sitter. I was both drunk and speeding and this patrolman in Water Valley put his face in the window, sniffing around six old boys all soused and hollering. Guess who he was. He had his ticket book open and his gun hand on the butt. Oh he had some live ones. But he took a long look, went white in the face. Walked quick back to his black-and-white chariot all whipped around and ass-important with way high antennas, and just eased off ahead of us, like now, Captain, go ahead and arrest me please. All our gang, me and two of them who'd serve in the spoils of the Republican administration in three years, got soberer but I was white in the face, too, until I told them who that cop was, and they almost broke the car laughing, hooting. A charmed day all around.

But that's when I learned the fellow had gone off into lay preaching and multiple deaconage around small county churches. I got white in the face as he was, all those pictures racing back from fifteen years ago, and *the* picture, the sickest. He did lay preaching along the white supremacy line, they said, not unusual for the race killers getting dug up nowadays by a reporter from the Jackson paper, the *Clarion Ledger,* and a special prosecutor out of the state attorney general's office after forty-five years and more. I don't believe I joined in the howling with the others in my van.

Somebody said something like all that is required for evil to prosper is the silence of good men. I count myself one of those. Too many of us stayed *good Germans,* a term I first heard in Eighth Army, Chosin Reservoir, 1950, staying quiet when a heinous thing is about like Hitler. The rest only knew him for a coward in the Guard, just now in the worst face-to-face you could pull on him. On race matters I remained quiet. You can't overestimate the difficulty of my Guard command, largely filled by boys sympathetic to the rioters but serving John Kennedy much against their instincts. We heard this was a police action at Ole Miss, but there were eventually thirty thousand troops in town, tents everywhere, a way station for the movement of troops to south Florida during the Cuban missile crisis. Wild boys or insurgents from the Klan of neighboring states were dropping railroad cross ties into the windshield of Army Reserve troop carriers from the overpass on Jackson Avenue. Still, I sent the order down that if any live ammo was discovered off their belt clips there'd be hell to pay. We were pure bayonets regardless of provocation, just like the federal marshalls who were trapped inside the Lyceum with Meredith courtesy of a bulldozer driven against its door by the apostles of the lunatic General Edwin Walker, who led the assault himself with a goddamned cavalry sword. It was a miracle no more than three were killed, among them James's father, a man I never put eyes on.

Our governor was Ross Barnett, a purebred mule-faced jackass rabble-rouser, about states' rights and sovereignty, but when I was a young captain I did not think he was such a bad sort. He was *our* jackass, was the issue. Nevertheless I dressed my command and told them their asses belonged to the federal government and me, rough as it was. You had to keep an eye on them. You never knew what mean little bastard would break ranks and try to make a name for himself.

I told this to James at Smitty's café just south of the courthouse and looked into his kind Canadian face, a face that had mesmerized me into this revelation over a good breakfast, eggs, country ham, redeye gravy, grits, the best big light biscuits. He ate the same as me, listened courteously without interruption. Then I saw the new look to him and knew that if the point of this story was that I killed his father, he would kill me on the spot with still the courteous look. It had been a long time since I had killed a gook or two. Not very long for him. Iraqis, the church organist.

The man was courtly. He out-captained me. We were just talking acquaintances, then, I don't know how he did it. Suddenly when I got to his man in the tree that night nearly half a century ago, of all things I thought of the Lord. I mean Our Heavenly Father. I leave the Lord alone since Korea and hope He'll do the same for me. You have to hand it to Him, He's done a damned pro job of evaporating these last centuries. I can't tell you the bodies, the pain. What was that about? Well, we turned South Korea Christian, and now our labor gets shipped off to them, Zenith TV and all. But it's not worth one gut-shot private, one lance corporal from Wyoming with a sucking chest wound. What Lord? What wondrous ways His works to perform?

The secret spoke itself like a tired bad ghost walking out of my throat.

Then for a while I didn't see him, only heard about the acts. I had peace for half an afternoon. But then my hands were bloody. My calm had a frown on it. Yes I'm going funny. This peach schnapps ain't doing it for me.

He made love with Goodie with a writhing ardor she'd not experienced, perhaps, ever.

"For the love of God, thank you," she whispered. She put on her kimono and white slip-on keds. Her body was remarkable. Without exercise except for five minutes of work and standing an hour around machines that would have perfected her in a Baptist hospital gym. Or remarkable because he stared at her as through a magnified pipe, and straight past her to their familiar replicants in a museum of devolution until the final sullen corpus, his man, stood at age twenty with the Ml Garand in his hand, a clip of live ammo snuck into its chamber, all the auto fires and tear gas and flares in the air, students shouting curses from as deep in them as the very heart of rot in Old Dixie. Punk Guardsman, punk city cop, his conversion to the Lord Jesus Christ and bolting out hymns, earning thereby the right to walk among free men, even preach to them, the low son of a bitch. But he must have felt a bona fide hell at his shoulders these years, or something right around the next door he opened, especially after the firebombing of the little church where he had stood recently. Was the man his man, or was the man himself? What a stupid meditation.

He left two days later for the archives in the attorney general's office in Jackson, three hours southward. The sunroof of the Mazda Miata was open. On the CD box was Led Zeppelin, *Houses of the Holy*. This sound like the reunion of a battalion in steel walls. Intense moments in Iraq, his sick mother. He needed more hate. Soon he was not rightly human. He could imagine himself howling on the street corner of a burning city. His eyes were wide. Purpose, what purpose did he serve against the lassitude of grief that filled his mother and himself all those years? Their avoidance of the topic and word *Mississippi*.

He found himself speaking aloud in French to his dead mother Celestine. In your hands how does the finish of this vendetta feel? He asked her. He recognized that all the earthly goods he's heaped on Goodie, *Teresa* more now, woman of tears, were meant for his mother. He'd just bought her a new car, Saab SUV sculpted like a space shuttle. These days, like millions of the talentless, she'd developed pretentions to art photography. This black wagon would hold her leather and canvas cases. You were nearly a saint, Mother, and I deserted you, he spoke. Now "Hey Joe" by that Mozart of the electric guitar, Jimi Hendrix, grabbed and dragged him to Iraq, lolling beside the 105 as he watched men burn in their T-34s on the red horizon. *Allons enfants to this good hell.*

Unsolved, said the state. Unsolved means all senses hover, loom, linger, harken. Nobody, however, knows a thing for sure. But I do.

So his Teresa sleeps as his nightmare it moves across the meadow, hooves in wet clover, toward the charred ruins of the little church. Canarsis's piano still stands, only half consumed, only half dead. The man, a sixty-four-year-old tattooed deacon and lay preacher. Destiny run toward him. James had the .38 and the wheeled propane and napalm flamethrower in the car.

Now in the cold January twilight he looked the man full in the face and told him to walk. The man had a round white ordinary face, more youthful than James expected. He held a pistol but James told him to throw it away and the man complied.

"Let's walk to the pier where they found Jimmy Canarsis and saved him. You may have heard about his success on the concert circuit. He began at the Castellow Ford Center. Then Memphis, Philadelphia, New York."

"Yeh. Why are you speaking these words?" asked the man, whose name was Dee Gale.

"Because Canarsis is so beautifully different from such sorry jackasses as us. Wouldn't you like to have lived in complete innocence and made as much of your gift as he has, nearly burned to death?"

"You the man who burned the church?"

"Well, I did not finish. You seem to want something remaining in it, too. You came back to the charcoal. What would that be? Your pilgrimage?"

"It had a good true spirit to it, that giant boy on a piano that seemed like a kid's toy measured to him. He brought God down from heaven with his music."

"You killed my father, holy man. What was your favorite hymn? A man like you."

They walked around the dam in silence. No creature stirred, all cabins were empty, the house ranger dulled like a sloth as he watched the evening news, settling in to his Pepsi and Orville Redenbacher's sublime pour-over cheddar popcorn. The perfection of winter muteness, happily dead in the mind, his contented good woman close to hand. James imagined them in an alternate universe. The gun was in his right hip pocket, forgotten, the flamethrower easy on its wheels. They walked to the end of the pier in dogged duty. A beaver fell from a dead cypress with a loud percussive entrance to the water.

"'Just as I Am' would be the one. We all are worms with guilty secrets. He forgives all even though we are *without one plea*."

"You don't have one plea right now?"

"You notice I'm not screaming for help, like I could. I stand absolved."

"I stand as your delayed executioner."

"But I've got a feeling you've killed before. You stand guilty and unforgiven."

"Can you do something for me then? Can you make up a hymn about why it was necessary to kill my father?"

"He was one those outside agitators helping bring on niggers adulterating our way of life. I only say this about the shooting. If the state thought I was guilty of anything but delaying these niggers I'd of been brought up on charges a long time ago. After what happened you didn't find no French meddlers and liars in these parts."

The flames were already reaching him then, and they kept reaching him as the napalm stuck. James was amazed the man could stand so long without taking to the water. He used a boat paddle to push the surviving stump of Gale into the lake. But the end of the pier was still on fire and he left in moderate haste to his car.

I watched him afterward. He was a kind of friend, always at Smitty's talking over the good country vegetables, fried okra, collards, world-class cornbread. He had fantastic eyes, jarred awake like a man whose head had just been severed. He was the saddest man I've ever known.

I can't know what you've heard of these parts, but there is law. More of the sheriffs voted, not appointed, into office, are college educated in criminology. Whatever that vague science is worth.

But no man showed at his door, no man raised a hand against him. Three men he knew, I was one of them, voiced the wish very sincerely that he would vanish from these parts, as he had from Montana. But no sheriff told him this. When James had swallowed it all he was dead for a while. He was in the tomb although the stone had been rolled aside for his free walk around the water or to the Arctic. This state with only a million whites is one backyard, and it is solid mouth to ear. Faster than you could trace it on the Internet, certainly faster than the sheriff's office women could find it on those grandmother computers, the worst is known, the gossip is dead-on to the comma. The lynching of blacks by vigilantes is gone forever, hope to God. We have a new aristocracy and they are black men. Morgan Freeman, B. B. King, Muddy Waters, the ghost of Robert Johnson making his deal with the Devil at a crossroads on Highway 61. But we are a state that still loves the vigilante. The climate is ripe for vengeance.

Franklin James became friends with a black emeritus professor out of Rust College in Holly Springs. Amos Pettigrew. They shared some subject, it was unclear what it was for a while. Pettigrew seemed to hold sway over whether James stayed, fled with or without Goodie, destroyed himself, or lived abundantly, propelled like a bird from the opened tomb into wild freedom. Pettigrew was a calm force for both James and Goodie. She did not know she might be deserted for a while or for good. I saw Pettigrew's old Buick in their drive many times. James told the man his whole story. Goodie was much afraid. The terror was all over her. She began a series of very expensive shopping trips. James, the killer, said nothing about this mania. He just stared at the bags. She acted as if the purchase of some choice item might be her soul and she could catch it and hold it in a shopping bag. Some of the bags she never touched, although they were full of goods, jewelry, God's own amount of purses.

Dr. Pettigrew had degrees from Dartmouth and Yale. He had worn himself thin striving against the darkness in young blacks. He had left his heart in the college. Now he was a hoarse and skinny man, going to frail. He knew every living fact about the struggle for civil rights in this area, every night attack, bombing, miscarriage of justice, even every fistfight. I don't know what afternoon exactly he told James he had burned up the wrong man. The right man was dead of natural causes. He had killed a man who emulated the dead one, dressed like him, had the same tattoos, the same voice, and was even fiercer and louder about his lay preaching and deaconry church to church with the biblical evidence for white supremacy. Two churches had obtained restraining orders against him, a first within anybody's memory.

When I noticed the yellow motorcycle was gone for several days, I crept up to their bedroom window, yes, like a common Peeping Tom and at my sadder age. I *had* to peep and eavesdrop. What I saw I call pornography, or some order of necrophilia. She was lying on the bed in a black nightgown revealing an amazingly fit nudity beneath. She did not move for an hour, as if commanded to lie still by a man out of sight. But James was long gone. I could not believe that frozen specter was all about grief. That's why I said pornography, some militant sexual exercise. I was guilty I saw her. My hands felt heavy when I crept back to the highway. They were bloodier and bloodier.

Rangoon Green

Rangoon Green
Trophy Holder, Third Place in the National Storytellers Tell-Off
Murfreesboro, Tennessee, 2011

YOU MAY HAVE HEARD OF MY BEHAVIOR AT MURFREESBORO LAST YEAR when they announced the winner, runner-up, and next, third, that would be me. Of course I made a noise. The winner, a long-haired creature with a lute who read barefoot, slept with one of the judges, and I know it truly because I saw her disappear into his trailer at ten thirty the previous night. Second was the old bushy man who *lived* in Murfreesboro. He circulated a fancy brochure about his wins not only here but out west and up north. His wife made cheese sticks, the pepperish kind, and got a tin of them to each judge. If that ain't cheating take me out to the pasture and shoot me. I'm still not over it. I don't get over robbery quick. If ever.

After the second propane fire here in Oxford the marshalls came to my door at the liquor store near the airport, right next to Supreme Used Auto, which I also own as well as the bail bondsman office straight across the street. Yes, women do sleep in the cars of Used Auto, but that doesn't make it an operation, a brothel. Men do come to them in the cars, but that is trespassing. If they have the keys to the autos, my right knows not what my left is doing. I cannot control sleepy women, poor gals down on their luck without the price of a motel, you can't say a thing. How could I organize sleepy women off the highway, as a lawyer said for me once?

On the mean-o-meter, if there was such a contraption, all right, I might score high. But much of that is rooted in the acne on my face and shoulders. When I finally got to a skin doctor, he told me about recent discoveries about vitamin A that would have cleared me up, but it was far too late. I don't look that bad except for the big pit on the left cheek, and there we have some serious ugliness. As a boy I hid my face behind the barn while others pissed and jacked off on each other. I have been called Frankenstein, Wolfman, the Flying Pitface. But what brought the marshall was the history of serious fireworks I had in the army, stations and bases in Texas, California, Michigan, and Georgia. Yes, true facts reveal I barely missed a court martial and did receive a dishonorable discharge from the bastards but that was twenty-five years ago, for making two oil drums rise a hundred feet with a propellant in my keeping. Just old boy fun but not to the sullen-ass army.

This smug Marshall Root, whose Montana ass shall be lined up for gutting after I have a word with my sidekicks Tico and Rez. The one Latino as it sounds, and the other named for his hesitancy to ever leave his bass boat and trotlines on Sardis Reservoir boat launches ten miles north at Coontown and sixteen miles west on Clear Creek, passing over the famous glory hole for bass, Tobby Tubby Creek. English for a long unsayable Chickasaw name centuries old. You can take centuries old and cram it. I don't care a thing about naught but today. You get into your golden history and you just walk around with this paralysis of mud on your boots, ask me. Another marshall, Bitters, lording it over me, put a word on me such as I made him write down. Smell this diction: hypermnesia. I got red knowing he reviled me and my unswept liquor parlor. My woman in the back where we live ever lazy except in the science of nooky.

It's plenty of room amounting to a five-bedroom home, two full baths, halls, kitchen, oversize pantry, wide screen porch where no mosquito or gnat penetrates. You ask about my woman, Louise. Well there she sits. Good figure, foxy in the face, some kind of coiled searching curls in her hair, shiftless as a hound dog in the song that eternal shaker from Tupelo, Elvis Presley, sang. She says she's even kin to the man, and there is one rule when you hear this claim. The claimer is not worth a shit, but they want the throne. I do not beat women. My father's violence toward my mother cured me forever of that notion. But Louise is hesitant to move even while looking cross-eyed at a fly that got in the front screen door after some long-jawed whiskey customer has let it in. I say the fly on the end of her nose can be setting up his fly stand and tuning his fiddle and she'll stay trans-fixed before she moves to another cube of air that might be flyless. After all my pains making the place ladylike for her, making it double the catalog lacey look so it would not be viewed as just a hell of a butt to a liquor store. Two HD televisions, purple drapes with cord pulls, satin sheets. And an even better set up on Lake Pickwick on the Ten-nessee River, which is flat-out a condo. We sit with the mighty there. Judges, expensive Memphis lawyers, a whiskey preacher out of a crystal cathedral, televised on Sunday. Well, I mean one, Dr. Quarles the Fourth, who could put away a bottle of Stolichnaya Saturday night and you'd watch that cathedral service Sunday morning, he'd be coming on strong fresh as a rose. Louise will loiter, but that figure of hers gets into action and you forgive and forget a host of sins. She can't warm a pot of peas and who cares.

Did I tell the truth to Marshall Root, was I afraid, so fraidy that I caved into Marshall Bitters? About the propane missile that wound up in the city hall bathroom? Oh no, not on your ass. Fear don't hunt here especially when it's anybody at the counter in tie and coat. I wonder if the man knew I was marking him for death or at least serious maiming when he held me there with his badge out, *blah blah blah*. Of course I was guilty, but guilty only of a little fun. We don't have a lot of raw fun hereabouts. And it was copycat, as far as that goes, except I started with fire in the army a good long time before these church fires began a dozen years ago. Let me put it this way. The army wanted me to work with fire and demolitions, then they did not, snuck to my back and called me down as some lame kind of example, an attack of conscience suddenly, oh no, what have we created in this master sergeant?!

And named Goon Green, formally Rangoon, because my mother liked rain and thought monsoons were a romantic weather period in the far-off gaudy East. Ignorant sow. Never said she wasn't a good woman. Just that she was an ignorant sow and I cannot imagine another kind of mother. A smart, kind mother I don't know what you're talking about. But I did at last come close to killing my father when he was beating on her. That earned me the road and a duffel sack. The old man thought it would make me all sad but it was the happiest day of my life. That night I blew up his pickup outside the eatery where he flirted with a woman with big titties.

One side of my face is good looking and I was holding that half toward the marshall, saying, "I'm not only innocent, you will see a lawyer if you come back. The damage to my reputation as a businessman will come to many, many thousands, I mean you even being around."

Not only the bondsman office, out of which I run bounties, too, sits across the street, but the big pawnshop is mine. Louise helps a little, shuffle, shuffle, moan, moan. I never heard anybody moan serving a customer like this woman. Goes against her looks, you understand. I free her to be a laboring feminist but her spirit is all fettered, an old-fashioned gal. Oh but liberated to hell when you show her a vacuum cleaner. "It ain't elegant," she says.

I can look a man in the eye and make him squeal. I can look a man fleeing from bond collapse and cry with his arms around my ankles. I began the pawnshop several years ago when I noticed the crack riffraff hanging around the corners of our fair little city. The Tunica casinos, where fat Wisconsin women play like they're in Las Vegas, are an hour and a half away, but broke riffraff spreads out in a great radius topped by Memphis and bottomed by us. Let me say others saw them as riffraff, and these suspicious persons were picked up and prosecuted on the old vagrant charge when they couldn't show fourteen cents in their pockets. But they also came with ridiculous merchandise on them if they could get to me before the cops got to them. I saw money in the trees while others saw just a nasty forest. This money tree might also include two gambling lawyers from the army in town. Well, they've got mini tape recorders, police scanners, fancy or antique pistols I need not know the getting of, as well as supreme boats with large engines. At least six in this town have lost everything to the casinos. They come to me for money. I can look their wife square in the face while I cut their husband's throat, as a figure of speech, of course.

Before that Marshall Bitters got off the bastard went so far as to use the word *maffick* on me, and I asked him what? three times, the last with the curse he deserved. It means *to celebrate*. The marshall knew enough of my history to step off. Come around speaking *maffick* at me. He left confused. I was not confused at all.

I had my fingers in at least four pies, and here I'm not counting the boyhood fun Tico, Rez, and I had constructing that V-1 missile from the propane tank. The shell on these mothers is not strong enough to penetrate the ceiling and roof of even a flimsy church like the Free Will at the end of Van Buren East. You have to know liftoff angle and be certain your power is large enough to begin right off. This you do not obtain with merely a propane tank just lying there. Well, I did even better and got a SCUD that penetrated two roofs. City hall was an accident, but I will accept the admiration for it. I wish two lawyers had been working late and found this flaming tube in their lap. You ask why. Because it could be done. I did not think the marshalls would be at my door so fast, but I knew they didn't have anything definite. Just tidying up a few loose ends. This loose end I told I would fold him five ways and stick him where the sun don't shine. I look at people and they *stay* looked at. I've never laid hand on a bond jumper. They jump right back in the car with me, shivering. See, the bad side of my face, pitted cheeks and nose, does work for me. I've taken such as I was given, no whining, and manufactured a man nobody messes with, no brag. That side of my face also worked for me when I got the fingers in the pies.

Wilkes Bell is a common drunkard except he wears Armani and other Italian suits, aristocratic shoes of a deep grained shine so you know it. And subtle thick-weave ties. Has thick light hair, you know, tossed this way and that and curled back from his forehead. Rich delta daddy in chemical fertilizers and rice. And while he was at the university thirteen or so years ago he was an art student and even now had paint on his skin when he was in the store sweating through his suit. You could smell the liquor coming out of those pores. My nose is trained for your lush. Half of those sleepy women who bed down in the cars of Used Auto are lushes, of course, and some of their boyfriends. One day Wilkes Bell staggers into the liquor store and whispers, that is mildly screams, a secret he had about his person in a big Ziploc bag. Lord help me if it wasn't forty or fifty thousand dollars of his uncle Anse Burden's money. He wasn't certain himself, since he'd scrambled around in it for a few night's drunks. His uncle had left it with him for safekeeping, what a made fool this uncle was, and he was thinking to catch up on his tab here, $6500 with interest, and let the money hide with me in my freezer. When he described his uncle as a down-at-the-heels lay minister I feared nothing. So the damned fool leaves it with me and starts staggering around replenishing his thirsty liquor cabinet with the blurred math he always had, meaning a 20 percent markup on every bottle for me, and I do this stupid playacting as I delicately lift the money bag and take it to the kitchen. Funny part is, the boy had such an attitude about himself he thought I was being used by him, I mean this unbreakable attitude. Hair tossed back and forth like some genius conductor and sweat popping out on his forehead like fury. Well, when they walk right into the vault with money for you, you take it. He asked this sum minus his tab be refrigerated against the IRS or other long noses and I said you have it, I'm like an eagle on it.

He said it was the last of his uncle's preacher money. Maybe he didn't hear me say, "Indeed it is." He couldn't understand anything anyhow, you know that stretched careful way the very drunk have when they think nobody suspects but they are sober. My god, this boy lived in that outfit, always in a play doing sobriety over and over, the fool. So you know what a colossal gift he was to anybody needing an edge. You didn't need much but to fake complete assurance it was business us usual.

Soon enough he flat out told me he was burning things. The church fires up and down the river were all over the papers and television. I doubted he was fit to take off from his labors at the bottle, this kid could do two a day, but he kept talking, in that god-awful shrieking whisper he thought was most confidential. Sure it was, all the way to Louise's ears and the ears of Tico and Rez on the back loading dock in this large whiskey palace, working the airport and the filthy alumni who can't get rid of their lucre fast enough when they're here buying memories, all of them in some form of Colonel

Rebel, the mascot, who looks like he could put away more than his rightful serving. If you want to know, I might not look it, but I could be half these sporting fools in button-downs and penny loafers and executive jets.

Not to get off my story, I listened to him about burning and it began to ring true. Because when he isn't lying he takes a long time combing a part in his sweated-up hair, like he wants nothing to impede his veracity.

Still, how could he manage to do all that climbing and heaving of his demolitions and accelerants and stay out of suspicion all by his drunk self? Then it snuck out that he didn't. I spotted somebody in the parking lot preparing to enter the shop and quieted him. The man wanted a golf cart to buy or rent and I kept a fleet of Harley-Davidson carts just next to the entrance to College Hill Road where lies the golf course. I don't have a trade that doesn't prosper.

But all through his histrionics I was in a state of delight because I do hate a church. I've been cast into darkness by many a preacher for the booze and the Used Auto. Isn't it funny I get along fine with Dr. Quarles the Fourth at Pickwick in the condos and chicken-wing joint, although his massive church was also exploded. No dead, as with the big Roman Catholic cathedral. I say I was delighted, I was in fine fettle, anxious to get back to hear Bell's whispery screaming and believing it.

Our good buddies the firebugs had a wonderful supply of napalm from some loosely guarded armory, I'd say the National Guard at any of a dozen bases. They're even more prone to accidental leakage than our fine army, which is a laugh when you say *security*. You can't imagine the waste in our services. There's not a lost and found office big enough. I should know it, I worked this lostness personally for five years. Before they caught on to me. A small nation could whip California with just the crap that rolls off a convoy or an army railroad caravan. I know an old boy took home a fully operating .50 cal and ammo for a souvenir when his time was up. Now that is class.

But back to ready delight. I gave the man after the golf cart a good buy. If you keep a part of your trade fair then they'll stand in line to be cheated next time. Et cetera with the drunk Bell boy.

He had got all mysterious but had two half gallons in front of him on the counter. He was hinting at something but was too drunk to get the right hint in, so I got immoderate. What in hell are you trying to say, just say it, you overdressed sputtering fool! So thick drunk he didn't even take this insult in, although he knew I wanted the secret from him. Thing is, he didn't give it to me promptly, and swore this business was very tight and dangerous. So next day I had my car curbside across the street just to watch what unfolded out of his grand apartment on the square. Soon enough, Wilkes Bell came down the stairs followed by a gent of middle age but holding it well and with that unmistakable rigor in the back you get from serious military time. They can't help it. They don't even know how to slouch anymore. A suit on them looks like a costume from a foreign nation. I guess it's us lowly sergeants that get familiar with our slouches. Yes he stepped along in something rich, Brit, *bespoke*. I learned that term from Mrs. Ferguson in Cape Girardeau, Missouri. You could hear his heels click across the street, a man in a clicking contest when all they were up to was eating at the Bottle Tree Bakery on West Van Buren, bagel, lox, cream cheese. Big deal. Or you would've supposed it was because heel-clicker was deeply studious, and drunk (yes, eight in the morning) Bell was trying to ape his manner like an earnest monk. I knew our older fellow was the other fireman. He had hard eyes and that sort of dismissal of everybody in front of him so as soon as they quit helping him they ceased to exist. A major hate engine in him set on fast idle when it wasn't wholly engaged.

Well I eased off to my much lesser acres without being seen, of course. If I play the better-looking half of my face right folks simply forget me, and I don't mind, I work in the murk just fine. The other side makes people drop their dinner fork. I don't mind, I just hate my parents for not having the drive to get me better treatment. They didn't have the drive to learn their own language. I got my decent English from a middle-aged blonde woman with good legs who took pity on me and my temporary passion for books. I was so depressed I had no passion that lasted long. But she lasted long, Mrs. Ferguson. I wanted a style and she came near giving it to me. Another life. I'd been a harmless drudge at everything. Just lucky, I guess, best of both worlds even though my freedoms came late. I have finer points due to Mrs. Ferguson. You will see them, along with brotherhood, compassion, mercy. But I do hate church and loved the broken hearts all warming themselves by blackened rafters, warm stone, and melted glass.

But know we are speaking of two years while I remained innocent as a lamb, as to fireworks at least. Yes, I lay in wait like your alligator or your mule, who had a long mean memory that'll all of a sudden flash out and catch you guessing with your underwear down and a hoof print dead center of your forehead. A gator twenty years until the time is perfect to eat a flamingo. This creature, tell me not, knows it has longevity. Even if what you have is a slug with little arms and one long slosh of a tail with vise-grip jaws. I lie in turds to accomplish the right moment. Even the promise of what I'd do to these specific turds, the bond jumpers, is enough, if I have that side of my face to them. Oh I'm licensed to carry a .357 Magnum revolver, but it's never used. I believe the jumper knows I've yet to use it and hastens to the backseat of the car not wanting to be first under the gun. The only fights I've ever had were with two women. I guess they thought I'd be a gentleman. Some shocked fool standing on tradition. They slugged me. But hit bad once, almost everbody sits down and asks the quickest route to jail. And I did swat them good.

I'm working on a children's story as well as my entry to that corrupt gallery in Murfreesboro, Tennessee. If I detect certain biases I plan to be not only assertive but persuasive. I don't care if third's the highest I ever placed. Many a listener told me I was the clear winner. Explosion bears repeating. I love being a bad loser. I got a hard-on for unsportsmanlike. I get to mock both fire-setting Bell and partner and the angry, miserable sheep inside what used to be the doors of their houses of worship. But why, why, why? you ask. A grown man with my skills, how can I stoop to this like the others wreaking havoc.

Poetry, I think, is the answer. To live that zigzagged deathlessness of the poem, as taught me by Mrs. Ferguson. It's how you know you're young, you're a gamer, and bantam rooster, your face in a curl of loogie-launching at the law. And that is paradise, to confuse the police with half their eyelids down over yellow eyes. Flies on their head, lazy waddlers who'd rather do nothing except compare their

muscles, shoot at the range, and beat the heat with beers and chattering wives in their cheap-ass project houses where they all, except
the chiefs, commiserate about their punk salaries and hard service.
   I had my time in glory with these people, or their military
equivalent in Georgia. The charge: blowing up useless surplus shit
on the firing precincts, harming red dirt. Experimentation. I'm not
kidding. I was too old for a juvenile delinquent and what's more
a master sergeant. The brass knew my projects had been going on
weeks before they decided they needed a whipping boy to take the
higher brass's eyes off another big scandal of their own, and that
would be a wife-swapping club fueled by the liquor of Uncle Sam.
Yellow-gilled loafers. I was at least employing my skills in the future
guerilla actions of Their Man's Army. Blowing up a few gasoline and
ancient artillery barrels, launching a short arc missile, things to save
some of our boys' lives woeful down the line. So a bus ticket to ride
I got at age thirty-two and a reaquaintance with my father in his
putrid lounge chair. A letter arrived and I didn't have to tell him
about the dishonorable proceedings because the old woodpecker got
to the mail and opened the letter addressed to yours truly. I picked
him up by the shoulders and came close to killing him, but it was
the worst day of my life because he never stopped laughing and the
old lady called me a rottener name every time I swatted my honored
patriarch.
   So I was sent into all parts of trade by necessity until I had
constructed my own realm, which I did here in the swanky back end
of my liquor store. Oh, I had fun with the bonds and the jumpers and
the drunks charging way over their head, taking care of the blurred
math for them. It is always a hoot to see a lush get an attitude about
charging booze, as if he's earned a pricey berth and can't be bothered
with small change. Still, he's overcharged and doesn't even scratch
his head, because he's weak and guilty and feels he owes the world.
Or he sees the pitted side of my face and my unnegligible bulk in
arms and legs and understands it is not good to call this man a liar.
   On the other hand I have been bemused by this burning. I
know Bell doesn't have the drive. He's been to the drying-out clinics
about four times, then promptly appeared at my counter like a boomerang that came the world around, stopping in exotic clinics long

enough to make off with their terry-cloth robes, a thick oozy warm for his travails through the shakes. The man has worn these robes with, say, "Palo Alto Chemical Dependency" or "Dr. Fang's Heat Cure" on their front pockets to the store, and shower sandals like such as you and I have never even *seen* to buy. I've given him dribs and drabs of the money, less his tab, which could launch a small satellite into space.

I understand he's now in constant quarrel with this uncle, but I fear little from a lay preacher running from the IRS.

Now comes a hard pass for me to set down but I feel it necessary you even know the, well saltier parts of this man who was robbed down to third place in Murfreesboro and for the last two years failed to place. See here, you now have gay hillbillies and phony hillbillies who've studied in the drama department in Knoxville or Louisville. Yes, Asheville, too. It's not fair that these ringers win. But I was a good loser to these privileged little weasels anyway, and as an artist I withdrew to my studies on my long-awaited children's book. Me and the wife have no children. But I've made a story for the little ones a goal all my life, and I know what moves, what bores them. It's a bookish town and I join right in. I was once with a friend, a writer, and we visited the great historian Shelby Foote in his Memphis mansion. I'd brought a gift crate of good whiskey to him, which he deeply appreciated. He showed us his working study, his foolscap and the nibs on his pens, which he ordered from the only place in the world that carried them anymore, a town in New Jersey. So I obtained for myself the staffs and nibs, ink and mini blow-dryer that completed the kit of the Civil War master and go about my slow but careful work. The antiquarian process slows the head until the absolutely correct word comes to it, so it is slow going and brain beating. I stay in my study and dress in a business suit, with tie, for hours, hours. This child's tale is not all for kids, but one of hurt and early hardship, which the boy works through with wiles and slyness. I can give away that much. My wife is charmed I'm in there looking good and working so hard. If it's good enough I might even publish it myself instead of having some far-off New York printer steal his cut.

But here is the hard pass, much harder to tell than *Who's Laughing Now?*, the child's book. Now five or six years ago we had several odd fogs come over the town. You couldn't find my liquor store, the airport shut down, it was unsafe even to drive until about ten in the morning. I'm writing. If I come out of my "den of the scribe" in my suit and catch a woman customer waiting, I could be irresistible to her. Some of the wimmens, they like rough faces and boldness. Ahead of myself here. These fogs kept up but one morning I heard a plane buzzing out of it with fog thick as soup and wondered how this pilot ever got clearance when the tower itself was shut.

Then who comes in all sprawling and emaciated, whirling his rich thick mane of hair around but Wilkes Bell, drunker than I've ever seen him. Instantly he's asking for the money in the freezer bag in my kitchen where no man goes. It's just a thing with me. I tell him it's out gaining interest in Harley-Davidson stock, which was true about the thirty K he had remaining, and that you just don't move that money around, it's got to stay to grow just like a seed. From the little scripture I know I cited Christ in favor of interest when he said the master had reprimanded the man who hid his money in fear of the master and congratulated the man who put his money out to make money. Some of the money *was* in H.D. stock and climbing. Then he told me the plane that just left was his uncle Ray flying to the bedside of a dying pilot he'd known in that old Iraq war of ninety-one. The man has no money and it's all my fault! he cries out. I'm quiet. Not quite a man of stone. Then quit drinking and I'll see what I can do, I tell him. At which he goes berserk and ends this flailing drama by begging for a bottle of Wild Turkey. His thirst is approaching the danger point, he says. People could get hurt. Sure, by your throwing up on them and/or falling off your balcony, I say, handing over the bottle. He left with two.

Then he spoke with his back to me. "Do you know who blew up the storyteller's stage in Murfreesboro, Tennessee?" he asked. I gave a long pause, I governed it. "No, but I wish I did. That place needed refreshing, a real makeover."

"I went up and saw you tell your tale," says Bell.

"Well, you went but were promptly thrown out for drunk before the competition started."

"It made the Memphis paper, which I'm sure was its aim. This drunk is more aware than you know. It wasn't till after your tale telling that I was fully wise to your coming on as a homey old pea picker. It didn't work. Whoever blew that pitiful stage up might pray for certain of his acquaintances staying quiet. For a half column of newsprint. It wasn't very mature or original."

He'd had one or two nips from the bottle, but this is the most forceful I'd ever heard him. The change took me aback. I went mute, then placed my hand on an original billy club I'd made from a child's bat. This action surprised me, because I never intended to harm Bell. His business was too good and just too interesting to give up. I believe I was scared.

"And you and your broomstick-up-ass buddy *are* mature, of course."

"We are constant, you hunk of burning white trash."

He walked on out, a changed man, a man with sudden convictions. The fog lay out so thick he disappeared into his dented Saab SUV with only the sound of the door to give him away, ten in a July morning. This fog, I say, I've never seen the likes of it. Curling around getting thicker like in a stew pot. But none of this is the embarassing part, which came almost immediately. After Wilkes Bell's car left, some other car rolls into the lot and a form walks to me slowly. At one or two times in a man's life he fears everything in his world. Such was this figure closing to me out of the insane weather; I swear I saw hell walking and shook. But it was only a woman. I'd worked myself up to a lather.

Here's my secret: I lick the sweat off women.

And I do sing as I lick, it's an involuntary thing with me, a lullaby or children's graveyard whistling. I believe it proceeds from the id part of Freud's teaching. I saw droplets of sweat or fog or both on this delicious young lady's back. I was still in my formal composing suit, which in afterthought might have reminded her of Wilkes, and I was around the corner and in a deep suck *thitherto*, a word I'd been working out lately in the child's book. My arms around to that sweet depression above her rump as the back convexes itself, my tongue busily tasting, my senses way heated and wetness spreading down. Well, she did take offense, but she was too stunned to take immediate action. I've had two who returned the licking, beside themselves, and then turn sick. I tell you that if my woman Louise was up front, which almost never happens, I'd be doing the same thing.

She shook me off with surprising strength, but then I remembered she was a dancer and aerobics instructor. I offered my handkerchief and quickly said, "You're so wet, beautiful, and sad!"

From fury she changed to a broken creature who was simply lost as to how to act.

"You ought not to do that. Maybe you think I'm somebody else."

"You came in once before. I can tell you're normal. Some women suffer from unceasing sweats. I know you because you came in once and Wilkes Bell talks about you in words sublime. I'm a writer and a yarn spinner myself."

"You don't call that horrible licking attack anything but crime."

"I'm sorry but something that sweet can't be a crime."

Well, she drilled me with hatred in her eyes and then she did almost collapse.

Women's throats in the summertime, that perfume and randy ooze the fairer sex has that we don't. So I've out and said it, and it's nothing I can help and lucky nobody's turned me in to the law. Five of them positively enjoyed it, and never knew they would until I was across the counter fast as a werewolf and as thirsty for salt as a sponge. Oh I lick them.

This woman was Charlotte Barrios, girlfriend to Bell. She'd never been here before.

"I'm sick with worry about him. Something's come over him where he thinks the end is near. He's nothing but woe and morbid surrender. He is changed to an upright corpse and just stumbles along."

"Miss, that's the normal style. He was just here saying those kind of things and hurling around like an actor from a great tragedy. For god's sake, he's a drunk, Charlotte."

"Who are *you*? You with that huge bow tie. Bob Cratchit? You can't just . . . *lick* a woman without . . . consequences."

"It's not my choice, Charlotte. It's an old compulsion. I've had treatment."

"Well you need more. You're lucky. . . . What is *wrong* with him? Where had he gone?" She was all to pieces again and I knew I was safe.

"I've a feeling he will keep to a small radius unless somebody else is driving. Wilkes is one for *diablerie*," I said, taking charge in my composing suit, my best shoes and shirt. I matched that ass Bitters for obscure names.

She just stared at me.

"I was so worried I drove over to the delta to see if his folks could help. It's no secret he's been a mess for years."

They're all hopeless trips. He speaks of them. He speaks of you. I know."

"Fuck you. You *can't* know."

The cursing surprised me, but then I looked at the full buffed bod under that warm-up suit of hot pink, and it didn't. How did Bell ever hang on to this?

I get a good neck sweat of my own eye-drilling her right back and by use of the eye on the good side alone I see her as a long picture of bare beige woman. Christ, if I'd had a golden youth to pour all over her. My eyesight was your abstract impressionism, probably. Maybe he painted her nude? The idea almost brought on another dire need to werewolf her.

"No, I never was his model," she answers, then sits in the counter chair, moving and crossing her legs for most of an hour. "We met when I saw him in a drenched suit with a brown paper sack of liquor six years ago in the Grove near the art department, maybe early October. Skinny where if he ate a full meal he'd look like a snake that swallowed a biscuit whole. That old cliché. I pitied him and told him he'd get in trouble. No liquor allowed on campus. What got me was his courtesy even messed up as he was. His big gray eyes so concerned for my well-being. You knew he was from blue bloods. His voice was beautiful. He said he had a weakness for painting, painting those fires, in fact painting was *all* he had, my man, and that day we met he was too drunk to remember where the Fine Arts Building where he'd spent four years was. I've seen him lose his car for an hour and a half after we tried to attend a Tulane football game.

"He told me his father despised him, was rather proud of it, then told me he was capable of great harm, his father was lucky. His *courage* struck me. Never did he complain of his own misery, which was constant. When I guided him to his own show that first afternoon, I saw he was a good draughtsman but had not broken out to another dimension. Maybe he was on the edge of it. As in dance when you do a skilled presentation of the movements, but not the true movements. He felt deeply and gave directly to the poor. Was wonderful with black children.

"Said he knew what I was thinking about his work, how it was not *there* yet but that life, not study, would give it to him and there was a black burning maw in the earth that ate the spirit of people and spat it back in the image of frozen brick and glass. In short, churches. He also said we did badly at peace and needed catastrophe closer by to stir us to life. These United States had made too many artifices between life, dirt, and blood, and every day we should do a good turn to a poorer person and give this person our flesh, dirt, and blood. In our world people were waiting earnestly for a happy deep-blue square of death."

"Whoa?" I say.

"He was not a reincarnationist. He was assured of *misincarnation*, where millions had just missed being born to their correct art and spent their days in sorrow wondering what was wrong. When what was wrong was that they were forced into occupations and beliefs they did not match, unhappily squirming toward their correct skill, even their correct bodily shape and health, and most of all, the fact that they were at one neither with their skills or their loves."

"He had *time* to think all this up? Or did he have a teacher? I never heard it, and we chewed the fat for hours over one bottle of single malt, Charlotte—"

"Wilkes said he was born into yet another category, perhaps the worst. That is getting born *almost* into your right form, almost a painter or almost a happy, loyal son. He squirmed every second, he stared and glared, he lay in cotton fields drunk under the stars in two-thousand-dollar suits. Suits to put a good face on his misbirth. To help his fellows and especially the black children see that you could bear bad luck in style."

"Please, this is quite enough talking. Have some water, lady. Frankly, old Wilkes, for all the hours we talked, was not that original a man. He was all over the place drunk but at the bottom of it, dull normal dressed up and forever wanting that next drink—"

"No!" Now she was angry. I was baffled why. "He drinks *because* he was a friend of the poet-philosopher William Blake, but he's better than Blake, I think. The Misgenitor is the villainous force in this world, he says."

"I see more sweat on you neck. Could I—"

"God, no! I can't believe he spent time with you. You hold the money of his uncle in bondage, you with the tongue, and that queer, what? old-timey *poet's* suit, if that's not misborn, you horrible old fuck."

"Woman, you should—"

"You shut up! You don't deserve to be in the same room, the same town, on his road. Now he's just out there lost in the damned fog. Someday his painting will become as natural as rainwater to him. He tries, he hurts himself so badly for it. A mystic in the middle of yahoos."

Her voice was rising and I heard Louise rising in the back. I was in a state. If she had come out front I'd have swatted her. Privacy reigned here.

"Lady," I said, "whoever told you you were that interesting? Come in my store. I am not a goddamned ear you work on till it's callused all over."

But then God, there's always a woman. Those death-row-marrying kind. She'd been up for nights and couldn't do anything but talk like one of those heads guillotined and fallen in a basket. That weird fog creeping outside.

The price you pay for some harmless licking.

Some months later Green was back from another storytellers convention in Tennessee and had not even placed. He did not speak to his common-law wife Louise for a week. He took to drink himself for the first time in his life. You could then hear him cursing in impotent rages through the curtains and back in his domicile connected to the liquor store. He would peep through the curtains or push only his face out through them if he heard a familiar voice at the counter run by his men Tico and Rez, who spoke very little anywhere, any day. The disattached face was red and puffed like the ass of a baboon, fearsome, fearsome and foreign even to customers who thought they knew him. When he heard Wilkes Bell baying for vodka he was way back in his "study" with the book but he was out of the curtains instantly and rushing around the counter in his jockey briefs, tall and gangling, specked by liver spots and sagging teats, sparse white chest hair. Bell was shocked into a long fart and a near blackout. Green dragged him back through the curtains as four other customers watched with a quick sickness. Green drew up a beach chair and pushed the floppy Bell into it.

Then he hauled him and the chair over to his desk to read the Wikipedia.

The No. 76 was an incendiary grenade based on white phosphorus and used during World War II.

The design was the suggestion of the British phosphorus manufacturing firm of Albright and Wilson at a time when the UK faced possible invasion by the Germans. . . . It would be used by organized resistance units as part of a last-ditch attempt.

It was a glass bottle filled with white phosphorus, benzene, a piece of rubber, and water. Over time the rubber dissolved to create a sticky fluid that would self-ignite when the bottle broke. The grenade could either be thrown by hand or fired from the Northover Projector, a simple mortar; a stronger container was needed for the latter and the two types were color coded. As any breakage of the glass would be dangerous, storage under water was recommended. Like the sticky bomb it did not engender much confidence in its users.

Mark 77 bomb.

The MK-77 is the primary incendiary weapon currently in use by the United States military. Instead of the gasoline and benzene fuel used in napalm, MK-77s use kerosene-based fuel, which has a lower concentration of benzene. The Pentagon has claimed that the MK-77 has less impact on the environment than napalm. The mixture reportedly also claims an oxidizing agent, making it more difficult to put out once ignited.

> *Use in Iraq and Afghanistan.*
> *MK-77s were used by the U.S. Marine Corps during the first Gulf War and Operation Iraqi Freedom. Approximately five hundred were dropped, reportedly on Iraqi-constructed oil-filled trenches. They were also used at Tora Bora, Afghanistan.*

Green held Bell by the back of the neck, forcing this matter on him. Bell was shaken but he had the vodka open nevertheless and nipped, then raised his head enough to drink from the saving bottle.

"Read, son. You read this and maybe your saint uncle'll see his forty K even though you drank it up long ago. I saved you by the investment."

"Why am I reading? What investment?"

"Even in these lame prime-rate times, you're a lucky-assed loser. And you know damned well what you're reading. I'm warning you."

"Please. Get your hand off so I can get drunk enough to read, Goon. Items of fire. Items of fire. Napalm, phosphorous. Where's the joy here? Your face. You're *drinking*?! God, do I look as bad as you? Red ass of an ape?"

"I'm not used to it. But you shut up and read."

"I will read."

He read about Greek fire, naptha, and thermite, thermate-TH3. Then he read about the fat bombs project, WWII, proposed against the Japanese whereby these winged creatures attached to incendiaries would fly into wooden homes and castles. Wilkes Bell wore horn-rimmed spectacles, pulling at his sweated yellow collar against his pink tie, his throat well wet and slightly yellow itself. Pondering soft hawk's face near emaciated. He felt Green at his shoulder not as a sodomist. He drank a long one from the Stolichnaya and wondered what the proper reaction would be to remove this long naked threat from his back. He chanced a look sideways and never completed the word *no* before Green was fastened on his neck and licking with such force it felt subdermal.

Bell reared up shaking away Green's mouth but the witless man still licked the air.

"God, man! Is this the end of the world? It was only women up to now. Anse got the last one to drop charges, insane bastard!"

Goon stood bereaved but mean in the face while his woman could be heard bellowing in a separate grief about a kitchen grease fire. Green ignored her as he tucked a loose gonad back into his briefs. Loud sad world and stinking, hog flesh and smoke. Both men standing thigh high in its wreckage. Mutual scholars and addicts of fire. Just over the north hill a jet screamed down to concrete. Out in the store the premium brands were pushed forward for these wealthy alumni and their sparkling second wives.

"I ain't myself," Goon apologized. "Where am I, what's that burning smell?" Neither man turned to watch or hear the woman, her bare feet and legs scattering beneath the pan she held. Both deaf by liquor, Bell in an appalled trance.

"I believe your house is nearly on fire," said Bell.

"Mizz Ann always manages. Good woman but got large in the ass on me."

"Goon, you got weird prominent titties. Be kind. You have much to worry about."

"These pages you read. That's your scripture, ain't it? Say you never get caught, s'how you work. Now I'm up on you. Got you in my sights. You tell Mr. Max Petraeus watch my smoke on the next pyrotechniques!"

"I'm telling you, you might already be dead for that propane rocket in the primitive church."

"Dead how? Do you believe I fear any man in this town? Look out that window and you see maybe a fifth of my empire, fool."

"I see a car lot, a bait shop, beauty shop, bail bonds office, a fleet of golf carts. Why are there iron bars on the bond building? I thought you were so tough and pro you could talk the shotgun off a maniac."

"I can in fact. But I want to give back to the community. The office is a home for battered women at night. I found the one in the back through my work there."

"I believe that as much as I believe those three whores prowling the used Cadillac section are flying nuns."

Another executive jet, purple and gold, squeaked and stormed with blowback, made its keening cry as it turned toward the radio shack. It was game day, LSU richlings poured in, the noise of two tigers aiming squarely at the liquor store, where on the airport side Tico and Rez, with Bell's painterly wit, had made a great billboard, with and deep, "FIRST STOP LAST STOP" bordered by the fierce helmets of the Southeastern Conference, whose boasted brutality and speed had long ago raised a sport to religion.

The kitchen fire was on the walls, Green yet clothed in only jockeys and Cole Haan brogans. He turned with low interest to the kitchen, walking like an unconvinced zombie to it even as Louise screamed louder. He slammed a door behind him. Bell managed a swat of vodka huge enough to straighten him out most genially. Next he knew the door opened on white smoke, dense but no flame. But both of Goon Green's shoes were on fire. Not so that Green noticed. Backwater Mercury blasted down by antiaircraft rounds.

"Look down," said Bell.

"Why? Well just fuck it." He stomped himself left and right. Success at last. "Now what danger to my person were we talking about."

"Petraeus. A man who does what he says."

"I would put it another way. Say this: With what I know I can bury the both of you. You drunks can't wait to tell a secret. Mr. Petraeus ought to kill *you* for starters."

"He really doesn't care that much. But he won't stand for mockery. This is twice now. The armory at Millington, maybe Hattiesburg, too."

"Didn't I ever tell you the fact our government military is just plain stupid. Sure, you've got your experts. They move shit around and make noise. But they lose things and steal things right and left. You've got majors simpler than a cow, and a cow's not good at anything but hiding her calf."

"So you stole from then blew the sides out of two armories."

"Impossible. I've got witnesses I was nowhere near, whenever they went off."

"But you made me read the pages. The point was? Was any jackass who can move a mouse can build a bomb. And you're in the big league now. But I asked you before. Where's the joy? What makes you put a foot on the floor when you wake from the bed?"

"Like you with booze? The next drink?"

"Like me with booze, with art, with Max. My woman. My dear uncle. Really good raisin bran at midnight after a bender."

"What a list. Somebody might mistake you for busy."

"They're not going to mistake you for breathing if you don't stop. Now give me Uncle Ray's money."

"No can do, not now. Your unc gets nothing if any harm comes to me. And both of you get bad, bad assfucking big houses."

Bell stood sodden with alcoholic sweat that made his suit feel heavy and absurd, a deep-diving outfit with globe head, lead pants. At once he felt the ghost of violent corn-holing in all this gear, weighted perfectly for bitches of the pen. He was out in his Porsche speeding up to leave the precincts.

At this moment a belch of fire raised most of an unpowered plane over the radio shack so you could see it over the smooth-lawned north hill whose south descended to a line of hangars for the new jet port. The explosion was terrific but seemed to be without human consequence. Bell was so used to exploding churches behind him and deaf from vodka he remarked it not at all.

No screams played out. The accident seemed to raise no further interest than a random column of swamp gas. Bell was far into his own land and recited as one hypnotized several facts from the pages he'd just seen in Green's house.

"Napalm . . . invented by Harvard president James Conant and colleagues at MIT Dupont, and Standard Oil . . . mixing napthenic and palmitic acids with gasoline produced a Vaseline-like yellow paste . . . burned slowly, stuck to materials . . . could not be put out. Water only splattered this jellied gasoline . . . hit the side of an edifice, run down it, find every opening until it consumed itself."*

Green, like any nondrinker after nearly a full bottle, had sprawled out cold in his "study" recliner, smelling of burned leather, his brogans, still smoking, pages spread over his lap and strewn all over the room. The unreconciled gonad had crept out the slit of his jockeys again. The liquor bottle clutched by its neck as in a lewder Norman Rockwell village hearth-warmer. His woman then stood over him. The hang of Green's hammer was no less a thrill and she knew secrets he guessed she didn't, despite the mumblings to Tico and Rez. She was frightened seeing him drunk the first time and by the close explosion over the hill he had slept through. She was a woman slightly more handsome than rough-edged, spoke proper English, knew how to dress and show her long legs in slitted skirts that made Goon and other men hot around the forehead and lap. What she looked upon, in his shorts and burned shoes, was not a feast of love unless she followed his lead and poured down the whole bottle.

When she was on fire in the kitchen he showed no urgency saving her and did little but become a shoe torch when the last grease was slung out of the pan. The smoke detector was screaming, the stove wall burned, but it was *her* hand on the extinguisher when she remembered its existence. Next that fancy lush Wilkes Bell was leaving fast, the explosion erupted. There must be a string flowing through these events but she could not find it yet.

Goon was no sloppy man but look at all the ransacked pages off the clipboard on his lap. This moment marked a bad, a maybe terrible thing, she was certain of it. And not much else.

*Please see publisher's note.

"Reading and writing train our people for logic, grace, and precision of thought, and begin a lifelong study of the exceptional in human existence. I think literature is the history of the soul. Writing should be a journey into worthy perception."

—Barry Hannah

Publisher's Note

The publisher gratefully acknowledges Brad Watson, Howard M. Lenhoff, and Elizabeth Kaiser for their invaluable contributions in compiling this volume, and Jack Pendarvis and David McLendon for the extra eyes and ears. And Richard Howorth, for all of this and so much more.

Wilkes Bell's dialogue regarding napalm on page 455 is taken from James Bradley's *Flyboys* (New York and Boston: Little, Brown & Co. and Back Bay Books, 2003, p. 215). We gratefully thank Mr. Bradley and his publisher for allowing us to use these words.

The following pieces from this book originally appeared in other publications. "Trek" originally appeared in *The Arrowhead* (Mississippi College) in 1964. "Water Liars," "Love Too Long," "Testimony of Pilot," "Coming Close to Donna," "Return to Return," "Midnight and I'm Not Famous Yet," and "Two Gone Over" originally appeared in *Esquire*; "Knowing He Was Not My Kind Yet I Followed" in *Black Warrior Review*; "Mother Rooney Unscrolls the Hurt" in *The Carolina Quarterly*; "Fans" in *Atlanta Weekly*; "Ride, Fly, Penetrate, Loiter" in *The Georgia Review;* "Even Greenland" was originally published as a chapbook by Barry Hannah in 1983. "Evening of the Yarp: A Report by Roonswent Dover" originally appeared in *The Quarterly;* "Hey, Have You Got a Cig, the Time, the News, My Face?" in *Santa Monica Review;* "Drummer Down" in *Southern*

Review; "Uncle High Lonesome" in *Men Without Ties;* "A Creature in the Bay of St. Louis" in *Sports Afield;* "Sick Soldier at Your Door" in *Gulf Coast Review* and in *Harper's.*

Text and titles have in certain cases been altered since the original publication.

From *Self-Portrait: Book People Picture Themselves*
from the Collection of Burt Britton

Barry Hannah (1942–2010) was the author of twelve books: *Geronimo Rex*, *Airships*, *Ray*, *The Tennis Handsome*, *Nightwatchmen*, *Captain Maximus*, *Hey Jack*, *Boomerang*, *Never Die*, *Bats Out of Hell*, *High Lonesome*, and *Yonder Stands Your Orphan*. His work was published in *The New Yorker*, *Esquire*, *Harper's*, *The Southern Review*, *The Oxford American*, *Gulf Coast Review*, and many other magazines. His achievements in fiction have been honored with an Academy Award in Literature by the American Academy of Arts & Letters, and he was nominated for the American Book Award for *Ray* and the National Book Award for *Geronimo Rex*, which won the William Faulkner Prize. He also received the Arnold Gingrich Short Fiction Award for *Airships*, and his body of work has been recognized with the PEN/Malamud Award for Short Fiction.

Hannah was born in Meridian, Mississippi, in 1942, and grew up in Clinton, where he received a Bachelor of Arts from Mississippi College. He went on to earn a Master of Arts and Master of Fine Arts from the University of Arkansas. Hannah was director of the MFA program at the University of Mississippi in Oxford for three decades, also teaching at the Iowa Writers' Workshop, the Sewanee, and Bennington summer writing seminars, and held teaching appointments at many other colleges and universities. He passed away on March 1, 2010 in Oxford.

Sign reads "Tonight Only, Mark Twain Opens for Trini Lopez.
'I'll Be There Before the Next Teardrop Falls.'"

Courtesy of Susan Schove Phillips
and the Oxford Lafayette County Literacy Council